SO LONG,
PRINCESS

SO LONG,
PRINCESS

BARBARA
BROOKER

William Morrow and Company, Inc.
N E W Y O R K

Library of Congress Cataloging-in-Publication Data

Brooker, Barbara.
  So long, princess.
  I. Title.
PS3552.R6578S6   1987   813'.54   87-7766
ISBN 0-688-06938-X

Printed in the United States of America

First Edition

1 2 3 4 5 6 7 8 9 10

BOOK DESIGN BY BRIAN MOLLOY

First, Mother; my two daughters, Suzy and Bonny;
Robert Brooker, my true Prince Charming;
especially, Dr. Carolyn Gracie—
In memory of my father, Barney Rose

ACKNOWLEDGMENTS

Special thanks to Fred Hill, my agent, who never gave up and always says, "Keep writing"; Pat Golbitz, my very brave editor with an eye and a heart; Alan Rinzler, who showed me the way; Bonnie Nadell; Katherine Knecht, my best friend; and Phyllis Koestenbaum for her encouragement.

Thanks also to Doris Ober, Adam Bersin, Robert and Richard Rose, Stanley Levin, Jill Hamilton, Jerry Astrove, Arlene Gemmil, Alan and Patty Axelrod, Arthur Robinson and Virgil Whitley, Arthur and Shirley Cerf, Barbara Brenner, Donald Alex, Elayne Epstein, Nancy Klein, Donna Madison, Lorine Greathouse, Kit Cameron, Judy Camp, Gary Carson, Marlene Levinson, to my friends, who know they're my friends. To God . . . whoever She is.

SO LONG,
PRINCESS

CHAPTER ONE

Anyways . . . my name is Lisa Perlman, and you don't know what I've been through. For five years I've been writing this novel about a Jewish princess who grows out of it. Oh, God . . . it's ten to three . . . time for Dr. Kenner. . . .

I hurried up the hill, fixing the Walkman over my head . . . Mozart so beautiful . . . my hair getting all curly from the San Francisco fog. God, the city so pretty, all pointy and sparkly. I walked fast until I got to the blue Victorian house. I went inside and climbed the creaky long stairway, carrying my paper bag to breathe into in case I had an anxiety attack.

In the waiting room I turned on the green light to tell Dr. Kenner I had arrived. I took off the Walkman and sat down on the lumpy red couch. I looked through an outdated *People* magazine, not really reading it, planning what I wanted to talk about that day. . . . You'd think I'd feel fulfilled and everything . . . the novel finally finished . . . but I still felt lousy. What's there to be so happy about? Forty-two years old and still shlepping to the psychiatrist, a single parent, celibate, not a pot to pee in. And what if the book . . . ? Feel like I'm walking on a high ledge. Can't look down. Anyways. . . .

I looked out the window at the tree all bent from the storm, the same tree I'd seen so many seasons grow on, until I heard the door open.

"Come in now, Lisa," said Dr. Kenner.

I got up real fast. As I rushed toward her I tripped over the loose strap on my Famolares . . . what a klutz . . . I feel so big . . . okay, Lisa, so you're tall . . . so what?

Dr. Kenner's office smelled like roses. I glanced at the long-stemmed red roses in the crystal vase . . . probably from one of her thousands of suitors. Wouldn't you know?

I settled back into the leather chair, crossing and uncrossing my legs and clearing my throat. I tugged at my pink leg-warmers, then I raised my head and concentrated on my eye focus. Dr. Kenner adjusted her lilac shawl around her shoulders, then the tiny, frayed pink satin pillow behind her back. Her wide-set, intelligent brown eyes were clear and she has long curly brown hair, not mousy brown like mine. She looks more like a fashion model than a psychiatrist. And what great-looking shoes, cranberry lizard with little ankle straps, not to mention the cranberry stockings. Even the plants were lush, not like my plants, which no matter what I did were always half rotten from some rare disease. The rose-colored room was as soft as the inside of a dream.

I pulled more Kleenex from the box. The Kleenex stuck to the box again.

After a long silence I said, "I hurt."

"I'm sorry," said Dr. Kenner in her soft voice.

I cried quietly for a while, shredding the Kleenex into little pieces, the tears flowing through my fingers. I smiled nervously and looked up.

"I finished my novel yesterday."

"That's wonderful," said Dr. Kenner.

"I mailed it to my agent." I hesitated and looked away. "Five years. Five years," I repeated, "and all those drafts . . . Lester hocking . . . I mean, you know Lester North is a heavy-duty agent . . . really believes in me, all that . . . even so, it's been awful . . . so lonely and all . . . everyone treating you like you just got off the boat. Anyways, I hope that Lester likes it . . . at least will send it out." I shrugged indifferently. "You never know with him . . . I mean, it has to be perfect. Though definitely this is the last time I'll rewrite. Twelve drafts are enough . . . and I don't know how I did it this time, with David leaving and all . . . the abortion. . . ." I put my head down and tore the Kleenex up into little pieces. "Over two years . . . I still miss him . . . the bastard."

"But you finished the novel in spite of that. Doesn't that tell you something?"

"Probably the novel won't be right," I quickly said. "Never be published. Anyways, why should anything go well in my life? It never has. Even my kids are always hocking . . . Jenny is always telling me to fuck off and Amy is always calling from New York and telling me to get my act together . . . even her boyfriend Adam tells me. . . . God, what act? Why do I have to get it together? For what? Who cares? And my agent—you know, Lester North—is always saying that I'm no Jane Austen." I stopped talking and looked at the seashell collection and tried to get my cool. "I feel like I'm living behind a rainbow . . . I reach for it . . . I get close . . . so close . . . but then it disappears . . . goes away." I sniffed a couple of times. "Not to mention David . . . who got tired of waiting for me to become a star."

Silence.

"All those years David cried he wanted a child . . . my child . . . until I got pregnant. . . . So what did Mr. Starfucker Art Dealer do? He looked at his gold Rolex and said in his so-deep throaty voice, 'I have a Schnabel opening. Get an abortion by Friday.' "

Silence.

"So there I was in same-day surgery with the rest of the deadbeats . . . shuffling down the hall, zonked on Valium, in the *shmatte* paper slippers . . . while Mr. Abortion Pro read *Art in America*."

Silence.

"I hate him! I wish I had jumped off the gurney and yelled. 'Fuck you! It's my baby! You can't take it away! It's my baby!' But I didn't. Then I guess everything in me broke . . . just went bonks . . . the sadness all coming out . . . wonder if the ache in me will every go away?"

Dr. Kenner nodded. Finally a sign of life. Shit. Why does Dr. Kenner always have to get all silent when I need reassurance? Honestly, it's something. I looked down at my fingers, so ugly and wrinkled at their tips . . . probably from typing.

"Anyways . . . the neighbors still look at me funny. Especially at the end of the day, after writing for several hours, when I go for my fast walk. I'm still so shaky I have to hold on to the houses. Now the novel is finished and I don't know what to do . . . what to do. I'm out of money now. Oh, I still have a little left from Daddy's trust. But I have to get a real job now. Pay off my bills," I said.

"Write, just continue your writing," said Dr. Kenner softly, her long, delicate fingers fluttering as if arranging flowers. "Begin another novel. Write something fresh."

Write, shmite! What the hell does she mean? Doesn't she know how hard it is? That you don't just pull a book out of the air? That I have to have more in my life?

"I don't know what to write . . . I mean . . . if I—"

"You know a lot about art," she said quickly. "The art world."

"I hate the art world! Phony as a three-dollar bill . . . you don't know the half . . . I'm telling you, a bunch of swank snobs wearing name tags and . . . God, not once do you ever see a midget or a fat person invited to their precious museum openings . . . it's all bullshit. My old friend Leo used to call the collectors art masturbators."

"Leo?"

"You know, Leo . . . the collector . . . he's been dead nine years . . . taught me a lot . . . left me the David Park painting . . . the one I sold to help pay for Amy's college. . . ."

"Oh, yes . . . Leo. Well, you're talented. There are so many ways you can go and still continue your writing."

"Anyways," I said real loud, annoyed at her Goody Two-Shoes stuff, "I was at the Berkeley Museum at this really great sculpture show . . . you should have seen Eva Hesse's stuff . . . I've been looking at her work for years. . . . God, it blows me away . . . it's really strange . . . all these weirdo nets and strings and ropes . . . all tangled and twisted and everything . . . broken things . . . yet . . they're whole . . . I mean, one whole thing. . . ."

"Sounds interesting."

"I read she had a terrible fear of abandonment . . . this father thing . . . when her father died and her husband left her she went all bananas . . . then her lousy luck with a brain tumor . . . all those operations . . . then dead at thirty-four . . . but she left work like you wouldn't believe . . . something true."

Silence.

I nodded and lowered my eyes. "I'm lonely. If it weren't for my cat Anny . . . I don't know . . . ." My voice broke and I bit my lip. I could hardly see through my dirty glasses. They were all smudged from the tears. But I was so nearsighted I was used to not seeing.

Why doesn't she say something?

"I'm lonely," I repeated, looking at Dr. Kenner anxiously. "And I'm not supposed to be lonely. Not the Jewish princess. Ex-princess." I chuckled and smiled quickly. "Though I don't think I ever really was a Jewish princess. Just a role I made up . . . I mean, everyone was always saying I looked like a tall Natalie Wood . . . you know, stuff like that. . . . Mother wanted me to be a princess, so I pretended I was a princess."

Another long silence.

A siren wailed outside and a long streak of light trembled across the rose-colored carpet. I waited for Dr. Kenner to say something but she didn't.

"Write," she repeated. "That's your center. Keep in touch."

"Do you really think so?" I asked eagerly.

Dr. Kenner nodded.

I shrugged and sniffed a few times. "Yes, I guess so. It's just that I always think God will tap me on the shoulder and say, 'Move over, Lisa Perlman, I've made a mistake in roll call.' " I hesitated and looked up. "You know, like everyone is going to find out."

"Find out what?" she asked gently.

I took off my glasses and rubbed my eyes. God, my right eye was driving me batty. All I need now is a lousy twitch.

"Oh, that I'm a fake. That I can't write, that I only pretend to write."

"All artists go through this."

Oh, what does she know? I thought. She just wants a really neurotic writer for a patient. Can't she see that I'm just ordinary? That I play roles? God, all I need is a dumb shrink.

The telephone rang. I almost jumped a mile. I hated it when the telephone rang.

I twisted my hair around my forefinger while trying to appear as though the ringing telephone didn't bother me a bit, that I wasn't at all furious that somebody had dared to interrupt my session. Cool it, Lisa. Don't get hysterical.

I sat there with this smile on my face, counting the rings, until

Dr. Kenner smiled sweetly and said apologetically, "Four rings means an emergency and I have to answer it."

I nodded and pulled at my sock.

"Uh-huh, of course. Go ahead, I understand." I smiled, murmuring that I didn't mind at all, that of course she had to answer the telephone. So while Dr. Kenner spoke quietly on the telephone, I covered my face with my hands and sobbed, my tongue curling under the roof of my mouth so that it wouldn't hang out. Something about my tongue came loose when I cried. Finally Dr. Kenner finished talking. She made a poo-poo big thing about adjusting her shawl, her pillow, and we both cleared our throats a lot. While I pretended that I had blanked out, wondering if she would remember where we had left off, Dr. Kenner adjusted her shawl once more, shifted her position, and faced me. She didn't say anything, so I went ahead. For what I'm paying, I just went.

"Anyways . . . so I write," I said, making my rubber face. "Big deal. What good is it? Everyone thinks it's such a big fucking deal, such a magical thing. That I'm some kind of cuckoo." I paused and scratched my foot, then tossed my long hair back like the Clairol Girl does. "My family treats me like I'm a freak . . . you know, like your elevator doesn't go all the way up. They always wanted me to be someone else . . . that's why I spent all those years sitting in the closet, reading novels and dreaming about castles, romance, the whole shmeer. Anyways, at Passover they seat me next to poor Aunt Sally, who shakes her head and talks to herself. Or my stepfather hocks why I don't get a real job. Mother thinks I'm this failure person because I'm not married."

"You've developed different values, priorities. Just because yours are different doesn't mean you can't love your family."

"Uh-huh . . . sure . . . anyways, my fucked-up family . . . my wacko brother Bruce . . . real black-sheep stuff . . . thirty-two and never worked a day, every minute detoxing from some biggie drug, went through Daddy's trust . . . Mother gives him an allowance that would choke a horse! . . . I try to help him, you know, give him support . . . let him know I care."

"What's the latest on Bruce?"

"He's at the Betty Ford. Mother says he got hooked on Darvon—you know, from his headaches."

"That's good that you help your brother."

"God, Daddy's probably turning over in his grave. Poor Daddy
. . . worked like a dog at Universal . . . had these big dreams.
Then whammy! Died at lunch over a bowl of chili con carne!"

"Hmmm."

"Every night at dinner Mother would yell her head off that I was
a liar, then accuse me that I was playing up to my father and couldn't
do anything right, that no wonder I was a wallflower, why couldn't
I be more like Suzy Mendelson, and Daddy'd just sit there with the
headphones over his head, listening to his ball games. Bruce would
whine and smash toy cars. My grandmother, God rest her soul,
talking to herself and then Mother would scream, 'Don't slump,
Lisa! And watch your diet. You're a big girl.' And I'd squint my
eyes until everyone shrank into tiny dots and I covered my ears so
I wouldn't hear Bruce whimpering. . . ."

Silence.

"Seems like everything is always going away . . . never there
. . . you know what I mean. That's why I keep real close up . . .
you know, in me. . . ." I dabbed at my mouth with another Kleenex and made a grave face. "So . . . anyways . . . I feel like a
butterfly inside a glass jar trying to get to the airholes on the top.
But I can't get out. I can't. And I'm afraid I'm going to die."

"You're afraid to live," she said softly.

I took off my eyeglasses and with the bottom of my pea coat I
cleaned them. Only they turned out more smudged than ever. I put
them on anyways and took a deep breath. I slumped farther in the
chair, crossing and uncrossing my legs. Dr. Kenner leaned slightly
forward. She knows that when I put my head down and slump I
have something to tell her. So I took another deep breath.

"I can't get an orgasm—you know, the big O—I mean, I've had
sex with a couple of men since David . . . with this thirty-five-
year-old dentist—God, he could go all night—and this frozen-food
salesman—poor thing, his thing was so small you could stick it in
a keyhole. So what was I supposed to do?"

Dr. Kenner uncrossed her legs. Her stockings made a swishing
sound. A giant horsefly floated by the window.

"In fact, I never reached orgasm, you know, with David. Not
that he ever noticed. In all the four years, did the man ever once

say 'Lisa, are you coming?'? Besides, I was too busy performing for him, doing all his poo-poo things, his baby licks. Ass licks." I looked away. "Not to mention having to stop in the middle—just when I was about to come—and put on my stupid red four-inch-high heels. Can you believe? The stupid high heels turned him on . . . and God, all the nursie and baby games. Sometimes I would get so exhausted from playing his games, not to mention a perpetual headache from my face being down there all the time. . . ." I stopped talking and covered my mouth with my hand. I hurt, really hurt . . . like the hurt in me was coming up, like every nerve in my body was all raw.

Finally I said, "I'm not frigid, though . . . I think a lot about sex. In fact, I dream that I'm making love to a no-name stud who is fucking me like mad, and I'm orgasming all over the place—in airplanes, supermarkets, all over the place," I said, crying now.

Dr. Kenner's face was expressionless. What a time to leave me hanging.

"No wonder I'm angry. Why shouldn't I be angry? Look at the rotten men I've picked. I mean, you think it was a joyride . . . twenty, all virginal, marrying Charley Berkowitz . . . the heavy-duty prince, the big plumbing tycoon . . . then after this big storybook wedding . . . flowered chuppa and everything . . . white roses . . . there I was on my wedding night, all breathless, hot as a pistol, my legs all spread to Timbuktu, whispering, 'Put it in now, put it in' . . . then nothing. He got all still and everything, said he couldn't do it because he'd made a mistake . . . didn't love me . . . the next day dropped me off at home. Back to the closet I went, part of me gone, split off. Charley's name never mentioned again . . . Oh, God, I don't want to cry."

"That was an unfortunate experience. But it's time to let it go."

"I try, but I can't. Whenever I'd be with a man, just as I was getting close . . . I'd think about Charley . . . white roses . . . then everything would stop."

"That's because you're afraid of closeness."

"Guess all that sex got stuck in me, buried way up in me. . . . God, sometimes I wish I could hold my breath, then let out all the sex."

Silence.

"All those years being Mrs. Arnold Perlman . . . living in the lousy suburbs, the long sultry days doing the hostess thing, schlepping around the pool in my rubber thongs, like slow dreaming . . . making bird calls . . . sitting in the laundry room, writing my dreams . . . painting . . . while Arnold Pooey drank like a fish. Meaner than a coyote. Believe me, I'm glad he took a powder— good riddance! What a lousy lover he was . . . half the time he had the runs or was on the telephone with his mother . . . wasn't playing with a full deck . . . in all these years he never once made an effort to see the kids . . . or paid a red cent . . . the big man . . . got away with murder . . . a miracle Amy and Jenny aren't nuts . . . I mean, they're great kids . . . I did my best . . . I . . ."

She nodded. Twice.

"Amy, a heavy-duty journalist in New York at twenty-one . . . living with her Adam. . . ."

"How's Jenny?" asked Dr. Kenner.

"Still selling used cars . . . her Auto Jen business is going real hot . . . working part-time at Saks . . . though I wish she'd go back to school . . . at eighteen she belongs in school."

"Just give her time."

"What have men done for me anyways?" I sighed and put my head down. No way am I going to talk about this lousy orgasm business anymore, not with Dr. Kenner's funny looks. For what I'm paying, she can talk now. You've talked enough, Lisa. I picked the crud, cereal or gum or something, from my coat sleeve. After a long silence, Dr. Kenner adjusted the pillow behind her back.

"About orgasm," she finally said. "When you accept yourself and meet someone someday who cares for you, really cares for you, and you trust him, aren't afraid of your feelings, you will have orgasms if you want to. You're a very sexual woman."

How does she know this? I thought suspiciously. Everything the woman knows.

"Anyways . . ." I sneezed a couple of times, wishing my eyes would stop boinging all over the place, that I could get the hang of the eye contact thing. "Now that I've finished the novel, guess I'll hit the employment agencies. No way am I ever going to sell art again . . . had it with the Junior Leaguers whining about their Vassar days and their Picasso prints . . . if only I could go back to school, get a Ph.D. . . . oh, God, my prospects are so bleak . . . and the men situation . . ."

"You have lots of choices now," said Dr. Kenner.

"I don't know any men, no one, though I hate them anyways," I said sullenly. "But Larry Segal—you know, my little writer friend— said I should put an ad in. Isn't that depressing? But I'm sick of talking all night to my girl friends—I call them telemoans because we complain so much—my big whoopee going to Miz Brown's Coffee Shop and yakking with the regulars."

"Hmmm."

"Marcie Kaplan says she meets a bunch of nutso men. She's really pretty, too, you know—real tall, slender, dark short hair and dark eyes. . . ."

"When you're ready, men will find you. And when you begin working, get out in the real world, you will meet men."

Sure, sure, easy for her to say. Look at her, all thirty-five and beautiful, a professional person. What does she know about menopause? Not to mention that I'm all hung up on the fucking tranquilizers she started me on.

"Anyways . . . who cares about the men thing? . . . I have more important things to worry about . . . like my book. . . . God, what's going to happen to my book? What if it doesn't get published? If . . . and I can't write anyways . . . I hurt too much. . . ."

Of course Dr. Kenner was silent. But I wouldn't say a word, not one word, until she does. Wait this one out, Lisa, exert some control . . . don't be such a fucking lily. I tilted my head kind of to one side and took off my glasses. I stared at the boring Japanese watercolor, bending my fingers way back, playing this little house, some dumb grammar school game. My knuckles made little popping sounds.

"Can you write without the agony?" Dr. Kenner finally asked.

Write without the agony? Who the fuck can write without the agony? Is she crazy! Why does she have to ask such a profound question? Of course implying that I should write without the agony. That if I had my shit together I could. Probably thinks I enjoy my agony, that I'm this neurotic person . . . oh, fuck all this ingst and angst . . . it's driving me nuts. Now what am I supposed to say?

"I'll never make it with anyone." I sobbed. "Not to mention my periods stopped—early menopause, my gynecologist says. And I miss the periods, the lousy cramps . . . part of me gone." I sobbed. I watched the sunlight break out patches along the floor. "Anyways . . . I fly in my dreams. I swear I do. I give a couple of pushes with my feet and up I go . . . my arms all outstretched . . . I float on top of the air. . . . God, it's something."

"Let's talk about that next time," said Dr. Kenner. She gave me her twice blink, the signal that my fifty minutes were up. I looked around for the clock. Probably she put it in the plant aquarium. Always moving things. Of course the next patient won't be as interesting, Lisa, you know that, so who cares that the time is up? In fact, today I won't look behind the wicker screen and see who her next patient is. I sat up staring at the dumb housefly and adjusted my thick sunglasses over my eyes. I got up quickly and put the Walkman on, almost tripping from my shoes sticking to the carpet and also my foot was asleep. As usual, by the door, which Dr. Kenner kept locked, I stood like a nebbish, a sicky smile on my face, while Dr. Kenner for the hundredth time explained gently, like I was some kind of nut, how to turn the three locks, first to the right, then twice to the left. Finally, after thanking her, for what I don't know, and holding her gaze a moment with my eye focus, I left and ran down the stairs, glancing behind the screen and hating the young blond woman reading a magazine.

Outside I blinked against the bright sunlight. I felt drained. I wondered if I would ever feel normal, feel like a woman, a writer, a person, be like the other women wearing espadrilles and walking leisurely down the street, their eyes calm and their walk serene, not all toppled over and carrying a paper bag. I stared at the roofer shingling the house across the street, his muscles rippling and everything. When he smiled I turned away and hurried down the street.

CHAPTER TWO

So a month passed and still I hadn't heard from Lester North. Probably he hadn't read the novel yet, or maybe he was getting ready to call me and tell me it was awful and that I might have to rewrite it. . . . Anyways, I was more nervous than ever, especially with the job-hunting. Going from one employment agency to another was no easy thing, believe me, not at my age, with a masters yet in creative writing, and an unpublished novel. Nothing to show for all the years, God, I was depressed. Not only was it awful, but actually embarrassing. Especially this one day when a horrible fat girl with a dark moustache, a Susan Abrams I think her name was, was clocking me during a typing test. It was my third try. I was sitting there in the testing room, hardly breathing, having a horrible hot flash, my fingers all stiff, praying to God that I wouldn't make any errors. But I made eighty-two errors. And while I was explaining that I was just nervous and all, this horrible Susan looked at me suspiciously and said that she couldn't send me out on any job interviews, that besides not being able to type I appeared weird, too nervous. At that point, I don't know why, but of all things I began crying and blowing into my paper bag, oh, it was awful, so embarrassing. I sat there crying and blowing into the bag, with my head between my knees, until Susan brought me a Dixie cup of water, then asked me to leave.

I didn't know what I was going to do . . . probably sell art for Shirley Plotkin's gallery. I dreaded selling art, though; it brought back too many memories of David, all that art and everything. Anyways, there I was this gray November day, sitting at my typewriter, writing a sex poem. God, I was getting hot. My eyes were closed, the Walkman playing Vivaldi, so when the phone rang it took me a moment to get out of my world. I pulled off the Walkman, the cord all tangled around my arm, and picked up the telephone.

"Hello," I murmured, barely.

"Lisa . . . it's Lester."

"Oh, Lester," I said, cheerfully, but dreading what he had to say.

"Good news," he said, his voice all silky and everything.

My heart leaped.

"Can you come to my office soon?"

"Lester, what . . .?"

"I sent out *Princess* to Avalon Publishers, and Walter Avalon likes *Princess*. He wants to contract you."

"Uh-huh," I said, trying to sound cool, not surprised, but almost ready to drop dead. . . . Suddenly I was floating . . . flying from the darkness into a golden light.

"Are you there?"

"Yes . . . I'm just so—"

"All right," he interrupted impatiently. "Come to my office in about an hour."

After I hung up, I sat there for a moment and cried. Just cried. Then I began jumping up and down, running in place, and screaming, "Oh, God!" until my daughter Jenny came into the room, along with her usual group, Char, Robin, Fariba. Jenny and the girls, all eighteen years old, had gone from grade school through high school together. They hung out. Mostly at my house. The girls even kept their diet foods and hair blowers at my house.

Jenny, the ringleader, looked concerned.

"Are you crazy again?" Jenny asked, giving the other girls a look.

"Crazy? Of course I'm crazy, but now my craziness will pay off! You'll see! Lester North sold my novel! It's going to be published. Published! I'm going to be a famous author!"

Jenny began screaming now, along with the girls, who were jumping up and down, too, murmuring, "We always believed in you . . . we never thought you were crazy."

When everybody quieted down, I called Amy. Amy answered.

"Amy! It's Mom."

"Are you depressed again?" she asked anxiously.

"No!"

"Do you have your retainer on? You sound funny."

"Amy! I'm never going to be depressed or lonely again. Guess what? Lester North sold my novel to Avalon Publishers, to—"

"What? My God!" she screamed. "Adam, come to the phone. God! Oh! How great! Mom! We always knew, I always knew, that you could do it. God, oh, God, I'm so happy." She began crying then. Adam, her boyfriend, on the other extension, said, "I always believed in you, Lisa. Always! In fact, just about every day I lit candles for you at St. Patrick's. You're one strong lady. And now that fucker David will eat crow."

"Won't he, though?" I agreed.

"Oh, God, I'm so happy. Happy," I repeated. "Now I can send you money, Amy, pay off your NYU loan."

"Amy could use a new coat with winter coming up. And we could use some things for the apartment."

"I'll be in New York for Christmas," I said happily, "and I'll buy you what you need. And we'll go to the Russian Tea Room for caviar and vodka."

"Right on!" said Adam.

"Mom . . . I'll make a hair appointment for you with Mr. Guy. You've got to look good."

"Yes. Do," I agreed.

"Lisa, before you hang up, someone wants to talk to you," said Adam. So while Adam went and tortured Lucy, their cat, enough so that Lucy let out a series of squeaks on the phone, I mooed and cooed baby talk to Lucy. After Amy and I told each other how much we loved each other, and I agreed I would stay with them, I hung up.

Next I dialed my mother. My hands were trembling by now.

"Hello . . ."

"Mother!" I shrieked. "Oh, God, Mother, I'm so excited, I could die! You won't believe!"

"What! Do you have a date? Have you met someone?"

"Mother! Lester North sold my novel to Avalon Publishers!"

"No!"

"Yes!"

"God, oh, God, Lisa!"

"God . . ."

"God . . . oh, my God!"

"God."

We cried a lot and everything. I agreed that after my appointment with Lester I'd go to Mother's house for dinner. I said of course I didn't mind if she had a few relatives over. . . . What did I care? I was too happy.

So, while Jenny and the group helped me dress, all deciding I needed a total do-over, that I was a mess, I stood there luxuriating in this dream, my ego expanding everything, changing before my eyes. After the girls made up my eyes and teased my hair until it stuck out like one of those Hollywood rejects on a game show, Jenny instructing me that I should look like a glamorous authoress, Jenny and the group drove me to Lester's office on Union Street.

I climbed the long flight of stairs, slowly tossing my long, dark hair over my shoulder, telling myself not to appear anxious or the least bit flustered. I brushed a piece of lint from the brown velvet riding jacket, making sure that the suede pants Amy and Adam brought me from Italy weren't twisted at the waist . . . praying to God that Lester's obnoxious poodle, Harry, wasn't there. God, the dog's a mental . . . bites everyone. And I was terrified of dogs. All I needed was a dog bite. And I left the paper bag at home, but, just in case, I had a Zanax. Lester was enough to deal with without the stupid dog. He's a tough number. As easily as he can cajole, he can bite your head off . . . and we had had some bad times together.

Lester's office was cluttered with best sellers, piles of manuscripts all over the long table. As usual, Lester was on one of his many telephones. He smiled and pointed to the leather chair across from him. He was wearing a cable sweater and Gucci loafers without socks. His round baby face appears much younger than his forty-two years. Already, Lester North was reputed to be the best literary agent in the country. We had been together for several years now, and Lester had always believed in my work and in my novel.

Anyways, while I sat there, pretending to fuss with a spot on my beige leather spats, I listened to Lester speak, his voice smooth as silk, to some client of his, chatting about screenplay this, foreign rights that, until at last Lester, after promising to have lunch soon, hung up.

I stood quickly and went over to him, trying not to trip on anything, or appear too anxious. Lester hated it when I appeared too neurotic or anxious. Especially when I would send him one of my neurotic notes, or call crying or something.

I kissed him on the cheek. I could see there was a flicker of emotion in his shrewd brown eyes.

"So, Lisa," Lester said, leaning way back into the leather chair and lighting an imported cigarette.

I concentrated on my eye focus, pushing back the long wave that fell sulkily over my eyes. I frowned contemplatively.

"We did it. I just took a shot and sent the manuscript to Walter Avalon. He loves the novel," said Lester, looking pleased, then exhaling a long stream of smoke. "Sees big things in it. Wanted to know if you're marketable, too. I assured him that you are. So you'll have to be on your best behavior," he said, squinting his eyes at me suspiciously.

"Uh-huh, sure."

"It's going to be big. Big," he murmured.

"Uh-huh."

"You'll receive a ten-thousand-dollar advance, a three-book option. With each book the advance will go up."

"God."

"God is right. It's a good contract," he said, looking pleased as punch.

"I'll say. I still can't believe it."

"Well, believe it."

I'm telling you, it was all too much for me, so I sat there, trying to appear real cool, thanking God that the tranquilizer was working, thinking that I could pay off my American Express card and that awful man from the bank won't look at me so funny anymore, and the children will talk to me with respect, not be so damned bossy, and the neighbors won't whisper about me when I walk by, and . . . . David, he'll die, absolutely die.

"Now, you will have a lot of work ahead of you, Lisa," said Lester, looking stern again. So Lester lectured me about how I would have to be very professional, develop a really professional persona and all that, and that I couldn't send any neurotic notes or poems to Avalon Publishers, that they wouldn't stand for it.

"Certainly not," I assured him.

"See, Lisa, hard work pays off," he finally said, his face brightening. He offered me one of his European cigarettes, and even though I don't smoke, of course I accepted one, not inhaling, but holding it right.

"And you don't look over forty, thank God," he said. "In fact, I assured Walter Avalon that you're a beauty and very marketable, and that you'll do well on the talk shows."

"Thank you," I said. "Oh, Lester, thank you. I don't know how I can ever thank you. . . ."

"When *Princess* makes it big, you can buy me a Hockney," he said, smiling and pointing to the reproduction on the wall.

"Oh, my . . . for sure . . . a Hockney."

"Believe me," he said, looking businesslike again, "next year this novel will be in the market . . . then I'll work on the movie deal," he said. "So, see, Lisa, all your work and suffering are worth it." He chuckled and his face was dreamy. God, underneath all the savvy hardness, Lester North is a softy. I was so happy I wanted to die, absolutely die. I was just about to cry when Lester took the wind out of my sails and said, all business and everything, "Next week the contract will be here. Ready for you to sign. But Walter wants to meet you . . . talk with you. You'll have to go to New York. Avalon, of course, will pick up your air fare. But you'll have to make your own hotel arrangements."

"Yes . . . yes . . . my daughter Amy . . . I'll stay with her," I said excitedly. "I'll leave right before Christmas."

"Good!" he said. "Now . . . take a few days off, enjoy this. But then, remember, Lisa, you're going to have a lot of hard work ahead."

"Uh-huh." What does he mean hard work? After all, the novel is sold and all. But I was too happy to say anything. So, after Lester called a taxi, I floated out of his office, not feeling my feet, just floating out on a dream. Didn't even mind when my heel caught on the old tear in his carpet and I almost fell flat on my face. Already had my voice changed from a somewhat breathless sound to a heavy-duty lower tone, as I instructed the taxi driver to drive to

25 Seacliff Avenue. . . . I couldn't wait to see the expression on my stepfather's face.

I rang the doorbell, humming and wondering if this is what happiness is. . . . Finally after three chimes, la, de, da, Mother answered the door. Mother is a petite woman with honey-colored, very short hair and a madonna-pale face. She was wearing an emerald green taffeta hostess gown.

"Lisa!" She rushed toward me and we exchanged our air kiss. "My God," she repeated. "I'm so proud of you . . . proud," she repeated, hugging me again, more than she'd ever hugged me in my life.

I stood there in the hall, murmuring, "My God . . ." wrinkling my nose from the familiar smell of lemon wax.

"I knew you'd do it . . . we always believed in you," Mother said, tears in her yellow eyes.

So who was I to argue? For once, she was happy with me and I felt damned good.

She took my hand and pulled me down the hall and into the living room. I walked carefully so that I wouldn't slide or fall on the heavily varnished parquet floors. When we stepped into the large living room, everyone stood and applauded. Can you believe, Sidney, my stepfather, a nice man, a good tennis player with a round face and gray kinky hair and a fleshy nose like it had no bone, shouted, *"Mazel tov!"* while Uncle Maury, a fat man with Sad Sack eyes, in the furniture business, with his Polaroid camera took pictures, and Aunt Pearl waving her handkerchief, and my fucked-up brother Bruce letting out his Donald Duck laugh. Even Sidney's gross daughter Fat Susan and her drippy husband, Keith, a chiropractor who always grabbed you and cracked your back, and crazy Aunt Sally, were throwing kisses.

Mother had gone all out. These were the relatives who for years wouldn't talk to me and refused to loan me money when my car was repossessed and my two teeth blew up and I needed root canal, and Uncle Maury repossessed my furniture. But Lisa, I told myself, let bygones be bygones. This is the moment you dreamed of. So I stood there quietly, practicing my eye focus and shaking my hair, telling myself to be calm, that I was above all this, and then I went over and kissed everyone, everyone murmuring that they always knew I'd do it and how much they believed in me.

Bruce, who'd just returned from the Betty Ford Clinic, dressed to beat the band in a red and white argyle cashmere sweater, Italian-cut pants, as wide as he was high and, kind of waddling, came over to me and whispered, "Break a leg, sis, fuck 'em all."

"Thanks, Bruce, I appreciate that," I said, thinking he didn't look so hot, like his eyes sunk way back into his head, and so pale . . . like all the color sucked out of him. His right eyelid drooped slightly and his small nose, kind of beaked, was a little lopsided, making his fleshy face look sort of crooked . . . off. He stuffed a hundred-dollar bill in my hand.

"God, Bruce, you don't have to—"

"Buy yourself something . . . get your hair done," he said impatiently.

"Thanks."

"I'll get you more . . . when I can. . . ."

"Don't worry."

"You're a star, Lisa . . . a fucking star."

God, I was sad, so sad, that I wanted to bawl right there or go into my closet or something. Sidney was at the bar, shouting, "The big authoress! At last she's earning a living, thank God!" and Mother was telling him to shut up and then everyone began talking all at once, Aunt Pearl in her gravelly voice repeating *"mazel"* and knocking on wood a lot.

"What does the authoress want to drink?" said Sidney, mixing drinks at the bar. Uncle Maury was still taking pictures. "Oh, vodka over. Two green olives, please."

"That's a strong drink for a lady," said Mother disapprovingly.

"Mother, please!" I shouted. "Do you mind if I want to celebrate?" God, I was getting so angry I started to feel all tingly. Whenever I would be at Mother's I would get an angry feeling.

Aunt Pearl said, "Leave the girl alone, honey, it's an occasion." Everyone looked at each other, giving their funny looks, and after a moment of silence, Fat Susan, kind of lisping, her mouth stuffed with caviar, said, "So, Lisa . . . tell us. How did this all happen?

It's all so exciting. Isn't it exciting, Keith?" Keith nodded and looked kind of shamefaced.

I just kind of shrugged and helped myself to another caviar sandwich, wishing that Bruce would stop his Donald Ducking and that Christopher, the family pet, some kind of weird pedigree, would stop begging for prawns. God, it was noisy, everything echoed. Mother never put carpets on the parquet floors because she said Christopher didn't like carpets. Anyways, there I was in my moment of glory, on my second martini, feeling lightheaded, especially with the mixture of alcohol and Zanax, dipping prawns in the hot sauce. They all murmured that I was so talented and everything, while Mother argued at the top of her lungs that her side of the family was related to Jack London, and Aunt Pearl argued that it was her side. After I gulped the martini and began a third one, I began talking about how I was writing a really important novel, that I had aspirations for maybe a Pulitzer Prize, that eventually I wanted to write a screenplay, that my life was about commitment, and on it went. Everyone was oohing and aahing, knocking on wood and talking at once. "I don't get the princess bit, though," said Fat Susan, stuffing a jumbo prawn into her small mouth.

"What's there to get?" I said, tossing my hair. "A pathetic person who defines herself by her husband's achievement, lives off him, has no self."

"Shame," said Fat Susan, patting her husband's hair. "I know some girls like that."

"So what's so terrible about being a princess?" said Mother, refilling the nut dish.

"*Nu*, not so terrible," said Aunt Pearl.

Susan smiled.

"Listen to Lisa!" shouted Bruce, popping nuts into his mouth. "She's had two husbands."

"*Oy*, and such husbands," said Aunt Sally. "Shouldn't happen to a dog."

Bruce let out this awful cackle, a slow-rising laugh.

"Everyone quiet! Lisa speaks!" said Sidney.

"Well, just read the book. You'll see."

"I hope it has a happy ending," said Fat Susan, brushing a nut from her red woolly dress, glancing at her tank watch.

"Actually, it's a tragic book."

"*Oy*, don't we have enough tragedy in the world?"

"I hope it has a lot of sex!" said Uncle Maury, looking at Pearl like a child looks at a parent for approval.

"Everything's so psychoanalytical these days. Just give me a good story," said Aunt Pearl.

"That Danielle Steel's wonderful, so deep," said Fat Susan. "I read every book she writes."

"I bet you do," I said, my voice screeching, shaking my glass so Bruce would pour me another drink, "My princess leaves her Gothic monstrosity and lives happily forever without 'Blue Boy' in the tank. Burns her Visa card. Goes to college. You know . . . looks for a more meaningful existence . . . in her . . . not through others . . . men."

"*Oy,*" murmured Aunt Pearl, shaking her head.

"Is the book about your life?" asked Fat Susan.

"All writers write about their lives," said Aunt Sally.

"Not really," I said, my voice rising above everyone else's, agreeing the book was about my life. "Sure . . . maybe some . . . but I've fictionalized quite a bit."

"Truth is stranger than fiction," said Keith seriously.

"Amen," said Bruce. "Lisa's life would make HBO."

"Maybe you'll meet someone now," said Fat Susan.

"Please God," said Mother.

"A rich man . . ." said Aunt Pearl.

"Knock on wood," said Aunt Sally.

"Our Marjorie Morningstar'll make it yet," said Uncle Maury.

"Please God," said Aunt Pearl.

"I don't want to—"

"Never mind! Once you make it, the men will be climbing the walls to get to you," said Fat Susan, nodding positively.

"You can flush all men down the toilet," said Aunt Sally, nodding her birdlike head and popping a bunch of nuts in her mouth.

"Anyways, *nu,* Bruce," said Uncle Maury, "how's it going?"

"Nothing. Nothing much," said Bruce, dipping another prawn into the cocktail sauce.

"Bruce is recuperating," said Mother, emptying an ashtray.

"He's been on vacation," said Sidney, laughing, then looking at Mother sheepishly.

"They say all the big movie stars go to the Betty Ford," said Aunt Pearl, knocking on wood again.

"Celebrities . . . a lot of nice people," said Mother, nodding approvingly.

"Shmaltzy place," said Bruce.

"Movie stars! Movie schmars!" said Aunt Sally. "If you ask me, they're all a bunch of drunks."

"For your information, Sally," said Mother, "they have a waiting list a mile long."

"Cost a bundle," said Sidney.

"Anyways, let's all pray Lisa will meet someone," said Fat Susan.

"I'd die happy," said Mother.

"Enough with the dying!" yelled Bruce.

"You'll die soon enough," said Uncle Maury.

So while they discussed the glory of being a princess, Fat Susan arguing that Lady Di has it made, and Bruce Donald Ducking and the dog throwing up prawns and going wacko, I sat there half zonked, feeling no pain at all, until Mother's housekeeper, Birdie, came into the room and announced dinner.

I felt a bit dizzy. Bruce helped me to the dining room and whispered that he had some good stuff, which I guess meant grass or something.

We all went into the dining room. God, the dining room was so beautiful! Mother's decorator, Woody, had decorated it in apricot silk moire, and it was like Versailles, not to mention the centerpiece, which was a Steuben swan filled with apricot-colored roses, and little pink candles glowed.

So while everyone argued about who was going to sit next to me, I sat next to Aunt Sally, who was shaking her head a lot and murmuring that she didn't know what all the fuss was about anyways and that everyone could go to hell. After everyone was properly seated, Mother rang the little glass dinner bell, complaining like crazy that good help these days was hard to find, until poor

Birdie, a tiny, wiry black woman with hawk eyes, shuffled in carrying a silver tray larger than she was. Birdie waited patiently while everyone helped themselves to roast beef and asparagus and all kinds of goodies.

"Birdie!" shouted Mother. "Take that dog out of here! He's driving me crazy!"

"Meat's tough," said Aunt Sally.

"Oh, leave my dog alone," said Sidney.

"Eat, Lisa," said Aunt Pearl. "You're a toothpick."

"Bruce, put more gravy on your meat," said Mother.

"He doesn't need it!" shouted Sidney.

So Birdie carried poor Christopher, yelping like crazy, from the room while Uncle Maury stood and took more pictures. Sidney told Mother not to shout so, that it wasn't necessary to shout, that her shouting scared the dog. And Mother shouted back for him to mind his own business, while Aunt Pearl said that she never heard of such shouting and Uncle Maury told her to mind her own business. Aunt Sally, poor thing, her false teeth making the funniest clacking sounds, complained about the meat and said that as far as she was concerned, everyone was crazy. Mother and Bruce were whispering their in jokes about the family. When Fat Susan poked and pounded Keith on the back and told him not to eat so fast, that he wasn't going to a fire, he almost choked to death, everyone bringing him water, God, it was awful. By now I was almost in a stupor. I hadn't eaten a thing. I was too excited. Everyone began asking me again about writing, if it was really true that writers have to suffer, if maybe a husband would help, if I drank like this all the time. Mother assured them that I didn't drink at all and that usually I didn't dress so freaky. Fat Susan said that she loved my style, that it was arty, and so it went, Aunt Pearl telling Uncle Maury that if I can write a book, their son can. All this arguing about nothing, God, I can't stand it. Suddenly I wanted to run out of there. For as long as I would remember, everyone always argued about everything, would even throw things at and hit each other. No wonder my stomach hurt. Anyways, I was just about ready for the paper bag when suddenly Bruce stood and rapped the water glass with his spoon.

Mother gestured for everyone to be quiet. Bruce's face was as red as his hair. His small mouth was pursed and he looked very serious.

"Let the boy speak!" said Aunt Pearl, smiling toward Bruce.

"What's all the fuss about?" shouted Aunt Sally, shaking her head like mad.

"I want to make a toast," said Bruce, holding up the wine glass and smiling at me. "A shmaltzy toast to my sis, Lisa, who is making us proud."

God, I was on the verge of tears. Everyone raised their glasses and smiled at me. Uncle Maury took more pictures. I blinked from the flashbulbs.

"Thank you, Bruce," I managed to say.

He pressed his lips tightly together, rapped his glass with a spoon, then looked around the room, making sure everyone was quiet.

"I'd like to make an important announcement," he finally said. He paused, looked around again, then said in a low voice, "At our next family dinner I want everyone to meet my lover, Mark. I'm coming out! I'm gay."

Dead silence. You could hear a pin drop.

"You'll get over it!" finally said Mother, looking frozen and glaring at Bruce. "Sit down!"

Bruce remained standing, nodding and smiling.

"Right on!" I yelled, clapping my hands. At last Bruce stood up for himself.

"Kids," muttered Uncle Maury. "Anything goes these days."

"What difference?" said Aunt Pearl, shrugging and smiling at Bruce. "As long as he's Jewish."

"They make wonderful cooks," said Aunt Sally.

"We eat out!" snapped Bruce.

"Gay, shmay," said Aunt Sally. "Who the hell cares as long as Mark Whatever-His-Name earns a living? Bruce doesn't earn a living."

"Living!" yelled Sidney, all red-faced. "Now I'll be supporting two faggots!"

"Shut up!" yelled Mother.

"The woman is putting me in the poorhouse," complained Sidney. No one was listening to him.

"Everyone keep quiet!" shouted Bruce.

"It's the trend now, *taka*," said Aunt Pearl.

"*Dynasty*'s full of gorgeous men," said Fat Susan sanctimoniously and looking like she was smelling something.

"Clichés!" I yelled above the racket. "People are people! Loving is loving!"

"Right on!" shouted Susan's husband.

"We'll talk about this later!" ordered Mother, poking Bruce and glancing at me.

"Mother! Bruce is over thirty. It's his business!" I said, furious. "It's wonderful when you know who you are. . . . Gay is loving."

"You and your lousy women's libber ideas!" she screamed.

"Lisa's a liberal," explained Sidney to Susan, who was slurping ice cream.

"Liberal, shmiberal, in my book you're all nuts," said Aunt Sally.

And then everyone began arguing at once, Bruce Donald Ducking and Mother's oval face all scrunged and angry-looking. God, I felt awful. Who cares what Bruce does, anyways! Good for him. God, wouldn't you know, on my one night of glory, Bruce had to fuck everything up. So while Sidney and Mother argued—screaming, actually—about what a rotten kid Bruce was, that he wasn't going to support some faggot Mark, that supporting Bruce was already putting him in the grave, Mother began crying, while Aunt Sally murmured again that everyone could go to hell.

I felt the rash starting on my face, and my hands were shaking. All I need is for them to see my anxiety attack. Fat Susan and Keith were looking at me, then whispering. Thank God Birdie carried in the cheesecake on a big plate and Uncle Maury took more pictures. I told everyone that I was exhausted, that I had a heavy writing day the next day, and that I had to get going. After everyone made a big thing about how I was going to get home, Bruce finally offered me a ride in his new Jenson.

So there I was sitting in this sports car, really a class job, holding the brown paper bag filled with the leftover prawns and dinner I hadn't eaten, complimenting Bruce about his speech, his courage.

"Now," I said, "You can get a job . . . not have Mother support you anymore. . . ."

"Mind your own business!" he screamed, jerking the car. If I hadn't had the seatbelt on, I would have gone through the windshield.

"Bruce . . . I—"

"Always a troublemaker . . . always watching. Have you made such a way in the world?" he said, calming down now.

I didn't answer.

"I just thought—"

"Don't think so much."

After a long, awkward silence, I asked, "What does Mark do?"

"Do? Mark does what I do. We sit and watch my saltwater fish." He put another tape in. The music was so loud I had a headache. "We sit and watch the fish—so beautiful—and we get stoned, then we go out and eat sushi . . . God, it's wonderful."

"Uh-huh."

"I'm not lonely anymore."

"Oh, that's wonderful, really wonderful," I said, suddenly crying and not really knowing why. "But a relationship," I said, "can't help loneliness. It's something you have to work on yourself."

"Oh, cut it out! I'm not in the mood for your introspection shit. A little therapy and you think you know it all. I've been in analysis for twelve years with Dr. Heindrich, who studied with Freud. A real Nazi shrink. So don't give me your bullshit." He gunned the motor and began driving faster while shouting obscenities in German, screaming heil this, heil that, God, I was scared. I prayed that he wouldn't crash. My luck . . . just on the brink of fame and I'll die yet, so praying was necessary. After all, Bruce had cracked up four perfectly good sports cars. The last one almost did him in . . . wired jaw, months in the hospital.

"Heil! . . . Dr. Heindrich," he said, enunciating the "ich," "is wacko . . . but he suits me fine," he said, lighting a cigarette with one hand. "He tells Mother and Sidney that I'm sicko and I get what I want. All Dr. Heindrich does is *ja, ja* this and fart. What a creep." I remained, of course, quiet, still praying for my life, until Bruce, thank God, stopped safely in front of my house. I slammed the car door and rushed up the stairs, shlepping the paper bag of prawns and caviar. Boy, was I glad to be home. I hugged Anny. Quickly I undressed and got into bed, wearing my torn frog nightgown, promising myself that with my first royalty check I would buy a new wardrobe, maybe even some sexy underwear.

I curled under the covers, in my usual prenatal position, clutching the heating pad. I closed my eyes, floating into the sea, into my dream, where I was walking across the stage, wearing my Yves St. Laurent black skirt with the slit along the side. When Dick Cavett held up my novel, *Princess,* I smiled. While Cavett stammered about how *Princess* changed the sexual climate of the country, I blew kisses to Amy and Jenny. The applause was deafening. I floated into the darkness . . . silver birds squawking . . . caw . . . caw . . . caw. . . .

CHAPTER THREE

Wouldn't you know it? The one day I fly, New York has the largest snowstorm in history. And me, so afraid of flying . . . but I told myself not to get all hot and bothered, just to keep cool. That the pilots know what they're doing. The San Francisco airport was pandemonium two days before Christmas. Everyone was rushing here and there, carrying reindeer tote bags filled with brightly wrapped Christmas gifts, and wearing holly corsages inside their lapels.

I hurried toward TWA, Gate 30, my black Von Furstenberg duffel bag slung over my shoulder. I could hardly believe that I was at last a bona fide authoress on my way to meet my publisher, Walter Avalon, and my editor, Shana Goldsmith. Gee, I was floating, aware that my midcalf black cape and slouch black hat and red leather Russian boots were dramatic.

So there I was feeling so good, smiling, even glancing back at the men, my cape floating behind me, until, at the bomb check-in, the buzzer went off. What a pain. There I stood, a sicky smile on my face, kind of chuckling and making jokes, while removing my silver dog chain belt, Navajo wrist cuff, silver earrings, everyone giving me funny looks. Phew! It was awful. The mean-looking porter went through my duffel bag and my briefcase until I was cleared. Practically running to the plane, I told myself that I wouldn't be afraid, that I had already taken quite enough tranquilizers, already felt kind of zonked, and that I would sleep on the plane. Besides, I could see that there were plenty of nuns and babies on this flight, always a good sign, though my feet were beginning to get numb and my mouth felt numb, you know, like when the dentist gives you a double shot of Novocain.

But could I help it? All those years spent in dark closets and basements. The anxiety had grown into this phobia thing, and now I was afraid of birds, elevators, balloons, planes, grocery stores, banks—anything moving or enclosed, you name it. But with a frozen smile on my face, when I stepped into the plane, I even chatted with the two stewardesses, who made a big thing about my cape, as if flying for me was an everyday occurrence. The plane was packed. As I tried to locate my seat, which was in the back of the plane, I tried not to shove the lady in front of me, who moved like a snail. I felt like I was going to faint. Finally I located my seat. Yuk . . . it was in the center of the aisle, and, my luck, next to a lady diapering a baby in her lap, while shouting Italian to three toddlers playing with rosary beads and eating crackers. Excusing myself, I removed my hat and tossed my hair. I smiled at the horrible children, then slumped into my seat and quickly snapped the seatbelt.

Wouldn't you know? Either I would be seated next to a coo-coo doing crossword puzzles, or screaming, sticky children. Why not next to that man over there, wearing the trench coat, with the silver hair, holding the nice leather briefcase? I practiced my eye focus until at last we made eye contact, but then I flushed and turned away and closed my eyes, as though I was going to rest a moment. I imagined following the man in the trench coat into the john, downing my pants, and fingerfucking a lot. Lately my sexual fantasy had been going wild, but plenty of time for that later, Lisa . . . after the book is published. Plenty of time.

So while I sat there, my teeth clenched, thanking God a lot that I had taken out the maximum insurance, the Italian children sucking pacifiers and crying like mad, at last the seatbelt sign went off. I kept my eyes straight ahead on the open cockpit, staring at the pilots, making sure that they didn't get shot or anything. By the time we landed after hours of circling Kennedy Airport, I was so glad that we were on the ground I even thanked the pilots for such a Class A flight.

Kennedy was a mess. For at least two hours I stood bleary-eyed waiting for my luggage, again making eye contact with the man in the silver hair wearing the trench coat, until at last I spotted Jenny's red Naugahyde suitcase with my somewhat stained bra strap hanging from its side.

Finally, I got into a taxi and instructed the driver, in my best know-it-all voice, to Amy and Adam's apartment on West-Seventy-sixth Street between West End and Broadway. I settled back into the seat and glanced out the window. The snow was falling like mad, so beautiful, all white and everything, the houses covered by snow and lit by Christmas trees. It was beautiful. I was so excited that I was breathing funny. Finally, when the taxi stopped in front of Amy's apartment, I paid the driver, who was still telling me how he drove twenty-two hours a day so that he could support his crippled son in music school. I overtipped him and shlepped the suitcase across the street, trying not to slip in the ice, feeling a bit hurt that Adam and Amy weren't in front waiting for me. Oh, well, kids. Why should they? So damned cold. So I managed, somehow, to drag my stuff down the stairs, holding my nose against the row of garbage bags. At last the kids buzzed me in. I dropped the luggage and ran down the smelly, dark hall, screaming, "Amy . . . Amy . . . I'm here . . . I'm here . . . Mom's here! . . ." Finally I saw her, God, so beautiful, this tall, lithe girl, wearing two sets of leg warmers. Still, she walked like a ballerina, feet extended. All at once we were both screaming. We rushed into each other's arms, hugging like mad. God, she felt good. A bit thin. Too thin, I thought. I could feel her bones underneath her two thick sweaters and her arms felt like sticks. Then we stepped back and looked at each other. "God," I repeated, touching her face, her beautiful chestnut hair hanging past her shoulder, her nose so acquiline, "You look beautiful. . . ."

"Oh, Mom," she said softly, her green eyes filled with tears. Too long for a mother and daughter to be apart.

"Stop Godding," said Adam, standing behind Amy.

"Oh, Adam," I said, hugging him. "Oh, Adam, it's so good to see you."

Adam and Amy had been living together since NYU. Adam was a handsome, theatrical-looking boy.

"C'mon, Lisa . . . let's get out of the hall. All your yelling will get us kicked out yet."

So I followed the kids, as I call them, into their apartment. It was so warm in there I felt like I was stepping into a sauna or something.

After I screamed, "Lucy!" and hugged this ugly, huge cat, who hissed at me, its tail all puffed up and everything, and raved about how wonderful their apartment was, how really New York and with-it it looked, at last I sat down on their beanbag chair.

God, they looked good . . . so really beautiful. The walls were covered with museum posters, and Adam had made built-in book-cases.

"I'll fix some coffee," said Adam.

"Take off your hat and coat, Mom," said Amy. "Let's have a look at you."

I removed my cape and hat, Adam and Amy gave each other a look, then squinted their eyes at me. Amy looked worried.

"The hair, Mom, I'll have Mr. Guy from CNN come over in the morning. He'll shape your hair."

"A little toning, Lisa. You have a lovely figure but I can tell that you need toning."

"And don't wear those clothes to Avalon tomorrow," said Amy. "I'll loan you my Perry Ellis." Suddenly I felt shy, at a loss for words, even kind of shameful, suddenly overwhelmed. It had been so long, over a year, since I had seen Amy. I began crying. Adam and Amy gave each other one of their looks, only the kind that intimacy knows. Amy's beautiful green eyes narrowed suspiciously and she said, almost in baby talk, "Mom . . . c'mon, have some coffee. You must be tired."

"And Lisa," said Adam, glancing at Amy sideways, "you have to be together for tomorrow. You can't cry or behave this way when you go to Avalon."

"Yes. Yes, I know. I'm just feeling kind of emotional, I guess." I glared at the awful cat.

For a while we sat sipping our coffee and chatting quietly. From upstairs, I could hear someone singing opera, along with the sound of violins and a lot of thumping.

"Everyone in this building is with the ballet or opera or something," explained Adam.

While Adam and Amy cooed and mooed, whispering in each other's ears a lot, I sat and stared at them, trying to catch up with time. "Adam and I are going to have bambinos. Lots of bambinos. As soon as Adam finishes law school."

"I hope they call me Lisa and not Nana," I said, laughing.

"C'mon, Mom, Adam and I made a room for you . . . and there are rules, so let us explain."

So I managed to get out of the lousy beanbag chair, my knees creaky, while Adam and Amy showed me my room, which consisted of a large closet Adam had so cleverly transformed into a room for Lucy. "You know," he explained, "in a New York apartment, we have to be careful with the litter box. So that we don't get roaches—or rats."

"Uh-huh," I agreed, looking at the closet, which was taken up mostly by this enormous, three-story wooden house Adam had built for Lucy's litter box. On the top of the house were three glass portholes so that Lucy could climb up and look out while she was doing her doo-doo thing.

"Don't worry, Mom," said Amy, looking worried. "The litter is chlorophyll, and Adam bathes Lucy every day in the bathtub and rubs her with Calvin Klein cologne."

"Uh-huh," I nodded, murmuring how really clean the house was. What's wrong with that, Lisa? So he has a perfume and cat fetish, at least he has a capacity for caring. So anyway, the kids had this sleeping bag, I think Amy's old camp sleeping bag, all laid out on the closet floor next to Lucy's litter house. I told Adam again how really clever the house was and assured them that, of course, I didn't mind sleeping on the floor next to Lucy.

"And Lisa," said Adam, looking kind of sheepish, but his turquoise eyes sparkling, "we don't mean to be selfish or anything. But please don't use any of our shampoo, cologne, or . . . you know, sundry items. Amy and I are on a very strict budget."

"Oh, God, Adam, did you have to tell her?"

"You told me to!" he said, his voice rising. They glared at each other. So while Amy frowned sympathetically, looking as if she was on the verge of tears, I assured them that, of course, I understood and that I had brought my own things.

"It's so nice of you kids having me and all," I said, feeling on the verge of tears myself.

"Never mind," said Adam, his face brightening, Amy still giving him dirty looks. "We love having you. Just that we have certain rules here, with studying, working, and school."

"Of course," I said. "I think it's wonderful."

"So let's go over the rules. May as well now," said Adam, glancing sheepishly at Amy, who was still frowning. "No coffee grinds in the sink . . . empty the garbage . . . and Amy and I like to sleep late. It's our vacation. So please don't use anything in the morning until we get up. And don't feed or touch Lucy. She's a nervous cat."

So after I agreed to everything, I sat in the beanbag chair, my feet out, waiting for my turn in the bathroom. The apartment was really cute. So in. With all the framed museum posters on the walls and the bookcases. The two typewriters. God, I was proud of Amy, already a journalist at CNN and supporting herself. God, I had been holding it for so long I thought I'd die. . . . So carrying my frog print makeup case and red flannel nightgown robe, I went into the bathroom. The bathroom was so tiny that when I sat on the john my knees hit the door. When I bathed, Lucy's cat hairs floated on the top. But so what, Lisa? You're here. Probably the most exciting time in your life. Next time you'll stay at the Plaza. For sure, soon all this struggle will be over, and anyways, it's so wonderful being with the kids.

So after I applied the placenta cream to my skin and brushed my teeth, keeping everything neat and separate from their things, I went into the room. The kids were cuddled in bed, mooing and cooing, doing their guppy kisses and making puppy sounds. God, it was cute. I went over and kissed them good night, assuring them that I wouldn't disturb them in the morning. Then I went into my closet and somehow got into the sleeping bag, the bottom sticking half out the door. That awful Lucy was sitting like a tiger, watching me and hissing. But I was so tired that soon I closed my eyes and listened to the street sounds, sullen horns pounding the traffic, the rattle of things, odd sounds, brazen sounds; finally I fell asleep.

When I awoke it was so still I couldn't hear a thing. So I turned on my stomach and peered out into the room. The kids were still sleeping, entwined in each other's arms. This hideous Lucy was glaring at me from the porthole again, doing her thing. The heater was hissing and the room was getting hot. The windows were frosted and outside it was white. Today, the day when I would meet Walter and Shana. . . . I lay there luxuriating in the glory, my legs so numb I couldn't move anyways, until, thank God, I heard Adam murmur something to Amy and they both sat up in bed.

"Lisa, are you awake?" asked Adam.

"Yes."

"Did you sleep well, Mom?" said Amy, looking concerned.

"Wonderful," I lied.

"How's Lucy?" asked Adam.

"In her house," I said.

"Quite a cat, isn't she!"

"Yes, never have I seen such a cat . . . she makes Anny look like a neb."

So I lay there while Adam and Amy went to the bathroom, holding my nose against the awful stench. Adam and Amy were laughing from the shower. Kids, how wonderful, I thought, remembering myself at twenty, virginal and scared, spending most of my time inside the closet, reading romances, and crying a lot. God, it was awful.

At last they emerged, sometime later, wearing layers of leg warmers, sweaters. So finally I rose, my legs creaking, and went into the bathroom and showered and dressed.

We had coffee and ate bagels and lox, while Amy and Adam discussed at length that they didn't think I should wear the brocaded brown velvet vest.

"It looks too Berkeley . . . too post-hippie, Mom. You're a sophisticated, classy lady."

"But I like it, Amy. It's different."

"Leave her alone," said Adam, looking protective. "She has style. She can carry it off." So after they decided that I could wear what I was wearing, Mr. Guy from CNN, the biggie hair stylist, arrived.

Mr. Guy was a tall, slender, youngish man who looked a bit like John Travolta. He was wearing a long fur coat, and carried an alligator case, I guessed for his scissors and stuff. After he greeted Amy and Adam, oohing and aahing like mad about what great style Amy had, something about the special way she wore her leg warmers and how great her braid was, he came over and shook hands.

For a moment he peered closely at my face, pushing my head this way, that, Amy and Adam murmuring "Do something, do something." Finally Mr. Guy removed his coat.

"Please wet your hair," he said somberly.

So I went into the bathroom and dunked my hair under the sink, only the damned sink was so small my head got stuck. But, thank God, I got it out. Then, shivering, a towel around my neck, my hair dripping wet, I sat down on the chair, placed in the middle of the room. Mr. Guy, without even a mirror, began cutting. All the while he gossiped with Amy about this layout, this shoot, various celebrities. While Adam played tiger games with Lucy. After some time, Mr. Guy began blow-drying my hair. After he finished that, he instructed, "Now, shake your head. That's right. To the right, to the left, up, down." Adam and Amy were shrieking, how great I looked, how the haircut had changed my life, how awful, even dowdy they said I had looked when I arrived.

Indeed, Mr. Guy had cut my hair beautifully. God, I really loved it, so I stood there, oohing and aahing and murmuring what a genius he was, shaking my head every which way. You know, like those girls in the television ads, running slow motion through a meadow, their hair bouncing all over the place, then landing in perfect shape, like that.

Anyway, I paid Mr. Guy an absolute fortune and Amy made up my eyes, Adam standing close by, of course, instructing just how much shadow, liner I needed. Until, at last, I was ready. Christ, it was almost noon. So I put on the cape and Amy's cashmere gloves.

"We'll wait with you on the corner until a taxi arrives," said Adam, putting on his earmuffs.

Amy smiled adoringly at Adam, so after Amy and Adam exchanged more guppy kisses, which was a kind of sucking of their bottom lips, and made more puppy sounds, we went outside and walked to the corner. The wind was howling like mad, but the city was so beautiful and white, and the skyscrapers tilted into the darkening sky. People dressed in furs or heavy winter coats, and scarves wrapped around their faces, rushed down the street, some disappearing down the steps into the subway station. A million Santa Clauses, ringing big brass bells, and kids, and strolling musicians, crouched on the street corner, and the charred smell of roasting chestnuts from the corner Sabrett stands fell into the air.

Finally a taxi arrived. I kissed the kids good-bye.

"Remember," Adam said, looking all concerned, "don't say 'God' or 'heavy-duty.' "

"And don't give that funny stare with your eyes," said Amy.

"Cool it!" shouted Adam over the traffic.

"Break a leg!" they said, crossing their fingers.

So I got into the taxi, wondering, what funny stare?, Instructing the driver to go to Avalon Publishers at East Fifty-first Street.

It was warm inside the lobby of the big brownstone building, thank God. I shook my hair until it hung full around my face, and I just stood there a moment, taking it all in, trying to keep cool. Already, though, I could feel myself shrinking, like a part of me was getting lost. God, that's all I need was to become this nerdish, passive thing. So get hold of yourself.

They like your work, so they'll like you. . . . While I was assuring myself with all this bullshit, I rode the rickety elevator to the fourth floor. I stepped into a small reception room, smiling toward the girl sitting behind the large desk.

"Lisa Perlman," I announced, glancing at the best sellers inside glass cases, thinking that someday mine would be there.

"Oh . . . Ms. Perlman," said the girl, smiling cordially and coming out to meet me. "Let me take your coat." We shook hands, and the girl took my cape. "Mr. Avalon and Shana are waiting for you. Take the stairway," she said, pointing to a side door, "and then walk up two flights, turn left, and Shana will be waiting for you at the top of the stairs."

"Thank you," I said briskly, smiling.

So carrying the briefcase and clearing my throat a lot, I climbed the stairs, telling myself that I felt great, that I was this authoress and all, until at the top of the stairs I looked right into Shana Goldsmith's sharp blue eyes. God, she was really something, a really petite, really heavy-duty chic New York lady . . . long dark hair, pointed features, and so confident. She was wearing a gray straight ankle-length skirt and gray suede flat boots, and a big black sweater, and around her neck a Paloma Picasso necklace. You know the type, real attractive, like she could step up anytime and hold an audience.

She extended her hand and smiled. "I'm Shana Goldsmith, your editor."

"Yes, yes," I said, smiling and shaking her hand. "I'm glad to meet you."

She nodded. "Let's go see Walter now," she said crisply. "He's waiting in his office." So Shana led me into this huge—enormous, actually—wood-paneled office. I nearly died, dropped dead on the spot, when I saw this really stunning, and I mean stunning, tall, slender, middle-aged man with olive skin, large dark eyes, and a thick shock of the most beautiful white hair I had ever seen. He was wearing one of those sharp pinstriped suits with a vest and a jazzy white silk shirt with French cuffs. I was in love. He, Walter, walked toward me, his eyes appraising me in one quick glance, and kissed me European style, I guess is what they call it, two kisses, one on each cheek.

Then he kind of pushed me back a bit and said softly, "Yes. You're beautiful. We can do a lot with that face."

For once I kept quiet. But suddenly my feet and hands felt so big. I stood there looking into Walter's eyes until Shana said, "Sit down. Over here." So I sat down in this leather chair placed in front of Walter's desk, clutching the stupid briefcase on my lap, looking at Walter, who was sitting behind his desk now, still staring at me.

After this long silence, the awkward kind, too, I said, "I'll work very hard . . . very hard . . . I want you both to know this . . . and thank you for the chance. . . ." I stopped talking, though, because I was sure they gave each other a funny look and no one was talking anyway. So I waited, held out on the eye focus until Walter said, "Go with Shana into her office. She wants to talk to you. Then we'll go to lunch."

I rose and walked slowly across the large office and followed Shana into her office.

In her office, she began explaining how she wanted a best seller, that her time was very valuable, that my *Princess* could be a best seller if I listened. That she wanted a princess better and bigger than

Judith Krantz's *Princess Daisy*. Oh, God . . . After I assured her that, of course, it would be better . . . that I understood perfectly, a part of me wondered why they had bought my princess. After Shana talked more about some of her famous authors and how impossible most of them were, how if it wasn't for her they wouldn't be famous, she said at last, "C'mon, let's go to lunch."

We went to this French restaurant, the kind that has walnut paneling, pink tablecloths, and silver decanters filled with little imported flowers. The waiters moved like they were gliding, and the women, all gorgeous, were wearing expensive furs and clothes.

I could hardly believe it . . . not that I hadn't been to some heavy-duty places, but here I was being dined and courted by Walter Avalon. My princess had gone farther than I had thought. So after we were seated and after several swank-looking people stopped by the table and Walter introduced me as his budding new authoress . . . then Walter ordered lunch, beginning with endive, fresh asparagus. Finally, Shana and Walter exchanged another one of those looks and Walter said, looking at me sternly, "Now, when you talk . . . please address your editor, Shana."

"Yes, yes, of course," I said. I laughed nervously, hating myself for being so scared. Shana was fussing about a chip in the wineglass and looking mad.

"This is so exciting," I said, looking from Walter to Shana. "I want you to know that I'm looking forward to working with such a fine editor." God, it was sickening how I was carrying on, but I couldn't help myself.

"Eat your endive," she said. "It's really excellent." So I picked a bit at my endive salad, uncomfortably because Walter, on my left, kept staring at me and it was making me nervous. Not my best side, either. Finally, between courses, Shana said, "I like some of your scenes, Lisa, and your writing is not without charm. But"—she pressed the palms of her delicate hands together and looked contemplative—"compress!"

"Yes," I said, smiling. What the hell does she mean, 'compress'?

"The car scene is good . . . the beach scene . . . but your princess—"

"Yes," I said eagerly.

"Younger, I want her younger!" she said, taking another bite from the endive.

My heart sank.

"Younger," I repeated, nodding.

"Younger," replied Walter.

"Younger definitely," finally said Shana. She glared at me for a moment and when she was finished chewing, she looked at me sternly. "Your audience are the women in Iowa who are folding diapers, and they aren't going to be interested in an unglamorous woman dragging around, introspecting."

I nodded. "Of course," I said. "I'll make her younger." I chuckled, looking from Walter, who was eating his chicken, to Shana, who looked more than annoyed.

"And too much introspection," she repeated, her voice rising. "As I said, your readers don't care about the psychological interpretations. So I want you to expand. Expand," she repeated, opening her eyes wide. "You know, move from the inside to the outside."

"Action!" demanded Walter, looking kind of mad, too. Shana nodded.

"Yes, action. Yes. I know what you mean," I quickly replied, beginning to feel really sick.

"Let the psychological stuff shine through the action."

"And younger," I said, nodding and smiling.

"Younger and more action," agreed Walter, chewing his asparagus. "Maybe a gun scene. For a really smash ending. A whodunit ending," said Walter, excitedly looking at Shana. So while they discussed over their asparagus just how I should end the book, I picked at the fish, telling myself that this was all necessary, that they certainly knew what they're doing, that, after all, who am I to tell them to take their book and you know what?

"Okay. Now," said Shana, finally looking at me again, her eyes narrowed, "figure out the gun thing and definitely class up the names. I don't like the names. And absolutely no children in this book. Do you understand?"

"Yes," I said.

"Judith Krantz doesn't sell over a million copies because she has children running through her book."

"No, of course not."

Walter nodded.

"Glamour sells," said Shana.

"And change the title," said Walter. "Maybe something about virgins, or madonnas, or blood."

"Yes. Yes, of course."

"And you must compress time," said Shana, pressing her hands together. "Do you understand?"

"Yes. Of course. Time," I repeated, feeling almost dizzy now.

"And more narrative," said Walter.

"And remember the action," reminded Shana.

"Yes. The gun," I agreed. "Don't worry about a thing."

Then I was sure—positive, in fact—that Shana and Walter gave each other this really funny look. I sensed that I was caught between some odd thing between them, maybe an argument, whether or not it was professional or personal or whatever it didn't matter, but I had the idea that maybe Shana hated the book and Walter wanted it. Something like that, though whatever, I knew that I was in for it. That it wasn't going to be easy. I picked at my food, just because I knew Shana and Walter were watching my every move, and it wasn't nice anyway to leave all this food, but God, I could hardly eat a thing. So when the waiter removed the dishes I was relieved. Finally, two waiters rolled over a cart making a big thing out of lighting some exotic fruit. Walter finally said, looking at me again, "Nice face, don't you think, Shana?"

Shana shrugged indifferently. "She'll be good on talk shows."

So while they discussed me in third person, I assured myself that this is the way it is, that I'm a trouper, that I would write them a much better book than Judith Krantz ever dreamed. So, finally, after lunch we went outside. The damned snowstorm was going wild, and though only afternoon, it was so dark that the traffic lights were on.

I kissed Walter good-bye. I couldn't help it. I liked him so much, felt his sensitivity underneath all the theatrics. Shana, buttoning her mink coat, still looked stern.

"Remember, send us the new outline," she instructed, "so that we can see the new plot."

"Yes, yes," I said, exchanging one of those phony kisses with her.

"Action" reminded Walter, his eyes twinkling.

"Yes, action!" I shouted above the traffic.

So after we yelled "Action!" and "Go to it!," I began walking, just walking, not hearing the pounding traffic, not feeling the cold. My feet were so numb, anyways. And I felt kind of nauseated and, God, the anxiety was starting, my arms tingly and that awful numb feeling in my mouth, you know, like Novocain.

I'm scared. What was I going to do? How am I going to do this action, glamour thing from my ordinary life? Little did they know that my life was inside a glass jar. But I should have been more assertive, not so passive and meek.

But what else could I have done? Nothing, I assured myself, walking faster now and crossing the street against the light. You'd better read Judith Krantz. Figure out how to write glamour, action. No more shleppy princesses tear-jerking and introspecting. Or curtains. And believe me, if you don't write it the way they want you'll be one of those bag ladies lying over there on the steps of St. Patrick's Cathedral. Poor things. I stood there, the wind turning my face all blue, when a wave of sadness came over me, so big that I ran up the steps and went inside St. Patrick's.

For a moment I just stood there, it was so beautiful. The cathedral was a golden glow from the thousands of candles flickering. As soft as prayers. Red and white poinsettia plants decorated the altars and saints. After a while, I went and sat down in a front pew. For as long as I can remember, I was fascinated by churches. Maybe because of all those years inside dark closets and basements. I sat there praying for my princess and the children in San Salvador for the longest time, at least until I stopped shaking. Then I went and stood by each saint and lit candles. The candles were so beautiful, their flames flickering like tiny stars in a dark sky. God, it was the most wonderful experience, so golden and still. The echoes and the prayer chants, the incense and the way the candlelight shadowed the saints.

Soon the anxiety began to subside and I relaxed, letting the disappointment settle into my bones. . . . I would just have to create a character . . . after all, isn't that what being creative is? . . . Of course you can do it. So after I lit a whole bunch of candles, finally I knelt by Saint Teresa, asking God not to forget me, at least to see me through this one, that after this book I would promise to write like crazy, and if I make it, to support all the bag people. After a while, my knees hurting, I tiptoed from the cathedral, feeling all emotional and everything. By now the city was pitch black. The people rushing along the streets were shadows and buildings all lit up for Christmas shone like gilded stones. I couldn't wait to see Amy and Adam and talk to them.

Of course, they were waiting for me, just dying to know everything. Before I could tell them, though, and just as I was about to remove my coat and plop into the beanbag chair, Adam asked politely, looking somewhat guilty, if first I wouldn't mind waiting outside for about half an hour, that he and Amy had to finish something. Of all times. So after standing in the dark hallway, shivering and holding my nose against the stench from the garbage strike, finally Adam called, "Lisa, you can come in now!"

After I told them the whole story, while crying and carrying on about how awful Shana was, and that I didn't know anything about guns, sex, action, that I hated their story and wanted mine back, that I wouldn't write it, Adam yelled at the top of his lungs, God, even Lucy went and hid under the bed, "Do what they want! Don't start fucking around! You're in no position to get difficult! Wait until you're famous!"

"Mom, I agree," said Amy, looking furious. "Don't start all your shtick. I'm warning you. Do what they want."

"What if I can't," I said, sobbing like crazy, "It's not my book anymore. I'm not a machine."

"You *are* a machine!" they both yelled. "Don't start that horseshit stuff. Or Lester North will kick you out. And then what?"

So after they both lectured that I was a neurotic, so impossible, not to mention self-destructive, chaotic, crazy, all the usual, finally I lowered my head and promised I wouldn't fuck up.

"Fine," said Adam, sighing like an exhausted parent sighs after a long argument. "Now, tomorrow is Christmas Eve," he said brightly. "I've made reservations at the Four Seasons. Where all the publishers go. You'll love it."

Sure, I thought, for what it probably costs, I'd better love it. Oh, God. But so what?

"Oh, wonderful," I said.

"And afterward," said Amy excitedly, "Mary Chase, the fashion photographer from *Vogue,* is having a party."

"Wonderful."

"And, Mom," she said, her tone cautious, "there'll be a lot of writers, film critics, really celebrity people."

Uh-huh, I thought, wishing I could go home. Suddenly I was homesick. Who wants to go to some Mary's stupid old party? But I had to. So I smiled and repeated, "Wonderful." That night, since the storm was so bad, we stayed in and decorated the pathetic Christmas tree. While Amy and Adam wrapped oodles of presents for Lucy, I stayed in the closet. Finally, doused from tranquilizers, I fell asleep, dreaming plot, wondering about guns.

Christmas Eve. All white and everything. The snow was so beautiful and the snowflakes were spinning softly. The city looks so peaceful that it's hard to believe that people starved on one end of the city and luxuriated on the other. For most of the day we stayed inside, holding Lucy up to the window a lot so that she could see the snow. Then we played Twenty-one. In late afternoon on Adam's new IBM Selectric, I started writing new plot ideas for *Princess,* writing and writing until I felt the high I always felt when writing, a peaceful high, the world all yours, like swimming underwater, everything so still, and you can see real clear. Only now my princess was gone, twenty-five years younger. I wondered if I was separate enough, if I wasn't still so attached to my old princess. Anyways, for the rest of the day, just for exercises, I wrote these poems in stream of consciousness about darkness, about damp, wet rocks and golden seas. Until Amy and Adam said it was time to go to the Four Seasons.

Of course, wouldn't you know that the heating system was broken, and such a fancy, shmancy restaurant, where all the hot publishers go, colder than a witch's tit, so that the management was passing out these heated crocheted shawls. Ugly, too, so ugly I was ashamed to wear it over my Yves St. Laurent black tuxedo suit . . . the one night I get all decked out, I end up with a nebbish shawl. Not only that, earlier Amy and Adam had an argument and now they weren't talking. So there I was, eating this good liver pâté that cost a bundle and dousing myself on vodka. God forbid I should look at the kids, so I glanced about the room, smiling at the pilly-looking people. What all the fuss was about I couldn't figure out . . . the restaurant looks like an overgrown chrome cafeteria, all glitzy and ugly and all these heavy-duty-looking patrons wearing big furs and jewels. Not even talking to each other. So quiet that when Adam belched—a little one—everyone turned around. If everyone was so happy, why the hell would they be here on Christmas Eve, freezing to death?

While Amy and Adam gave each other more dirty looks, kicking each other a lot under the table, I picked at the salmon mousse, whatever the hell it was, trying to decide whether or not to order another martini. Already Adam and Amy were looking at me funny. What the hell, it's Christmas. So I will. By now I was on the fourth martini and feeling no pain. Ready to land. At least the depression was going away. What really got me all depressed again, though, was when four sicky-looking waiters, shivering like mad, probably from flu or something, came over to the table and sang "Silent Night, Holy Night." God, I wanted to bawl right there. But of course we smiled and thanked them. Adam whispered that I would definitely have to leave a biggie tip since it was Christmas, because the waiters were so poor. What the hell does he think I am, not poor? Kids. Oh well . . . let them be. I smiled, when suddenly Amy, who had been pouting for most of the night, leaned over the table and half covered her mouth.

"Look, Mom! Over there. No, don't turn around, but sort of . . . yes . . . that beautiful blond girl. She's the new author. I saw her on a talk show . . . she wrote that best seller . . . you know, the Russian romance. The movie's coming out. Isn't she beautiful, Mom?"

"My God, that's Walter Avalon and, I imagine, his wife."

"We told you not to look," said Adam, hissing at me. "Don't be too obvious."

"See, Mom. That'll be you."

"She's so young," I said wistfully. "No more than early thirties."

"That's not so young," said Amy.

"It is," I said, gulping my martini.

"It's not," said Adam.

"Do you think that's her husband?" I asked Amy.

"Probably," said Adam.

"Isn't Walter Avalon handsome?"

"Incredibly," said Amy.

Then Walter caught my eye, did this up thing with his eyebrow, not really a lift, but an acknowledgment. I smiled.

"He saw you," whispered Amy, looking pleased.

"Good. Be seen," said Adam, nodding approvingly.

"But all the rewriting. Oh, God."

"Stop whining," said Amy.

"I agree," said Adam. "Just do it. Read the Russian romance."

Then the four sicko waiters crowded around Walter's table, singing "Silent Night." I could see them from across the room. The girl's eyes were shining and she held hands with the blond man.

I was becoming more and more depressed and I could hardly eat. And then the four waiters wheeled over the cart with one of those tall silver ice buckets and a champagne bottle sticking out.

"Compliments of Mr. Avalon," said one of the waiters.

"Oh . . . nice," said Amy.

"I'll say . . . Dom Perignon '67," said Adam.

The waiter gave me a note.

"*Princess* is next," the note read. "I haven't lost one yet. Best, Walter."

Soon we were giggling, practically drunk, and finished the entire bottle. I smiled back at the short, bald man at the next table with a red face and wearing a green velvet jacket and plaid kilt. Finally, thank God, after some terrible dessert lit up with fire, the four waiters brought the check on a silver tray, making a big thing like it was the crown of England or something.

After Adam added up the check on his calculator watch and whispered, "Two hundred and twenty-three dollars plus tip," I didn't know what I was going to do. I had about one hundred and ten dollars in my purse, most of which Bruce had given me. How did I know this lousy dinner would cost an arm and a leg? But I didn't want the kids to know that I didn't have the money. So I took a

chance and used my overextended American Express card, praying
to God that the waiters wouldn't check on Christmas Eve.

Anyways, I was so glad when the waiters brought back the tray
that I didn't mind at all paying the two hundred and sixty dollars.
Not every day you have a chance like this, the kids and all. So I
assured the kids it was worth it, and while we assured each other
that the food was fabulous and definitely the best Christmas ever, I
was not only in a bad mood and freezing, but I felt kind of sickish.

For what seemed like hours we waited in front of the restaurant,
practically freezing to death waiting for a taxi. The city looked empty.
Each time a taxi drove by, Adam ran into the street, blowing the
tiny gold whistle he wore around his neck. Until at last a taxi stopped
and we all jumped in. Adam bargained with the driver, agreeing to
pay double because of Christmas. At last we stopped in front of
this swank building on the East Side.

"You'll love Mary," said Amy in the elevator. "She's the best
fashion photographer in New York. Does all the shoots for *Vogue*.
And she's your age, Mom, and her lover is a famous film critic."

"Imagine," I said, hating Mary already.

Amy rang the buzzer. Mary opened the door, a drink in one
hand, screaming, "Baby!" and hugging Amy. Mary was a small
woman, about forty, with short brown hair and one of those sassy
faces with good bones and ambitious eyes. She was wearing white
satin chinese pajamas and a pearl necklace that reached to her knees.

After Amy introduced me and Mary gave me a quick appraisal,
I followed them into the living room. It was one of those large
living rooms with a lot of cute little windows all frosted from snow.
The room was painted a chic color, a kind of salmon. On the walls
were Mary's photographs of famous people, along with Chagall
and Miró prints. Teeny-tiny chairs, salmon-colored, too, and little
silk couches were set about the room, and on the tiny-teeny tables—antiques, I'm sure, French, probably—were *objets d'art,* porcelains, mementos. Christmas carols played softly from a stereo
somewhere, and a fire roared in the teeny-tiny fireplace. Anyways,
so there I was in the middle of this heavy-looking crowd, not
knowing a soul. So I went over and stood by the buffet table, laden
with silver chafing dishes. For the longest time I stood there wear-

ing my most princess expression, kind of like I'm somebody, too, and, oh, God, this is boring, picking the sequins from my vest, until this tiny, slim girl with long stringy brown hair, kind of mousy-looking with an intense face and squinty eyes, came over and extended her hand.

"Heather Weisberg. Vassar," she said.

Uh-huh. What the hell is this Vassar bit?

"You're Amy's mom. And a writer," she said approvingly. "How exciting," she continued, while looking around the room.

"Yes," I said, shifting to my other foot.

"I'm a filmmaker," she said, looking suddenly interested. So while I did this big thing with eye focus and feigned interest, Heather went on about the ravages of creativity and how she was suffering for her art, how her loft was all drafty and all.

"How interesting," I finally said.

"Yes," she said, opening a silk raggy purse she wore crossed over her chest and slung low on her hip. "But I've suffered like hell."

"Hmmm . . . know what you mean."

She blinked several times, blew her red nose. "No one knows what an artist goes through . . . no one."

"No."

"It sucks."

"You're telling me."

"On top of it," she said, blowing her nose, "my fuckin' loft has no heat and I've been sick all year."

"Oh, my . . . must be hard."

"Thank God for Daddy. My daddy owns several department stores, so he phoned down to Small Appliances and told them to send me fourteen electric heaters."

"My, nice having a daddy."

"Daddy's been so supportive. He donated a bundle to Vassar. And Vassar went wild over my latest film—a Lilliputian romance."

"Interesting," I murmured, wondering what the hell a Lilliputian romance was.

She darted her tongue over her small lips. "My agent, a ballbuster, says my film doesn't have a mass market. She's trying to fuck me over! The dyke! Fuck her! Little does she know, Daddy has pull at Paramount."

"Wonderful," I said, flicking the sequins and sipping the hot toddy . . . bitter as hell.

"What's your book about?" she finally asked, squinting her little eyes and looking around the room.

"A Jewish princess."

"Plenty of those around New York," she said, kind of snickering like she was above it all.

"Guess so, but she's—"

"See that man over there?" she interrupted, pointing to a decadent-looking man with gray, silky, long hair.

"Uh-huh."

"He's Stanley Gold, the film critic."

"Oh, yes, the one who—"

"He loves my film," she said, looking at him reverently.

"The Lilliputian thing?"

"No, my new film about abortion in Venezuela. It's hot . . . really hot."

I was just about to talk about myself when this fat woman wearing holly in her hair and a red felt dirndl skirt rudely stepped in front of me and dragged Heather away. So there I was again, feeling sicker than ever. I mean, I felt awful, like I was disconnected from the world. Everybody looked so unplugged. And what the hell I was doing there with these lulus in this teeny-weeny apricot apartment I didn't know. So I meandered through the crowd, smiling, nodding, like I was having this merry old time, watching Mary flit around the room repeating in her fake southern belle drawl little catchphrases like "It's wonderful, isn't it?" until at last I spotted this really serious-looking group of people, so I shoved my way through this other group who looked out of it, kind of frowning like I couldn't care less, and stood on the edge of the group, murmuring "uh-huh" a lot as if I was in on their conversation, until this film critic, this Stanley person, drunk as a skunk, monopolized the conversation and began raving about Al Pacino's film *Scarface,* insisting that it was a work of art, violence in its best sense, and then going on about how no one knows how to review a film except him.

When he talked he pushed his face real close and his eyelids hardly moved, and he kind of drooled.

A scrawny blond woman with suspicious eyes and a writer pushed herself in front of him, her shrill voice rising above his, and complained about how awful it is sharing a word processor with her famous actor husband. Meanwhile, the hostess flitted around and introduced everyone not by name but by their profession.

I'm telling you, as far as I could see, they were all a bunch of swank lulus. So while they crabbed about elitism and Jewish princesses, I nodded and squinted my eyes, doing my invisible shrinking until Heather Weisberg came over to the group. After kissing everyone, she announced to the group that I was contracted by Walter Avalon. Suddenly everyone stopped talking and looked at me as if I was a person.

"What's your novel about, dear?" asked the scrawny blonde.

"About a Jewish princess."

"Sounds like Walter," said Stanley, laughing.

"A riot," said Heather, addressing Stanley.

"It's a very serious book," I said.

"Who's your agent?" he asked.

"Lester North."

"Ahhh . . . Lester. He'll get a movie deal out of this." And then while Heather went on about what a cliché the Jewish princess is, I explained that my novel was a serious story about a really hot Jewish princess—until the film critic began talking about how sick the talk-show circuit is and the lousy agents.

No one was really talking to anyone . . . like they were having monologues with themselves. I wanted to get out of there. Hold Amy. Connect. Finally, thank God, I found Adam and Amy in the back hallway, arguing about Cuba with some weird-looking fatso man. I told them I wanted to go home, that I didn't feel so hot.

God, was I glad to get back to the kids' little apartment, even Lucy, who wore a big red bow around her neck. After I waited an hour, practically dying, for my turn in the bathroom, Adam decided no one would get up Christmas morning until Adam yelled "Go!" Only then would we get up and open our Christmas presents. Later on Christmas Day we would go to Grand Central Station and ride the train to Adam's family in Westchester. After we all hugged good night, the kids exchanging a million guppy kisses, Adam squeezing my arms and whispering "Let's get those muscles up," I got into my sleeping bag, shivering from the flu. The heater was hissing softly and the snow falling and Lucy was doing her doo-doo house thing and the toilet was clanging and soon the creaks settled into the night. And I thought, at last, the next day we'd all have a nice white Christmas, a real family gathering.

The next morning I woke first. For a while I lay there, all scrunched and everything, until Adam yelled, "Go!" Quickly we all rose and, still with sleep in our eyes and in our nightgowns, we crowded around the nebbish tree. Adam was holding Lucy and Amy took pictures.

The heat was hissing and Lucy meowing. Like she did when a kid, Amy sat cross-legged in front of the tree, shouting out orders about taking turns opening the gifts. Without her makeup she looked like she used to, a young child with old eyes. And an old voice. I wanted to kiss the freckle on her baby finger.

We began opening presents, going oohhh after each one, crying and stuff. Though I felt hurt when Adam and Amy laughed at the one-hundred-dollar check I gave them. "God, Lisa, we have a whole drawerful of your bum checks."

"Gee, Mom, you don't have to give us money."

"Sure, sure," I murmured. "Anyway, keep them. Someday they may be worth something."

"Adam will, believe me," said Amy, a possessive look in her eyes.

Anyways, I opened typewriter cartridges, notebooks, a lot of pencils, a new cat mug. While Amy loved her new shell earrings from Jenny and the new sweater set from me, Adam oohed and aahed about his scarf and mittens.

For at least an hour, Adam opened Lucy's packages, each time squeezing Lucy and holding her head high in the air, kind of stretching her out like an accordion, so that she could see the toys or something, I guess. Afterward, while I dumped the papers in a box, promising that I wouldn't use the bathroom until they did, we called Jenny, who screamed over the phone that she had fallen in the street on her tongue, no less, and now her tongue was hanging out. Next we called my mother, who wanted to know if Adam and Amy slept in the same bed. For the rest of the day I wrote, while Amy and Adam played Monopoly. God, it was nice. Finally it was time to leave for Grand Central Station, so that we could get to Westchester in plenty of time for Christmas dinner.

The evening was a riot . . . a hoot. The Bernbaum family's house, a large modern redwood and glass house, sat on two acres of white snow behind tons of fir trees. Even a pond with frozen ducks, like a picture postcard. Adam's mother—ex-Amish, wears the bonnet, the whole bit—and his father, they adopt Mexican orphans, from the earthquake. These poor kids were running all over the place. The smallest boy, Roger, about ten, was smashing toys while this Robbie the Robot machine squawked a horrible sound and the two little girls, wearing red organdy dresses, clutched Cabbage Patch dolls. And during dinner, stuffing our faces with turkey and ham while Jane talked about the horrors in the Mexican camps, a priest, this Father Donald something, every minute made us recite prayers. So, believe me, I was glad when we left and arrived back at Adam and Amy's warm little apartment. For a long time we sat around drinking coffee, the snow falling softly and making the windows all white.

"Are you in love?" I asked carefully.

"We're going to have little bambinos," said Amy, gazing adoringly at Adam.

"Not until I finish law school."

"God, a nice Jewish boy in law school . . . Nana will die."

Adam smiled.

"But I do think Amy should get her career off the ground before bambinos."

"Oh I want a career . . . definitely. I want to produce, write . . . be on camera. Maybe an anchorwoman. But I'll never go through what you've gone through."

"Amy's got it," said Adam, winding his watch again.

"I know Amy's worked her way through college, a long haul. But marriage and children right now will slow her down."

"Oh, Mom! Just because David fucked you over doesn't mean I'll be fucked over."

Adam put his arm protectively around Amy, called her guppy lips . . . puppy or something . . . and they kissed, as if kissing away my folly.

"Oh, I guess I just worry . . . worry endlessly. I don't want Amy to drown in diapers, then on the analyst's couch," I said, smiling apologetically. "I don't mean to interfere—"

"You're so analytic," said Amy.

"Stop worrying, Lisa," said Adam, looking disgusted. "It upsets Amy. Especially that you're alone . . . poor . . . she—"

"Sure. Okay."

Anyways, Lucy peed on top of the clothes lying in my open suitcase, and Adam practically beat the poor cat to death. I was leaving the next morning, so I finished packing and then when the kids were at last in bed and sleeping I squished myself in the bathroom and prepared for bed. Finally I was all tucked into the horrible sleeping bag, Lucy snoring beside me. Christmas past, I closed my eyes and slept.

The next morning a storm like you wouldn't believe . . . probably the worst in New York history. Decked out in my cape and hat, carrying more stuff than when I'd arrived, I waited in the smelly hall with Adam and Amy. The airport bus was picking me up any minute, while Adam was telling me what a heavy-duty lady I was and Amy lectured me to get to work and hang in there, assuring me that she'd come home soon. So I smiled and pretended that I didn't feel sad. But the sadness settled in my bones, a sadness like I'd never felt. It weighed me down.

When the airport bus arrived and Adam helped me shlep everything, I took one more look at Amy and began clutching her, murmuring for her to eat more, that I worry that she's anorexic and, God forbid, I don't want an anorexic child.

After promising that we wanted to see each other soon and that I would get it together and that I would write a really good novel, I got into the bus. I kept my head down so that I wouldn't look back.

CHAPTER FOUR

Over a year later—fourteen months, to be exact—one of those windy March days when the leaves are turning all gold, I was in my den, Walkman over my ears playing Mozart, writing a really hot sex scene with my princess and this wacko gun salesman. I'd spent days at this horrible gun shop in the Mission District while this hoodlum with greasy hair, bad breath, and a long scar on the side of his face showed me which guns were best for suicide, murder, robbery, pretending I was so interested, even flirting with the yucko salesman, until one day I got it! I mean, the whodunit ending—sleaze . . . blood . . . an ending that'd knock your block off.

So, thank God, finally I was almost finished rewriting *Princess*. And I couldn't wait to get *Princess* out of my life. The fourteen months rewriting, changing everything, were a nightmare. Because I was writing their *Princess,* not mine, I had a tough time knowing what was real, what wasn't. But Walter wanted a gun, so I gave him a gun. Walter wanted perversion, so I made the sappy count a pedophiliac. You name it, I wrote it. But I felt invisible, so far away from myself—like the real me lived behind the words, the words only little pictures. And when I thought about my old princess, breathy and searching, now glitzed up, a twenty-two-year-old moron, this awful feeling would come over me—so big it scared me—up to my skin, so close, sometimes my skin felt prickly . . . and I'd want to kick the walls in, kick them in . . . and call Walter and say no soap, fuck you. . . . but then I'd quickly assure myself that rewriting was the name of the game, that I was just putting in my dues, and that all authors went through this. And I'd get all soft when Walter wrote these long, wonderful letters raving about how wonderfully sleazy *Princess* was and that she'd take the world by storm and complimented me about my raw talent and about how happy he was that I'd gone commercial.

But the waiting for Shana's approval on the chapters I'd sent months before was enough to drive you up the fucking wall. The waiting took on a life of its own. At least loneliness has a place, a yearning, a missing—but waiting is so long, empty, like time stretched out. Ordinary sounds become a separate world. Anny's purr, Jenny's hair blower, a bicycle bell, the swish of Mrs. Strauss's broom, the roar of a jet, a squawk of a bird flying low, the rustle of a tree closing the day. But just to get through the long months, the isolation, hormonal highs, lows, I'd live this pretend life, pretend I wasn't horny as hell and that I didn't have bills up the gazoo and that isolation was necessary because I was writing this biggie novel.

In the early morning, before writing, I'd go on my usual walk to the Chinese bakery for my lousy pork bun, passing the nebbish trees, pretending I was on some exotic island, touching the peat moss growing along the bark like yellow velvet, imagining the fog a damp kiss. At the corner I'd usually buy a paper, but I'd never read it, because my mind was too full of plot. After eating the pork bun I'd go into my darkened den and after studying the outline pinned to the cork bulletin board, next to the pictures of Amy, Jenny, I'd begin writing. The words poured out of me, came real fast, but I felt upside down because they didn't belong to me. But I'd keep on writing until the mailman's hum, and the shadows crept all vertical.

At night, after writing all day, sometimes just to get out of the house I'd dress up, do this number, make up my face real wild, fix my hair, and go and sit at Miz Brown's Coffee Shop and talk to some poor retard person about my writing problems and listen to Frank Sinatra records. Or I'd go to the twenty-four-hour Xerox place and yak with the Chinese boy while he Xeroxed my pages, the Xerox fumes going up my nose.

I'd force myself and go to the Golden Venus Gym because the kids chipped in for my last birthday for an aerobics class for women over forty. God, I hated the class, jumping up and down on the trampoline with all these idiots while dopey John Travolta records played "Saturday Night Fever." God, it was an awful time . . . the waiting made everything seem slowed up . . . like a slow dream.

Anyways, I finished writing the last chapter and sent the new

Princess to Avalon. God, I wanted *Princess* published so badly—was all I thought about, dreamed about—like its publication would make all the waiting, all the years, something real. I could hardly go into a bookstore. When I'd see some crappy book spinning in a gold case I'd start crying and have to blow into my paper bag and people would look at me like I was this goony bird. At night while lying in bed I'd watch Alexis fall down the stairs in *Dynasty* or Krystle all tied up. Then after talking for hours with my pathetic tele-moans—Marcie Kaplan going on about the various sizes and shapes of penises, Sandra crying about her lousy sex life and that she and Peter never had an orgasm—I'd zonk out on Zanax, pretending I didn't have dreams.

Jenny was comforting . . . I mean, the poor kid had put up with a lot . . . all those years I was wacko over David, she'd done the laundry, cooking . . . but now she wanted her own apartment, was looking . . . and it was time . . . we were getting on each other's nerves.

But between Jenny's working part-time at Saks and running her Auto Jen business and spending most weekends at her boyfriend Kevin's apartment, I didn't see much of her anyways.

Amy—still living with Adam, who'd graduated from law school and was working for a Madison Avenue hot-shot entertainment-law firm—called every week. She was doing well at CNN . . . was writing more . . . just fashion copy, but nevertheless writing . . . and she'd talk a lot about her dreams of becoming a writer and producer.

Two months later I still hadn't heard a word from Avalon. When I'd called Lester and asked him what the problem was, he screamed at the top of his lungs that I should be more patient, that a good writer knows patience.

I put off getting a job. . . . I still had some advance money left, a little income, and I wasn't in the mood for going to the employment agencies and taking math and spelling tests. And selling art was still hard . . . reminded me of David. Besides, I only wanted to write. So I'd decided I'd try for the magazine scene again. Write a piece about singles. I interviewed a nerd single guru who calls himself King Puck—yep—thinks he's Shakespeare. Ugly as sin. He runs singles workshops . . . makes a bundle, too . . . you bring a pillow, a candle, old fears . . . and for three hundred dollars, cash on the line, he promises you'll come out with a mate. I told Mr. Puck that I was writing this piece about him on spec, so you bet your sweet boots he agreed to let me sit in free on one of his workshops. God, it was something else again. You'd die. A regular midsummer nightmare—everyone was lighting candles and lying on their pillows, singing a sappy little song about finding your puck. A lot of crying and feeling each other up while this schmuck ranted like Hitler about happiness and finding your "g" spot.

So anyways, a few days later I was at the typewriter writing up a storm about old King Puck when suddenly in the middle of the page something came over me, and I started writing about Eva Hesse. Almost breathless, all the impressions, feelings I'd kept hidden about the art world coming loose . . . and the words were coming so fast the words were coming out all backward . . . and before I knew it I was writing a scene . . . 1969 . . . at the New York Whitney Museum's big exhibit, "Anti-Illusion," where Eva Hesse was the only woman artist exhibiting with all these biggie superstud minimalists . . . Andrea . . . Tuttle . . . Heizer . . . Bochner. God, it was something. I could see the crowd . . . hear the Rolling Stones . . . and God, everyone in the art world was there, all the superstar artists . . . de Kooning . . . Rauschenburg . . . Johns . . . Stella . . . the star collectors . . . the Robert Sculls . . . dealers . . . Ivan Karp . . . Leo Castelli . . . you name them, they were there . . . critics . . . matrons . . . patrons of the arts . . . they were all there. God, it was exciting . . . like someone else was writing and I was watching the crowd, so close . . . the peeling leather jackets . . . feathers . . . beads . . . velvet jackets . . . mink worn over slumped shoulders . . . Andy Warhol, his silver painted tennis shoes, holding his tape recorder. . . . But Eva Hesse's work . . . that was something . . . the sculptures were huge things made of knotted ropes and strings, cheesecloth, all kinds of weird material, twisted and hanging, nothing formed or connected, yet order from chaos and chaos from order, everything changing, like growing.

After a while I was so excited I had to stop writing, and my hands were shaky and I was getting that numb feeling in my mouth. So I went into my bedroom, still shaking, and pressed my face close to the mirror. My eyes were larger, like they had seen past me, and my face all flushed. And God, I was scared, because the feelings were so big and I knew I'd write another book . . . about Eva Hesse . . . one I'd feel . . . that was true . . . about a woman all broken inside . . . full of hurts . . . yet able to work and create whole work . . . believe in herself . . . able to say when she was really down, "Art is my weapon." So that night I couldn't sleep . . . my mind was really going at it . . . pressing . . . how I'd go about writing the story of Eva . . . in her voice . . . open in New York . . . and her first meeting with Tom Doyle . . . then flash-backs to her life in Germany . . . then back to New York . . . her days at Yale Art School . . . what was going on in the art world . . . the middle of the book with her marriage to Tom Doyle . . . their ups and downs and breakup . . . the death of Eva's father . . . her deep depression . . . illness . . . her best work . . . then death . . . and sewing through the story, Hesse's vision, her commitment as an artist and a woman. That's what I'd do . . . how I'd structure the book . . . I'd call the book *Eva*.

So the very next day right after the pork bun I got out the old grocery carton marked "Eva" and started the long, tedious job of sorting the pages, clipping the notes. From art books I'd copied names of museum curators, collections Hesse's work was in, critics who'd written about her, friends, colleagues who knew Eva.

For the next couple of months every morning with the yellow legal notepad by my side I'd check off the names I'd called . . . some I couldn't reach . . . some wouldn't talk to me about Eva . . . some said, "Lisa Who?" . . . or said that Eva Hesse was too obscure. But I'd managed to get through to a cousin of Eva's . . . I'd even tracked down her doctor at a New York hospital . . . and a close friend of Tom Doyle's. I'd made endless calls to the curator at the Berkeley Museum, a nice woman who was very interested in my project and said that she thought Eva Hesse was an important artist and wished me luck. Also, Nick Thompson at the Oakland Museum led me to an old friend of Eva's who lived in Berkeley . . . she invited me over to her house and let me read some of

Eva's letters along with a couple of Eva's art notebooks.

Anyways, that morning the writing was flowing, and I was really on, into the scenes, when I realized the phone was ringing. I'd forgotten to turn on the answering machine. Almost scared me to death. As if I'm not nervous enough. Removing the Walkman from my head and trying not to shake, I answered the telephone.

"Hello . . . hello."

"Lisa! It's me. Mother."

"Oh, Mother, hi."

"Are you working!"

"Of course I'm working. What else would I be doing?" I replied irritably. God, what does she think I'm doing in here all day? No one ever takes me seriously.

"I thought we'd have a little lunch. Maybe you'd take a break," she said carefully.

"No. I can't."

She sighed and then I sighed, and after we let out a series of exasperated sighs, she finally said, "I have some wonderful news!" Gee! I perked up. Maybe Uncle Sol, may God bless his soul, is . . . well . . . after all, he is almost one hundred, and I am his favorite niece and all . . . God, I could buy a word processor. Most of my advance was gone by now.

"I spoke to Selma Rosenblatt this morning. You know my friend—"

"Yes. Yes, I know Selma," I said impatiently.

"Anyways," she continued, "Selma has a really handsome . . . gorgeous, she says . . . nephew . . . not to mention affluent." Mother's voice dropped lower. "Made millions . . . millions, with some wine called, I think, pink pop, something like that—"

"Mother, I'm not interested."

"Not interested! What's not to be interested?"

"I have too much work. I'm struggling with my new book, Mother, and I don't have the energy," I explained, my voice rising. "Nor does he sound particularly interesting. Anyways, I'd like to think about this."

"Think! Think about what? That you never go out, that you lock yourself in all day in that filthy room, writing God knows what?

That years are going by and I don't see a novel! They say Danielle Steel turns them out every month. Everyone is talking about you . . . the whole family."

"Mother, please! Let's not get into the family. I couldn't care less."

"Of course not. It's obvious that you don't," she said with a sniff.

After a long silence and more sighs, Mother said, "Believe me, this Harry Wolfstein is eligible and only fifty. And Lisa, don't get mad when I say this, but only a mother will tell you the truth. Believe me, but you could use some fixing up . . . after all, you're still pretty, reasonably young, but no woman your age, even you, can afford to go around looking the way you look."

"What do you mean, 'look'?" I challenged, on the verge of screaming.

"Well," she said cautiously, "those funny pink socks, do you have to wear pink? And those long earrings."

"Mother! It's my style! Who do you want me to look like? Fat Susan? Or my ugly cousin Frieda? Yuk!"

"No need for your remarks. She's happily married."

I sighed.

"So, you're lucky that you have this chance. Where else are you going to meet men . . . eligible men? At those sicky poetry meetings you go to? Or those creepy intellectual groups? Didn't you have enough with David? Didn't he teach you a lesson?"

"Mother! I don't want to discuss David."

"No, of course not. Never do you want to discuss anything you're wrong about. I warned you about David. The minute I met him I could tell by his rat eyes and that weak handshake that he was a louse! Believe me, I knew the minute—"

"Mother, please!"

After another brief silence, Mother said, "I'll send Birdie over to clean your house, you can't have a man over in that mess. Mess," she repeated, sighing some more.

"I don't want Birdie over, Mother, she throws out my papers. So leave me alone, will you? Stop butting in and let me get back to work."

So we chatted a bit longer, Mother gossiping about her friend Sylvia Finkel, then about how awful the fall fashions were, on and on, until finally I promised that I would, at least, talk to Harry Wolfstein.

After Mother's phone call, not only did I feel angry, but no way could I go back to work. Maybe I should meet Harry Wolfstein. Certainly enough time had passed since David. And probably I'm beginning even to look celibate. At my age I should be having lots of sex or something. I began pacing about the room, feeling disjointed, picking up paper clips from the floor. What was I afraid of? I know I'm not frigid. Even Dr. Kenner agreed. Maybe that's why the writing isn't going so well, trouble pulling out the character. Oh, sure, I could write the action, even sleazy sex scenes, no biggie. But something wasn't happening. Probably because I'm not living the material. Though Flaubert didn't live the material, got the idea for Emma Bovary from a tiny newspaper clipping, I assured myself, still feeling disconcerted.

I went over to the window and opened the shutters. So bright outside. All the neighbors were watering their patches of lawn across the street, wearing their rubber thongs, and calling their dogs. As usual, the light hurt my eyes. For so long I had been writing in this dark room. The sky was silvery, almost metallic. I watched an ordinary-looking brown bird soar gracefully, then waver about as if hesitating, then finally dip its wings this way and that.

My next-door neighbor, Dr. Strauss, a retired dentist recuperating from a heart bypass, was watering the box of marigolds on his porch. As I watched Dr. Strauss carefully watering his marigolds, his face intense, I wondered if all this grand passion and action I was writing was just that. Only fiction. For the movies. Not at all like Dr. Strauss's marigolds. Every day Dr. Strauss watered the marigolds. Sometimes his wife, Doris, a pretty woman with white hair and a nice smile, would step onto the porch and together they would discuss the proper angle for the pictures. For fifty years they had been together and every day they came onto the porch and watered the marigolds. As I watched them talking gently to each other, Doris stepped out of the sunlight so that Dr. Strauss could take the pictures.

I watched a bit longer, thinking that love maybe after all is not such a complicated thing, and went back to the typewriter. I put the Walkman back over my head. Couldn't write without the music. I made some notes, always I was making notes, changing things. I glanced at the cat calendar hanging above my typewriter, marked with chapter numbers. The wall was filled with memos from Shana, a Xerox copy of a check from Walter, a few hang-in-there notes from friends, a couple of photographs of Lucy, Adam, and Amy, a drawing of my princess, what I think she looks like . . . a picture of Eva. I began writing the next scene in *Eva,* feeling glad to be back inside the novel. A party—1964—in Andy Warhol's loft, the Factory. I kept on writing until I couldn't write any more. I stopped writing and watched the way the patch of light was hanging along the wall, then broke into little pieces, finally falling onto the floor. This meant that it was late afternoon. I had learned to tell time by watching the way time falls into the shadows. For a moment I sat there, feeling tired. Whenever I stepped out of my books into my world, I felt empty, sad. Suddenly I missed Amy, not really missing, because missing is wanting back something you had. It was more about what we hadn't had. Not that I hadn't tried my best and all to be a mother. But what did I know about being a mother? God, the poor kid. Never had I really been a mother. Not the real kind. No magicians at birthday parties. And Amy always had to sew on her own camp labels.

Then at seventeen she went off to NYU and never came back. Sometimes I had nightmares that twenty years from now some sappy game show would present me with my estranged daughter and, while cameras would be poking into our faces and organ music playing, me an old lady slobbering all over the place, Amy screaming how she hated me, yuk! What a nightmare. Anyways, I pressed my push-button phone, cursing the stupid access numbers, until, thank God, Amy answered. "Hello."

"Amy, it's me, Mom."

"Mom! My God, what's wrong? Are you depressed? Have you heard about your book?"

"Depressed! Why should I be depressed? Just because I want to talk to my daughter? I just missed you," I said sheepishly.

"Your voice sounds funny," she said suspiciously. "And you're breathing funny. I know that something's wrong."

"I'm not breathing funny. It's my allergies," I replied defensively and on the verge of tears. "I only wanted to talk to you and hear your voice."

Then, would you believe, I heard this muffling sound and I was sure the other extension was picked up.

Finally, Amy said, in her most maternal tone, "Mom, I'm not in the mood for your complaints. All Jenny and I hear lately are your complaints and how hard everything is for you. God, Mom, you're always talking about yourself. Never do you ask me about my job." She hesitated, I heard more muffling. "Adam and I decided that, as much as we love you, that we aren't going to give in any more and listen to your complaints. It's not healthy, Mom," she said, her voice dropping.

"Uh-huh. No, it's not . . . I understand," I murmured, feeling hurt but trying to sound cheerful.

"And Jenny calls and cries. Gee, Mom, she's only a child, and do you think it's fun for her to see her mother in a dark den? And she says it's filthy. For over a year now you've been rewriting your book, and Adam and I find that strange. And Jenny says you're dirty, too, and that you never wash your hair."

"I can't help it!" I said, crying now. "What do you want me to do?" I said, my voice rising. "Kill myself?"

Amy sighed. "Let's not go into that again."

After a brief silence, I said, "How am I supposed to get out when I have no money, no car? Or anyone who believes in me?" I said with a sniff.

"Oh, Mom . . . I believe in you . . . I really do . . . It's just that I want to see you go out . . . not have life pass you by . . . and, Mom," said Amy in a careful tone, "your book is taking such a long time. Maybe you should say something to Shana or—"

"Say something! What do you expect me to say?"

"Be assertive!" she screamed. "At least ask her why she takes so fuckin' long!"

"Sure! Sure! Easy for you to say, twenty-two and glamorous . . . and a career ahead of you."

"Stop it! Mom, stop it. I can't stand it when you whine."

So, after we both sighed for a while and I pulled myself together, finally I asked, "How are your classes?"

"Oh, okay," she said gloomily. "But going to school and working is hard. New York is tough, so tough you don't know. Don't know that the other day I fainted in the street from hunger. If a really nice man hadn't helped me into a coffee shop I could have died."

"Maybe if you eat more . . . don't starve yourself so you look positively anorexic . . . believe me, only a mother would even tell you this. You look all yellow and your bones stick out . . . and I don't care what Adam says. You look awful!"

"She looks hot," said Adam. "She's not too thin."

"Oh . . . Adam," I said nervously. "I didn't know you were on the line."

"Hello, Lisa," he said impatiently.

So after I asked him about his new job in the biggie Madison Avenue law firm, trying to be all cheerful, Adam, somewhat appeased, said, "Someone wants to talk to you."

While my telephone bill was going to the sky, and Adam tortured Lucy enough so that the stupid cat let out a series of horrible screeches on the phone, Amy lectured me some more about how I shouldn't be so depressed and that I definitely should meet a man.

After I agreed, Adam put in his piece, too, saying in a huffy tone that he would from now on appreciate it if I didn't call so much and that if I did call to be more considerate, please, that I was upsetting Amy and it took him two days to get her over me. I felt so hurt. Then after they covered the receivers, probably having a meeting about me, I apologized.

"Act like a mother," said Amy.

"It's not good for a kid to have a kid for a mother," said Adam with a chuckle.

"No, I know," I said meekly.

"Maybe you should see Dr. Kenner more."

"But I can't . . ."

"Call us when you're in a better mood. Adam and I are depressed." And click went the phone. Just like that. Click.

For a second I sat there still holding the receiver to my ear, thinking that maybe Amy's right. That I should get out more, scoop up some life. I hung up the receiver, feeling kind of low, missing Amy, so I decided to do a giant cleanup. I started straightening up the den, getting my papers in order, vacuuming like mad, telling myself that I had to get out more, not be such a recluse, until the bag blew up.

So that night while I was sitting cross-legged on the edge of the bed, polishing my toenails purple, Jenny shouted for me to pick up the fuckin' telephone. God, that kid, someday, when I'm rich, I'm going to send her to one of those finishing schools where she'll wear a uniform and say, "Yes, ma'am." I picked up the receiver.

"Hello."

"Lisa?"

"Yes."

"My name is Harry Wolfstein. Selma Rosenblatt asked me to call."

"Who?" I asked, thinking that he had a nice voice.

"Selma Rosenblatt. Oh, didn't she call and tell you that I was going to call? I'm terribly sorry."

"Oh, Selma, of course. Yes, my mother told me. Nice of you to call," I said in my most charming voice.

"My pleasure," he replied.

We both chuckled and murmured something sappy about how nice it was finally to talk to each other, that neither one of us ever went out on blind dates, but that since Selma Rosenblatt is such an okay lady that it was okay.

Then, after an awkward silence, I couldn't think of a thing to say . . . not one thing. Nothing interesting, that is. Until finally, when I couldn't stand the silence, I asked, "Do you live in San Francisco?"

"Yes. Now I do."

"Now?"

"Since my divorce six months ago."

"Oh . . . I didn't know," I said in a grave tone.

"Oh, that's all right," he said.

"Do you have children?"

"Jonathan's four, Benjamin five. Also two grown daughters from a former marriage . . . plus grandchildren."

"God, all those children will keep you young."

He chuckled. "Bee Bee, my ex-wife, is twenty-five years younger than me." He laughed nervously. "So that explains the babies."

"Imagine," I said.

"Yep. I raised Bee Bee. I knew when she began taking those photography classes, then the Women on the Run jogging classes, then the feminist workshops, I knew that Bee Bee was on her way out. I tried everything. Everything. From spas to fur coats. Even bought her a camera and a tripod, trying to encourage her. But then . . ." He hesitated. "Bee Bee is a beauty."

"I'm sure."

"And I'm worried. All those guys out there, the fortune hunters and all . . ."

"It sounds like she can take care of herself."

"That's what I'm afraid of."

I kept murmuring, "I know what you mean." Then there was another long silence, God, he got me into a bad mood.

"Aunt Selma tells me you're a writer."

"Yes."

"How interesting. I've never dated a writer before."

"Oh . . . writing is a garden variety vocation."

"Not true!" he insisted. "You must be different from the ordinary woman . . living from your imagination," he said wistfully.

"Where do you get your material from?" he said, his voice lowering.

"From my imagination. Or from experience . . . . a blend, I guess," I said nervously.

"Love it," he said, his voice all silky.

What the hell does he love? I wondered.

"Would you like to have dinner Thursday evening?"

"Yes," I said. "That would be fine . . . Thursday evening, I mean."

"Sevenish?"

"Fine."

"Is that your beep, or mine?"

"Mine has a funny sound."

"I'll let it go—I'm talking to an interesting woman."

"Uh-huh. Thanks."

"Is there any special cuisine you prefer?"

"No . . . not at all . . . you choose," I said.

"How about Thai food?"

"Oh, wonderful," I said. All I need now is some parasite. God, I hated all those Eastern spicy foods.

"Thursday then."

"Wonderful," I said. "I'm looking forward to it."

So after I gave him directions that, I'm sure, were all wrong, and again we agreed how wonderful Selma is, I hung up.

Thursday arrived. A light rain still fell over the city, making it shiny and so beautiful. The Golden Gate Bridge appeared an orange shadow that dipped over the darkening ocean. All day I sat writing *Eva*. Thank God, I was really hot. The material was coming easily. Mother drove by in her gold Porsche at least twice, dropping off little cakeboxes tied by white string, just in case, she said, along with flowers and some little canapes that Birdie made. Toward late afternoon, when I was just about a basket case, Jenny and her usual entourage, Char, Fariba, and Robin, came in and pulled me away from the typewriter.

"Tonight you really have to look good, Mom. You can't go around like this anymore. Look hot."

So while I soaked in the bathtub, the soap and sing radio stuck to the wall, listening to Mozart, I closed my eyes and rested my head against the red vinyl lip pillow. My legs rested on top of the faucets, and soon the anxiety floated away. But I couldn't shut off my mind. I wondered what Avalon thought of the final rewrite . . . why I hadn't heard from them . . . I'd call again next week. Then my mind turned to *Eva* . . . rethinking a scene . . . *Princess* faded.

Anyways, after soaking in the bubble bath, the plastic turtle put-putting all over the place, at last the alarm went off and the girls were pounding on the bathroom door, shouting that it was time to get out.

So after I put on the Calvin Klein panties and lilac see-through bra, I blow-dried my hair. The waves fell silkily over my face. Next I put Vaseline on my thick, dark eyebrows so that they would be all slick and straight, and then applied the placenta cream to my face. I put on the white velour robe and went into the bedroom. The girls were sitting on my bed, smoking and stuff.

"What's that smell?" asked Jenny, wrinkling her nose.

"Rose perfume," I said defensively, glancing at myself in the full-length mirror.

"Phew! A really with-it lady doesn't wear rose perfume. Wear Opium," said Jenny. "You can use mine."

"Yeah," agreed the girls. "Rose perfume is dorky."

So like a dummy, I stood there while Jenny sprayed Opium all over me. Then finally I dressed in the black Kamali trousers, and put on the black Kamali sweater with the large shoulder pads, and my silver Navajo wrist cuff and the usual long silver earrings.

"Those lavender stockings are for the boonies," said Char, cracking her gum.

"I like them," I said, wondering why I always had such a tough time being assertive.

"Now turn up the cuffs of your pants," said Robin, a tall redhead wearing a leopard blouse and tight black leather pants. They shook their heads, no less, as if there weren't a thing they could do with me. While I stood there in the center of the room, asking them how I looked.

Jenny looked first from Char to Robin to Fariba and asked, "Well, what do you think?" They looked at each other cautiously. "Well, I'm not sure," said Charlene, a tiny girl wearing a Mohawk haircut. On the side of her blond shaved head, she had painted a black circle. Her head was tilted in contemplation.

"She needs more shadowing and blush to bring out her cheekbones. She has really high cheekbones."

"Yes," they murmured, squinting their eyes.

"And a nice mouth. Small but full," said Robin.

So I stood there, while Char, a cigarette hanging from her mouth, applied more eyeshadow and lined my eyes. Finally I looked at myself in the mirror. Not bad. Not bad at all, Lisa. For years I hadn't worn makeup. Now my eyes, shadowed in gray charcoal, looked all dreamy and lined, Egyptian. My lips were kind of frosty and pouty.

"She's hot!" they agreed.

"Oh, who cares?" I said, turning several more times in front of the mirror.

"Oh, don't go into your feminist shit," said Jenny, wearing a tight frog tee shirt and red heart earrings. She placed the makeup carefully back into the porcelain box monogrammed "Jenny." "We've heard it a million times, all your shtick about men. Shit, Mom. Give it your best shot. Who knows? You might even enjoy yourself."

They laughed.

"Stop chewing gum, Jenny, and talk to me with respect."

We were just about to start one of our awful arguments, really awful, when, thank God, the doorbell rang. I jumped a mile. My heart was beating fast.

"Sssh," the girls said.

"Don't run," said Robin, looking all worried and everything.

I walked slowly toward the door, telling myself that it was only a date, feeling generally like some kind of dork.

I opened the door.

A tall, slim, tan man with salt-and-pepper Afro hair took my hand. "Hello, Lisa," he said.

"Oh . . . hello, come in," I said, stepping into the hall.

We stood in the hall murmuring how nice it was finally meeting each other, each of us trying not to look each other up and down. Not bad, not bad at all. Geez, I was pleasantly surprised. He was wearing a preppy-looking tweedy jacket and beige gabardine pants. His eyes were dark and intelligent-looking.

He followed me into the living room, and I quickly put the chair in front of Anny's litter box.

"You have some interesting . . . very interesting, in fact, art here," he commented, looking at the contemporary paintings.

"From my art dealing days," I said.

"Did you paint any of them?"

"That one over there," I said, pointing to the large canvas of a nude woman.

"Interesting," he said, standing in front of it, his hands folded behind his back, a really serious expression on his face.

"I guess a writer paints, too."

"Oh . . . well, I paint some, but for me words are like paintings . . . upside down." I stopped talking because he was looking at me funny. I warned myself to be careful . . . not to talk about myself so much.

"So," he said, facing me, "why don't we have a drink at the restaurant."

"Oh, yes . . . of course," I said, trying to put on the jacket, damning the shoulder pads, my arm caught in the sleeve. God, I felt shy.

As I got into Harry's Mercedes, a 450 SL painted bronze metallic, I pretended not to notice Jenny and the girls practically hanging from the front window, or that the Strausses were standing on their porch, or that half my jacket was caught in the car door.

I sat back in the lamb's-wool seat and waited until Harry snapped his seatbelt. When I realized that he wasn't going to help me with mine, I struggled with the damn thing, hardly breathing, for it was so tight across my breast.

After some time, I said, "Nice car . . . though I'm not interested in cars, this is very nice."

"A lot of people think it's tacky driving a Mercedes, but mechanically it's such a good car. . . ."

"Yes, I can imagine."

So, on the way to the restaurant, we didn't say much of anything. Mostly commented about how really beautiful San Francisco is . . . or about its wonderful cool weather. Things like that. Every so often I noticed that Harry glanced in the rear mirror, sneaking looks at himself, probably.

We arrived at the restaurant, set high on a hill overlooking the city. The rain had stopped, but the city was draped in a hazy silver fog, the clouds dropped low, almost touching us, and the sound from the foghorns made me shiver.

It was so dark inside that I kept blinking trying to adjust my eyes to the dark. After two tiny men wearing white turbans and gold-brocaded jackets removed our shoes, we were seated at a low table on the floor, leaning against huge velvet cushions, just dozens of cushions. When our drinks came we clinked glasses, each murmuring something sappy about blind dates were full of surprises. God, could it be that I actually felt chemistry? Especially after a second martini, I felt no pain. I was having so much fun, laughing and everything until Harry ordered a dinner with dozens of courses. He had really nice strong hands and a silky voice . . . and I almost died, felt butterflies in my stomach, when he said, "You know, you have a strong physical presence. I'm sexually attracted to you. And I'm not easily attracted." Oh, God, what do I say now? Kind of smiling and tilting my head a lot, I smiled up at him.

"Oh, that's a very nice thing to say . . . but how can you tell?"

"Oh, believe me, I can tell," he said softly, looking at me intently. "Your body movement drives me wild. You have a lovely body."

"Oh, God," I said, pushing my hair from my face. "I feel so . . . so awkward."

"We'll have to do something about that," he said.

By now I was so bombed out by drinks, not to mention the spicy food. So I just relaxed, telling myself that it felt pretty good being hot and bothered. I began to feel more relaxed. Harry lit a long brown cigarette and inhaled deeply.

"You know," he said, his leg pressing against mine under the table, "you're fascinating. Something interesting about you . . . a kind of sexual energy."

"Energy," I repeated.

He laughed.

"You could do worse," Harry said, taking my hand. "I'm no kid, but every day I look in the mirror and say, Harry Wolfstein, it could be worse. A good business. Flat stomach."

"Worse," I repeated, my feet touching his.

So, while Harry told how women were driving him crazy since his divorce, that he really got off on an elusive woman like myself, how his wife was a real Jewish princess, "of the worst kind," he said, how she was costing him a bloody fortune and how his kids were all gifted so they had to go to special schools, I just kind of kept pushing the wave back from my eyes while pressing my thigh against his.

"At Harvard . . . when I went to Harvard," Harry was saying.

"Oh, Harvard . . . I'm impressed," I said.

"I majored some in English . . . not bad in writing, either," he said with a chuckle. "What are you writing about?" he asked softly.

"Oh, about a woman's growth."

"Growth . . . what does she grow into?" he asked, looking amused and pressing his leg against mine, harder now.

I sighed.

"Oh, into this really heavy-duty lady."

"You're a heavy-duty lady," he said, his eyes twinkling mischievously.

"Uh-huh. Thanks."

"What about sex? Don't you need sex scenes?"

"Not really. I have plenty of sex scenes," I said, tossing my hair. "Though, maybe if I really need a biggie, I'll let you know. . . ."

We both laughed. "I've been celibate over two years," I confessed, feeling shy and turning away.

He looked at me kind of funny. Like maybe he didn't believe me or something, or thought that I was putting him on . . . you know how men can be.

"You're putting me on."

"No, I'm not kidding," I said, feeling hurt.

"Why?"

"Because of my writing. And also, I was getting over someone important in my life." I snapped my fingers and said, "I can't just forget, well, you know."

He assumed a very grave expression on his face and nodded. "Yes, I know what you mean, sensitive people are like that."

So, while we were both being so grave, I was wondering if I should go back to his house after dinner, or wait for a couple of more dates. But, what the hell, what was I saving it for?

Harry whispered that if I wanted some sex scenes he would teach me.

"Let me expose you," he said, looking intent.

"Expose me?" I said, feeling shy again.

"Yes. I have a feeling that you haven't been made love to . . . really made love to."

Oh, God, I was about to die. Just from the burning feeling, from Harry's eyes, not to mention the way his hand so smoothly, gently, was caressing my thigh.

"You need a lot of caring, of loving," he said.

"Don't we all?"

"No, not all," he said. "But I can feel your sensitivity. Your vulnerability," he said, his voice dropping. "And your sexiness."

So, at this point, I definitely decided to get off the sex subject. For most of the evening, anyways, Harry had dropped little sex hints, you know, using words like "hot" or "spot" or "sexual," little things, nevertheless there. Finally, after drinking endless amounts of jasmine tea, Harry said, "Let's go."

I nodded, murmuring how much I had enjoyed the dinner.

In the car we didn't say hardly a word. Except maybe when a couple of times I mentioned how pale the moon was. And it was a kind of chipped pale thing lounging in the dark sky. The air smelled muggy, like maybe we were going to have an earthquake.

In the elevator, one of those creaky jobs that you wouldn't want to get caught in during an earthquake, Harry kissed me, a great kiss. I could really tell he was some lover. Not one of those wet, guppy kisses. But a really hot, smooth kiss.

His penthouse overlooked the San Francisco Bay. It was so dark inside I had to hold onto Harry's arm. Harry lit a fire. The firelight cast a golden glow and I could see that the shadows from the flames were hanging along the walls.

I was getting all turned on. By how smooth Harry kissed. By everything, the music, some sensual, Brazilian beat. The only thing that bothered me, and I told Harry so, was this really awful-looking standard poodle Harry called Prince, who kept close to Harry and was drooling all over me.

We sipped brandies and made small talk. Until Harry kissed me again. This time I put the brandy down and wound my arms around his neck. I closed my eyes and gave him my movie-star kiss . . . for so long that part of me had been dead. God, it was sensational.

"Lisa . . . Lisa, this is hot kissing," he said. "Really hot kissing. I never before—" I kissed him again. Hard. Kissed him so hard we couldn't breathe. And suddenly Harry Wolfstein became this other person, not a stranger, but all the no-name studs of my dreams. I couldn't stop. I was burning. Harry pulled off my sweater and unhooked my bra. For a moment I covered my breasts, I don't know why, maybe an old reflex, kind of modest, I guess. But when I looked into Harry's eyes, I began taking off clothes until I stood naked in front of the fireplace.

"Oh, my," he whispered, looking so intense. "You're beautiful . . . what a beautiful body. . . ." As quickly as possible then, before I could say jackrabbit, he had his clothes off. His body, bronzed and muscular, had a slim waist, long legs, full, pale buttocks . . . oh, God, he felt good. We danced naked in front of the fireplace, our bodies swaying slowly to the sensual Brazilian music. Harry was caressing my body, his hands gently tracing the curve of my waist, along the thighs. He was whispering in my ear how fuckable I was, how hot he was for me, and that I was a damned exciting woman. Hard to believe with all this passion going that I felt a kind of shyness. Like no way was I going to let him know about my real burning side. Finally Harry contained himself no longer, lifted me, actually carried me down the long hall into his bedroom. He lay me down on top of his bed, on his downy quilt. Anyways, I felt all funny, so burning between my legs, like something came loose in me, like that thing that had grown tight inside me for so long came loose now. I raised my legs and wrapped them around Harry's back, drawing him into me. My head was tilted way back, and my eyes were half closed. I was whispering, "God . . . Harry . . . please fuck me now . . . now. Fuck me hard." When I felt him enter me, deep inside me, I shuddered from the sheer ecstasy. God, it felt so good. I pressed my legs harder against his back, my hands on his buttocks, while whispering for him please to fuck me harder now.

But hardly was he inside me when Harry stopped kissing me. He pressed his face into my shoulder and his body went stiff, kind of a long spasm, then he didn't move at all. I was still moaning, fuck me more, rocking back and forth, but Harry was all still and I didn't feel anything. I mean, Harry wasn't hard anymore. This I could tell. I thought I would die. In fact, I didn't know what to do. His body just felt like dead weight on mine. I dropped my legs slowly down, like embarrassed things, and kind of made a flutter of my hand, like I was pushing away the hair from my eyes. What happened? Could it be my fault? Did I turn him off? Or did he have a heart attack? It was quiet, so quiet that I could hear the beating from my heart and the buzzing from Harry's electronic wristwatch. From the living room the Brazilian music was still going, a sultry echo, and something was dripping from the bathroom—a slow kind of drip, a rustle from the blanket, the stupid dog breathing like mad. I could feel the huff of air coming in from the open window, and it smelled like rain. A long slant of light coming from somewhere, probably from across the street, breathed under the curtain. I could swear that Harry was sleeping, his eyes closed.

Finally, when Harry's stupid electronic watch began playing "Love Story," of all songs, and I almost began crying, bawling from sheer frustration, loneliness, Harry stirred and let out a yawn. He rolled off of me and said, "Babe, c'mon, I'll take you home. Tomorrow, early, I have a biggie publicity meeting for my pink pop campaign."

"Uh-huh . . . oh sure," I said, pretending that I was stretching from lavish exhaustion. He patted my thigh and said something about how pink pop was a winner, that it would keep Bee Bee, a ballbuster, and the kids in style. After a long silence, Harry, mostly yawning, turned to me for the first time and asked, "Did you come?" I nodded, but I didn't look at him. God, I wanted to say, how could I? There wasn't time, that he was definitely a wham, bam, thank you, ma'am guy, that he didn't even know how to feel or how to hold a woman. Thank God it was dark in the bedroom, because I didn't want Harry to see me crying.

After Harry went and brought me my clothes, somehow I managed to get dressed. After Harry was dressed, now in corduroy pants and a Harvard sweat shirt and his tennies, I could hardly look at him. When he turned on the lights, he said, "You're so beautiful. I love to see a woman after sex . . . all flushed." Can you believe, he actually thought that I was flushed from his lousy lovemaking, not because I was damned angry.

"Do you want anything?" he said. "Perrier . . . Calistoga? . . ."

"No . . . no, thank you," I said, walking toward the door. "I have to get going. A busy day tomorrow for me, too."

"Oh, yes . . . I don't want to intrude on your schedule," he said, smiling nervously.

In the car, driving home, I didn't say a word. Not one word. I just looked out the window, the tears rolling down my face. Finally Harry said something like, "Are you all right, or just tired?" I still didn't answer until he pulled up in front of my house.

"Don't walk me up, Harry."

He took my face in his hands and kissed me lightly on the mouth.

"Catch you later, babe."

I don't know how I got upstairs. I went into Jenny's room, tiptoeing so I wouldn't wake her. Her room smelled of hair spray and perfume. Robin was sleeping in the other bed. I kneeled by Jenny's bed, hardly breathing. I pulled the blanket over Jenny's shoulder. She still slept with her fingers curled under, her old Raggedy Ann doll next to her.

I kissed her one more time, then went to my room. I undressed quickly, still not turning on the lights, like maybe light would make me feel the sadness. Quickly I slipped on my frog nightgown, plugged in my heating pad, and got into bed. The rain tapped against the window, and the foghorns made a lonely sound. But the moon was there. It was.

CHAPTER FIVE

After the Harry Wolfstein episode I put an ad in the *Bay Guardian*'s Personals column. After all, what'd I have to lose? The men couldn't be any worse than the wackos I'd been meeting. I'm telling you, they got worse instead of better. Wasn't that I didn't try either. God, I went out with Marcie Kaplan's rejects—all out to lunch. Even with Aunt Pearl's furrier, Sheldon Moskowitz, who was so hard of hearing that over our fish dinner he kept shouting "What?" then carrying on in a loud voice about his impotence problem and that he was having a splint put in his thing. And to top him, at Judy and Harry's wedding, over Oysters Rockefeller this, la la that, I met this silver-haired dentist everyone was fussing over. While we cha-cha-chaed, he whispered in my ear that I had great breasts so that in his book I was A-OK, because he was definitely a breast man. I'm telling you, enough to make you sour on men.

So it wasn't such an effort putting in the ad. And my ad was no big deal actually, nothing really heavy or emotional or implying that I was chomping at the bit. It simply read: "Ex-Jewish princess seeks company of male genius." So about a week later, when the letters from the ad arrived, I went into my den and tore open the large manila envelope stamped, *"Bay Guardian,* Box 203," all charged up, telling myself not to breathe so loud, and began reading the letters. And God, you should've seen how many letters I got, you wouldn't believe. A riot. Letters from garbagemen who had the hots for Jewish princesses, shrinks, three social workers, one with herpes, one political activist who wanted me to go to Guatemala with him and farm, and one writer who said he wanted a suicide pact. You name it, they wrote it, and they all wanted a Mrs. Robinson who could sew, knit, cook Chinese and French, speak several languages, and with a sense of humor yet, and all claimed themselves geniuses except for one: Eric Blumberg, a fifty-one-year-old mathematician on the faculty of U.C. Berkeley, who wrote in a neat handwriting, the letters as tiny as little hieroglyphics, that he was an ex-genius and that he wondered about the "ex" in my ad because, like anti-Communists, he said, once a princess, always a princess. But that he didn't care if I was a Jewish princess, because he liked them all. And then he went on to say that he had raised two grown sons and that he liked walking, talking, eating, and that he told funny jokes sometimes. I laughed out loud. Sounds like fun, I thought. Probably I'd call him, but God, I didn't know if I had the nerve. After all, I'd never done anything like that before. So, carrying Anny in my arms, I walked around the room in circles, discussing out loud with Anny about whether or not I should call this Eric person. But why not? You're sick and tried of writing sex scenes all day and up half the night talking to Marcie Kaplan on the telephone about her fucked-up lovers and certainly no Prince Charming is going to drop into your life. No way, José. Make things happen or you'll end up like poor Laura in *The Glass Menagerie,* all books, playing with your glass animals. And anyways, I was ready because I was climbing the walls, hot as a pistol, still dreaming at night that I was lying naked by the sea while faceless men made love to me, or every day staring out the window at the two gorgeous hardhats shingling Mrs. Nelson's roof across the street, practically drooling at the muscles in their bare backs. Nor could I spend the rest of my life going to the mailbox and wait for Shana to send me the edited chapters. Months would go by before she'd edit a chapter, and then she'd send me one of her lousy memos, complaining about my typos, that she was exhausted and needed another vacation. "Time to change my life," I said out loud.

I went quickly to my desk and looked at Eric Blumberg's letter, squinting at the tiny telephone number scrawled in the corner of the letter. I began dialing his number, clearing my throat so that my voice wouldn't squeak, and assuring myself that if he didn't answer by the count of six I'd hang up. "Hello," answered a man in the softest voice I've ever heard.

"Is Eric Blumberg there?" I asked.

"Speaking."

"Hi . . . my name is Lisa . . . Lisa Perlman . . . you know," I said, kind of laughing and telling myself not to sound so nervous, "the ex-princess . . . the *Bay Guardian* . . ."

"Oh, yes."

"I've never done this before, I mean put an ad in—"

"You'll get used to it," he said in a matter-of-fact tone.

"Oh, you don't understand. I put the ad in because I'm a writer and I needed some material. Otherwise I'd never do it."

"Well, it's okay," he said. "I've done it several times . . . and I've met some attractive women. Some I didn't like, some I liked, some who didn't like me."

"Why do you answer ads? Doesn't a Berkeley professor have a full social life?"

"Of course," he said, speaking precisely. "But sometimes I get tired of meeting the same people."

"Uh-huh. I know what you mean. So, I guess if you're not looking for anything, ads are all right. But you wouldn't believe the letters I got. Seems like everyone in the world is looking for a relationship, for a special thing. And it doesn't exist anyway."

"What kind of writer are you?" he asked, not commenting about relationships.

"Fiction."

"Impressive."

"My first novel's been sold to Avalon Publishers," I said, nervously thumping the pencil on top of the desk. "I'm just waiting for my editor to finish editing the book, so it can get published. You don't know what I've been through . . . I—"

"What is it about?" he interrupted.

"About a Jewish princess, about her rise and fall."

"I thought you said you were an ex-Jewish princess," he said, laughing.

"I am, but the book is fiction," I said defensively, thinking that his laugh was warm and rich, not one of those icky fake high-tech laughs. "The book has nothing to do with me. Not anymore."

"What is it about?" he asked.

"About a person who doesn't feel anything—except in her dreams—imagination—nothing real—everyone expects her to be something she isn't. Anyways, when the princess finally finds out she isn't a princess and God, everything happens to her. Anyways, it started out as a serious book, but my editor, this nutso woman, wants more sleaze, less introspection, so now my princess is a glitzy mess. But after all," I went on, speaking faster, "it is my first novel—"

"Is it about your life?" he persisted.

"Not really," I said impatiently, thinking that something about his probing made me uncomfortable. Probably one of those smart-ass professors . . . thinks he knows everything about everything.

"Anyways," I quickly said, "now I'm writing a biographical novel about Eva Hesse."

"I saw her work years ago at the Berkeley Museum. An interesting artist."

"Very. Also an interesting woman."

"Uh-huh. What makes her interesting?"

"Her courage. Her total belief in her art. Her vision. Anyways," I quickly said, wanting to change the subject, his silence making me nervous, "what kind of mathematics do you teach?"

"I'm mostly doing research now. I teach a few graduate courses."

"I've never known a mathematician. I'm terrible at numbers. And I know this sounds silly . . . oh, I'll ask anyway. Do two plus two ever make five?"

"Sometimes," he said in the same matter-of-fact tone.

"It all sounds impressive," I said, nervously twisting my hair around my finger and thinking that this man really sounded nice and low-keyed.

"So does writing a novel," he said seriously. "And I'd like to talk to you about that some more. So why don't you drive over to Berkeley Saturday evening and we'll go to a clarinet concert."

"I don't drive at night. My eyes aren't so hot. And, besides," I quickly said, "I'd rather have you come over to my house." I laughed. "Guess I still have some of that princess stuff in me. After the concert, if you feel like it, if the moon is right, why don't you give me a call and come over for a drink. I'll be home writing, anyways. I have a deadline."

"Okay," he said hesitantly, stretching out the "kay," like he was thinking it over. "I might do that, Lisa."

"Good, because I'd like to talk to you, too, hear more about your

work . . . and about the university. . . . I want to go back to
school someday and get a Ph.D. in English lit. Sorry I'm talking
about myself so much. Usually I talk about myself a lot, I guess,
because I haven't found anyone else as interesting."

"I noticed," he said, laughing again. "But it's okay. I'll call you.
What's your phone number?"

"Phone number . . . oh, sure . . . it's 922-1936."

"Good. I'll call you."

"Uh-huh. Fine."

"Bye-bye."

He hung up.

After I hung up, I thought, okay, you did it—not bad at all. I
enjoyed talking to Eric Blumberg. Something about his soft, mod-
ulated voice and confident tone and the silence between his words
interested me, and he sounded with it. But, who knows, he could
be a creepo, too.

The following Saturday night was raining like hell, one of those
dismal nights when you want to get into bed with someone and
cuddle. Anyways, Jenny was at Kevin's for the weekend, so I moved
the typewriter into the kitchen, where it was warm and bright. I
sat at the table with my bag of chocolate chewies, Anny on my lap,
typing over a passage I'd been working my ass off on, a flashback
with Eva and her father in Germany. But the work was moving
right along and I was humming to Beethoven's Piano Concerto
playing from the living room stereo. God, the music really did
something to me, made me feel all dreamy. I imagined myself in a
white chiffon dress dancing with a fabulous Greek. So I was feeling
pretty okay for a Saturday night, though the thunder and lightning
gave me the creeps. But I kept on writing and humming, occasionally talking to myself—I did that a lot while writing—until I got
pretty tired. By 11:00 P.M. I figured that this Eric Blumberg was a
no-show, so I decided to call it a night and go to bed and finish the
bag of chewies and watch the rerun of *Holocaust* . . . maybe call
Marcie Kaplan again . . . maybe chew the fat with Larry Segal. . . . I turned off the typewriter and began picking up the
dropped pages from the floor and stacking them on the table. From
my kitchen window I could see Doris in her kitchen, and Cole

Porter music was drifting from Joe and Richard's window. I liked
the neighborhood sounds, the rattle of Doris's pots and pans, and
through the vents I could hear the Pons arguing in Chinese. Anyways, I was locking the kitchen windows when the telephone rang.
God, I nearly died a thousand deaths, jumpier than a jumping bean.
So I ran into the living room, calling out, "I'm coming . . . I'm
coming" like someone could hear me and answered the phone. It
was Eric Blumberg, explaining that the concert had let out late and
asking if he could still come over. I said, "Sure, why not," thinking
that this genius person must be really hard up. But I figured what
the hell, I was in the mood for an adventure anyway, what did I
have to lose? Was my life such a fantasy island? Such a ball? So I
tidied up, even watering my two pathetic yucca trees. And I changed
from my drecky frog tee shirt into Jenny's Norma Kamali red
sweater, leaving my sweats on. Almost forty-five minutes later, the
doorbell rang. I took a deep breath, telling myself not to get all
tripped out, that it was all in a day's work, and ran to the door. I
opened the door, smiling this sicko smile, murmuring some sappy
thing like "at last we meet," while this genius person, carrying a
paper bag under one arm and a big black umbrella, grinned like he
was so amused about something.

My first impression of him was that he looked older than he
sounded on the telephone. Maybe it was the dull porch light on his
face, or that he had this pilly expression on his face. Anyways, he
was kinda short—about my height, actually—and he had this darkish hair that stuck out wildly all over his head. He was wearing
steel-rimmed glasses, and even though it was dark in the hall and I
couldn't see his face clearly, you could feel his dark, intense eyes
taking everything in. He shook out the big black umbrella, just
taking his time like he had all the time in the world, still grinning
and letting the water drip from the umbrella before leaning it against
the wall. "Could be worse . . . at least we're presentable," he said
somberly, and shrugged his broad shoulders nonchalantly. He came
in then, still not looking at me, and strutted right into the kitchen,
just like he owned the place, a real pill, nervier than hell, I thought,
following him.

"Do you have a wine opener?" he asked, opening the paper bag
and taking out a bottle of wine.

"I don't drink wine," I said.

"Well, I do," he said soundly, opening the kitchen drawer.

"Anyways, you'll never find one in that mess," I said.

"I can see that."

God, just what I need, a clean freak. "Well, when I'm writing I don't have time to clean drawers, you know," I said, feeling ridiculous chattering because he didn't seem to be listening.

"Oh, here we go," he said, pulling out this wooden opener that Amy had sent me last Christmas. And then without a word, in one swoop, like he was so efficient at everything, he pulled out the cork, and dropped the cork in the trash basket.

"How about a glass?" he said, looking at me intently and grinning.

"Sure," I said, opening the cupboard and looking for a glass that wasn't chipped. I put the glass on the kitchen table and he poured the wine.

Still grinning, he said quickly, "Let's go into the living room."

So he went into the living room, and I followed along, thinking this guy's really a trip and has nerve galore. He put the wineglass on the coffee table and took off his corduroy jacket, folding it neatly over the chair.

"I'd like to turn the volume up."

"Go ahead."

"One of my many obsessions," he said on his knees, fiddling with the volume. "I like good music clear. There! Bach's Concerto in A Minor . . . o . . . kay."

He sat down on the black leather chair next to the yucca trees while I sat across from him on the white, moth-eaten sofa.

"So," he said, glancing at the paintings, "I see you like contemporary art. Though I figured if you're writing about Eva Hesse you were involved in contemporary art."

"I love art."

"Did you paint these?"

"Oh, some. That portrait over there," I said, noticing that his shirt cuffs were frayed and that he bit his nails down to their quicks. Yet there was a scruffy elegance about him.

He nodded. "I wanted to be an artist."

"Uh-huh."

"What does that symbolize?" he said, pointing to *Fear of Success*, a tall wooden sculpture.

"Well, you see, the figure is a woman—"

"Kind of Giacometic," he said.

"Yes, in a way, and see how she holds the dollar bill, like throwing it away. She's afraid of success."

"Are you afraid of success?" he asked, looking at me curiously.

"Not consciously, but fear of success is instilled in women."

He looked reflective.

"I was trained to get married and say no more than 'Pass the butter, dear. Is your shirt ironed all right, dear? Is that good, dear? Did you come, dear?' Never be more than dear Dr. Poo Poo's wife. Die without knowing myself."

"Interesting," he repeated, looking at me curiously. When he talked, his wide, full mouth curved upward, revealing the most even and gorgeous teeth.

"Anyways, most of these paintings, sculptures, are from years ago when I began collecting."

"I can't get into contemporary art. I don't understand it."

"I'd think you would . . . a mathematician."

"Mathematics is about concrete ideas. No room for the abstract."

"Abstract?" I repeated. "Picasso says art is the lie that understands the truth."

He smiled. "Art is art. Some good. Some bad."

"That's like saying apples and oranges. Art is more than that. It's not about something. It *is* something. Conveys feelings. Anyways, your letter says you like classical music," I finally said, annoyed by his cool confidence and silence.

"Yes."

"I do, too. Obviously." I pointed to the shelves filled with classical tapes. "Beethoven and Mozart are my favorites, but I prefer Mozart."

"Beethoven is more complex," he said positively. "More interesting."

"Oh, but Mozart is more emotional . . . has a better emotional range, don't you think?"

He didn't answer. He stroked Anny for a while and sipped his wine, every so often throwing his head back and closing his eyes like he was concentrating on the music. Not bad-looking. It was an intelligent face with strong bones, and in the light his hair, which I had thought was dark, was reddish. He took off his glasses then and laid them neatly on their sides on top of the table. His eyes, without his glasses, were even darker, and his nose was well . . . okay . . . Romanesque, but the bottom of it looked squashed or like it had been broken. Probably a fight . . . he looks like the type who gets into fights.

"I have a cat, too," he said, sipping his wine and not caring that Anny was walking over his lap.

"Oh, you do? I love cats," I added, relieved that he wasn't going to continue talking about Beethoven. "What's its name?"

"Max," he said simply.

"Do you have a house?"

"Yes, I have a house."

"Where are your sons?"

"My son Ian lives in Berkeley with his girlfriend, Dianna, and my other son, Joshua, is twenty-four and in medical school at Princeton. How about you? Do you have children?"

I nodded. "Amy is in New York. She's a journalist for CNN, and Jenny is probably going to move out soon. She's been looking for her own place. Right now, she's working at Saks and selling used cars. But I'm trying to get her to go back to school."

"Children," he said, sighing and shaking his head like he had the weight of the world on his shoulders.

"They're something, aren't they?"

"Sure are," he said, smiling and looking reflective. "I wouldn't want to be without them. I wish I had more."

"So do I."

"Do you have family here?" he asked.

"My mother and brother. Do you?"

"My father lives in Chicago and my brother Herb teaches physics at Columbia, a few nephews and cousins in the Bay Area. My father is eighty-five years old and recuperating from a recent heart bypass."

"You must be close to your family."

He nodded. Then he got up and began fiddling again with the stereo, turning the knob back and forth while complaining that the sound wasn't just right and that I should get it adjusted. "As I said, one of my obsessions," he said, sitting back on the chair.

"Is your work an obsession, too?"

He looked thoughtful. "I've worked on something important."

"What?"

"I've worked out the mathematical theories that developed the cellometer."

"Cellometer? What's that?"

"It's complicated," he said impatiently, but then his face softened as if he thought he might have offended me. "It's an instrument for measuring cells. Controls the way cells reproduce."

"You mean . . . God . . . could it control cancer . . . AIDS?"

"A long shot. The cellometer is still in the early stages . . . experimental . . . still has a long way to go. . . ."

"How many years have you worked on this?"

"Twenty."

"God, you're a regular Einstein."

He smiled.

"What mathematical theory—or should I say process—developed this?"

"It's too complicated to explain," he said, looking somewhat gloomy. "But it's called the optimal theory."

"Uh-huh . . . What is it?"

"Well . . . it means a lot of things," he said, looking more animated. "Picture balls . . . just plain old billiard balls, floating in a box."

"Uh-huh."

"Imagine the balls . . . they're moving in all directions," he said, sitting forward. "All over the box."

"Uh-huh."

"And I take photographs of them . . . successive photographs so I can see the configurations in their speed, figure out how to get to every position from every configuration."

"Configuration. What do you mean, configuration?"

"Think of the world . . . system of planets."

"That kind of configuration. I see."

"Can the same configuration occur again?" he asked, looking at me with the look of a patient teacher.

"Why wouldn't it?" I said.

He smiled.

"It has to be proven. That's what I'm working on. Order comes out of chaos. A lot of other factors you wouldn't understand."

"You mean, if you found a way to control the configuration, the planets could be controlled, too?"

"Maybe."

"God . . . it's something."

"Anyways," he said, shrugging nonchalantly, "all this and more led to the cellometer."

"God," I repeated. "It's something. Really something."

He shrugged, lit a cigarette. Took a couple of drags, then put it out in the ashtray.

"What does the cellometer look like?"

"I'll show you," he said, taking a narrow gold pencil from his pocket. He drew the cellometer on the back of my *Art Forum* magazine.

"It's beautiful," I said, admiring the graceful cylinder.

He smiled.

"You've really contributed something to science. Your work is important."

"It's also timing . . . intuition. A good scientist works on the right thing, selects the right question for investigation. It was there waiting for someone to find the chance."

"Oh, I do know. It takes perseverance . . . risk. . . ."

"There's still a lot of work to do," he said, looking distracted and dropping the pen on the table.

I laughed. "God, I advertised for a genius, and I got one. But why would you answer an ad?"

"Same reason you put one in. Something different."

"Like looking for a Rembrandt in a garage sale."

Silence.

"Have you published a lot?"

"Some."

"Any books?"

"The book I'm known for is titled *Cell Control*."

"Interesting title."

He didn't answer. "Tell me about your work," he asked, looking very serious and watching me intently.

"Next year *Princess* will be published. My horrible editor . . . slow as a snail . . . is only halfway through editing."

He smiled.

"I changed the story a lot."

"Why?" he asked softly.

"Why? Well . . . it's my first novel. The first one's a toughie. And if I don't, well . . ." I sighed.

"Once you get that first one published, you won't have to compromise."

"No," I said, feeling uncomfortable by his intense stare.

"How did you become interested in writing the biography of Eva Hesse?"

"Hesse . . ." I repeated, nervously tapping my foot, "well, she went through hell . . . you can see it in her work. If she'd been a man, her work would be a household name. Women are still fucked over in the arts."

"Sounds ambitious," he said, looking at me seriously. "How long will the book take to complete?"

"If I'm lucky . . . you know, work every day, not get any diseases . . . all that . . . well, about a year . . . at least."

He looked reflective, then asked, "Have you published anything before?"

"A couple of pieces about art collectors . . . I mean, I got a lot of rejections . . . breaking into the magazine scene is hard. But I published a piece 'Do Midgets Collect Art?' "

"Midgets? Why midgets?" he asked, half grinning.

"I wanted to show that the art world is more about patronage and less about art . . . keeps out a lot of people who are interested in art . . . who are made to feel like the art is too big for them . . so I interviewed a couple of midgets who collect art."

"Interesting," he murmured, shaking his head, stroking Anny, who was walking over his lap.

"Are there many women mathematicians?" I asked.

"For some reason, no," he said. "I work with one at Berkeley. She's a fine mathematician. But she's too involved in feminist issues."

"That's what men say when a woman is in their field. They always put the woman down."

"I'm not going to get into that," he said, picking up the wineglass and stretching his legs.

"Anyways," I said, "I want to write an important book."

"What's an important book?" he said gently, looking at me patiently, like a parent sometimes looks at a willful child.

"Oh, great truths. Emotions. I think emotions mostly," I said, wondering why he was staring at me. "When the emotion shines through the words . . . like a Rothko painting," I added, my voice fading because he was watching me so intently and it was making me nervous. But what was I supposed to do, sit there like a retard? One of those intellectual poops who thinks anyone besides Flaubert is a hack?

"What's wrong with small truths?" he asked softly, rolling the wineglass between his hands. "Doesn't a good story evolve from a small truth, from a germ of something?"

"Well, that's debatable," I replied, annoyed that he was challenging me again. Smart ass, I could tell. One of those smart asses. "Small truths grow into big truths," I said, wondering why he was looking at me like I had the wrong answer. "But I don't really want to argue the old art versus life thing . . . God, that's a bore." I sighed. "Everyone always carrying on about that. . . ."

He smiled as if he was amused and, after an uncomfortable silence, he said, "I had a dog named Judy, but she went away."

"Judy!" I said, laughing out loud and surprised by his abrupt switch in subject matter, his eyes twinkling mischievously, his playful tone.

He laughed, too, his mouth curving up over his teeth, and when he laughed he half closed his eyes and I noticed when he leaned back in the chair, how nice his body was, broad and thick. "The other day I was walking in my neighborhood and I saw Judy, who lives with another family now, and she passed me like she didn't know me, didn't even stop."

"Oh, no," I said, really laughing because something about this guy was a riot, really funny, sure you have to listen for it, because his humor is subtle, hidden underneath his plain little stories, but it's there, inside his soft, detached tone, and if you listen carefully you'll pick it up.

"And Miriam Adler brings me chicken soup and she's trying to find me a wife. So far no wife."

"Who's Miriam Adler?" I asked, still laughing at the deadpan expression on his face and the way he suddenly threw in the name Miriam Adler like improvising pieces of his life.

"Jacob Adler's wife."

"Jacob Adler?"

"The Nobel Prize-winning physicist I worked with; he created the bubble chamber."

"What's the bubble chamber?"

"A container . . . the particles leave tracks . . . so you can see matter . . . never mind," he said impatiently.

"Oh, matter . . . sure . . . I understand."

He looked solemn then. A melancholy about him . . . not visible but underneath . . . slow, in the stillness of his eyes.

Then we just started talking, mostly about what foods we like, sushi opposed to Thai, or whether or not we believed in reincarnation, Eric arguing that life stopped with death and things are as they are while I argued that life weaves through death and that life is about perpetual change. And then he talked about how much he loves traveling and about growing up in the back streets of Chicago, and the days he worked his way through college. And then we talked about films and both agreed that we loved Woody Allen. Then we exchanged more stories, Eric laughing like crazy while I described my first meeting with Shana and I laughed while Eric, with the same deadpan expression on his face and detached tone, described one of Miriam Adler's dinner parties when she'd fixed him up with a fat Russian mathematician who belched all night and screamed in Russian. While he told his story he used very few gestures, almost as if his stillness was his drama. Everything he did had a special meaning: the way he'd shake the glass before sipping the wine or throw back his head at an especially beautiful passage of music, sighing and closing his eyes as if he were inside the music.

I was slightly intrigued, at the same time troubled by his silence. A knowing silence, like he could see in me. And as I continued talking about my writing . . . Amy . . . Jenny . . . my body moved slowly, deliberately, like I was slow dancing and my hands moved faster because the chemistry between us was so strong it made me uncomfortable. Surprised me. Because at first I thought he was a scrungy intellectual with a pilly face, but as the evening wore on and he talked more, I knew he was different. Unusual. Not the ordinary Joe Blow. Maybe not the most handsome creature in the world, hardly Robert Redford. But the guy's got something. A silent sex appeal. Something special hidden underneath the silence.

When he stopped talking, I asked him how long he'd been single.

"Fourteen years," he replied quickly. And I could feel his whole mood change, like a sudden quietness came over him and his expression changed, from one of cordiality to a quiet gloom.

"How long were you married?" I persisted, trying to know more about him.

"Ten years," he said, sighing and looking far away. God, a real Sad Sack, one of those I-still-love-my-ex-wife freaks. All I needed. "My wife got crazy, suddenly one day said she didn't love me and then she took off. Became a born-again Christian. So I raised the boys."

"Oh, I'm sorry," I said, observing the yearning in his eyes, a look a child has when he loses something and wants it back.

He shrugged and looked away. "I should've married Deborah. She's such a wonderful person."

"Why didn't you then?" I asked.

"I guess I wasn't in love with her . . . and there were things I didn't like. I tried to get over them, but, well . . . things . . ."

"Oh. Shame."

"Anyways, she met someone else." His voice drifted off, and for a second he looked far away and I could see the loneliness in his eyes.

"How long did you go with her?"

"On and off for a couple of years," he said nonchalantly.

"What did Deborah do?"

"A poet . . . unpublished . . . I never read her work, but my friend Holly Rheinhardt—an English professor at Berkeley—says she's good. Anyway, she was such a wonderful person. And she loved me so much. I tried to love her . . . no chemistry, I guess."

"Sounds heavy."

For a second he rolled the wineglass between his hands and looked all still, like contemplating something. "I've been sleeping with a woman once a week . . . for years now . . . but I'm not involved." He looked at me intently, like waiting for my reaction.

"In my book, that's involved. Very involved," I said. "Involved enough to see each other once a week. And how can you separate sex from emotion?"

"Good sex is a gift. A very rare thing," he said, looking at me like I was a naïve child who didn't yet understand the ways of the world.

"Well, a once-a-week love affair wouldn't do it for me. It's too conditional . . . limited."

"No, you're the kind of woman who would expect a man to fall instantly, totally in love with you."

"That's not true. I don't know if I'd want that."

"You're clever."

"Clever?"

"Clever with words, uncomfortable with pauses."

"So fill them in."

He laughed.

Silence.

"I want to get married someday," he said, looking tense. "God, I want to get married. . . . I hate being alone."

"I don't. . . . I never want to get married again. Not until my career takes off and I'm financially independent. Besides, Arnold Perlman was enough."

"What happened?" he asked softly, looking sympathetic.

"Nothing happened. That's the point," I said, laughing like it was funny. But I was angry. "I married him on the rebound, anyways."

"From what?"

"Oh . . . I don't want to talk about it."

"Oh."

"I left a five-acre mini-estate with a Buster where I did my princess thing all Puccied and blah-blahed to death, plus a gardener, a pool sweeper, the whole shmeer. But I didn't like him much. And he hated kids, including his own. We haven't heard from him in fifteen years."

Eric didn't say anything. Just watched me, as if waiting for me to say something more, but I didn't want to. And the way he watched me, so silently, his eyes all still, made me uncomfortable.

Anyways, when the thunder broke and the windows rattled, I jumped and then a blue streak of lightning bolted silently across the room.

"Lightning scares me," I said, hugging my waist.

"It's beautiful," he said softly. "Nothing to be afraid of. It's beautiful."

He paused a moment, watching me curiously.

"Have you always been afraid of lightning, thunder?"

"Guess it's one of those childhood fears."

I laughed nervously.

I stopped because he was still watching me and I was angry that he was looking in me. But then he resumed talking about the new lawn he was putting in, his garden, about the tough semester he was having, and about how his graduate students weren't doing as well as he'd hoped.

Anyways, Vivaldi's "Four Seasons" was playing, and the rain slashed hard against the windows, rattling the shades. We sat quietly. Eric drank more wine, his eyes half closed, listening to the music. When the music stopped, I said I had to get up early the next morning and that it was getting awfully late. So Eric stood quickly, shaking out his jacket before putting it on. He put his glasses on and ran his hands through his hair, which was sticking straight up. At the door he held my hand and looked at me closely, like he was thinking over something, evaluating something.

"Lisa Perlman," he finally said, his eyes like little dark secrets, "I enjoyed meeting you. . . . You're unusual," he said in a tone like he was assessing a term paper. "Quite lovely . . . beautiful, actually. But your ad was deceiving because you're still a princess . . . full of hopes . . . dreams," he said, looking at me wistfully and at the same time frowning disapprovingly. "You're climbing a mountain and I'm coming down one. This spring I'm going on my sabbatical."

"Well, you don't have to marry me, you know. We could be friends," I said, irritated—angry, actually—that he assumed I'd even be interested in him, and to tell you the truth, I wanted to say "Bug off, creep, you're not my type anyways," but I didn't want him to know I was hurt—disappointed, so I smiled and said formally, "It was nice talking to you, too . . . and lots of good luck with your work."

He moved slightly toward me and then I sensed that he wanted to kiss me, because he had that look in his eyes like a young boy has before his first kiss. But I moved away and said in my coldest tone, "Thanks for dropping over. And again, good luck." I opened the door then and he stepped out onto the porch. It was still raining, but not as hard, and the air smelled muggy. And, without looking at me, he opened the big black umbrella and ran down the stairs, disappearing into the night.

After I shut the door, I tried not to think about Eric Blumberg, but I was angry that this stranger had spent half the night at my house—then assessed me like I was some student he'd failed. And calling me a princess, how dare he, I thought, like he knew something about me that I didn't . . . well, whatever it was, I thought, turning off the kitchen lights . . . a nervy guy, pompous as hell, and that I don't need. But when I went into the living room and saw the imprint of his firm body, still freshly pressed into the leather chair, I knew that something about this man, this stranger in the night, made an impression on me, a damned strong impression, too, and it bothered me. Why I didn't know.

CHAPTER SIX

The following Friday, at 7:15 A.M., I was in my den writing *Eva,* drafting a scene in Eva's South of Houston Street loft. She was working on a huge sculpture hanging from the ceiling to the floor, a black ball caught in an intricately woven net. A difficult scene. When suddenly my den door opened and Jenny burst into the room.

"Mom! Didn't you hear me calling you?" she demanded, looking at me through eyes full of sleep and clutching a hair blower.

"No . . ."

"Well, take off that fuckin' Walkman," she said, pulling her lilac satin Jean Harlow negligee closer to her body. "Amy called twice. Says it's an emergency. Wants you to call her."

"My God!" I said, jumping up from the chair and untwisting the Walkman from my head. "My God!"

"Don't get excited, Mom!" she said, looking at me as if I were nuts. "It's not an emergency emergency, just one of Amy's usual emergencies."

"Okay," I said, sighing with relief. "I'll call her back later."

"Your typewriter woke me again," Jenny said irritably and yawning. "Can't you wait until seven-thirty? I need my sleep."

"No, I can't," I said. "You know I have a schedule. That I begin writing at six forty-five. Close your vents."

"Give me a break," she said disgustedly, wrinkling her nose and glaring at me.

"You can stand it," I said, smiling at her.

"I can't wait to move out," she said, looking away and then back, watching me for a reaction.

"I bet," I said, thinking that she looked so funny, so old and yet so young in the negligee, her hair sticking out all over.

"I'm still looking . . . but the rents are so high. . . ."

"Uh-huh. If you're living alone," I said carefully, "you don't need a big or real expensive place."

"Who'd you think I'd be living with? I'm going to live alone."

"Well . . ."

"I know . . . you were going to hock about Kevin—"

"No, I wasn't. . . ."

"Kevin and I had a wonderful time last night. I had three wonderful orgasms," she said, yawning again.

"My God!"

"What my God?"

"I've asked you not to talk about your sex life with me. Not every detail."

"Don't rag me about Kevin, Mom. You're always ragging on me about my hair, my weight."

"My God."

"And stop saying 'My God' every minute."

"Jenny, please!" I said, really getting irritated. "I have work to do."

She yawned one more time, then said, "What shall we have for dinner tonight?"

"Fish . . . vegetables."

"Not tofu again. I'm sick of tofu. Dodie, this lady at Saks, she's old, almost fifty, about your age, in menopause, too . . . every minute she's borrowing my Motron, says tofu isn't good for you."

"Oh, all right. Jenny, can't you see I'm working?"

"Dodie carries a sack of shoes because her feet get swollen. She says if only she'd listened to her mother and married the nice Jewish chiropractor she wouldn't have swollen feet. So, Mom, you should get out more."

"Out, Jenny! I'll talk to you later."

She blinked a few times, rubbed her eyes, then said, "Heard from that professor?"

"No."

"Tch . . . tch . . . Amy and I think if you fixed yourself up more . . . You should see Dodie without makeup—awful! With makeup she's a beaut. Make a list—I'll get you some makeup on my discount."

"Jenny, please! Do you mind? I'm working on an important scene. I don't like being interrupted."

"Give me a break!" she shouted, then slammed the door so hard the window rattled.

I felt like slamming the door, too. Jenny and I were getting on each other's nerves. When she was home, the constant whir of her hair blower, the tinny sound of the punk music, her phone ringing at all hours of the night, people inquiring about her cars, all kinds of voices echoing in my sleep, Fariba, Char, and Robin always there, using my bathroom, my things, giving me funny looks. God, I loved Jenny so much, missed her when she wasn't there, and resented her when she was there. So believe me, I was relieved about the apartment. Glad . . . and sad.

"Kids," I said out loud, putting on the Walkman and deciding I'd call Amy at two my time. Probably she wants to complain about Adam. Lately Amy'd been complaining a lot about Adam . . . or sometimes she'd read me her assignments, little pieces on swimwear or shoes. But when I'd correct something she'd get mad and hang up. Anyways, I began writing, and soon I was in New York, 1962 . . . the sound of traffic . . . the smell of paint, glue, turpentine . . . echo of cement floors . . . arguing, voices rising . . . the wind blowing . . . rattling. . . .

Three weeks and the genius hadn't called. No matter how many times I told myself he's a horse's ass anyways, who needs him, I was bewitched, bothered, and bewildered. When I'd gone to the library and looked up Jacob Adler's bubble chamber, I'd looked up mathematicians and discovered that Eric Blumberg was a biggie. A long article in *The American Scientist* magazine said that Eric Blumberg at twenty-three years received his Ph.D. from Princeton and was known for his good work in generalizing the pontrayagen maximum principle and had written *Cell Control* at twenty-six. By thirty years old he'd been awarded several prizes. Other articles went on to say that physicists, physicians, biologists, anad mathematicians were studying the cellometer and its effects on immunosuppressing diseases. Eric was published in over thirty scientific journals, cited one hundred and twenty-two times. Hard to believe we met through an ad. Yet it figured that Eric Blumberg would do something different, unpredictable. Anyways, if he didn't call me, certainly I wasn't going to call him. As Marcie Kaplan says, if it's meant to be, fine . . . if not, *sayonara*. Besides, I had more important things on my mind than Eric Blumberg. Like my writing.

And poor Bruce. He was in one holy mess. He'd smashed up the Jensen. Mother said some drunk ran head on into Bruce's car, hit and run. By a miracle, Bruce wasn't killed. Broke his nose, some cuts, shock. I'd visited him at the hospital. He was okay now, but he was in debt up to his eyeballs. Seems before he'd gone to the Betty Ford he'd been buying illegal medications. That's how Bruce explained it to me. Ran up a big tab. Now the sharks were after him. Plus, when Mother and Sidney went to Carmel for a few days to rest, their house was robbed. Mother's jewelry, furs, rugs. Bruce was really upset about that. For when Mother was upset, Bruce was upset.

After the accident, Bruce moved from Marin to San Francisco. He wanted to be closer to the family. I hadn't seen him since he'd moved. So I decided to surprise him with the cookies Jenny'd baked.

Carrying the tote bag and wearing my jogging suit I'd painted with flowers and frogs, I began walking to Bruce's condo on Lake Street, not far from my house. I waved to old Mrs. Nelson, shlepping along in her walker, all dressed up in a beige woolen coat with four wooden buttons and a matching veil. Farther along the street, I chatted with the Strausses, wearing matching jogging outfits and holding hands. I'm telling you, regular lovebirds.

As I got near Lake Street, overheated and breathing like a dog in heat, hot flashes! . . . lousy! . . . like weights pulling you down . . . lately they'd been driving me up the wall. . . . I spotted the light blue Victorian-styled building and the separate little pathway that led to Bruce's condo. I opened the little wooden gate, thinking the pathway lined in pink azaleas charming. The fog lay so low, in little thick patches, but you could see the sun through them. The foghorns were blowing in little mists and sounded so utterly lonely that for a second I stood there shivering. I rang the doorbell, untangling the Walkman from my head, deciding that if Bruce wasn't home I'd leave the cookies on the doorstep, maybe walk to the Marina Green and jog around the track with all the jogging studs. But then I heard Bruce's heavy footsteps. Bruce opened the door.

"Lisa . . . hi," he said, looking surprised, hugging me.

"Bruce! I'm so glad to see you," I said, kissing him back, noticing how much weight he'd put on. "I was going to call you first . . . but . . . oh, here! Jenny baked chocolate chip cookies . . . especially for you."

"Thanks," he said, lifting and dropping his shoulders, looking pleased, and taking the tin of cookies. "Don't just stand there, Lisa. It's cold. Come on in. You're just in time. I ordered a pizza. I was so hungry I couldn't wait for dinner."

I went into the little hallway. It smelled of fresh paint and Bruce's cologne. Bruce walked ahead of me, kind of waddling, as if his body were too heavy for his small feet.

"What a lovely place," I said, admiring the all-white combination living and dining area, pullman kitchen, a long glass aquarium. Two black cocker spaniel puppies were sleeping in a large cage.

"It's nice. Mother is decorating it. She still has a lot to do. . . . If you stand to the side of the window, Lisa, you can see the tip of the Golden Gate Bridge."

"Yes . . . and those fish . . . so beautiful."

"Some of those fish," Bruce said, frowning and pressing his lips tight, "cost me as much as three hundred bucks apiece."

"What are the dogs' names?" I asked, kneeling by the cage.

"Paco and Pico."

"So sweet."

"I just got them. Don't tell Mother."

"What happened to the cats?"

"Mother gave them away . . . without asking me, just came over and gave them away."

"Anyways, Paco and Pico are adorable," I said, ignoring his sudden gloom.

"They're cute," he said, shrugging. "I might give them away. Get a couple more cats."

"Oh."

"Cats are clean. Go in the sandbox. Mother'd probably buy the sand at I. Magnin. . . . What do you want to drink, Lisa?"

"Oh . . . diet Coke . . . if you—"

"Diet Coke coming up!" he said happily, taking a can from the icebox.

"Thanks."

"I'll set the table," said Bruce, waving me away. "Make yourself comfortable."

"I'll peek around."

"Go ahead."

Everything was neat, in its place, sparse, like hidden. In the tiny white kitchen, the jumbo appliances . . . toaster oven, coffee pot, in a crock pot every kitchen utensil imaginable, you name it, everything shiny, unused, displayed like in a model home. Above the icebox hung a large empty cork bulletin board, with little colored thumbtacks stuck in. On the glass and chrome coffee table, set between two white loveseats, was a book titled *San Francisco*. On the cover a picture of the Golden Gate Bridge. There were sparkles on the ceiling. A couple of prints Mother and Daddy had bought on one of their trips to the Orient hung above the fireplace. The double bed, in the small bedroom, was neatly made up. A huge television set next to a bookcase filled with neatly arranged opera videos and old movies. On one shelf were lots of books about medicines and insects. A framed plaque hung above the dresser, a tribute to our father, Lou Roseman, for thirty-five years in the movie business. As I read the tribute, I felt sad, A part of my father I hadn't really known.

"Lisa," Bruce yelled, "the pizza is hot!"

Bruce folded two blue linen napkins and put them next to Mother's blue and white plates.

"Hope you like anchovies."

"Love them."

"So, what's new with the book?" he asked, helping himself to a thick slice.

"Slow. It's going slow."

"You'll make it. You're a star."

"Not a star. I'm not a star."

"Just the other day I said to Mother, 'You watch Lisa. She'll climb right to the top.' "

"There's no top. Believe me. . . . What's new with you, Bruce?"

"Nothing . . . nothing much." He shrugged.

"Nothing?"

"Not yet. Nothing. I keep busy . . . I do a little housework . . .

take the dogs out . . . nothing much." He wiped his damp forehead with the napkin, then took another slice of pizza from the box.

"I love this aria," he said between mouthfuls, nodding his head to the music.

"*Marriage of Figaro* is my favorite opera," I said.

"It's shmaltz."

"Bruce, how's your money situation? You know," I said, lowering my voice.

"Mother gave me some of the insurance money from the robbery. So the assholes are off my back."

"That was awful . . . the robbery, I mean. Poor Mother."

"Eat your pizza, Lisa," he said impatiently, patting his forehead again with the napkin.

We didn't talk for a while. The music echoed over our silence. Bruce ate the pizza slice, picking off the peppers and sausages, eating them last. He popped open another diet Coke can.

"When I get my driver's license back I'll get another car . . . a Porsche this time."

"You don't have a license?"

"They took it away. . . . Don't look so surprised! I was arrested for drunk driving."

"Your license was suspended?"

"Revoked."

"God, Bruce, when you've been through so much . . . worked so hard to—"

"The night of the accident Mark and I had a fight. I went crazy . . . went to a neighborhood bar. Drank saki. Took the turn at fifty . . . no seatbelt . . . hit the guardrail. Woke up in the hospital with a million tubes. I was still drunk."

"God."

"Now I go to a state methadone clinic . . . and it's great. Better than the Betty Ford crap. A bunch of assholes. A bunch of crap!" he said, his voice rising. "That fucking place cost me a fortune. The more neuroses you got, the more money."

"I'm glad you're getting help. I—"

"My counselor, Dr. Singh . . . he's a Ph.D., not a medical shrink.

But he's better than that lousy shrink Dr. Heindrich! This guy's really helping me. He's the director of the clinic. A brilliant man. Younger than me. He's Indian. Really smart. I'd like you to meet him, Lisa. He's really smart." He nodded twice.

"Uh-huh. Great. Sounds good."

"And Mother says to me, 'How come you go to that dark, dirty person?' "

"My God."

"The only shrink I've even given any credence to. She's always ridiculed my shrinks. With due respect to Mother, though," he said, snickering, "they're all a bunch of assholes. But Dr. Singh is helping me. So what does she have against the man? He didn't pull me out of the house, drag me to the clinic. I chose him." He wiped his forehead again with the napkin and his face was turning red. His voice was sharp, on the tip of a scream.

"So every Thursday morning on the dot, seven A.M., Mother calls me and she says"—he went on, imitating Mother's high voice—" 'Isn't this your Dr. Ding-a-ling day?' It's not funny, Lisa."

"I know . . . but . . . Mother means well. You have to laugh. You—"

"I do! Believe me, I do. But it's not easy when every morning she asks me to come for dinner . . . of course, never Mark. And when I say, 'I can't, Mother,' the voice drops ten octaves and she says, 'But I'm cooking pot roast and noodle kugel.' "

"All the things you're not supposed to eat."

"The other day she was making one of her famous remarks about the gay people, about how they're all sickies, I turned to her and said, 'I'm gay, too, Mother.' "

"What did she say?"

"She said, 'Well, you're not like that.' You know. So I just let it go. What's the use?"

Silence.

"Mother's like a dymo labelmaker . . . everyone has a label. She'll be watching television, and she'll say everyone is sick or . . . everyone has a label . . . except for the dippy blonde on *Wheel of Fortune*. Mother loves that program. She's damn good, too."

"Uh-huh."

" 'Do something that makes money,' Mother's always saying. But I might do volunteer work at the convalescent hospital."

"That might be good. You know a lot about being cooped up, about nursing . . . might lead to something. The best reward for work, Bruce, is that you get better at it . . . not the money."

"I like the old people; they like me."

Silence.

He got up from the table then and opened a tiny drawer in the small walnut buffet table, once in Mother's breakfast room. "Before I forget, Lisa, I want to give you something. One of the kids at the clinic gave it to me. For luck. This is from Africa. A rhinoceros made of malachite. It'll bring you luck."

"It's lovely," I said, looking at the tiny green rhinoceros. "It's lovely. Thanks."

"Do you want to take the rest of the pizza home?"

"Sure."

"Good!" he said, looking pleased. "Maybe you could have it tomorrow. Leftover pizza is good." He wrapped each slice neatly in foil, then put the four pizza slices into a Ziploc bag.

"There!" he said, his lips tight, pressing his forefinger along the top of the bag, making sure it was sealed.

"Thanks, Bruce . . . I had a wonderful time."

"So did I," he said, lifting and dropping his shoulders. "I enjoyed it."

I kept my hand on the little rhinoceros a second longer.

That evening around nine o'clock, I was sitting in the living room writing in my journal and feeling pretty low about Bruce. As usual, Jenny was at Kevin's for the weekend and I was feeling restless. I was sick of staying home on Saturday nights. Earlier, I had killed some time talking to Marcie Kaplan on the phone about her latest lover who couldn't get it up, and then I called my psychic, Philip Shultz, who said to hang in there, that things got worse before they got better. And then for a while to Larry Segal, my friend the writer, who talked about how the publishing business was fucked. Anyways, suddenly I put the journal down and I went into the den and took Eric Blumberg's letter from the envelope and went back into the living room. I dialed his number, dialing quickly before I changed my mind, assuring myself that he probably wouldn't be home on a Saturday night anyways, but he answered on the first ring.

"Hello," I quickly said. "This is Lisa . . . Lisa Perlman."

"How are you?" he said, sounding glad to hear from me.

"Fine, thank you. I was just sitting here reading and thought I'd call and—"

"I'm glad you called," he said quickly. "I've been home working. My graduate students have kept me busy this semester."

"Why don't you come over?" I suddenly asked.

There was a brief pause. "Why not?" he said in that matter-of-fact tone.

"Good. And Eric, would you please bring a bottle of vodka? I feel like getting smashed."

"Be there at ten."

After I hung up, I started tidying the living room, filling the ice bucket, and thawing the rotten cheese that'd been in the freezer for God knows how long. I turned on the stereo, making sure that the classical station came in clearly. Then I changed into the pink cable sweater Amy had sent me and I put on my long silver hoop earrings. I brushed my hair back off my face and wound it into a chignon and stuck a rose from the bouquet in the vase into the chignon.

When the doorbell rang, I quickly answered it. Eric, wearing the same beige corduroy rumpled jacket and white shirt, looked at me like it was the first time he'd ever seen me. He came right into the kitchen, strutting like the Prince of Wales, and took the bottle of vodka from the bag.

"Oh, thanks," I said, "I don't drink usually, but I felt like a martini . . . a hard day, family hassles."

"You look great," he said, staring at me and ignoring my distress. He put some ice into two glasses and poured a hefty amount of vodka.

"Thanks, you look great, too," I said, clicking my glass against his.

"Good," he said. "Now that we both agree how great we look, let's listen to some music."

We went into the living room and sat down on the sofa. The

music . . . I think Handel . . . was soft and beautiful and the room was nice and warm. Eric sat slightly away from me, like maybe he felt kind of shy, too, and when I wasn't looking, I could feel him looking at me.

"How's your father?" I asked, rattling the ice in my glass.

"Oh, he's doing okay, thanks . . . complaining about his medications . . . it's shitty getting old."

"Oh, I don't know about that. Depends on how you perceive getting old," I said, enjoying looking at him.

"Old is old," he said with a shrug.

"Anyways, I'm never going to get old. My fiction will keep me young."

He smiled indulgently, like one smiles at a wishful child, and he clicked his glass again. "To your fiction," he said softly.

He wasn't wearing his glasses that night. Up close his eyes were even darker than I remembered, and I liked the way the quiet took over his face when he was talking about his father.

We talked some more then about his father and about how important it was to have family around you, then I told him a little bit about Bruce and about how hard it was for me to get close to people because my family had never been really close. He listened attentively with that quiet on his face, sipping his drink or nodding, his somber eyes always watching my face. I was starting to feel more relaxed—kind of high, actually—and the chemistry between us was so strong, I was afraid to touch him. After a bit Eric put his drink down on the table and touched the side of my cheek and looked at me with the most gentle expression.

"I like to look at you," he said softly and smiling. "You have a beautiful, intelligent face . . . a funny face . . . your nose is a little crooked and everything is a little off, but it's a beautiful face."

"Thank you," I said, feeling pleased and moving slightly away from him.

"And you're smart," he continued in the same soft tone. "An unusual smarts. You use words in the wrong places and you mispronounce Mozart and Tchaikovsky and you talk way too much because you're afraid of silence, but you're unusual and interesting."

"Please don't analyze me. Just kiss me," I said, putting my drink down on the table and surprised at how aggressive I was.

"Lisa," he said softly, his finger caressing my nose, "we're going to get involved." So, okay, the guy's one of those cocky types, but what was I going to do, argue we wouldn't get involved? God, I was popping like popcorn, dying to kiss the guy.

And then he kissed me, at first lightly and then he kissed each cheekbone, then the tip of my nose, then on my mouth again. It was a kiss like I'd never felt before, not one of those wet guppy kisses or contrived passions, but a real kiss, deep and strong, and when the kissing became wilder, I felt those little pinpricks going up my legs, going up all over my body, like little yearnings that had been there for so long and were just coming out. I tightened my arms around his neck and pressed my body closer to his body, because I wanted to climb inside of him, my hand moving slowly along the inside of his thigh, finally touching him there where he was hard. He kissed me smoothly, deftly, like a dancer who knows the steps, but underneath his passion and expertise was a gentleness, so exquisitely sensual that I felt like tearing off my clothes and doing it right there on the floor. But like you hold tight to a ledge before falling, a part of me held on to myself. Until after a while, when we stopped kissing, Eric sat back and looked at me.

"I love the way your face is all flushed like a young girl's," he said softly.

"I like the way you kiss. Very much," I said.

"Let's go into the bedroom," he said. I got up and he followed me into my bedroom.

Beethoven's "Moonlight Sonata" was playing, I'm not kidding, and the moon was so low it looked like it was going to fall right into the room.

"I'm a little shy," I said, explaining the dark. "It's been a long time."

"That's okay, I'm shy, too," he said, undressing quickly. "And it's always that way the first time."

I pulled down the window shade, leaving enough of it up so I could see the moon. And then I began undressing quickly, and closing my eyes so that I wouldn't see Eric's naked body. I was afraid to see it because it was probably too beautiful. I pulled back the quilt and got into bed. The sonata was almost over and the moon was so bright you could see it through the shade when Eric got into bed. I held my breath, still keeping my eyes shut so I'd keep back the part of me that wanted him to tear right into me. When Eric kissed me gently on the shoulder and I opened my eyes and put my arms around his neck we kissed, and our bodies moved slowly together, and Eric, still kissing me, got on top of me. He went inside me then, quickly, like he wanted to reach the bottom of me. I liked the way his body felt on mine, strong and heavy, perfect inside me, like he was made for me.

"Your cock feels good . . . so good."

"It's all yours."

"I love that, Eric . . . so good."

"You feel like honey . . . like I thought you'd feel. . . ."

"More . . ."

"I could make love to you all night."

"Do then."

"Can't get enough of you," he said, holding me tight.

"Hold me more. I love to be held."

"You've come to the right place," he said, holding me tighter.

"Kiss me again, please."

He kissed me tenderly. "So beautiful . . . you're so beautiful," he murmured. But I pulled back a little, trying to pull back, so I wouldn't let go, like holding on the edge of something real tight, just before falling, like when you don't want to look down. And I didn't want to let go . . . let him know I was falling . . . and I couldn't stop kissing him, touching him, just touching him everywhere. I loved the feel of his skin and the way between kisses he'd whisper something sweet in my ear, or touch my hair. My legs were shaking, shaking real hard, I guess from feeling so much, because I'd never before felt what I was feeling that moment, with Eric deeply inside me. It was just the most perfect thing, not just because of our bodies and all that. It was something deeper, like the chemistry between us had touched something deeper in each of us, something we both knew had only started and, God, it felt good, so good. "I want it in all night, way in," I whispered.

"Like this?"

"Yes . . . harder . . . more . . ."

"Oh, God, Lisa. You're good, so good, the best I've ever had."

"I am?"

"Like I dreamed, like I dreamed."

I whispered something in his ear.

"You're terrible," he said.

"Be terrible," I said.

"Like this?"

"Not bad," I said.

"Okay, how about this?"

"Better."

"I knew it would be like this . . . I knew it . . . I could feel it . . . when I first met you. . . . I think I was afraid of you. . . ."

I laughed. "Oh God, really . . . I'm glad I called you then, because I wanted you, too."

"I want to spend more time with you."

"We'll see."

"That's good. . . . Oh, God, Lisa . . . sweetheart . . . ride it . . . rare . . . you're a rare animal."

"A leopard, that's what you are," I said, my hand moving slowly along. "Creepy and still . . . and—"

"And you're beautiful . . . sexy . . . beautiful."

"I'm a butterfly, I live in a glass jar . . . but I don't want you to keep me in the jar."

"No, baby, I won't, I'll let you out."

"Eric . . . I've never felt anything so good . . . so hot. . . ."

"Do that again, Lisa . . . oh, my . . . No one's ever done that . . . even imagined such things. . . . You live in a jar thinking of things no one else thinks . . . unusual things."

And then our bodies were moving so beautifully together, like we were dancing, our special dance, slowly and sensuously. And I was burning, burning all over. So I closed my eyes, moving my hips slowly, slowly so Eric's cock would stay in me all night . . . all night . . . and then I was floating, floating, and I could feel myself letting go. So I stopped moving, lay still and opened my eyes, because I was afraid if I closed them I'd go under and lose the part of me I kept so close to myself, the part of me afraid to let go.

"Baby . . . don't hold back . . . don't hold back," Eric murmured, "I want you to come."

"I—"

"Don't hold back" he said, caressing my thighs. "I love those
long legs. . . ." And then he pressed deeper, and I was squeezing
his cock inside me, squeezing him so tight and for a second, only a
second, I felt this burning feeling go all through me, and I thought
I was letting go . . . letting go, so I forced open my eyes and
thought about white roses and the moon outside and then the hot
feeling stopped, got all stuck in me, my hands caressing the backs
of Eric's thick thighs, my hips moving up and down, watching
Eric's face. His eyes were closed and his mouth was slightly open
and he was calling my name, calling "Lisa . . . Lisa . . ." over
and over again. "Come, come . . ." then I felt his body shaking
and he was moaning and his cock was moving in and out of me
fast, then slow, and his heart was pounding so hard I could feel it
through my skin. We kissed hard and long, our mouths pressed
close. I murmured things in his ear and held him tight, so tight,
until his body became still, all still. We lay there quietly for a while,
not saying anything, just touching each other all over touching
everywhere until our breathing got slower and then Eric slowly,
gently pulled his cock out of me.

After a while he got off me and I lay in his arms, my head on his
broad chest, enjoying the feeling of his warm, strong body against
mine. The music had stopped long ago and the room felt chilly so
I pulled the quilt over our bodies, looking at Eric's moody face all
shadowy in the moonlight. Anny was howling from inside the house,
and the soft sounds from our breathing gently moved the stillness.
Eric held me close to him, so tight I couldn't move, and he kissed
me again, and again our mouths pressed in long, warm kisses. I
was feeling kind of jumpy and my legs were still aching I guess
from the little hot pinpricks between my legs because I hadn't let
myself go, hadn't allowed an orgasm, and I wished I could turn
myself upside down and spill out all the sex stuck inside me. Spill
it out. I wished I could.

After some time Eric said softly, "What are you afraid of?"

"Afraid?" I repeated.

He didn't answer.

"Just because I didn't fake, scream 'I'm coming! I'm coming! You wonderful prince!' you think I'm afraid. I'm not afraid, Eric. I just don't trust you yet."

"It's okay, sweetheart." He pulled me closer. "But you have to trust yourself."

I didn't answer, pulled away. Eric touched me gently along my thigh.

"Does it bother you I didn't have an orgasm?" I asked, angry that he was making a thing about it.

"I guess if you did I'd like it better. But it's your orgasm—all yours."

"Next you'll tell me to relax."

He pulled me closer.

"I felt like I was just about to let go, but then . . . well, you don't understand a lot of things about me . . . it's hard for me to let go."

"Don't worry about it," he said, kissing me on the mouth.

"Anyways," I said, wrapping my legs around his and holding him tighter, "I don't want to talk about orgasms."

"You don't have to."

Eric stroked my hair then, touching me gently all over my body, his fingers softly exploring my body, until he said, "I'm going to close my eyes now and try and work through a mathematical problem I'm working out . . . so you go to sleep."

"What kind of mathematical problem?" I asked, kissing his mouth.

"It's complicated . . . you wouldn't understand."

"Try me."

"Okay," he said. "Let's see . . . I'll start with this: A prime number is a whole number, other than one, that can be divided without remainder only by one and by itself. Thus the first ten primes are two, three, five. . . . Now, you do it. What are the next numbers?"

"Oh, sure . . . five, seven, eleven, thirteen."

"After seventeen," he said gently, caressing the inside of my thigh.

"Nineteen."

"Is twenty-one a prime?"

"No."

"Why?"

"Because three times seven is twenty-one."

"Go on."

"Twenty-three."

"And . . ."

"Twenty-nine."

"Good," he said. "Very good."

"Uh-huh . . . so prime numbers are infinite."

"You say there are an infinite number of primes," he corrected.

"Uh-huh."

"Why do you think so?" he asked.

"It'd seem to me that as the numbers become larger they'd shrink, and what shrinks, expands, and begins again. It's hard to explain."

"You have your own logic, but you're right. Euclid proved they're infinite."

"Uh-huh. Interesting." His cock felt warm.

"A few months ago a student of mine discovered a Mersenne prime."

"Mersenne?"

So Eric began explaining prime numbers, that the first Mersenne prime is three, and then recited the thirtieth Mersenne prime and then explained twin prime this, twin prime that, and about how prime numbers become smaller or larger, then about the Ornstein theory, about the catastrophe theory, and more about the balls floating around the box, ergonomics, the cellometer, really getting into it, like I was just an ordinary genius and understood exactly what he was talking about. And as he recited more equations or an anecdote about a colleague or student, his soft, even voice contained a vitality I hadn't heard before, and then he couldn't stop talking, like he was in another world. He went on talking, reciting, more equations and proofs, theories, and God, it was something, while I murmured, "Uh-huh, sure, I understand." I watched the moonlight fade into a cold light, shadow Eric's strong profile. I lay my head on his chest, and between more explanation about primes, we kissed or touched each other gently, until finally Eric closed his eyes and lay still, so still, yet I could hear his mind still thinking, figuring out his little numbers, his mind ticking like a little bomb, ticking away, and I wondered if Eric was as complicated as the little letters and numbers that filled his mind that gave him a special view of the universe beyond. Finally, after some time, when the moon was only a chip, hardly there, I closed my eyes, wondering why Anny was crying.

The next morning when I awoke, Eric was still sleeping. I liked his curly hair on the pillow. He slept on his side, with one arm over his head. It seemed oddly natural that he was there. For most of the night we had held hands, or Eric kissed me in his sleep, murmuring my name, and we slept together like we had always slept together. I got up and quickly went into the bathroom, brushed my teeth, and washed the night from my eyes. I put on this old shleppy red bathrobe the kids gave me, wishing I had some floaty lilac thing, then went into the kitchen. I fed Anny her meow chow stuff, then I took out of the bread box three stale croissants, along with two linen napkins. I put them on the pink lacquered tray. Without my glasses, I was bumping into things, coffee spilling all over the place. God, what a mess. Finally I got everything together, even put a bud vase with a wilted rose on the tray, and I went waltzing down the hall balancing this drecky cat tray, tossing my hair and humming, like bringing breakfast on a cat tray was no big thing.

When I came into the room his highness was sitting up and reading a *New Yorker* magazine. He smiled at me. "Good morning," he said softly. His eyes were full of sleep and his hair stuck out all over his head. I felt kinda shy . . . different, like the night had worn off.

"I thought you'd like some breakfast," I said, trying to sound like bringing breakfast to bed was an ordinary thing for me, and put the tray between us.

He smiled. "That's very nice of you . . . but you don't have to please me. You please me quite enough already."

"Oh, I'm not trying to please you," I said defensively, feeling slighted. "I just wanted some breakfast." He drank the coffee then and began dipping a croissant into the coffee, eating hungrily and silently.

"When are you going to show me some pages from *Princess*?" he said, finishing his coffee.

"Oh, I never show anyone my work."

"I understand," he said, smiling at me. "But just two pages? I'm interested."

"Well, maybe . . . just the first two pages," I said, ambivalent about showing him but at the same time wanting him to see my work.

So I went into the den and took the first two pages from the top of the manuscript and went back into the bedroom and gave Eric the pages. I lay down beside him and watched his face while he read the pages. He held the pages away from his face like maybe he was farsighted. His face remained expressionless and after he read the first page, without looking at me or changing his expression, he put the page on the bed and read the second page. He finished reading the second page, then turned and looked at me with empty eyes and I sensed a silent disapproval.

"How far are you in the biography of Hesse?" he asked, trying to sound polite.

"Oh . . . I'm still in the drafting stage . . ." I answered reluctantly, annoyed that he hadn't commented on the pages. "But Lester thinks *Princess* is going to be a best seller . . . maybe a movie, important enough to win something, maybe an Academy Award. You just have to read the whole book."

"Your first book, and you want an Academy Award," he said softly, looking at me as if I were a ridiculous child. "It's a long shot. Try going for small things. Not so big."

"Wouldn't you want the Nobel Prize?"

"Mathematicians can't get a Nobel Prize," he said gloomily.

"Why not?"

"Oh . . ." he sighed, kissing the side of my face. "The story goes that there was a rivalry over a lady's hand between Alfred Nobel and the Swedish mathematician Gosta Mittagleffler."

Before I could protest, Eric kissed me and before I knew it he was taking off my robe and kissing me all over my body, all over it. And when he went inside me so quickly—God, he felt so good for a minute I thought I was on the verge of letting go, but the morning light was so bright and I didn't want him to see that he made me feel like I'd never felt before. So I held him real tight, enjoying him but not letting go. "Come, baby, come," I whispered. And I began moving my body like I couldn't get enough of him, whispering all kinds of things in his ear, until I felt his body stiffen, like a spasm kind of, and then he was quiet, so quiet, hardly moving at all, not even kissing me, just like he turned off, turned off. I dropped my legs slowly and then I kissed him a couple of more times, but something was wrong, was off between us, and I wondered if Eric had sensed I was holding back.

"I thought we'd go see the penguins today," finally I said, kissing his sullen mouth. "The park is so beautiful and I love the penguins."

"I have to get going, Lisa, I have work to do."

"Oh, please . . ."

"Is this a battle of will?" he asked, looking at me coldly.

"No, of course not," I said, trying not to show I was annoyed that he was leaving so abruptly. A pain in the ass, I could tell already, tell my prince was going to be one of those complex jobs. Trouble ahead.

He got off me and his eyes were averted. He went over to the chair then, where he had dropped some of his clothes, and began dressing, his eyes still averted.

"I have to get going," he repeated, buttoning his shirt. "I have a lot of work to do."

"Sure, I understand," I said quietly, covering myself with the sheet, "I have work to do, too." But I wanted to scream at him, scream how dare he leave me so abruptly and turn on, then turn off me like that, and that I wouldn't allow it, I wouldn't. But I didn't. I simply got up like nothing in the world bothered me except finding my robe. And then when he was dressed, I followed him to the door.

He kissed me on the mouth, but his eyes were cold. I acted real cool, my tone all formal, like it didn't matter to me whether I ever saw him again. But I wanted to shake him loose and tell him that he couldn't turn me off like that, that I was angry. But when he said, "Work well . . . . I'll be talking to you," I said, "You work well, too," and smiled like a sap.

When I shut the door I stood there in the hall, feeling that sinking feeling, like everything under me was falling in, wondering if Eric was still seeing that once-a-week woman he told me about, why he suddenly ran off. Over my dead body would I be her replacement, fit into his little time slot. I'd vow celibacy and eat tofu forever rather than that. I pulled my robe closer. The Sunday morning lay all over the floor in streaks of grayish light. I hated the Sunday light. An empty, hollow light. I wanted to crawl back into bed, where it was still warm from Eric and try and get back the warmth because I felt colder than hell. I went back into the bedroom, wondering why he hadn't liked the two pages. I knew he didn't. And I had the emptiest feeling inside me, because when the moon went down he changed.

Later that afternoon I was in my den writing. I wasn't feeling so hot. Kind of low and my back was hurting. The wind was rattling the windows. I was struggling through a difficult scene, trying to keep Eric from my thoughts, push him away. Ever since he'd left I'd felt troubled, like a piece of me inside had broken off. When I heard Amy's voice over the answering machine, I jumped up quickly and answered the phone.

"Mom!"

"Hi! Wait . . . until the message goes off . . . there. . ."

"Is someone there?" she asked, lowering her voice.

"Of course not. Who should be here?"

She sighed.

"Hi, Lisa," said Adam.

"Oh, hello, Adam."

"We just thought we'd call and chat. Say hello on this wonderful Sunday," said Amy with forced cheer.

"Yes . . . yes . . . I was going to call you later. How's everything? Work? Everything?"

"Going great, really great," said Adam. "I have a few celebrity clients . . . the Doobie Brothers . . . a new word processor . . . a secretary . . . great."

"Lynn gave me some swimwear pieces to write for the show next week."

"Sounds good."

Silence.

"Have you heard from Avalon?" asked Adam.

"If I did, you'd be the first to know."

"Adam," said Amy in muffled tones, whispering. "Anyways, Mom . . . what've you been doing?"

"I'm working on *Eva*."

"How's it going?" she asked.

"Very well . . . I love working on the book. It's going to be hard . . . is hard . . . but I love it."

"Good, Mom," murmured Amy.

"Trouble is," said Adam, "no one's heard of Eva Hesse. I've asked around. No market for it."

"That's not the point, Adam."

"Gotta think of the market," he said.

"Mom, wouldn't it be better if you went and got a job . . . got out more . . . met people? . . ."

"This *is* my job."

Silence.

"Jen said you've met this professor," she finally said. "Eric Bloom—"

"Eric Blumberg."

"Well?" said Amy.

"Well, what?"

"Are you going to see him again?"

"Maybe."

"Don't let him think you're too anxious," said Adam.

"Or too disinterested," said Amy.

"Will you two stop?"

"When Jenny moves out, you'll be alone .   . and—"

"Kids, I've got to get back to work."

"Are you using the aerobics? It's good for stress."

"And toning," said Adam.

"Yes."

"Good."

Sighs.

"Amy, call me from work tomorrow. I'd appreciate it if you could get me some catalogues from the Museum of Modern Art—"

"Oh, we have a call coming in, Mom."

"I love you—"

Click.

CHAPTER SEVEN

Please God, don't let me love Eric Blumberg. God, I didn't want to. But no matter how many times I'd tell myself that Eric spelled trouble, definitely bad news, he got under my skin and I'd find myself thinking about his cool eyes, and when the phone'd ring I'd jump out of my skin.

Even though I'd been seeing Professor Shmatte four months—concerts, films, lectures—and we made love like a couple of banshees, I knew little about Eric. . . . I mean, Eric didn't let you know him, only gave what he wanted. We'd be having this real hot time and the next morning Eric would suddenly turn off, without a word, just run off, sometimes not calling me for days. And who needs that? Certainly I didn't . . . I wanted someone dependable. . . . I'd had enough with the I'll-love-you-later types.

Anyways, I hadn't heard from Prince Charming since the last weekend, when we'd gone for sushi, then necked all during this Spanish love film, the subtitles all screwed up anyways, and then after the movie we were in such a hurry to get to my place we practically did it in the car. God, it was something. But then the next morning, there I was still hot as a firecracker but Eric got all somber and jumped out of bed and took off, his shoelaces not even tied. And I hadn't heard from him since. So this time when he called, I'd decided I was going to say that I was busy and that I couldn't possibly see him for several weeks. But when that Thursday night lover boy called and in his soft, even voice explained that he hadn't called earlier because he'd been so very busy with his work, I kept the old trap shut, butterflies flying around my stomach, and in my most Lauren Bacall voice—husky laugh and all, enough to make you whoops—I said that I understood perfectly and that I'd been so very busy with my work, too. So we made a date for dinner and a concert the following Saturday evening. After the star professor yakked some more about how well his father was recuperating, then complained that he got a low assessment on the students' evaluation report and that he was kind of low about his work, something more about the optimal control theory, and then he said he missed me, we hung up.

I was excited, running around the house carrying on with Jenny about what I'd wear, acting like a regular nutso, but Jenny said to get it together, Mom, and that she didn't know what all the fuss was about anyways because she thought Eric was a nerd. But Jenny was like that with me, real protective, and she had only met Eric a couple of times on her way to Kevin's, so I didn't pay much attention. After all the months of looking for an apartment, Jenny finally found one nearby and she was moving out on Monday. So thank God she was busy with her own life . . . not too busy, though, to talk to her sister every day and give a blow-by-blow about Eric and about how I was mooning about the house, finally met a man I liked, because every minute Amy was calling me and bossing me about just how I should look, what I should say.

All in all, things were changing, going really well. I mean, not that writing *Eva* wasn't a struggle and a half, but I knew what I was doing and what I wanted to say and I loved the work and stayed close to the work. But the waiting for Shana was a mess and really affected my moods and when I'd recently called Avalon to find out what was happening with *Princess* they said Shana was out sick with dysentery and would probably be out for the holidays.

Anyways, the next afternoon I was meeting Mother for lunch, not that I really felt like it, but usually Mother and I had met for lunch once a week and I hadn't seen her for a couple of weeks. I had walked from my house and it was already past noon and Mother didn't like waiting. So I hurried along. But before going into the restaurant I looked up at the sky and the sky was the color of milk glass, really clear. I watched the swirl of dark birds float aimlessly like they had no place to go, until they disappeared.

I hurried into the restaurant then, one of those little places with more plants than tables. Mother was already seated by the window, which looked out on a nice courtyard with cherub fountains spouting water. As I approached the table, Mother gave me a quick look, a look like she wasn't really looking at me, but her eyes rapidly taking in every detail of what I was wearing. Mother never missed a thing.

We exchanged one of our air kisses, neither one looking at the other. Then I sat across from Mother, thinking how pretty she looked in beige and how young, God, like her face never ages.

Right away, though, before I could get my breath or open the menu, Mother frowned disapprovingly and shook her shoulders, like she was cold or something.

"Aren't you freezing, Lisa, with only that thin blouse? How can you go around like that? No one goes around like that. It's freezing."

"I'm not cold," I insisted, already feeling uptight but telling myself that I wasn't going to start with Mother. No way. Who needs that? I'd learned the hard way that arguing with Mother never got me anywhere. Made me angrier. Sometimes so upset I'd go home and sit in the closet.

"Why do you wear all that Indian jewelry?" she said, looking at me suspiciously and shaking her head. "Beatnik jewelry . . . that's what it looks like, Lisa. You're too old to wear such dangly earrings."

"I'm not too old. I have my own style."

"I see the girls and they don't—"

"You see Fat Susan wearing her horrible little button earrings, and—"

"Never mind! Her husband is worth a million dollars."

"If you don't mind, Mother, I'm not in such a hot mood today. So please don't start hocking about my jewelry. I have more important things on my mind. If you care to know, I'm plenty worried about my book."

Mother averted her eyes and pressed the napkin on an imaginary stain on the tablecloth, giving me one of her I-told-you-so looks, and making this tch-tch-tching sound with her tongue.

"Every day," she said, still tch-tch-tching until I was ready to scream, "I read about Danielle Steel. They say she turns out books like hotcakes. I don't know why yours is taking so long—maybe you should do something else."

"For God's sake, Mother," I said, trying to keep my voice down, because I was really getting angry, "you don't know this business, and anyway, I'm writing a serious novel. Not some romance."

"All right," she said, looking annoyed but pretending she wasn't, "but do you have to live like a hermit? If you don't mind my saying so, it isn't normal."

"Please stop with the normal. What do you think I'm doing, having a wonderful time?" I said, my voice rising now. "You think it's easy rewriting an entire novel with a crabby editor breathing down your back?"

She shrugged indifferently. "You chose it," she said in a singsong voice and giving me another I-told-you-so look. "No one could ever tell you a thing."

"Please, Mother," I said, sighing in exasperation. "Let's not discuss my book."

"Don't raise your voice, Lisa," she said, glancing nervously around the room, like she was afraid someone would overhear. "Everyone is looking. Always be a lady." She made this tch-tch-tching sound again, then sighed like she was exhausted. "For once, Lisa, can't we have a happy day? Talk about something pleasant?"

"Sure, happy," I said gloomily, thinking I'd better keep quiet. If I continued talking about the book we'd only end up arguing. Then Mother'd say I was ruining my life. That I should concentrate on getting a husband instead of writing, and oh, God, I'd get wild and we'd start and it'd be an awful mess. So better the silence. So we sat for a while in this uncomfortable silence, while the little angers I'd feel whenever I was with Mother came up over me. So I folded and unfolded the napkin in my lap, and looked out the window or around the room, telling myself not to let Mother get to me. But it was hard. She could drive you up a wall. Still she was with the tch-tch-tching and every minute checking the water glass for a chip, or the silverware for a smudge. Phew, her endless fussing with details . . . guess they took away the big things, the things she didn't want to face.

"So, Lisa," Mother finally said, taking a dainty bite from the roll, "what's new?"

"Oh, Mother, really," I said, shrugging my shoulders and pretending that I didn't know that she meant whether or not I had a date.

"Do you ever hear from Harry Wolfstein?"

"For God's sake, Mother, I haven't seen him for over four months."

"Still, he could call," she insisted, lifting and dropping her shoulders and pretending she was more interested in eating the roll than hearing about Harry Wolfstein.

"Sylvia Finkel tells me he's quite a catch."

"Not for me, he's not. Not my type at all."

"Type! Who's your type?" she said, frowning and wrinkling her nose. "That bearded art dealer? A nut!"

"Mother, please," I said, ignoring her remark. "I don't like Harry Wolfstein."

"Can't you go out with him anyways? Be friends, let him take you to nice places . . . you never know who you could meet. You have to be seen." Then she paused for a second and waved at some imaginary bug, watching me from the corner of her eye.

"Jenny tells me that you met a math professor," she said, frowning disapprovingly and watching me for my reaction, but I shrugged like Eric wasn't important or worth discussing.

"I hardly know him, but he's nice."

"Nice! You need more than nice!"

"Mother, please!"

"Professors don't make much money."

"I'm not interested in his money."

"Money is the most important thing. Haven't you learned that by now?"

"Mother, please—"

"You always pick the funnies, Lisa. First it's that art nut, now it's a math professor."

"Mother, please!"

"Money's the name of the game," she said, pressing her napkin.

"Mother," I said, sighing impatiently, "he is not just a math professor. He's a prominent scientist."

"So?"

"What do you mean, so? He's developed the cellometer, could be a breakthrough to AIDS, cancer. . . . He's been on the Berkeley faculty for sixteen years."

"Your Uncle Ted, on your father's side," she said, pressing the napkin, "is a famous physicist—"

"I find Eric attractive and interesting," I continued, not caring that I was interrupting her.

"Ask him if he knows Dr. Ted Roseman."

"Yes, I will."

"Ask him, Lisa."

"I said I would!"

"One name I've never liked is Eric."

"I like it."

"It's no picnic for a woman alone these days," she continued, ignoring my irritation.

"Depends on the woman."

"Even Sylvia Finkel with all her money and new face lift . . . and gorgeous too, Lisa—looks forty . . . is having trouble meeting the right man."

"She needs a face lift. She's a real pill."

"And at the rate you're going—"

"Don't start, Mother, please."

"In a few years you'll be fifty," she quickly finished.

"Fifty! So what?"

"So nothing! Wait and see if a man will ask you out in such a hurry . . . they want the young chickies."

That did it. At that point, no way would I continue this one. She's always pushing me into another marriage, always wishing some prince would rescue me. I wished we could talk about something else besides a man. Or how I look. Or that I could tell her that Harry Wolfstein was not only boring, but a lousy fuck. But she didn't want *her* daughter to talk about her sex life. Any mention of sex embarrasses her. She still believes in virgins and that smart women hold out for the right man. That behind every smart man there's a woman, that if you hold out in the sex department, you'll get the man, etc., etc.

"Lisa," she finally said, glaring at the poor waitress who was serving at the next table, "see if you can catch the waitress's eye and tell her we've been waiting entirely too long . . . honestly," she said, tch-tching.

"Mother, she'll be here in a second," I said, sighing and holding my breath, hoping that Mother wasn't going to start in complaining to the poor waitress. Not that Mother would get mean or anything like that, but when she'd start fussing, then asking for the manager, it was embarrassing. But then, thank God, the waitress brought our Cobb salads. After Mother asked the waitress to please check the draft coming in from the door, Mother looked at me and smiled.

"The salads look delicious, don't they, Lisa?" Mother said, nodding approvingly while peering closely at her salad.

"Yes, wonderful."

"So full of croutons and bacon bits."

"Yes, bacon bits. I love bacon bits."

"Eat, Lisa," she said, frowning and giving me that appraising look again. "You're too thin. And believe me, only a mother would tell you the truth. Men don't like thin women, Lisa. It's not attractive. And another thing," she added, talking faster now so I wouldn't have time to protest, "you should wear cover-up on your face. Your skin looks splotched, and Clinique has such nice cover-up. Always be well groomed. You never know who you'll meet around the corner."

She resumed eating her salad then, lifting and dropping her shoulders like she knew she was getting my goat, when suddenly this wave of compassion came over me, just came over me. Something about Mother's thickening neck—and the way she slumped over the salad and held her napkin so close to her heart so that the salad dressing wouldn't splash on her ultrasuede suit, making a big deal about the croutons—made me realize that Mother wasn't the angry tyrant I once feared, but only a fussy, aging woman who couldn't face her disappointments, wearing the complacent expression of an old princess ruling a monarchy of shattered dreams.

"Jenny tells me she has an apartment," Mother finally said after some time, patting her mouth daintily with the napkin and frowning disapprovingly.

"Yes."

"Why isn't she living with a nice girl?"

"She wants to live by herself."

"I don't like the idea, she's living alone . . . that horrible Kevin will park himself—"

"Don't worry, Jenny has a mouth . . . she can take care of herself."

"I hope it's decent," she said anxiously.

"It's nearby . . . a cute little studio. And I think it's great that Jenny can take care of herself financially."

"How, I'll never know," she said, tch-tching. "Must be a rathole."

"Mother! She makes a lot of money selling used cars. And she earns seven dollars an hour at Saks."

"Used cars!" She shook her head. "Never heard of a nice Jewish girl selling used cars. I'm embarrassed, too, when Sylvia Finkel asks me what Jenny's doing."

"She's learning a lot about business . . . nothing to be ashamed of. But I hope she goes back to school . . . finds a profession she loves."

"Better yet, she should marry a rich man," she said, shaking her head and rapping her knuckles on the table.

"What good did marrying a rich man ever do for me?" I asked angrily.

"Oh . . . you! You'd never listen to anyone," she said, pressing her mouth tight and giving me a disgusted look. "I never did like the look in Arnold's eyes or his fishy handshake."

"Oh, Mother . . . you thought he was wonderful."

"I did not! You wouldn't listen."

"All right Mother," I said, sighing and remembering when I divorced Arnold and Mother insisted that Arnold was a wonderful provider-father-husband and that without him I'd be nothing and she wouldn't speak to me for months.

"Anyways . . . Amy is doing very well. She loves being on-camera," I said, wanting to get off the subject.

"That's because Amy goes with the right kind of boys," she said, nodding affirmation. "That Adam is a darling boy. Such poise, manners. They make such a wonderful couple."

"I only hope Amy doesn't get married for a long, long time. Not until she gets her career off the ground. Not so dependent on a man."

"Oh, you women libbers are for the birds," she said, looking at me like I was crazy. "God forbid Lisa you should have the problems I have with my children. Believe me, you'd sing a different tune, wouldn't be so high and mighty. You'll be grateful for a nice boy like Adam, you can bring him anywhere. Lawyers make wonderful providers."

"Mother, money isn't everything."

"Since when?"

"My girls will earn their own money."

"They'd better," she said heatedly. "If you teach them not to get married, they'd better."

"I only want them to be independent without . . . expecting a man to—"

"Jenny, miss big shot! She has to buy Lancôme," she said, pressing the napkin on the table. "Walgreen's isn't good enough . . . and Amy, every minute, calling you collect. While you go around in those rags. They spend money like water."

"Oh, Mother—"

"They only call me when they want something."

"They don't. They love you."

"They're spoiled," she repeated, her voice rising.

"At least they work. More than I can say for Bruce!" I said, watching her face for some reaction. "Bruce should be working and not taking money from you."

"You raise your children, I'll raise mine!" she snapped.

Silence. I hated it when Mother started in on the girls. When I lost my cool. But Mother made me so mad. After a long moment, Mother looked at me. Kind of sheepishly.

"Bruce needs help, Lisa. You know he was born with an old heart . . . an old heart," she repeated, lowering her eyes, still pressing the napkin. "He could die any minute."

Then she got all quiet and her eyes looked so strange, like far away. And she kept pressing the napkin on her face, as if she were pressing away something. So I kept quiet, too, telling myself that I should know better than to mention Bruce. Because whenever I'd mention Bruce . . . in any way . . . the slightest criticism, Mother would get all weird, sometimes wouldn't even speak to me for days afterward. And this old-heart thing . . . for as long as I'd remembered, Mother would say, "Bruce can't play, leave Bruce alone . . . he has an old heart." . . . I was relieved when Mother perked up and gossiped some more about Sylvia Finkel, then about her fundraising symphony guild, nodding and murmuring "uh-huh" a lot, drawing flowers on the outside of my water glass. I looked out the window and watched the sicko pigeons doo-doo all over the fountain. Until, thank God, the waitress came over to the table and Mother ordered espresso coffee and caramel custards. So while we waited for the desserts, Mother carried on about how maybe I should sell computers . . . a good way to meet men, she said. But then it was strange . . . suddenly she got quiet. Kept twisting the wedding band around her third finger and looked at me shyly . . . like she was on the verge of some great confession.

"Lisa," she said finally in her baby voice, "next week—Thursday, actually—I'm going to Mount Zion Hospital. I'm having a heart bypass . . . a triple bypass, Lisa." She giggled then, relaxing and dropping her shoulders again, as if she had admitted some terrible breach.

"A bypass . . . a bypass," I repeated, my voice sounding so far away. "I didn't know you were sick," I said, feeling like I'd been knocked right off the ground, right off, and telling myself not to talk so fast, otherwise Mother would know that I was upset. She senses everything.

"Oh, I'm not really sick," she quickly replied, waving her hand again and giggling like it was ridiculous that I'd even think she was sick. "A few clogged arteries, that's all, Lisa," she said in a baby voice, "and Dr. Julian says that I don't have to worry about a thing, that Dr. Berman is the finest heart surgeon in the country. And you should see him, Lisa, he's a sabra," she said, blushing like a young girl.

When she said that, God, it was so sweet, and she seemed so vulnerable that I reached over and held her hand, at first lightly and then I really held it.

"You'll be fine, Mother, just fine," I repeated, hoping that Mother didn't notice that I was kind of stammering or that my hands were trembling. "In fact," I quickly added, pushing the hair from my eyes, "Dr. Strauss had a quadruple bypass only six months ago and you should see him, Mother, he's jogging every morning, Mother, imagine."

"A lot of my friends had bypasses," she said, looking more relaxed but like she wanted more affirmation. "Selma Rosenblatt feels better than ever."

"Oh, yes," I quickly agreed. "Everyone is having one. You'll be fine."

"Do you think so, Lisa?"

"I know so. And when you're in the hospital I'll take care of everything. I'll call Sylvia Finkel every day and give her reports about how you're doing, and keep a list which friends called, and I'll see that . . . oh, what's wrong?" I asked, noticing that her face suddenly got all sad-looking.

"Would you . . . well, Lisa, would you drive Bruce to his program?"

"Program," I said carefully, so that she wouldn't know I knew.

"Well . . ." She sighed. "When his license was suspended, though Bruce wasn't drunk, Lisa, that much I know," she quickly explained, pressing her lips tightly together, "Bruce has to go to this program for counseling . . . and I've been driving him, every morning at seven."

"Oh, Mother, you shouldn't be driving Bruce. . . . Why doesn't he get a car pool or—"

"The people there aren't responsible, Lisa . . . I've talked to Dr. Heindrich. Even he agrees," she said, pressing the napkin on the table again.

"Of course I'll do it," I said.

"Oh, would you, Lisa?" she said, her face brightening. "And make sure he takes his Inderol. He forgets. One other thing, Lisa," she said, lowering her voice and looking around the room, making sure no one else could hear, "I'll give you a postdated check payable to Bruce's dummy psychiatrist—whatever you call that Indian—but if anything should happen to me, don't pay him. He hasn't done a thing for Bruce. Bruce still sees that character, Mark," she said, lowering her eyes.

"Don't worry about a thing," I said, deciding not to tell her to stop interfering in Bruce's life again.

After the Bruce thing was settled, Mother seemed more relaxed.

I wished I could tell her that no matter what, I loved her and that I'd always be there for her, and that it scared me to think she might die. But I couldn't, just couldn't.

The words were stuck inside me.

So while we ate our caramel custards and sipped our espressos, Mother chatted on, happy as a lark about what she needed to buy for the hospital, then gossiping some more about Sylvia Finkel and Selma Rosenblatt, until finally she said it was getting late and that she'd drive me home.

Outside it was gray, really foggy. The sky had turned dark, and shadows covered most of the sunlight, making shadowy patterns along the sidewalk.

We drove home in silence, except when Mother would pound the horn impatiently or complain about the horrible traffic. Boy, is she an aggressive driver.

I looked out the window and counted the trees. I used to do that as a child, when I'd go with Mother to pick up my father at the airport. The fog was hanging from the trees like old lace shawls, like time, that thing that makes yellow into gold, gold into dark, into eyes that see back or way into the future. I could hardly believe that Mother was almost seventy-five years old and that she was going to have a heart bypass. And that she might die soon. Finally we arrived in front of my house. Mother made some critical comment about how my patch of lawn needed watering. She turned off the ignition. It was still, so still except for the ticking of the tiny gold watch Mother always wore on her left wrist. I put on my dark glasses. Mother was squinting because the stream of sunlight coming in through the window was in her eyes. She pulled the visor down and adjusted one of her pearl button earrings, and the silence between us was loud as a drum. I touched Mother's hand, feeling kind of self-conscious about it, but I needed to touch her, make contact with her. Maybe I was afraid that if I didn't, she'd die.

Mother turned slowly and faced me. Her eyes were wide and full of sunlight . . . the color of yellow glass. I took a deep breath and concentrated real hard on my eye focus. My eyes wandered when I was nervous.

"I want to talk about us," I blurted out, "before it's too late

Mother. . . . I want us to be closer," I repeated, my voice sounding so far away it didn't sound like my voice . . . someone else's.

Mother blinked several times, then tilted her head way back and put her hand over her forehead, like she was pushing away the sunlight. I could see the tiny blue veins through her skin, and the windows were all steamy. Probably because we were both breathing so hard.

She pressed the button, and the window on her side opened, letting in a gush of air. Mother opened her beige lizard purse and took out her lace handkerchief. When she shook it open, it smelled of roses. She pressed the handkerchief close to her face. At first I thought she was blowing her nose, but then I realized Mother was crying. God, hardly ever had I seen Mother cry, not even when Daddy died, or when Bruce almost died from an overdose. I didn't know what to do. I felt uneasy. So I sat there, making the popping sounds, helps me not to cry. Finally Mother took the handkerchief away from her face, a smudge of lipstick on her chin, and I noticed a tiny run along her beige silk stockings.

"I want to be close, too, Lisa," she said, so faintly I could hardly hear her, "but I don't know how. . . . I'm not like you young girls today, I don't know how."

When I realized how utterly embarrassed she was and at the same time sincere, it was like something in me came loose, like all the anger I ever felt for her went away and all this swelled-up love came loose. I hugged her so fast, a real hug, my cheek was against her cheek, and both our cheeks were damp from our tears. I could see way into her scalp where it was pink and where the makeup had worn off her cheek. I could see these dark age spots and definitely there was a lot of gray in her hair.

After we hugged, Mother kind of lifted and dropped her shoulders and giggled and looked away. Mother's seatbelt was locked tight across her chest so she couldn't move around that much. Her hand clutched the steering wheel and she kept turning the wheel as if she were still driving or needed to feel that she was still driving, going somewhere, because it was quite a moment. A moment we would always remember and never have back again.

"Every night before I sleep, Lisa, I pray you'll be happy. I only want you to be happy," Mother said, wiping my eyes with her handkerchief.

"I *am* happy, Mother. Maybe a little frustrated about my work," I said, "but I'm happy. I'm doing what I love to do."

She nodded, still staring ahead. "You'll make it," she said almost in a whisper. "It's the ones who never give up who make it. Your father always said that."

"Did he?" I paused, thinking that I wanted to know more about my father. "He loved you so much, Mother. He loved you so much," I repeated.

For a moment she looked so far away, like she was deep inside some dream. Her eyes were full of tears. "He was strong. Worked hard. Like you, Lisa. He was talented and worked hard like you, Lisa," she repeated. "And did you know that he was a wonderful photographer? Wonderful."

She applied fresh lipstick, then pressed her lips together with a Kleenex. She brushed off her skirt, not that there was anything on it. Just so the suede ran all the same way.

"Lisa," she finally said, "Macy's is having a sale on Fieldcrest towels . . . oh, and the nicest Wamsutta sheets. You can use a new toaster, too."

"Yes, that would be lovely, Mother."

I reached over and kissed her. Not an air kiss, either, more like when I kiss Jenny or Amy and suck in their cheeks.

"I'll call you tomorrow," I said, getting out of the car.

"Oh, Lisa . . . I almost forgot."

She gave me this silver tote bag that said "Clinique" on the front. "My girl at Saks . . . the sweetest thing, Lisa, gives me extra samples." She giggled. "Here, take them. And use some of the cover-up on your skin."

She smiled then, lifting and dropping her shoulders. And I was just about out of the car when Mother said in this little voice, "Hang in there, Lisa. Hang in, you'll make it. I know it. I can feel it," she said, shaking her shoulders. God, I almost died when she said that, I was so touched.

I jumped out of the car real fast. Mother drove off in the gold Porsche, spinning rubber, as Jenny would say.

I stood there, my heart beating fast, watching her car disappear around the corner. The German woman across the street was watering the lawn and shouting "*Ja . . . ja . . .* nice!" I ran up the stairs, waving to Joe, my next-door neighbor. I glanced up at the sky one more time. It was turning kind of dark again. The clouds looked puffy. About to burst open.

When I opened the door, I called Jenny. She had been packing little by little for days, moving things over to her new apartment. Cartons were all over the hallway. Jenny called back that she was in her room. So after I'd fed Anny and checked my messages, I went into her room. Jenny, wearing a lilac kimono, was sitting at the antique dressing table Mother had given her, preparing the ritual of making up her face. She looked up and smiled. "Hi, Mom," she said. "What's up?"

"Hi, Jen," I said, kissing her, loving the feel of her skin.

Cartons filled with her clothes, books, records were lined along the wall. Some filled with her old toys, stuffed animals. The Michael Jackson tape was so loud I couldn't hear myself think, so I turned down the volume, then I sat down on Jenny's lilac floral bedspread, watching her arrange the little boxes and pots of rouge in neat little rows, thinking that Jenny kept her dressing table as neatly as she used to keep her toys in her old blue vinyl toy box. Jenny liked order. She kept everything neat as a pin, from the socks in her drawer, folded and arranged by color, to the seashell collection inside the wicker baskets along the top of my old walnut dresser. Maybe the order made Jenny feel grounded.

Anyways, the rain was going like mad and the wooden shutters were rattling and every minute the telephone was ringing, and either Charlene's or Robin's or Fariba's voice echoed over the answering machine. God, I'd probably miss all of that . . . for a moment I felt sad.

"Where are you going tonight?" I finally asked.

"Kevin is taking me to a really expensive French restaurant," she said, powdering her face with a big pink powder puff. "It's our third anniversary." She stopped powdering for a second then and pointed to a single white rose inside a crystal bud vase next to a picture of Kevin inside an ornate, heart-shaped frame. "Isn't it

143

beautiful, Mom?" she said, her eyes all dreamy.

"Yes, very," I said, smiling at her.

"The first time Kevin and I made love he brought me a white rose. It's symbolic," she said seriously.

"Uh-huh."

She resumed powdering her face, pressing her lips tightly together so that the excess powder didn't get into her mouth. Lately I'd noticed that Kevin hadn't been calling her as much, and it hurt me to see Jenny waiting by her telephone. If only I could make her believe that she was talented, some way to influence her to go back to school, find a career she'd love. She was waiting for Kevin to fill in her empty spaces—the spaces between her and her father, all her hurts. I knew that pattern only too well. So hard . . . But before I'd start hocking her about school . . . work . . . I'd tell Jenny about Mother because Jenny and Mother were real close. In fact, Jenny is the only one in the family who knows how to handle Mother. They talked on the phone all the time. Jenny told Mother everything.

"Jen . . . I have something to tell you . . . about Nana."

Jenny stopped lining her eyes and turned quickly and looked at me anxiously, biting her lip like she would when afraid.

"Nana's going into Mount Zion Hospital next Thursday . . . for a heart bypass."

Jenny looked like she didn't believe what I was saying. Then she put her face in her arms and cried, her shoulders going up and down.

"She'll be fine, Jen," I said, quickly going over to her. "Look at Dr. Strauss."

"Mom," she said, her voice muffled, her tears streaking the powder along her cheek.

"Don't worry," I said, holding her tight. "Routine," I assured her. "Routine."

"Mom," she said, her head still buried in her arms, "leave me alone for a minute. Please, Mom."

"Okay . . . I'll sit on your bed."

Jenny cried softly, still covering her face. She never wanted anyone to see her cry, for as long as I could remember. Even when

Jenny was a little child, she'd cry alone in a corner or go off somewhere. So for quite a while she cried, her face buried in her arms,
crying softly, until finally she stopped, and quickly covered her face
with Kleenex. After she blew her nose, making a honking sound,
and dabbed her eyes with more Kleenex, she turned and looked at
me. Her eyes were swollen and shiny from tears.

"Poor Nans," she said.

"I'm telling you, Jen . . . she'll be all right. She's strong."

"Nans is frail, Mom," said Jenny, glaring at me and looking sad.

"Anyone who's been through what Nans has is strong."

Jenny shrugged, then resumed arranging her little brushes and
bottles, though she was still biting her lip and I could see the tears
rolling down her cheeks.

"You don't know Nans like I do," she said, looking reflective
and shaking her head. "She's very sensitive, and . . . it upsets me,
Mom, when you argue with Nans. God, Mom, Nans is an old lady
. . . so deal with it. . . . She'll be gone soon and you'll feel sorry."

"You're right," I said, a sadness coming over me, knowing that
what Jenny said was true. "Just today Nans and I decided that after
her surgery we're going to spend more time together, get closer."

"Good!" Jenny said, smiling and looking relieved. She faced the
mirror again, sucking in her cheeks so that she could apply blusher
to her cheekbones.

"So tell your boss at Saks next Thursday you can't work. Nans
wants you at the hospital."

"Of course, I'll be there," she said, putting her brush back into
the little Lalique antique box Mother gave her, closing the lid twice,
making sure it snapped shut. "I love Nans. She's such a lady, not
a dime a dozen," said Jenny, giggling. "A classic."

"Yes, she is."

"I love the way she zips her purse and spends an hour in the
bakery picking out just the right dessert for her little bridge
luncheons."

"Yes," I said, touched by how much Jenny appreciates Mother.

"I'm going to bring her a bouquet of red roses . . . she loves
red roses. . . . No one ever brings her anything."

"That'll be lovely."

I watched Jenny as she dipped a little brush into a pot of bright red lip gloss, then pouted her lips so that she could brush on the gloss. After that, she turned her face from side to side, looking at her profile in the mirror, making sure the makeup was perfect. Then she got up and changed the message on her answering machine, saying in her deepest voice that she wouldn't be home until Monday. She turned on the yellow hair blower, expertly maneuvering the hair blower while her other hand twisted the brush along her hair.

"When am I going to see your apartment?" I asked, shouting above the blower.

She turned off the hair blower. "Soon . . . and oh, Mom, wait until you see it . . . it's so cute. I want your honest opinion about the color paint Kevin bought. He says he'll paint the whole apartment lilac. And Nana is giving me her Sears credit card and she said I could buy anything I want."

"You can have the cat mugs and cat trays and the blue towels."

Jenny, looking satisfied, turned on the hair blower again and finished drying her hair. Then she began brushing her hair, until her hair made a crackling sound.

In a way I was relieved that I wouldn't have to hear her phone ringing at all hours of the night or her hair blower or her constant interruptions while I was trying to write. At the same time, I felt the loss. Jenny and I had been together for a long time. Her sounds were a part of me. But it was time to let her go. I knew that.

"How's work?" I asked, careful not to sound too anxious.

"Okay," she said, wiping a smudge of eyeshadow from her cheek.

"The cars—"

"I sold another cream puff yesterday," she said, pressing her face close to the mirror.

"What's that?"

"A '64 Cad with fins. Everything on it. Beautiful Bob gets me good cars. He's a good source."

"Hmmm."

She turned and faced me, looking reflective.

"Mom, maybe you could help me with this."

"I'll try."

"This really nice couple offered me thirteen hundred cash. I'm asking sixteen. They want to take the Cad to the diagnostic."

"Oh, God."

"Uh-huh," she said, shaking her head. "I'm fucked. So I decided, if they want a diagnostic they can have the car for thirteen cash, providing," she said seriously, "when they take the car for the diagnostic, they leave their car with me and one hundred dollars—nonrefundable if they back out of the deal."

"Sounds excellent."

"After all, it's my time, too."

"Sounds good."

"I like the business part," she said, "but most of the people are flakes. But I'm making enough for my apartment. Kevin wants to go in with me now."

"Sure he does! After you've done all the work, getting the cars, establishing credit—"

"Oh, Mom—"

"You don't need Kevin. It's your business. If you can support school and an apartment, that's pretty good."

She began applying some white stuff to her face.

"Don't hock."

"Don't you want to learn more?"

She shrugged.

"You're talented."

"And you're my mother."

"I also know talent when I see it—or hear it, and time goes so fast—so . . ."

"What's that supposed to mean, Mom?" she said, not facing me.

But I could see her watching me through the mirror.

"It means that before you know it, you'll be twenty-five doing work you don't feel good about and depending on Kevin or some other man, resenting it."

"Just because that happened to you doesn't mean it'll happen to me."

"No one told me what I'm telling you, but even though I'm struggling, I have a profession . . . education—"

"You've told me all this, Mom."

"Jen, life goes by . . . fast . . . so fast . . . and school would open up a world for you . . . I promise. You'd develop yourself . . . in a few years have choices you'd never believe. . . . I don't want you to struggle like I've struggled, depending on a man."

"I know, I know. Give me a break. You've told me so many times. You repeat yourself."

"You could do so many things—drama, literature, teach, who knows?"

"I'm not interested in school, Mom," she said, shrugging her shoulder. "Don't rag me."

"But—"

"I said I'll think about it."

"Good. That's all I want you to do," I said, speaking quickly because I knew she was listening. I could see by the way she was biting her lower lip.

"In five years, Mom, Kevin and I might get married."

"Okay, so you have five years then for school. . . . Who knows what could happen in five years?"

"Okay, already, don't stress out on it, okay," she repeated, giving me a look that I had said enough.

She began brushing her hair again, but I knew I'd struck a nerve.

After she finished brushing her hair, she put the hairbrush back into its place and turned and smiled at me. She blinked several times.

"Oh, Mom, don't look so sad," she repeated, sighing like she had the weight of the world on her shoulders. "Give me a break."

"Oh, sure . . . I'm not sad . . . I'm really happy for you."

Silence.

"When are you going out with Professor What's-His-Name?"

"Eric Blumberg. Tomorrow night. We're going to dinner and a concert."

"Good," she said, looking relieved and holding her nails under the light. "Amy and I worry about you. You're too pretty to be alone, Mom. You're hot, Mom . . . you should see poor Dodie without her makeup. You look good for your age, Mom," she said, smiling approvingly. She took off the kimono then, revealing a black lace teddy and the edible underpants Kevin gave her for her birthday. I pretended I didn't notice. She slipped on the red satin

low-cut dress, so low-cut you'd die—a regular torch singer's dress—
and reached her hand behind and zipped it up.

"How do I look, Mom?" she said, looking at me anxiously.

"Oh, beautiful," I said, thinking that underneath her powder and
her heavy eye makeup, an exuberant youthfulness shone through
like a light through a dream.

"Well, don't get all sad about it. . . . Aren't you glad your child
looks good?"

I laughed.

"Which color do you like better: this pretty red . . . or the light
one?" she said, wiggling her nails.

"The red matches your dress."

"Do you?" she said frowning like she wasn't sure.

Then she sprayed perfume into the air so it floated over her like
a mist. And when the doorbell rang, God, you'd think an earthquake had just trembled the earth, because she started running around
the room, shouting that she wasn't ready, that her makeup wasn't
right, that her nails weren't dry, and would I please answer the
door and tell Kevin she'd be ready soon.

So I rushed down the hall and opened the front door.

"Hello, Kevin," I said, opening the door wide.

"How are you, Lisa?" he said, stepping into the hall and kissing
me on the cheek. "Fine, thank you," I said, standing on my toes
so I could reach him. Kevin is six feet tall and so slender you'd
think a strong wind would blow him away and he has these size
fifteen feet that could knock you over, I'm not kidding. But he has
a nice slender face with bright blue eyes and dark hair that is styled
like a rock star. Anyways, Kevin and I made small talk until Jenny
came into the room and then it was as if everything stopped, just
stopped, because they only had eyes for each other. Jenny gave him
the white rose and then they kissed. God, it was something to see,
really tender.

"Mom," said Jenny finally, "be sure and leave the lights on or
you'll be afraid of the dark . . . and, oh, be sure and lock the door.
I'll call you tomorrow from Kevin's." After I assured her I'd be
just fine and reminded them one more time to wear their seatbelts,
I shut and locked the door. I stood in the hall then, just stood there

motionless, breathing in the scent from Jenny's perfume, thinking that Jenny was all grown up, and wondering where all the time had gone. I went down the hall and into Jenny's room. Her room was all dark except for the little pink lights around the dressing table. I touched one of the little glass perfume bottles. I guess I wanted to touch her, just touch her. Her telephone was still ringing and the shutters were rattling. I picked up the old Raggedy Ann doll with the missing buttons for eyes and squeezed it, like squeezing back the memories of Jenny, sucking her thumb on a wooden swing, swinging back and forth.

"Last night was wonderful," I said.

"Yes," murmured Eric, pulling me closer. Sunlight was all over his face. Tiny rainbows. Our legs wound tight, our bodies close, my head on Eric's chest. We'd slept like that. All night, we'd slept like that. The night was still with me. A gust of air came into the bedroom and it smelled muggy.

"We were terrible leaving the concert last night . . . the Mendelssohn was so beautiful."

"I couldn't wait to make love to you."

"Me either."

"Did you like it better . . . Eric . . . I mean that . . . I came."

"Didn't you?" he said softly. He held my hand tight. "It was like our little celebration."

I kissed him back, getting a glow feeling, remembering last night, our lovemaking so tender, Eric saying he loved me, deep inside me, my body so hot the breath went out of me, letting go then, my legs shaking out all that sex in me, all out of me. Shook it out. Like floating, floating free. God, it was something.

"Baby, let's get up," said Eric, stroking my hair. "It's a beautiful Sunday. We can't stay in bed all day, we'll spend the day in Berkeley, I'll show you my office, we'll have brunch at the Berkeley Museum . . . dinner at my house . . . you'll meet Ian."

"That sounds lovely," I said.

"I want to spend more time with you, show you my world, maybe walk along the ocean." He kissed me tenderly.

"I'd love that," I said, moving my hand along his thigh. "Before brunch, though, I have to stop at the museum bookstore, pick up a catalogue. Let's look around. Hesse's piece is there."

"Okay," he said, "bring your work. I have my briefcase in the car . . . some papers to read . . . so if you want, bring your work. . . ."

"Good idea," I said, kissing his mouth.

After showering and dressing, we left and drove to Berkeley. In the car Eric was real quiet, but the Mozart was so loud that we couldn't hear each other talk anyways. I was content sitting close to Eric, my hand resting on his thigh, last night . . . close . . . it was wonderful. I looked out the window, enjoying how the sail-boats on the bay shone like little crystals, the water sparkling so blue, the color of sapphires. And the clouds floated down low over the bay and moved in and out and you could see the sky through them. Eric parked his Saab near the campus and we crossed the courtyard and went into the Berkeley Museum. I loved the museum. So open and airy and light, its twirling ramps and glass sky-lights, the sudden hush, the art lovers quietly observing a work. Eric shook his head in distress at the Robert Mangold exhibit, pro-testing that the paintings—lines—delicate circles—were not mathe-matical, about balance and spatial relationships, harmony, arguing that as far as he was concerned he didn't see anything and that he liked to see what was there, not imagine what wasn't there.

After an hour or so, we sat eating in the museum's courtyard. The sunlight made circles and crisscross patterns over the patio and half shadowed Eric's face, turning his hair auburn. Some children played tag behind the large Bottin sculpture, a maze of colorful painted squares and circles. Our espressos were steaming hot, and the croissants and fruit compotes fresh. Eric was reading some pages he'd taken from his beat-up briefcase, while I edited some pages from *Eva*. From the corner of my eye I watched Eric. While read-ing he sipped his coffee or touched my hand, but when he worked he hardly moved at all.

After a while he looked up and smiled.

"How's the new book coming?" he asked.

"Oh . . . all right."

"Let me see some pages," he said.

"Well . . . I don't know."

"Just a couple of pages, Lisa."

"All right, just a couple."

He read the pages, placing each page neatly in a pile.

I felt kind of nervous about Eric reading . . . I mean, after his silence about *Princess* . . . but he looked up a couple of times and smiled at me.

When he finished reading the pages he gave them back to me and leaned back in his chair.

"It's good, Lisa, I like it. Interesting material. But remember, use concrete language . . . hone it down."

"Uh-huh . . . more concrete."

"It's good, though."

"Thanks."

"C'mon, let's go."

We walked across the campus, quiet on Sunday except for some students wearing backpacks, Sony radios over their ears, on bicycles, rushing from or to study halls. Bells were ringing softly. You should've seen the trees—tall oaks, their leaves turning all yellow, glistened from the early-morning fog. And the sky so clear, like pale glass. Puffy clouds, so big, almost covering the sky . . . opened and closed like white rose petals, then closed gently . . . broke away . . . while a mist, delicately arched and full of light . . . pinkish . . . like a Monet painting, hung low over the bay. Eric walked quickly—long, sure strides, like you do when walking on your land, our shadows long in front of us. I loved the firm way he clutched his briefcase, his quick smile and wave when a student called out, "Hello, Professor Blumberg." I think I loved him.

At Evans Hall, a modern glass building, square Bauhaus style, we took the elevator to the fifth floor. The halls were quiet and smelled of Naugahyde. Every so often Eric stopped and pointed out the portrait or mural of Euclid, Fermat, Mersenne . . . other great mathematicians, finally stopping in front of a group of photographs.

"See," he said, "our math faculty. There's Seymour," he said, standing on his toes and pointing to a picture of a dark man. "You'll meet Seymour and his wife, Betty Ann. She's on the faculty, too.

And Andrea, that's the woman I work with . . . and Felix Mandel
. . . the Nobel Prize economist/mathematician. And . . . oh . . .
here I am," he said with a chuckle.

"You!" I moved closer.

"Fifteen years ago."

"Your hair is darker. And a beard. You look formidable."

He laughed. "I am."

"Are you?"

"C'mon," he said. He pulled my hand and led me into a large
sunlit room. A glass wall looked out to a sweeping view of the San
Francisco Bay, the Golden Gate Bridge a misty curve in the sky.

"Our lounge," said Eric proudly. "Where mathematicians meet
and ponder problems." Eric nodded toward a serious-faced young
man sitting at a table and doing card tricks.

"What kind of problems?" I asked, fascinated by the metal jigsaw
puzzles, some half done, set on brightly painted wood tables.

"All kinds." He shrugged impatiently. "Computer scientists col-
laborate . . . discuss complexity theory . . . make things work."

We walked down the long corridor then, the keys rattling from
Eric's key ring attached to his thick brown belt.

"My office," said Eric, unlocking the door.

The room was kind of small but bright with sunlight, and a ter-
race looked out to the same sweeping view. A long table set in the
middle of the room was stacked with papers. A desk over in the
corner. A couple of bookshelves. Photographs of his sons. A large
picture of Euclid.

"Everything is so neat," I said, surprised at the order.

He smiled, watching me intently, as a child watches when showing a parent some achievement.

"How beautiful," I said, looking up at the blackboard, scrawled
in white chalk with tiny numbers, letters, symbols, equations. "Like
some ancient scroll . . . or a Twombly painting."

"I'm not familiar," he said indifferently, watching me through
half-closed eyes.

"It doesn't matter," I quickly said, "this is very beautiful. All
these little numbers. Pieces of the universe . . ."

Our eyes caught. Eric came over to me then and we kissed. As quickly as he'd kissed me, though, almost like the kiss was a sudden impulse, he moved away and stacked some papers on the table, still watching me, his mind ticking, ticking.

"All those books," I said, going over to the bookshelves.

"My publications are on the middle shelf."

"All these," I said, looking at the thick volumes. "I'm impressed."

He shrugged and looked pleased. "I've done some good work. Look in that yellow binder, 'Cell Control.' Yes . . . that one . . . twelve years' work . . . ."

"May I?"

"Sure."

I flipped the pages, intrigued by the aesthetic beauty of the equations, delicate little arrows drawn through numbers, connected to letters, symbols, Eric's window eyes looking into the world beyond, into something so big.

"Your numbers are beautiful," I said, closing the book and looking at the blackboard. "Like little truths that fit into something so big . . . grand."

"It's not poetry, Lisa . . . you're talking in metaphors again," he said peevishly. "Speak in concrete language. Numbers have structure. Form. Mathematics is different from writing."

"Uh-huh."

"Anything can be well written. Anyone in the world can write and make something work. Mathematics has to be proven."

"But Eric, you can't write about anything and make it true. . . . Just because you write about something true doesn't mean that it's going to come out true."

"But in writing,' he said impatiently, "the work is the answer. In mathematics you find the answer first. Before you start working it out. There's no room for improvisation. You wouldn't mine for gold if you didn't know the gold was there."

"There's risk in everything. As Delacroix says, we all have to begin, otherwise how can we achieve an end? What happens if you're working on a problem . . . and your numbers don't work? What do you do, give it all up?"

"They fall apart in the middle, then everything turns to shit."

"Oh."

"Happened to me plenty of times," he said, shrugging his shoulders and stacking some papers on the table. "You learn to cope. In mathematics you have to be tough."

"So you're saying that you wouldn't give it a go until you have an answer?"

"Of course, yes—until I'm sure about what I'm investigating."

"I agree that structure is important . . . the stem of a flower . . . the frame of a house . . . but it's the music inside a sonata—"

"Look, Lisa," he said, sighing impatiently, "some other time I'd be happy to bullshit and fantasize with you about physics and prime numbers and philosophy, but I don't feel like talking about it now. C'mon, let's go," he said, his mood changing from solemnity to impatience.

He locked the office door, then shook the door several times, making sure it was shut. While driving to his house, he seemed distracted, like his mind was far away, ticking, ticking. Until the Saab stopped on Oakmont Avenue, in front of a two-story white-shingled house. Shaded by two large oak trees, the windowsills trimmed bright blue.

I followed Eric up the long pathway, admiring the little purple plants on either side of the walk.

The wide front porch, cluttered with bicycles, tennis rackets, skis, stacks of newspapers tied by white thick rope. The front door was open. So dark inside it took me a second to focus my eyes. Gray and white print drapes closed over narrow, high windows, forcing the sunlight outside.

"Careful . . . don't slip," he said, walking in front of me. "The rugs are being cleaned."

"What a nice room," I said politely, stopping in front of a wall of bookcases. Mostly philosophy, economics, mathematics. In the middle of the room were two couches, indifferent to arrangement, one covered with an old Indian blanket, a guitar thrown across the other and several chairs, interesting chairs, maybe from Eric's travels. A chess set on the pine table, the pieces on their sides.

"How lovely. Who did that?" I asked, pointing to a charcoal sketch of a nude.

"I did. A long time ago in art school."

"I like it."

He smiled.

"What's this?" I asked, picking up a cube with dozens of little colored squares.

"A Rubik's Cube."

"Looks complicated."

"It is."

"And what lovely rocks," I said, touching the beautiful rocks on the mantel. "And . . . oh, a piano."

"Play," he said. "No one ever plays that old piano anymore."

I sat down on the wobbly stool, bending my fingers, and then I began playing a few bars from "Liebestraum," my fingers stiff, the untuned piano tinny.

"That's nice, Lisa," said Eric across the room, watching me from the shadows. "Play some more."

"Oh, I can't. My fingers are stiff."

"You should practice. You have a nice touch."

"Do you play?"

"The clarinet."

Then on top of the piano I saw the wedding photograph. Eric with the dark beard, wearing a dark suit and tie, smiling at a beautiful girl with dark curved eyes and long blond hair.

"Megan," he said softly. He had this look on his face like a young boy wanting a shiny sports car.

"C'mon," said Eric, pulling me by the hand. "Meet Ian."

I followed him down a long, dark hall, past several framed drawings . . . nursery school drawings, Eric pointing out photographs of his father . . . his brother . . . into a darkish small kitchen with a brown linoleum floor, cluttered with wicker baskets filled with herbs . . . lemons . . . garlic . . . jars of pasta . . . pots, all sizes and shapes hung above the restaurant-size stove . . . notes and drawings stuck to the refrigerator door.

A tall—about six feet or more—husky boy with blondish loopy hair like Eric's and Eric's olive skin came over to us.

"Lisa, my son Ian."

"Hello, Ian. Nice to meet you."

Ian shook my hand, looking at me with Eric's same dark, appraising eyes. The space between his front teeth added a strength to his almost perfect features. Two tiny gold earrings in one ear.

"You're the writer."

"That's her," said Eric, dumping a bin of apples into the sink and turning on the water.

"Dad," said Ian, looking kind of upset, "I tried to call you at Lisa's, but you'd already left. I wanted to talk to you about something."

So while Ian and Eric, in low tones, talked, I went into the family room adjoining the kitchen, stepping over yellow plastic laundry baskets, filled with neatly folded laundry, black socks in one basket, colored in another, and metal buckets full to the tops with green apples. I sat at the plain wooden table, looking out at Eric's garden. A large garden shaded by apple trees, tall hedges, and shrubs. Some jutted out, coming out at you, others partly clipped back . . . everything in the middle of something happening. Tennis balls, a gardening glove, a hose, a pair of muddy tennis shoes, clues to Eric's domestic life, lay about the patio. The part of him you don't see but is there in the apples' shine, the baskets of laundry, the partly clipped hedge, the unshaped thing you can't see, but you know is there.

I saw the calendar with a picture of Einstein hanging over the desk and the name Emmy in Eric's tiny handwriting written in every Tuesday.

Who was Emmy? His once-a-week person? Or . . . God knows. I only knew about the time Eric and I spent together. But I felt a pang of jealousy.

"Lisa . . . come. I'll show you the garden," said Eric, kissing the back of my neck, then taking off his jacket and unbuttoning his shirt.

We went outside to the patio, Eric walking so fast I could hardly keep up with him, and every second stopped to pick up something . . . an apple, biting it, then throwing it over the bush . . . or picking up a hoe . . . or hose, checking it, then dropping it . . . checking and rechecking his domain.

"I've never seen a hot tub," I said, looking at the redwood tub.

"Well, this is a nice one," he said, lifting the top, the steam coming out in a big white puff. "Cost a bundle . . . took me a year to decide on just which one I wanted . . . a pain. But the kids love it," he said, banging the lid back down, then pressing his hand along the edges, pounding it so the top would fit.

"Warped. Max jumps on the lid," he explained, still pounding the top. "Off an eighth of an inch . . . fuck! In any event, over there, Lisa," he said, walking onto the lawn and motioning for me to follow, "all my land . . . up to here," he said, pointing to a wire fence. "I'm extending the lawn to there."

"That'll look nice," I said, my shoes sinking into the damp ground.

"You're stepping on the new seed!" he shouted. "Move over there, please."

So I moved, angry he shouted. But not wanting to make a big deal.

"And over there," he said, softly now, blinking against the sun and looking preoccupied, "I'm pouring cement . . . maybe a basketball court. Ian likes basketball. And up there," he said, pointing to the roof, "I'm adding a study."

"That'll be nice."

"Get my work out of the bedroom."

"Good idea."

He took off his shirt, dropped it on the ground. Then he fussed with this metal gadget attached to the long green rubber hose . . . one of those jobs that sprinkles water in a million different directions. He turned on the water. But only a trickle of water came out of the hose, puffing up.

"Damn!" he shouted, "damned rainbird. Returned it twice already. Fuck." He unscrewed the gadget from the hose, turning it over in his hand, looking at it closely, as if he were contemplating some great problem. "Can't be the rainbird . . . has to be the plastic tubing."

"Too bad," I murmured, trying to keep out of his way.

"Probably a kink in the fucking tubing," he murmured, on his hands and knees, scooping away the dirt. "Gotta take out this piece of hose . . . fix it . . . dig it back . . . a kink, probably." He turned around and looked at me for a second, the sun falling in his eyes. "I have to fix it. An hour or so and I'll have it fixed, Lisa."

"Now?"

"The water pressure isn't coming through the hose properly."

"Sure, okay."

"I won't be long."

So I went inside and sat at the wooden table, hungry as a bear, eating some stale corn chips from a chipped yellow bowl, doing a stupid crossword puzzle, still wondering who Emmy was. Until Ian came into the room. He was holding a thick gray textbook on chemistry. He sat down across from me, looking at me with watchful eyes.

"Your father is fixing the rainbird," I said, pushing aside the paper.

"He won't rest until it's perfect," he said, smiling and glancing toward Eric. "He's been fussing with that thing all week."

"It'll be a nice lawn—"

"Yes, it'll be nice," he said seriously and nodding. "Dad loves things to work. Has a green thumb, too."

"Probably good at everything he does."

Ian watched Eric through the window, watching quietly, like a parent silently watches a child at play.

"A chemistry major?" I asked, pointing to the book.

"Yes."

"Grad school someday?"

"I'm taking a year out after graduation and traveling first."

"Sounds good."

"Going with Dad on his sabbatical . . . most of it, anyways. Australia . . . China . . . on to India. . . ."

"How wonderful."

"I like traveling."

"Have you traveled much with your father?"

"Not as an adult," he said seriously, his eyes like Eric's. "When Dad taught at Cambridge, we traveled holidays . . . summers. Saw a lot of interesting places." He paused, then said, "A few years ago, Deborah, Dad, Josh, and I traveled through France. We had a great time."

"Oh, nice," I murmured, trying not to show the pang of jealousy that came over me, or my curiosity.

As Ian spoke about his travels, the new Ecstasy drug, genetics, the lab he was working in after school, his girlfriend Dianna, he watched Eric, still patting dirt over the long white plastic hose. Even from there you could just feel their connection. You could feel it. The way Ian's eyes darkened when he looked at his father. The possessive tone when he said "Dad," the suspicious way he watched me. He spoke articulately . . . like he'd been trained to edit his thoughts . . . and his mannerisms were those of a much older boy . . . like maybe he'd never been a child.

After some time Eric came into the house. There was a red vertical streak along his neck, and his face was flushed.

"I got it working. . . . Come on, Ian . . . Lisa. I want to show you."

We went outside. Eric's rainbird was spouting water, spinning thousands of tiny rainbows.

"Good, Dad, I knew you'd get it," said Ian, patting Eric on the back.

"Amazing what plastic tubing can do. Such a simple thing," he said, shaking his head, looking pleased as a kid with a new toy.

"It's beautiful," I murmured, watching the water gush from the lousy rainbird, sick of the whole sprinkler business. My shoes and sweater were soaked.

"Good, Dad," repeated Ian.

Long shadows lay across the yard and the sun was falling behind the trees. After Eric moved the rainbird a couple of times, placing it just so, his hair damp, we went inside the house.

"Do you want something to drink . . . or something, Lisa?" asked Eric, pouring himself a Perrier.

"Vodka, over ice."

Eric frowned and looked quickly toward Ian.

"You'll get drunk."

"Over ice, please."

"I'll have a beer, Dad."

When the phone rang, Ian jumped up and made a beeline.

Eric reluctantly gave me the glass filled with vodka and two ice-cubes and sat next to me, his Perrier in front of him, somberlike. While I drank the vodka, I could feel Eric's chill, the silent disapproval.

Ian, holding the receiver close to his mouth, talked softly to his girlfriend, Dianna, while Eric glanced toward the yard, the rainbird put-putting back and forth, water splattering the window.

"I love you, too," Ian said, then hanging up. "Dad, I'll see you tomorrow."

"Be sure and wear your leather jacket . . . it's cold."

"My leather jacket's at the cleaners. Haven't picked that up yet. Tomorrow . . ."

"Oh, Ian," Eric said with a sigh.

"Nice meeting you, Lisa," said Ian, shaking my hand.

"Bye-bye, Ian . . . nice meeting you, too."

"Sure thing."

When the front door banged, Eric shook his head, like shaking something away. "Children."

"Ian's a very nice boy. I like him."

"He's a good kid," said Eric, looking reflective. "I miss him."

"I know what you mean."

"That's life," Eric said gloomily, sighing and buttoning his shirt.

"Oh, Eric, wasn't it sweet when Ian was talking to Dianna and said 'I love you, too'? . . . so unashamed, direct."

Eric frowned and said quickly, "But she said it first. There's a difference."

"There is?"

"Yes. Now Lisa, I'm hungry. Are you?"

"Why don't you like Dianna?" I persisted.

"Ian is too young."

"Uh-huh."

"She's sick a lot and she's a terrible cook, too. Anyway, I'm hoping Australia will make him forget her."

"Oh, Eric, she's a kid. You're acting like a Jewish mother."

"I *am* a Jewish mother."

Silence.

"I made some cabbage soup. Would you like some?"

"Sure."

So we went into the kitchen, and Eric stirred the thick pink soup, with diced vegetables, in a big yellow pot.

"What's in that other pot?" I said.

"Mushrooms."

"Only three," I said, looking at three mushrooms blooming open inside boiling water. "What are they for?"

"My cousin Sasha had high blood pressure," he explained, looking kind of embarrassed, poking a long fork into the mushrooms. "A Chinese herbalist recommended the three mushrooms. And she's never had high blood pressure since. . . ."

"Do you have high blood pressure?"

"Sometimes . . . My mother died from high blood pressure . . . was always afraid of it."

"Ah. That's why you are—"

"But I take my blood pressure every day. Eat three mushrooms. So far, so good. Also supposed to prevent impotence."

"You don't have that problem."

"I don't want it. It happens," he said, shaking his head. "Soup's ready," he said, with a big ladle scooping the soup and pouring the steaming soup into two plain soup bowls.

"Looks good. All those vegetables, so neatly diced. Must've taken you days."

"I like soup," said Eric. "My mother always made soups. Sit down, Lisa. I'll bring the soup." I sat down at the wooden table. Eric brought the bowls of soup to the table. Then he turned on the stereo. Prokofiev's music burst through the house . . . so beautiful. The rainbird spinning a whirring sound, a da, a da, a da, a da in rhythmic gusts, water splattering the windows.

"Put some of this yogurt in your soup," he said, passing a white bowl filled with creamy yogurt. "It's good."

"Looks delicious," I said, smiling at him, thinking of him as charming as a young boy pleased with his first car.

We ate quietly. Eric ate with gusto, every so often glancing toward the rainbird and smiling approval, then nodding twice before eating again.

"The music . . . is beautiful," I murmured, enjoying the soup. "Prokofiev, isn't it?"

"Pro . . . ko . . . fi . . . ev!" he said, looking at me impatiently. "You mispronounced it . . . like you do Tchaikovsky, Mozart."

"Pro . . . ko . . fi . . . ev," I said, exaggerating the correct pronunciation, annoyed as hell. "You're always correcting me."

"I'm deciding whether or not you pass or fail," he said, laughing like it was a joke.

"I'm dropping the course."

"Eat your soup," he said, pointing with his spoon.

We ate quietly, our knees touching, until I asked, "Does Megan ever see Ian . . . Joshua?"

"Ian sees her from time to time. He likes her."

"Do you see her? Ever talk to her about the boys?"

"As little as possible," he said, his face close to the soup.

"She was very beautiful. I saw the weeding picture on the piano."

"She's still a fine-looking woman . . ." he said defensively, glancing again toward the rainbird.

"Were you ever happy?"

"For about three years . . . it was nice."

"What was she like? How did you meet?" I asked, jealous of the look in his eyes.

"She was my student . . . smart . . . complex . . . a little crazy— always wanted to be by herself. I always wanted to be with her. I was obsessed by her. But she never loved me. She told me that before we married."

"Then why? . . ."

"I loved her and I thought living an academic life with me, away from Kentucky musicians, back porches, she'd . . . well, change. Anyway, eat your soup. And besides," he said, touching my nose, "if she hadn't left, I wouldn't be here with you." He kissed me then, so tenderly, and a piece of cabbage stuck to his bottom lip.

So, trying to keep the conversation light, get off the subject of his wife, I asked, "Have you met any new authors recently?"

"The other night . . . at Holly's. A small party. I told Tom Farber—"

"Oh, God, I'd really like to meet him sometime. I admire his work—so economical. He knows his craft."

"Holly doesn't like Farber's work. She says he doesn't expand ideas."

"Why do ideas have to be expanded?"

"Because then they're only sketches."

"Renoir made sketches. You take your own ideas from the sketches. Develop them . . . interpret."

"I agree with Holly," he persisted, still not looking at me, tilting his soup bowl, "that writing should have form. And Farber writes about his friends . . . his life. . . ."

"D. H. Lawrence says never trust the reader, trust the tale. All writers draw from their lives . . . you take pieces and sew them together . . . like the numbers in your equations. Like you once pointed out to me. From a germ of something you shape the pieces into an experience."

"Look at Milan Kundera—he writes concrete language. If he writes about death, it's death."

"Well, that's Milan Kundera. I'm Lisa Perlman."

He shrugged.

He looked away. I wondered what happened, what made him change, suddenly angry.

Silence.

Rainbird da da da da spin.

"Would you like some Tofutti ice cream?"

"No, thank you."

"Or coffee?"

"No, thanks."

"I like ice cream. So if you don't mind."

"No, go ahead."

He ate his ice cream, scooping it from the side. Then he said, "I met a woman at Holly's house going through what you are. She's waiting for Random House to make a decision about her novel. A historical novel."

"Uh-huh. How interesting."

Silence. An awful silence. The kind between two children when playing some new game . . . each wanting to win . . . watching the other.

"Do you want anything else?" he asked, looking at me intently, like he was behind windows, keeping me out.

"Oh, no. Everything was wonderful," I replied. "A lovely day."

"I'll take you home then."

"Home? I thought—"

"I have work tonight," he snapped. "I like working at night . . . when it's quiet."

"Uh-huh. Sure, I understand. Let me help you clean the table, rinse the dishes."

"No, leave it."

So, just like that, we left. While driving across the bridge, Eric remained quiet. A distant quiet. But I could hear the noise in the silence. While I chattered about the research I was doing on twentieth-century art . . . then about the Borofsky show at the Berkeley Museum. In front of my house I said, "Don't bother walking me upstairs. It's been a lovely day and—"

"I want to fix your toilet seat. My tools are in the trunk."

"Toilet seat?"

"It's loose."

"Oh, you don't have to."

"I want to."

"Next week you can—"

"I'll fix it now."

So while Prince Charming, on his hands and knees, made a big thing about my toilet seat, I wondered if fixing it was an exchange for some guilt.

"There. The screws are in tight. When you lift it, be careful."

"It's fine," I said briskly.

"Next week I'll bring you a spice rack. It'll keep your spices in order."

"Uh-huh."

I walked him to the door. He looked at me, his eyes dulled. Closed off. Like he was looking at me through smudged windows. He kissed me. I put my arms around his neck really tight, kissed him hard, kissed, kissed. And, for a second, he was the Eric I knew in bed the night before. Like he started to loosen up. But then he pulled away and touched the side of my face, and his eyes were still closed off. Dark. Ambivalent.

"Work well," he said softly.

And off he went, down the stairs, two at a time, carrying his tools, his feelings locked tight somewhere inside him, inside someplace. He wouldn't let me know. I closed the door. "Some girls get roses, some get toilet seats," I said aloud. Maybe a lot on his mind. But then those pinpricks stuck in me, stuck to my skin, and this sad feeling came over me so big I held on to the wall for a minute. Until it went. I picked up Anny and rocked her in my arms. Then, carrying her, I went into my bedroom, undressed quickly, and got into bed. The side where Eric had slept still rumpled.

The wind was snapping against the window. The heating pad scrunged under me. So warm. Soothing the ache in me. I closed my eyes and retraced the day, playing it back in my mind like a reel of film, Eric's every word, gesture, every little silence, his silences opposite of his words, clues. And I remembered us in the car, walking across campus, hand in hand. The way he'd suddenly look away when I'd catch him watching me. His fast walk, on his knees patting the mud over the hose, patting it tight, neatly, listening to Ian and me, listening to every word, patting tight, assessing me. Something he wouldn't let go . . . trust . . . maybe love . . . a fear so big he shrunk us back . . . tight, closed . . . some old hurt buried deep in his silence . . like his feelings can't stay out too long. Are so big they can't hold on, stay out. So they go back . . . shrink back . . . into some little place inside him.

So I'd wait. Listen. Learn Eric like learning a complex and beautiful symphony. Because underneath him there was music. I could feel it . . . feel the music . . . and romance, as exquisitely pure as a white rose. So finally I fell into sleep, my heart in a bottle, floating out to sea, floating out to sea, Mozart's melody going around and around in perfect order. Around and around. The rainbird da da da da spinning a thousand rainbows.

The following Wednesday afternoon I was walking over to Jenny's new apartment. A brisk walk . . . a couple of hills, not bad. I liked to walk. Cleared out my thoughts. As I walked up a hill a wave of sadness came up on me. The next day was Mother's bypass and I was plenty worried. Mother was acting like she was going on a cruise or something. Even that morning Mother'd left her usual morning message on my answering machine, her baby voice saying "Good morning, Lisa," then offering a nice lemon cake and some new typewriter cartridges. Anyways, I was carrying a bag of things

I'd bought at the market for Jenny . . . just Mom things . . . toilet paper, Jenny's favorite cookies, vitamin pills, stuff like that. It was such a beautiful day. The sky so clear, a swoosh of blue paint, though the air was cold. I hurried along the street, for the bag was getting heavy, and that funny, clawing feeling went along my back. As I pushed up the hill, I imagined the patches of shadows crossing over the light, a large canvas of shapes. I looked at my watch . . . past five . . . would be home from work soon . . . what a day . . . one of those days when I wished I'd stayed in bed. That morning while writing, another tooth blew up, and I rushed to Dr. Cohn, who is kind of senile, for emergency root canal, and while he was working on me, he talked on the phone and dropped the phone on my head.

The night before, I'd been up half the night proofing pages from Chapter Five about Eva's first breakup with Tom Doyle and talking on the phone to my telemoans. Depressing. Linda had collagen treatments for the lines around her mouth and her face puffed way up and Sandra said she had writer's block and cried the whole time on the phone and Marcie, dating the youngies now, talked about her latest—a Biff something, a twenty-six-year-old, a whoop-de-do lover but cried for Mother and slept with the night-light on, and Larry Segal, depressed about his novel, was moving to Los Angeles.

I stopped at 120 Euclid Avenue. Several old Cadillacs with fins, strategically parked along the street. The apartment was set behind a large house, one of those mother-in-law units. I rang the doorbell, telling myself to act cool . . . like this was just an everyday visit.

Jenny opened the door. She was wearing a nice black suit and she had this nice smile on her face.

"Mom!" she said, hugging me.

"Jen! Oh, God . . . God . . ."

"Okay already," she said. "Here, let me take the bag," she said, looking into the bag. "Oh, thanks, Mom . . . you're so cute."

I hugged her one more time, then another. Kissed her again and sucked her cheek way in.

"Okay already," she said, flushing and looking pleased. "Enough."

"Oooooh . . . look how adorable!" I said, looking around. "It's gorgeous! And the lilac rug is perfect . . . Nana's old chairs. . . ."

"Isn't it," she said, looking so pleased and kind of giggling. She turned on the little stove.

"I'll fix tea . . . herbal tea," she said, filling the bright red teapot. "Dodie—you know, the older lady at work—I'm going to have you two for my first dinner . . . chicken with pineapple."

"That'd be lovely."

"I told Dodie you're a writer, and she's fascinated. She'd die if she saw your bird pants. You know, she wears French clothes. . . . But you have style . . . she doesn't."

"Thanks, sweet."

"Look, Mom," she said, opening her kitchen cupboards, "I lined the shelves with lilac Con-Tact paper."

"Beautiful. Everything is so neat. . . ."

"Nans bought me these adorable little cat mugs."

"I love them."

"Nans gave me the furry rug and the lilac towels . . . and see, Mom, your picture . . . Anny . . . Amy . . . Nans . . . Kevin . . . I'm collaging this whole wall."

"Good idea . . . but that's an awful picture of me."

"You always say that. I think it's beautiful."

"A garden . . . how lovely," I said, peeking out the narrow window.

"It belongs to the tenants. But I get to water it . . . walk their dogs."

"Uh-huh."

Jenny bustled about the little kitchen, making sure the drawers were closed, putting the mugs on a tray, her phone ringing like crazy, Robin's, Fariba's voices coming over the answering machine, the teapot whistling. She looked so pretty, so fresh. I looked at all her little things . . . clues to her . . . the cat calendar pinned to the wall next to the icebox . . . a grocery list neatly written on a yellow notepad . . . a pink flower inside the crystal bud vase, her beloved dressing table next to the bed . . . the little boxes of makeup arranged just so . . . the stuffed animals . . . her old Raggedy Ann doll on her bed . . . everything clean, shining, organized. Her world. A pride.

"Sit down, Mom," she said, pointing to the old beanbag chair. "I'll bring our tea."

I flopped on the beanbag chair. Jenny brought me steaming tea in the cat mug, with a fortune cookie. She sat on the edge of her bed. For a while we didn't say anything. We drank our tea, the steam flushing our faces.

"The tea is wonderful—kind of peppermint."

"Isn't it," she said, nodding.

"Wonderful," I repeated.

"Don't look so sad, Mom."

"Sad? Who's sad?"

"You're sad. I can feel it. I know you," she said firmly.

"I miss you . . . miss my Jen."

"Give me break," she said, looking both pleased and annoyed. "Stop with the missing every minute. . . . I . . . ."

"Can I help it if I miss you? And I'm worried about Nana."

"Nans will be fine," said Jenny, taking my hand.

"Do you think so?"

"I know so! She's strong. Like you, Mom."

Silence. The teapot still whistling. Footsteps outside. A dog barked from outside.

"I hope you keep this door double-locked—just the other day Nana told me about a rapist—and—"

"Mom!" said Jenny, letting out an exasperated sigh. "You'll never know what Nans did."

"Uh-huh."

"Yesterday she came into Saks and I helped her pick out robes and nightgowns. Everyone at work loves her." She giggled. "And, Mom, you know her hairdresser, Romy . . ."

"Yes."

"Nans made Romy give this boy my number. Seems Romy cuts his hair—the whole family—and Nans knows the family. Can you believe? Nans told me in case she dies she wants me to marry a nice Jewish boy."

"Oh, my God!"

"So this Ziegler dork already called me and he says, 'Hi, Jenny, your grandmother wants you to meet a nice Jewish boy and I have a gold Porsche, a gold American Express Card, a free trip to Club

Med, my own business, a VCR . . .' Can you imagine, Mom?"

"So, go. Will it hurt? At least he sounds like he has a sense of humor."

"I'll see."

"See what? Can't you let him take you to dinner? You never know whom you'll meet."

"Okay already. Don't hock—"

"You never know."

"Give me a break," she said, waving her hand. "You sound like Dodie at work. Every minute between the cramps and hot flashes, Dodie mumbles, 'Listen, kid, if only I listened to my mother and married the nice Jewish chiropractor, I wouldn't be shlepping, always shlepping with swollen feet.' "

"Well, it won't hurt to go. And what about school? Did you register? You know—"

"Okay already!"

Silence.

"What's happening with you and Eric Dork?" Jenny finally asked.

"Why do you call him dork?"

"He's so . . . well, conceited."

"It's just his way."

"He's lucky, Mom. You can see others, too. If I were you, I'd play it cooler."

"Yes."

"Amy says you sounded low on Sunday."

"God, nothing's sacred."

"Well, we both care . . . worry . . ."

"Anyways, Jen . . . the creative writing classes at State are excellent . . . and the drama . . . and you never—"

"I know, I know. . . ."

"Tch, tch, tch."

Jenny kissed me. "Let's open our fortune cookies, Mom!"

"Let's, Jen. Maybe inside there's a prayer for Nana."

CHAPTER EIGHT

Mother'd been in surgery for at least four hours. We were all in the coronary care unit waiting room at Mount Zion Hospital. Phew, it felt like I'd been through the wringer. At 6:00 A.M. Jenny and I had seen Mother before she went into surgery. God, it was something. She'd looked so little, not even like Mother, with her head all wrapped in a green cap and her arms tucked under a thick blue blanket. So many nurses, doctors, tubes, and IVs going, a megillah.

But even sedated, don't think Mother didn't notice I was wearing the Clinique cover-up on my face, even reminded me about the check for Bruce's psychiatrist. Touching the way Mother, even on her deathbed, tried to keep her ship going. Guess that's what holds her together. And what was really cute was when the doctors wheeled Mother on the gurney, Mother, though her eyes were closed, held up two fingers for the victory sign. Sidney, the minute the gurney was out of sight, crabby as hell, lectured us that Mother was a sick lady because we were such rotten kids, that I should get myself a decent job and a husband.

So anyways, there we were, all charged up from worry, while sitting in the overheated waiting room, Bruce's wheezing enough to jump you around, Sidney honking his nose every minute and muttering to himself. The old steam radiator was clanging and the wind outside banged against the windows. Bruce, as usual, was dressed like he was going to a Mafia funeral in a black pinstriped suit and blue necktie. Jenny sat next to me on the long Naugahyde couch, knitting a sweater, a green sweater for Kevin, and I could tell she was nervous, because she'd knit a row, then take the stitches off the needle and knit them on again. And every second she looked at her big pink Swatch watch that matched her bright pink sweater and pink button earrings. Sidney sat as far away from us as possible, doing crossword puzzles and yakking with this buttinski blond woman who was carrying on about how she had warned her husband, Sol, about too much cholesterol, while Sidney repeated that kids could put you in the grave.

Bruce looked terrible. God, I hadn't seen him since that day at his apartment. His mouth seemed smaller, like it had disappeared into his face, and his pale eyes looked so empty, like all the wishes had gone out of them. Only his carrot-colored hair retained a vigor almost garish next to his ghostly coloring. He sat real still, hardly moving, and yawning like everything was such an effort. Except he kept stretching out his fingers like he was reaching for something and his face was pointed like he was holding his breath, while Sidney every minute was getting up and pacing back and forth. Then Sidney would sit back down and stare straight ahead like his mind was a million miles away.

For most of the morning I tried to be Good Sister Sue, you know, keep everything going, conversing with Sidney about normal things . . . the latest airline crash, the rise in inflation. Or I'd run to the coffee shop for Bruce's cigarettes. But, believe me, it wasn't easy making small talk. We'd never been in one room so long together before. This was our first adult crisis. Because when Daddy and Nannie died, Bruce was so young. Anyways, there I was trying to be real in with Bruce, hanging on to his every word, while Bruce complained about the Betty Ford Clinic, saying that it was a rip-off and that he'd met some real stiffs there, and that he was going to sue them for his accident. A couple of times I went into the hall and called Amy, then Eric, who'd been a doll and insisted that I call him at the office. In his calm voice Eric assured me everything would be fine and that I should remain as relaxed as possible. I went back into the waiting room and sat next to Jenny, her knitting needles making a soft clicking sound, and took out my frog notepad and began sketching faces. I liked sketching faces. When I'd been especially anxious, I'd sketch faces, the faces coming out of nowhere, the lines pulling out my thoughts. I sketched Eric's face in a variety of angles, shadowing the planes and hollows of his cheeks, the darkness of his eyes. Eric was opening me up, letting out old things in me, feelings I kept in so long. And *Eva* was going well. The day before, I'd talked to Lester again about Shana and he said Walter promised that Shana was winding up *Princess*. Anyways, as I sketched, everyone was quiet. Sidney was sitting off in the corner of the room, now playing blackjack, slamming the cards on the table.

Soon I'd call Amy again. Poor Amy. She'd called at 5:00 A.M., crying and worrying about Mother. The nurses, before Mother was sedated, put the phone next to Mother's ear so she could hear Amy. God, Mother's poor heart, all clogged up . . .

"Goddamned doctors," Bruce said, looking at his gold Rolex watch and pressing his lips tightly together, much like Mother does. "Five hours already."

"You know that the doctor said it'd be at least six hours," I said, patting Bruce's arm reassuringly. "Takes time," I said.

"Poor Nans," said Jenny, looking at her watch again, then resuming her knitting.

"I have an idea," I said. "Let's give Mother a surprise seventy-fifth birthday party . . . with all the relatives, even the ones Mother doesn't speak to . . . maybe Amy will come home."

"Good idea," said Jenny, smiling. "Nans would love that."

"What do you think, Bruce?"

"Sure," he said, yawning and patting his mouth with a big cotton handkerchief. "Why not?"

"Settled, then. I think it's a wonderful idea and it's a chance to work on something together."

Then we were quiet for a moment. Sidney paced the floor again and Bruce swallowed a couple of pills with stale coffee.

"How are you feeling, Bruce?" I asked, careful not to sound too solicitous, or, believe me, Bruce would get snippy. God, you had to handle him with kid gloves.

"Oh, not so hot," he said, patting his forehead with the handkerchief. "I've got the headaches again."

"Try aspirin or jog," said Jenny, not looking up from her knitting, the needles going click, click, click.

"I can't jog, you know that!" said Bruce, his voice rising, fiddling with a gold money clip, once Daddy's, and counting out several fifty-dollar bills, then folding them and placing them back into the clip. "I'm not supposed to get overtired."

"Well, walking is good," I said. "Every day I walk, helps clear the thoughts and—"

"I walk!" he snapped, pressing his lips tightly together again, waving his small hands, like pushing away the air.

"Couldn't you walk to your . . . program?"

"It's too far. I can't walk."

"Well," I said brightly, "when I drive you to the program, afterward then we'll go walking . . . see the ocean. . . ."

"We'll see," he said gloomily.

"Not that I mind driving you, Bruce . . . but isn't there a car-pool . . . or—"

"Lisa! What do you think the program is . . . a country club? It's a fucking detox program. And do you think I'm going to get in a car with those rehabs? The place is filled with a bunch of nuts . . . criminals."

"Well, I'll be glad to do it," I said, smiling and nodding. "You'll see, Bruce," I said, putting on my dark glasses, peanut butter chew stuck to their rims. "Everything will come out roses . . . at least marigolds."

"Oh, sure . . . I wouldn't bet on it," he said gloomily.

"And . . . well, Bruce . . . I guess I shouldn't mention this now . . . here . . . but sometime if you would like to talk about Mark . . . maybe I can help you. Maybe even talk with Mark . . . explain—"

"Mark left!" he said, spreading out his fingers like grabbing air.

"God, I'm sorry, Bruce."

"So am I," he said, and for the first time I saw a gleam of emotion in his eyes, a spark.

"What happened?" I asked softly, careful not to sound too interested or he'd clam up.

"I'll tell you what happened," he said, lowering his voice and looking at me, his neck flushing red. "Mark got sick and tired of Mother calling every day and insulting him. Yes, insulting him. Always asking me if my friend was there, friend meaning Mark. And the straw that broke the camel's back was when Mother called Mark's boss, accused Mark of stealing her jewelry and eight thousand dollars. Huh! Little does she know that I stole her stuff . . . had it arranged . . . sold it," he said, laughing bitterly.

"Oh, my God," said Jenny, looking up from her knitting.

"Awful," I murmured.

"That's what you get for being nice to kids," said Sidney, slamming down the cards, shouting, "Blackjack!"

"Lay off, Bruce," said Jenny, looking apologetically at Sidney.

"Well, it's true! What do you want me to do, lie?"

"Mother's plenty mean, plenty mean," said Bruce, his voice rising.

"Sssscch . . ." said Sidney. "In front of Jenny yet."

"I've heard worse," said Jenny, not looking up.

"Shame," I repeated.

"Lisa, stop with the shame and listen to me!" said Bruce, sitting forward and gesturing for me to pull my chair closer to him.

"You don't know the half," he continued, looking more agitated. "Mother took away my credit cards, allowance, my new car. And I know it's because I wouldn't give Mark up."

"She took away your car because your license was suspended for drunk driving!" shouted Sidney.

"Ssssh," I said, gesturing for Bruce to quiet down.

"Nans's very generous," said Jenny, looking at Bruce sternly.

"She's plenty mean," repeated Bruce, dropping the money clip on the table, then snapping the rubber band . . . snap . . . snap . . . snap. . .

"Mother's not mean," I said. "You're just upset."

"He should be," said Sidney, looking disgusted.

"Poor Nans," murmured Jenny.

"A shame," I repeated. "But Bruce, if you had a job, you wouldn't have to account to her or anyone and—"

"Oh, stop with the job shit," he snapped, glaring at me. "You sound like those nutty social workers at my clinic—like that nut Dr. Singh—they don't know their ass from a hole in the ground. You're always hocking about working. I can't work! If I worked, I'd die. You know I was born with an old heart, Lisa. So why do you always hock me about working?"

"The big authoress speaks," said Sidney, laughing to himself and turning over the cards.

"Because I care, Bruce," I answered, ignoring Sidney.

"Mom cares a lot. So do I, Uncle Bruce. You'd feel better about yourself if you worked."

"Okay! Enough!" suddenly shouted Bruce, Sidney sssccching, then murmuring for all of us to keep quiet. Bruce patted his forehead with the handkerchief, then said, "Anyway, Mother's going to need me to help take care of her, so I might move back to the house."

"Mother has Birdie," I said.

"Birdie's a dip. The other day she broke Mother's lalique dinner bell . . . she's so careless."

"Lisa's right," said Sidney.

"And I'll help Nans," said Jenny.

"Kids! The day, when they help."

"Bruce, you go back to the house and it'll be curtains for you!"

"Mind your own business, Lisa!"

"Will you kids stop arguing!" shouted Sidney, glaring at us while the horrible woman shook her head. So for a little while we were quiet, Jenny knitting like crazy and Bruce aiming the rubber band across the room, then getting up to retrieve it.

"Sure takes long enough," said Bruce, looking up at the clock again.

"Takes time," said Jenny, knitting faster.

"What's the rush? You're not going anywhere," shouted Sidney, slamming down a card.

"Something must be wrong," said Bruce, looking at Jenny, then at me.

"Nothing's wrong, Bruce," I said, "I promise you."

"How do you know, Lisa?"

"Nothing's wrong," said Jenny.

"Try to relax, Bruce. You need to relax."

"Who can relax, Lisa?" he said, patting his damp face with the rolled-up handkerchief.

"Don't shout, Uncle Bruce," said Jenny.

"Who's shouting?" yelled Bruce.

"Everyone shouts," said Jenny, shaking her head disapprovingly, not looking up from the knitting.

"Pipe down," said Sidney.

"All I did was ask what time it was," said Bruce.

"Sssssch."

"No respect, the kids today," said the woman.

Then suddenly everyone got real quiet. It was almost four o'clock. I finished sketching Bruce's face with the pressed mouth, drooped eyelid, then Jenny's bright face, her ponytail circling around her waist, then Mother's small nose and wide, deep-set eyes, remembering childhood times with Mother, the Children's Symphonies, Mother and I shopping, blowing the fox collar on her coat, wishing I could be like her . . . but knowing I couldn't. Wouldn't. Then I drew my father's long thick black eyebrows, black silent eyes, my grandmother's long curved mouth, and suddenly Daddy's death came over me, over me so close I shuddered. I could see myself bending over Daddy's open coffin, looking at his face, feeling shy. Holding my breath, afraid he'd wake up and catch me looking at him.

I rubbed the tiny rhinoceros between my hands, praying for Mother and wondering if death was only a still-life portrait of life, when Dr. Berman came into the room followed by several doctors and nurses. He was wearing a mask around his chin and his mouth looked somber. He walked right over to Sidney and patted Sidney's arm. I held on to the edge of the chair, watching Jenny, knitting like she was knitting the world together, and Bruce, who looked like he was holding his breath, stood near Sidney. "Mrs. Lieberman is going to be fine," said Dr. Berman.

"God bless, Doctor," said Sidney, shaking Dr. Berman's hand. And then we were all knocking on wood and saying, "Thank God."

"You can see Mrs. Lieberman in about thirty minutes, one at a time. But she's not out of the woods yet. There was more valve-work than we anticipated, so we'll keep her in here."

When the doctor went out of the room, we all hugged, Bruce shouting, "Thank God!" Then we sat quietly until a nice, pleasant-faced nurse came into the room.

"I'm Marilyn," she said, smiling brightly. "Mrs. Lieberman's nurse. Mr. Lieberman is first."

After Sidney left, we smiled at each other, but we didn't talk. We couldn't.

When Sidney came back into the room with the nurse, I searched his face for some clue about Mother, but he only smiled and his eyes were sparkling. He went and sat down on the edge of his chair, leaning kind of forward like he'd leap at Mother's first whisper.

"Okay, who's next?" asked the nurse.

"You go, Lisa," said Bruce.

"I'm last," said Jenny, biting her lip.

"All right, I'll go," I said, smiling at Jenny.

I stood and straightened the crease along the front of my white shirt and pulled the backs of my pink stockings so that they wouldn't wrinkle. Holding my breath, I followed the nurse down the hall and into this large room. The room was kind of dark and all the beds were inside these glass cubicles. Nurses and doctors were all over the place. Over each bed were several heart monitors making beeping sounds, and they looked like television screens playing everyone's heart. As I followed the nurse, walking carefully, almost on my toes so my shoes wouldn't make noise, I kept looking at the machines because I was looking for Mother's heart. Everyone in the beds looked all the same, their bare chests covered with sheets, their heads wrapped in caps. But even before the nurse stopped in front of the cubicle, I knew it was Mother because I recognized her hand, I'm not kidding, her delicate fingers were spread way open and her wrist was raised slightly like she was trying to hold back death, and her fingers were curved like she was going to play the piano.

We went inside the cubicle and I stood by the bed. And as I stood there looking at Mother's puffed-up face, for a second it felt like the ground was coming up over me, so I held on to the bars of the side of the bed real tight and God, poor Mother, her face was so big, her features spread out like she had grown this other face and her mouth was wide open and her head was tilted way back and a long tube was down her throat and her skin was so white, like stretched out, so stretched out I couldn't even see the veins. My heart was beating so fast that I worried Mother might hear it, so I put my hand over my heart. "Can I touch her hand?" I whispered, trying not to let the nurse see that I was upset. The nurse smiled and nodded. I touched Mother's hand, at first gently, because I felt awkward and was afraid that the slightest touch would hurt her, then I held it, and the tears started coming out of my eyes and pouring down my face and I was crying then, and it felt good, because I was crying for Mother and the tears let loose the sadness, all the anxiety.

"I love you, Mother," I whispered. "I love you. Do you hear

me? I love you . . . hang in there . . . it's Lisa." I felt her hand squeeze mine then, I'm not kidding, maybe not really a squeeze, but I felt something, this little flutter, so I held her hand real tight and watched the heart monitor above the bed, making sure the squiggly lines on the screen were moving.

"Time to go. You can see her tomorrow," the nurse said softly.

I bent down and kissed Mother's hand and then I followed the nurse back to the waiting room. Bruce was waiting by the door and he looked so scared my heart went out to him. So I put my arms around his neck.

"Mother's fine, Bruce," I said, "just fine. Sure, her face is a little puffed up, but don't let that scare you. Just squeeze her hand so she'll know that you're there. She'll want you there, more than anyone else." When I kissed him, his cheek felt cold and I knew he'd been crying. He pressed his lips and folded the handkerchief into a triangle and put it into his jacket pocket. Jenny and I stood by the door, holding hands. Jenny bit her lower lip, and her hand trembled. After Bruce came back, his lips pressed tight, nodding like he'd had a secret, Jenny went in.

Bruce said he'd spend the night at the hospital. I assured him Mother would be fine. Sidney sat by himself. When Jenny came back, she was crying. I held her in my arms.

"Poor Nans, Mom, she's so brave."

"Oh, Jen, Nans will be okay. I know it."

Jenny rubbed her eyes with the pink cotton handkerchief.

"Do you think so, Mom?"

"I know so, Jen."

"Schmaltzy lady, your grandmother," said Bruce, smiling.

"I want to go home and make Nans something special. She loves my drawings. Frames my poems, too."

"That's a wonderful idea."

"Poor kid," murmured Bruce, looking sad.

"Go home, Lisa," said Sidney. "We'll call you."

So we said good-bye and Jenny and I left the hospital. We hurried to the car because it just started raining . . . not a fast, heavy rain but a slow, gray rain . . . a big clap of thunder shook the sky and made it all dark. Then the rain started . . . really started.

* * *

The holidays passed . . . so did Mother's crisis. But like life plays tricks on you . . . I mean, Fate can be a pill. A few weeks after Mother's surgery, Bruce had a heart attack—a whopper, the doctor said. Bruce'd been depressed about Mother . . . Mark . . . so I guess his old heart gave in . . . just gave in. Birdie and I would drive Mother to the hospital, Mother's bad leg bandaged up. Mother would sit by Bruce's bed, just sit there, her face real still, not talking or anything, just sitting there. Like the two of them were connected to Bruce's old heart.

So Bruce moved back into Mother's house and was recuperating in his old room, with the fish tanks, lying listlessly watching television programs about heart transplants on baboons, debarking dogs, desnoring husbands, you name it. I tried to talk to Bruce, even suggested that I call Mark and bring Mark over to see him, but he snapped my head off, insisting that he didn't want to see Mark and that Mother wouldn't let Mark in the house anyway. A few times I'd driven Bruce to his detox program, even sat in with him while he pounded pillows and threw chairs, but then Bruce stopped going, plain refused, saying that the social workers were all a bunch of nuts, even refused to see Dr. Singh. Just stayed home, watching the weirdo fish boinging around the tanks, his eyes all empty like the dreams went out.

Eric and I visited Mother on Sundays, and like Aunt Pearl says, Eric's a *mensch* . . . was real sweet to Mother and brought her bouquets of baby's breath and forget-me-nots. Eric was real nice to Bruce, too, talked to him so sensitively, even brought Bruce a book on saltwater fish, told Bruce a million stories about the saltwater fish he had seen in China. Bruce would tell Eric about his heart attack, then explain about his medications and all the heart procedures. God, he knew a lot about the heart. But Bruce's heart attack set Mother back. Somehow, though, she got the strength for Bruce . . . waited on him hand and foot. But her leg never got well. We would be careful not to mention Bruce to Mother because Mother's face would get real sad and she'd say that she gave Bruce his old heart.

And when Mother, wearing her apricot silk robe that matched the coverlet on her bed, complained to Eric about her swollen leg and the ringing in her ears, Eric held Mother's hand and in his soft, even voice he explained to her in detail about his father's symptoms and recovery until Mother felt better. And Mother said that she liked Eric, that he had nice, steady eyes and a strong handshake, though she thought his hair was entirely too long and wild.

A lot of afternoons I visited Mother, shlepping my typewriter and writing in my old room while Mother napped, but then childhood ghosts would come over me and my mind would go back, and I'd see me, a gawky girl wearing thick eyeglasses, hiding behind the door watching Mother and Bruce laughing, hugging, my grandmother at her sewing machine, her eyes dark and sad, her red swollen hands snipping thread with her big metal scissors, and my father reading in the green velvet wingback chair, the lamplight shining his hair silver, and I'd get weirded out, a sad feeling, and stop writing and sit by Mother's bed until she awoke. Or sometimes Mother would want to go downstairs and play the piano, so Birdie and I would help her down the stairs, into the living room. I'd sit by the piano while Mother played and sang out loud in her baby voice the old songs she used to play for Daddy, her heavy body swaying back and forth, her eyes dreamy. Then we got back to our routines and I didn't visit Mother as much and when I'd be with her nothing changed, only the sadness in her eyes deepened and made them seem darker, not so gold. We'd meet for our little lunches, mostly in Mother's rose garden, Mother eating silently while I chattered about nothing, careful not to mention Bruce or *Princess,* wishing that I could let Mother know that as a mother I, too, understood her sadness, feeling that lonely feeling I'd always get when with her because we didn't talk, didn't connect our feelings. But if I let her know that I knew about her sadness, it'd blow things open, change what we had, and we were used to our little lunches, our unsaid truths. So it was better that way.

Anyways, I was in love . . . really in love . . . don't ask me to explain it . . . just knew something different touched my life . . . lived in my air. I struggled to keep Eric separate from my work . . . my feelings for Eric were growing so big, at times I didn't know what to do with them . . . and my work would slow up . . . and the words came out only pretty little masks, covering what I wanted to say, couldn't get out. So I pushed the writing, working eight, ten hours a day, hoping the discipline would push open the words, let loose my feelings, so I could put them aside.

One Sunday after we visited Mother, Eric and I'd gone to a Bach concert at the Legion of Honor and it was beautiful, listening to the music and looking at the Rodin sculptures and at the view of the ocean and the Golden Gate Bridge. It was late afternoon after the concert when we came back to my house and were going to cook dinner.

We were lounging in the living room. I'd been editing pages from *Eva*. Eric sat across from me, scrawling equations on yellow sheets of paper, Anny walking all over Eric's lap and his dark blue flannel shirt was covered with Anny's white hairs. But Eric didn't flinch . . . just kept on working. When he worked he'd become motionless like his mind went far into some world and no one could intrude. I put down my pen and stretched my arms, then picked up a bottle of nail polish and began touching up my fingernails. The stereo was playing the most beautiful Beethoven concerto and the late-afternoon sunlight was streaking across the living room.

"Are you hungry?" asked Eric, stretching his arms and smiling at me.

"A little."

"Later I'll cook the fish," he said.

"Good. I'll help."

"Never mind . . . you're not so good in the cooking department," said Eric, stretching out on the couch, the papers falling from his lap onto the floor. "But you're good in other departments," he said, still smiling and shrugging nonchalantly.

"Do l get an A?"

"Plus."

I laughed.

"Let me see some more pages," he said, looking at me with a serious expression.

"It's only a draft . . . wait until—"

"Bring your pages and lie here with me," he said, patting the pillow.

"How's your work going?" I asked, closing the bottle of nail polish, gathering up the pages, and going over and lying beside him.

"I don't want to talk about my work," he said. I put my head on his shoulder, brushing the cat hairs from his shirt while he read my pages. A couple of times he smiled at me, looking pleased, or laughed out loud.

"This is good, Lisa, very good," he repeated, dropping the pages on the floor, kissing my cheek, and looking somewhat surprised. "Now you've got it . . . it's rich . . . has humor . . . concrete." He shrugged. "At least it's not the *Princess* crap."

"Avalon thought *Princess* was good enough to advance ten thousand dollars."

"Avalon wants potboilers, sensationalism, and from what I've read of *Princess,* it's much ado about nothing. You're better than that, Lisa," he said, looking at me sternly. "When you're soppy, your writing is terrible, but when you're honest, your voice is rich. Forget that *Princess* gig. Tell Avalon you're writing something better. Wait—"

"Lester says that *Princess* is a best seller," I said defensively, annoyed that he was always hocking about *Princess,* putting it down.

"Mencken said never underestimate the bad taste of the public," he said, laughing.

"I resent that! Besides, I need the money, Eric. After *Princess* is published, I'll tell Avalon I'm writing something new . . . but *Princess* is still a good book."

For a while, then, we didn't say anything. Eric lay still, with his arms tightly around me and my head still on his shoulder. But something bothered me. Sure, I knew his advice was sincere, that he was right about *Princess,* but detected the slightest tone of condescension, like maybe even a tiny resentment, almost as if I were some unruly, willful child he wanted to keep in place. But I bit my tongue, telling myself that could be my imagination and that listening to constructive criticism was new to me.

"Are you angry?" Eric asked.

"Why would I be?"

"I don't know. I can feel it," he said, kissing my ear.

"And I can feel your picking . . . your silent pickings," I said.

He didn't answer. Just lay still, looking at me with a softness in his eyes and gently kissing my forehead.

"Are you excited about your sabbatical?"

"Not really," he said, brushing aside my hair from his eyes. "Mainly you're the reason, but I made a commitment to Ian. But," he said with a sigh, "maybe the trip will give me new energy."

"How long will you be gone?" I asked.

"I'm not sure . . . maybe three months," he said, biting his nails. "I might cut my China trip short and spend most of the time in Australia. . . . I hope you'll be here when I get back," he said, kissing me.

"I'll be here when you get back," I said softly, my voice real up, like it didn't matter how long he'd be gone. "Must be interesting, stepping into other cultures . . . especially with your son."

He nodded. "When I lived in England and taught at Cambridge, the boys and I traveled all over the world."

"You miss the kids, don't you?" I asked. When Eric talked about his kids, his entire tone changed, and his eyes, usually so solemn, became all soft.

"Sometimes, when I look at pictures of the kids when they were little, or see the old milk stains on the rug, I could cry . . . they were so cute . . . I could cry."

"You and your boys shared so much together . . . all those travels . . . they'll never forget that. . . . What's that around your belt? God, it's poking me."

"Keys . . . to the office . . . house . . . and I bought this in a Hong Kong department store . . . see," he said proudly, removing the bunch of keys from his black leather belt, showing me a little red knife. "When you open it, it has forty slots . . . a knife for everything."

"Did you like knives, gadgets, when you were a little boy?" I asked, undoing his belt.

He shrugged. "I didn't like much of anything," he said gloomily, "except math and chess. I was a moody geek."

"Oh, I wish we had met—"

"You wouldn't have liked me. I was unsophisticated, awkward then, and you were probably a beautiful princess, the belle of the ball," he said, looking at me wistfully. "All the guys were probably in love with you."

"That's funny because I was really awkward and lonely. . . . I wished I had married someone like you instead of Arnold. . . ."

"You missed it," he said, looking suddenly far away, and I knew he was remembering his ex-wife. Whenever I'd touch the past he'd get silent and brooding, like he wanted the time back.

"What do you mean?"

"I mean having children with someone you love." He kissed me.

"Anyways," I said, "someday I'm going to travel."

"That's good. Traveling will help your writing," he said. "Your world is too small."

"My world is inside me, in here," I said, annoyed. "I write Paris from impressions . . . pictures . . . like painting an apple from a still life."

"Hemingway went to Paris," he said in a challenging tone.

"Paris was his backdrop, but he wrote his feelings. You can't write pain if you haven't felt pain."

"Everyone feels pain, you're not the only one," he said, looking at me critically, and I sensed the slightest antagonism in his tone.

"Experiencing and feeling pain are two different things. Feeling the experience takes some doing, digging in yourself, acknowledging your feelings."

"Feelings are feelings," he said gloomily.

"Don't be a pinhead," I said, trying to humor him, brushing back the curls that grew like loops along the side of his head.

"I'm exhausted," he said, sighing and putting his feet on my lap.

"You were born tired."

"Lisa! What are you doing? Why are you taking my socks off?"

"I'm polishing your toenails, they look awful."

"Sure, why not? I've always wanted my toenails polished."

"Anyways, Eric . . . you're always uncomfortable when I talk about feelings, yet you said we don't talk."

"I did say that."

"What does that mean?"

"That our talking is limited."

"Limited, of course, meaning me."

"Oh, Lisa, don't get mad. I think you're clever. . . ."

"I hate it when you say I'm clever. Like I'm this guile person."

"Guileless," he corrected.

"Guileless."

"I'm sorry. I shouldn't do that," he said, "but I can't help it."

"There! Aren't your toenails beautiful?" I said, blowing the polish dry.

"Beautiful."

"Now let them dry . . . keep your feet up . . . like that . . . that's a good boy . . . while I unbutton, right here."

"You're a terrible person, Lisa."

"Not as terrible as you."

"We're both terrible."

"Terrible."

"God . . . Lisa, that's good . . . farther . . . bite it a little . . . only a little . . . there . . on the tip . . . farther . . in . . . oh, God . . . Lisa, you're so good. . . . Oh, God . . . don't stop . . . easy . . . that's right. . . . Oh, God . . . don't stop! Lisa! Don't stop! My God! Why are you stopping?"

"I lost my contact lens."

"What a time!" said poopy pop, his hand frantically searching along his fly. "Here!" he said, showing me the tiny lens stuck to the tip of his finger.

"Thanks."

"Let's play, Lisa . . . you know . . . more play . . . the closet," he said.

"That, again? . . ."

"Yes."

"In a minute."

"And do this? . . ."

"Oh, Eric . . . my God . . . not here. Mrs. Nelson can see us. . . ."

"It'll make her young."

"Let's do your other thing."

"You're a terrible person."

I laughed.

"This is wonderful."

"Like the moon."

"Oh Lisa . . . you're hot."

"The moon is . . . full . . . warm . . . dark . . . hot. . . ."

"Press . . . up. . . ."

"Like this?"

"Higher . . ."

"More?"

"Lick."

"Like this?"

"Like that, you're doing great. Bite, there. . . ."

"Eric, don't . . . I'm shy. . . ."

"Shy, my ass."

"Your doctor's ass."

"That's me."

"More."

"You're so raunchy . . . and feminine . . . so . . . good. . . .
What are you doing with the pen?"

"Drawing a butterfly on your cock. There! A silver butterfly . . .
so beautiful," I said, dropping the pen on the floor. "Poetic."

"You and your poetry," he said, mounting on top of me.

"Oh, God, Eric . . . the butterfly . . . will fly away . . . gone."

"Tell me you love me, Lisa. Tell me, sweetheart."

"The butterfly is . . . it's—"

"Tell me."

"I . . . hate you."

"Hate me."

"The other way . . . yes, there."

"Whisper your dreams, Lisa."

"Yes . . . oh . . . yes, I love you . . . love you . . . love . .
oh, the butterfly is gone . . . love . . . oh . . . I love you."

CHAPTER NINE

March already . . . cold and brisk . . . the trees turning all purple and the sky sometimes bolted yellow. Maple leaves like puffed-up stars sprawled along the street. Like time does, it has a way of seeping through your life, hardly noticeable . . . but you can see it in the seasons . . . little changes.

As my work grew, I felt less anxiety, less need to please Eric. He became a part of my life, not the center. I stopped showing Eric my work. Held it close to me. I didn't want Eric involved in my work anymore, or his critical comments, perpetual suggestions, blue pencil marks . . . always wanting control of my language, thoughts, so that my work would reflect his ideals, fit his erudite world. I sensed an increasing resentment between us. Lately Eric complained his work wasn't going well. That he was afraid time was passing him by. He became moodier, especially when I was working on a difficult chapter and sometimes by choice I wouldn't see Eric for several days.

But we'd shared some special moments . . . really tender times. Sometimes during the week, after writing all day, I'd drive to Berkeley and meet Eric in his office and then we'd walk hand in hand along the campus. A couple of times I sat in on Eric's lecture with two hundred students and watched in awe as the star professor paced back and forth, dragging the microphone like a talk-show host, lecturing in his firm, even voice, scrawling equations on the blackboard. Afterward we'd go back to the French Hotel and drink espresso while reading our books, each lost in our thoughts. Or I'd drag Eric to the Berkeley Museum and while he'd silently observe the paintings and sculptures, shaking his head in distress, I'd explain the merits of modern art. But unfortunately I knew by then that loving Eric wasn't enough for me and that I wasn't about to spend the rest of my life idealizing and romanticizing the fucked-up genius, or I'd end up like my poor princess, always pleasing and living his expectations or until, like poor Deborah, he'd punish me for loving him too much, he'd give me some fatal flaw. But each time I'd pull back, tell Eric I didn't want to see him for a while, old superstud would get the hots again and call . . . ten, twelve times a day, exclaiming that he loved me, didn't want to lose me. Once in the middle of the night he came over, banging the door, waking the neighbors. And when I saw how utterly miserable my poor poopy prince looked, the bags under his soulful eyes, his nails bitten to nothing, scraps of paper scrawled with equations hanging from the pockets of his corduroy jacket, I got all soft. Because all he had to do was touch me and I'd go bananas. But then a couple of weeks later he'd be back with his bag of tricks.

So, after hours at Dr. Kenner's crying about Eric, my disappointment, my broken dream, Dr. Kenner in her soft, even voice patiently explained that Mother brought me up with the idea that all men were forever or never and that I should never have disappointments, and pointed out that even the most loving relationships don't make it often, have different goals and expectations, and that realizing what was best for me, what I wanted and didn't want, was my triumph, not defeat.

So for weeks I spent wakeful hours at dawn, walking around the house, carrying Anny, crying out the disappointment and the hurt so it wouldn't come out all at once. Until I decided that it was time to confront Eric. Before he left for Australia. And tell him maybe we shouldn't see each other, at least for a long while. If I didn't talk to him soon about what I liked, didn't like about our relationship, our love would only be a façade, grow all crooked as a diseased rosebush grows crooked along a garden fence.

That Friday afternoon, I was on my hands and knees waxing the old linoleum floor, shrieking at poor Anny, who walked in the wax, hurrying so that I could bathe and dress before Eric came over. So when the phone rang I remembered I'd turned off the answering machine. Thinking it might be Mother or news about Bruce . . . God, the *tsuris* at the house . . . I jumped up, almost slipping and falling on my face. I ran into the living room and answered the phone, holding the receiver away from my hair, sticky from wax.

"Hello."

"Lisa . . . Lester."

"Oh, God, Lester, how are you?" I said, picking wax from my hair.

"Good news," he said silkily.

"I could use some good news."

"I spoke to Walter this morning. He wants to see you in New York two weeks from Monday . . . discuss the publication. He wants *Princess* on the market by fall."

"Shana finished editing *Princess*?"

"That's what Walter says."

"God . . . I can hardly believe it!"

"Well, believe it," he said, chuckling. "Walter says Shana is just polishing, smoothing out, the final chapters."

"God, oh, God."

"See what happens, Lisa, when you're patient? You'll be a star yet."

"Oh, I don't care about being a star anymore. I just want the book published."

"It'll be published."

"But Lester . . . I don't understand. Avalon hasn't sent me the rest of the chapters for my approval. I haven't seen a thing . . . nothing since the eight chapters."

"Never mind! There's no time to start changing things . . . let's get the show on the road."

"But . . . the eight chapters were kind of flat . . . and then I wanted to change the ending . . . make it more believable."

"Look, Lisa," he said, sighing impatiently, "you're not writing *Madame Bovary*. You're writing a good commercial novel. Walter likes the book and that's what counts, so let him get it on the market. He thinks, and I agree, that *Princess* would make a wonderful movie. Leonard Serkin at Warner Brothers is interested . . . very interested," he said, chuckling. "Walter's arranged lunch with Serkin."

"Movie?"

"Yes, movie."

"My God!"

"Big. It's going to be big," he said excitedly.

"Big," I repeated. "But I'd like to see the final chapters, what Shana has edited."

"Never mind! Don't start in now! You've waited a long time. And they know what they're doing."

"But *Princess* is an important book," I said.

"It's not important! It's a good commercial novel!"

"Uh-huh, all right," I said, thinking, What's the use?

"That's a good girl."

Pause.

"Walter thinks the gun scene is hot."

"Hot."

"Honey, it's hot, a hot scene."

"I think it's contrived. God, it's not believable. That's why I want to—"

"It's not. It's hot! They know what they're doing," he repeated.

"Wait until you read what I'm writing now. About a sculptor, Eva Hesse. Her struggle, courage. The story is set in the sixties . . . in the art world—"

"Who the hell is Eva Hesse?"

"She's a very important artist . . . and she died at thirty-four, but her work made an impact, broke through minimal art."

"Write about someone everyone knows . . . Mary Cassatt . . . someone like that. But first let's concentrate on *Princess,*" he said, his voice lilting upward.

"Uh-huh, sure."

"Stop worrying, Lisa," he said gently. "Soon your troubles will be over. You've worked hard, Lisa. You're a good writer. Trust me. I believe in you."

"Thanks, Lester."

"Cindy will arrange your flight. Walter agreed to pay your ticket. So call the office next week."

"All right."

"When you come back, we'll celebrate."

"Uh-huh, celebrate."

"So enjoy yourself."

"Oh . . . okay . . . and oh, Lester, I guess I'll have to buy the Hockney after all."

"Honey, you'll have enough to buy three Hockneys."

"Uh-huh."

"Be a good girl."

"Yes."

"Call me from New York."

"Sure thing."

" 'Bye."

When I hung up, I just stood there, my feet stuck to the floor, not from wax but so full of happiness I was weighted to the ground. Not a night for confrontations . . . a good time. Especially when I was feeling so good, but I couldn't put it off anymore . . . otherwise things would just stay the same, never change. And change happens only when you push back the old stuff. But I'd see, I happily told myself. While I bathed and dressed I thought about what I'd say to Eric, how I'd say it.

When Eric arrived, looking crabby as hell, in a real snit, I didn't greet him with my usual movie-star kiss. I kissed him lightly, coolly on the mouth. He brought a bottle of wine and a bag of tiny chocolates wrapped in gold foil shaped in hearts. He put his briefcase on the kitchen table and took out the three facockta mushrooms and placed them in a little glass jelly jar.

"For tomorrow," he said gloomily. "I forgot them last time, and I feel kind of fluish."

God, those fucking mushrooms and his perpetual flu almost made me cry. I softened right up, got all soppy, and I put my arms around his neck and kissed him. So hard. After that, the big man fixed a Scotch for himself and a vodka martini for me and then went into the living room and sat on the couch facing "Fear of Success," glowing pink in the candlelight, Mendelssohn's Violin Concerto rising, filling the room. Eric took off his corduroy jacket, then folded it over the back of the couch. He was wearing a blue cotton shirt with frayed cuffs, white splotches on its front—detergent, probably—and his hair, really long now, stuck out more than ever. He kissed me lightly on the mouth, sighing like he was exhausted.

"Sorry I was late . . . my car isn't working . . . I mean, bad brakes . . . an ordeal," he said, sighing and looking away.

"You seem uptight."

"Don't talk about it or I will be," he said crabbily, gulping his Scotch.

"Guess what, Eric? You're not going to believe—"

"What, baby?"

"Lester called today. They want me in New York in two weeks . . . to discuss publication. . . . Eric, maybe even a movie! Can you believe?"

He picked up his drink and rattled the ice, shaking his head like he couldn't believe it. His face remained expressionless, revealing nothing, except his eyes were darker and I could see he was fatoozled, like he didn't know what to say . . . how to react.

"Wonderful, baby . . . wonderful," he said, a slow smile on his face, his voice slightly uneven, and kissing the palm of my hand. "Amazing," he said, rattling the ice a few more times. He looked at me tenderly, paused a second, looking reflective, then said, "I always knew underneath that blond personality there was a willful, determined woman."

"Blond personality!" I said angrily, pulling my hand away.

"Oh, Lisa . . . don't get upset."

"You just forgot to look under the blond wig, that's your problem."

Silence.

"Amazing," he repeated.

"Oh, stop with the 'amazing' every minute!" I said. "What's so amazing? You make me feel like I'm getting a book published because I have big breasts. I hate it!"

Silence.

"You'll make money now," he said somberly, "have public affairs—"

"That's insulting, personally and professionally!"

"Soon," he said, ignoring my distress and lighting a cigarette, looking at me as if I were a child he was explaining two plus two to, "your life will change. You'll see, Lisa. You've come a long way . . . what a year . . ." he said, shaking his head.

"The book won't change my life. *I'll* change my life. The book is separate. A separate thing. My work has nothing to do with me . . . us."

He sighed and said, "I think I'll have another drink." He got up and went into the kitchen.

The candlelight was flickering tiny pink shadows and the music was rising. Eric could be a pill, and I was disappointed . . . angry that he was so unwilling to take me seriously.

When he came back he sat next to me but didn't touch me. For a while we sipped our drinks quietly. Eric stretched his legs and half closed his eyes, like he was listening to the music, but I knew he was thinking about us.

"Funny . . ." he finally said, still not looking at me. He paused, sighed, and looked at me then, his eyes reflective, then said, "You know, Lisa . . . the woman I told you about . . . the writer . . . the one waiting for Random House . . ."

"Uh-huh. Yes."

"Funny, she's properly educated—Harvard—a gifted writer, I can tell by her letters . . . they're very descriptive, well-written . . . and she's very articulate, so writing is easier for her," he said in that assessing tone of his, "but if I were taking bets on who's going to make it, I'd bet on you."

"An obvious bet!" I said angrily. "And I'm not in any race. You are!"

He laughed. "O . . . kay."

"Anyways," I said, rattling the ice and glaring at him, "soon . . . in about three months . . . maybe four . . . I'll be finished writing the first draft of *Eva*."

"Wonderful," he said, looking at me curiously.

"*Eva* is an important book. For women as well as artists."

"I have friends who've written important books and they don't say they've written important books. Do you ever hear me say my work is important?"

"Maybe it's not. I think mine is."

"You're angry," he said.

I didn't answer.

"I'm low, Lisa," he said, looking kind of sheepish. "My work isn't going well."

"It will."

"Maybe not. All I've done for the past several months are jigsaw puzzles and word jumbles."

"Sometimes you need to do that . . . press the keys into new thoughts, ideas."

He shrugged and rattled the ice.

"Jacob Adler told me that there's a rumor in the department that . . . well, I might be up for a Fields Medal."

"Oh, Eric, how—"

"It's a long shot," he said quickly, shrugging again and looking sad. "I don't expect much from life."

"Nothing's a long shot. Certainly you deserve it . . . worked so hard."

"Don't humor me, Lisa."

Silence.

"Anyways, Eric, don't be too hard on yourself."

"My work is stuck," he said, looking away like he was embarrassed about confessing his anxiety.

"You'll get unstuck."

"I'll go to China, extend my sabbatical," he said, sighing gloomily. "Get some new ideas."

"Where? China?" I asked, hurt that he'd changed his mind about cutting his trip short.

"Nankai University."

"When?"

"After Australia."

"Uh-huh."

"I'm bored . . . need new ideas."

"How do you get new ideas?"

"Reading about mathematics . . . traveling . . ."

I sipped my drink, wondering how long Eric would be gone, but no way would I ask him. No way.

"Anyways," I finally said, trying to keep it light, "It'll work out. Your work will be all right."

"China will shake it out," he said. "I have to get away."

"Yes, that'll be good."

"I'm looking into my life," he said gloomily. "I'm not happy where I am."

"We're all exactly where we choose."

"That's not true," he said, looking at me angrily. "How about the famine in Ethiopia?"

"That's a sociological issue. I can't believe you'd compare your privileged unhappiness with such atrocity."

Silence. He drank his drink.

"Maybe if you'd face your fears, accept yourself . . . look into yourself! You'd find you're not as unhappy as you think you are. Get unstuck!"

"O . . . kay. I'm getting irritated now," he said, sighing. "You're talking *at* me—not *to* me. You're lecturing me."

"You say that when you don't want to hear."

"You need interaction lessons."

"You don't know what interaction is! Stop with the interaction this, the interaction that! We interact through sex. Now let's really interact!"

"What's wrong with sex?"

"You make me feel like a sexual object—like your favorite wine or restaurant."

"I don't mind being a sexual object," he said, half grinning.

"I do! I do! After the orgasm, the ball is over. We never talk . . . I mean, really talk. . . ."

"No, we don't talk," he said, shrugging.

Silence.

"There are a lot of things I could say . . . but don't."

"You keep me separate. Like your own little treat."

"When you get back from New York, I'll have a party . . . you'll meet my friends . . . Holly . . . Seymour . . . the gang."

"You mean now that I'm a published author, you can."

"Oh, Lisa—"

"Okay."

"Maybe we don't bring out the best in each other," he said, looking gloomy.

"Cheap shot, Eric! Maybe we only bring out the best in sex."

"So what's so terrible?"

"Nothing. But there's more. More than that, Eric. And anyways, we're too old for this, Eric . . . playing games, pretending we hate each other so we can love each other. It's a mess. And you're always picking on me, on the way I am. . . . Sometimes I think you hate me."

"Just enough," he said.

"Sicko."

"But let's not talk about us," he said irritably and looking uncomfortable. "You're always trying to get me to say things," he said peevishly.

"Oh, you're always uncomfortable whenever I even get close to talking about my feelings . . . you just don't want to hear them."

"Look, Lisa . . . you know what happens when you lecture me— I pull back."

"Fine. Pull back then. I don't think we should see each other . . . until you get back from your sabbatical . . . anyways, I'm busy with *Princess . . . Eva* now . . . and you—"

"Fine," he snapped.

"Okay."

"It won't kill me," he said, "if I don't see you. It won't kill me," he repeated.

"If it won't kill you, Eric, why do you always say you love me?"

"Because you always say it first and I'm too embarrassed not to."

"Not true!" I said. "That's not true, Eric! And a lousy thing to say to me, like what you said about Ian and Dianna."

Silence.

"So with you, love is never having to say you're embarrassed."

He laughed.

We sat quietly then. Eric bit his nails again and looked distracted. The candles burned slowly, the wax dripping, dripping. Finally, after a long moment, Eric turned to me and said, "You're right about something, Lisa. I try not to, but I'm insanely critical of those who get close to me. It's a disease that brings me a lot of grief."

God, when my poppy poop confessed that and looked so forlorn and all, so utterly miserable, I couldn't help it . . . I couldn't help it . . . I wanted to hold him close and rock him, just rock him in my arms like a baby, like a baby, but I didn't. Didn't dare. For he'd run away for sure. So we sat there, real quiet for a while, the candles making glowy circles on Eric's face. So pretty.

CHAPTER TEN

Three more days until New York. God, I was excited, ran around like a nut, picking up my cleaning, talking every morning with Amy about what clothes I should bring, agreeing that I'd splurge and stay at the Waldorf-Astoria Hotel . . . like old times, Amy said. But Eric . . . another story. I'd stuck to my guns and not seen or talked to him since that night at my house. I knew I made the right decision . . . time to change . . . not for him, but for me. But I missed him, missed him like crazy. So many times I picked up the phone, almost wrote him a note, but I didn't. That was my old pattern, and if I had, Eric would play into it and things between us would start all over again. So I just kept working and writing through the anxiety, pushing away the old impulses, like knots in an old ball of yarn. So even though I was excited about *Princess,* I walked around with this ache in me.

That Friday morning I'd taken a break from my writing schedule so that I could watch Norman Mailer on *World Authors* panel. I was vacuuming my bedroom, listening to Mailer talk about murder and art, yelling, "Go to it, Norman!" when suddenly the program went off the air. Then after a second of squiggly lines, the Modess girl tripping along a daisy field whispering soft days, the camera flashed to the Berkeley campus in front of Evans Hall. And there was my Eric, wearing his *shmatte* corduroy jacket, his hair out wild, blinking behind smudged glasses, reporters swarming around him, asking how he felt about being one of the three to receive the first Nobel Prize in Mathematics . . . the others . . . a Professor Liu in China . . . one in England . . . Eric shrugged and said in his nonchalant tone and deadpan expression he'd just received the telegram and hadn't yet had time to think about it. And then the reporters were asking Eric, cool as a cucumber, a million questions about the equations that led to the cellometer, while I jumped up and down like a maniac, crying and yelling "My genius boy!" until Eric waved and the program flashed back to Norman Mailer, still blah-blahing about murder. Then all hell broke loose . . . my phone rang.

"Lisa! It's Mother."

"Mother! God!"

"I was watching that horrible writer nut . . . what a terrible man . . . when . . . Lisa . . . I couldn't believe—"

"I told you, Mother! I told you Eric is a genius! Do you realize this is the first time in history a mathematician has been awarded the Nobel Prize?"

Pause.

"Lisa," she said, sighing, "he may very well be an intellectual, but a genius . . . I don't know. I haven't seen his IQ. And Nobel Prize or no Nobel Prize is no excuse to look like a slob. The man could clean himself up . . . get a haircut. Sylvia Finkel said—"

"Mother! Please!"

"Okay, okay, can't say a word to you."

"Mother, the man's won a Nobel Prize! The news is going wild. Oh, God, Mother! Another call is coming in. Wait."

"Those call-waiting beeps make me crazy. Call me when you're free."

"Later, Mother," I promised.

Click.

Marcie Kaplan beeped through, exclaiming that I'd been holding out on her, that she saw Eric on television and thought he's very attractive, then Larry Segal from Los Angeles called and said ads pay off, and Sandra, who said profs are fucked . . . Doris . . . Richard . . . Joe . . . the German woman across the street, yah-yahing to death . . . and then Amy screaming into the telephone that she couldn't believe it, the entire CNN crew on the other extension asking what Eric was like, the lousy wait call giving me a headache, Aunt Sally screaming "Coo coo," then hanging up, until finally the big man himself beeped through.

"Eric! My God! God! God!" I repeated, wiping my eyes on the bottom of my frog tee shirt.

Silence.

"Baby, I'm proud of you. Happy for you," I said, so choked up I couldn't talk.

"O . . . kay."

I laughed.

"Are you happy?"

"Not so happy," he said, stretching the so. "But I'm happy enough."

Silence.

"I don't know what to say! The news is going crazy . . . wild . . . about the cellometer . . . says researchers are studying the cellometer. . . might be a breakthrough to AIDS. . . cancer. . . ."

"Maybe."

"Wow! I told you nothing's a long shot! See . . . And you thought the Field Medal was a long shot! God! Hard to believe . . . boy . . . life is weird . . . you never know . . . and here you thought you'd never—"

"Listen, Lisa," he interrupted impatiently, "this evening Miriam Adler is having a press party. Mostly faculty. I'm giving interviews, so I'll be busy . . . but if you want . . . you don't have to . . ." he stammered, "I'd understand . . . but I'd like it if you were there . . . maybe afterward, we'll talk."

"Of course I want to be there. I wouldn't miss this moment in history. I'm happy for you!"

"Okay. Let me give you her address."

"Uh-huh. Let me find a pencil."

"Hurry."

"Okay," I said, grabbing a lipstick. "Shoot."

"Eleven Oak Avenue. Take the Ashby turnoff."

"Yes."

"Now, do you know how to get there?"

"Yes, I think so. . . ."

"Do you have gas in your car?"

"Yes."

"Get a map," he said. "About six."

"Okay."

"And . . . one thing, Lisa. . . ."

"Yes?"

"Everyone thinks we met at the French Hotel while you interviewed me about an article you were writing about scientists."

"You mean, they don't know we met through an ad?"

"Of course not," he said impatiently. "I have to be careful."

"Uh-huh," I murmured, annoyed.

"The university wouldn't approve."

"Sure. Okay."

After I hung up I stood there a second, my body all heavy, my face cold, wiping my eyes with the tee shirt, letting the news settle in, catching my breath. God, it was something. I still couldn't believe it. I was happy for Eric, God knows I really was . . . at the same time I had this weird feeling, couldn't put my finger on it . . . something gnawing at me . . . but I pushed it away . . . after all, I couldn't not see Eric on the most important night of his life . . . I couldn't do that. I'd really have to do a number, show Eric how happy I was for him . . . look really spectacular. And he did say he wanted to talk . . . and that was something. So things between us could work out. Still, I was bothered . . . because I knew everything had changed. . . .

I had a hell of a time finding a parking place, finally squeezing the Rabbit between two cars with Cesar Chavez bumper stickers. I checked my face one more time in the rearview mirror. I wore my black pleated trousers, white silk shirt, French-braided my hair, and stuck between the plaits pieces of black ostrich feathers. Long silver earrings. Carrying a single yellow rose wrapped in green tissue, covering my head so my hair wouldn't get wet from the rain, I ran down the narrow tree-lined street. The Adlers' three-story brown shingled house was set behind huge oak trees.

The door was open. I went inside, feeling kind of shy. The large hallway was crowded with lots of couples, on one wall a mural of Rome. The high-ceilinged living room . . . walls of bookcases, a fire burning in the fireplace . . . a mob scene. The press was all over the place, photographers taking pictures of Eric, who stood in front of a tall bay window, wearing a kind of *shmatte*-looking brown velvet jacket and a Prince Charming ruffled shirt, and cuffs, his loopy hair uncombed, the glasses still smudged. Ian stood next to him, smiling proudly. Eric was talking to a slight man with a thick head of gray curly hair and pointy gray beard and horn-rimmed glasses. So there I was, all scrunged into the crowd, fiddling with the feathers in my hair, watching my golden laureate, feeling mixed emotions . . . wanting to rush into his arms and at the same time, run away . . . even ashamed that I was feeling left out. . . .

Everyone there was a couple except for a few stray kids running through the room and up the long stairway. Waiters passed champagne. Men wore beards and corduroy jackets, looking kind of shlumpy, actually, but most had an elegant, graceful demeanor, like they belonged to a world used to goals and achievements. Something about the way they stood, moved, talked in low tones, occasionally a burst of solemn laughter, with their hands folded behind their backs or around their wives or girlfriends.

I was just about to take a deep breath and give Eric the rose when this rather stout short dark woman about my age, with long black frizzy hair, wearing a white gauze toga, came over to me.

"You must be Lisa," she said, her shrewd eyes quickly appraising me. "Eric said you were pretty. I'm Miriam Adler."

"Oh, how do you do?" I said, taking her hand.

"I love your hair!" she said, pushing my head to the side so she could look at the braid. "I should do that with my hair, don't you think? Will you show me sometime?"

"Of course."

"Isn't it exciting about Eric?"

"Oh, my, yes . . . 'exciting' isn't the word for it."

"Everyone was thrown off course," she said, her voice dropping into a confidential tone. "The first time . . . and the announcement in March . . . but Jacob heard rumors . . . that man knows everything. . . ."

"Uh-huh, I can imagine."

"That's Jacob over there," she said, pointing toward Eric, "the mousy one next to Eric with the gray beard. Honestly, he needs a haircut."

"He looks nice," I said.

"He's a shit! Don't ever marry a genius. After Jacob got the Nobel he got worse!" she said, tossing her long black Medea hair and narrowing her tiny black eyes.

"Oh. Uh-huh."

"Sixteen horrible years," she continued, lowering her voice and standing practically on top of me, "we've been on the verge of divorce. But Jacob's always so concerned about the department we never pick up the final papers. Who else would put up with him? I can't write . . . can't do a thing. He comes first. Though for my birthday present, Jacob arranged to have my poems published . . a small Berkeley press."

"Oh, wonderful!"

She sniffed.

"Eric tells me you're an art historian . . . written a few articles about the art world . . . that you're writing about . . . who was it? . . . that artist who took pictures of the freaks. . . ."

"No. That's Diane Arbus, and there's already a wonderful biography. And I'm not an art historian . . . but I'm writing a biographical novel about Eva Hesse . . . a sculptor."

"How wonderful," she said. "Eva Hesse . . ." she repeated, her voice drifting and looking puzzled, waving to a fat blond man. "Eric is such a love . . ." she said, turning back to me and looking at me curiously.

"Yes."

"Try the Almarado coffee," she said, kissing me on the cheek. "Pete's makes the best coffee in Berkeley. Eric and Jacob love it. And the cheese."

And then she turned away and talked to some dopey-looking couple carrying a screaming baby. So I wandered around the crowded living room, my eyes on Eric, still surrounded. Eric didn't see me. Finally I went into the dining room, a large room opening to the living room, and stood by the table laden with cheeses . . . pâtés. I smiled back at a group of women. One of the ladies, a small birdlike woman with short gray hair and wearing a fuchsia and yellow shawl, came over to me and introduced herself. She took my hand and brought me over to her group. I sipped the champagne, nodding while the faculty wives rattled on about their yoga clubs, the coming faculty ball, their husbands' tenures. sabbaticals, their kids' early Ph.D. programs, but my eyes were always on Eric. I could see him perfectly from where I was standing, especially watched when this very attractive—stunning, actually—petite lady, wearing a green silk Chinese jacket and handpainted doll earrings, dark short hair, rushed over to Eric and put her arms around him. Eric kissed each side of her face, his eyes half closed. Kissed her slowly, gently, affectionately, then twice on the lips. Then they hugged, a long, warm hug. My heart jumped. Because this wasn't any old kiss. No way. A familiar kiss. A lover's kiss. I excused myself from the faculty wives and pretended to cut some cheese, my eyes still on Eric and the girl quietly talking. And Ian was gone . . . probably left.

Eric looked up and our eyes caught. I waved. He came quickly over to me. I kissed Eric lightly on the mouth, aware the girl was watching.

"Congratulations, darling," I said, giving him the squashed rose.

"Thank you," he said, sticking the rose in his jacket lapel. "You look beautiful. I love your hair."

"Thanks. . . . Oh, can I read the telegram?"

"Sure, why not?" he said, taking the rumpled telegram from his pocket.

The telegram read: "In recognition of your outstanding contribution to mathematical theory and your part in the practical application of mathematics to the field of immunology, the Nobel Foundation of Stockholm on behalf of the Royal Swedish Academy of Science is pleased to inform you that you have today been voted the first Nobel Prize in Mathematics. Stop. Your share of the prize will be a gold medallion and a check for $122,000. Stop. The award ceremony will take place in Stockholm on December 10. Stop. Details follow. Stop. Heartiest congratulations. Stop."

"God, it's something," I said, folding the telegram and giving it back to him.

"It's okay," he said, stuffing the telegram back into his pocket.

I wanted to reach over and kiss the curls puffed out around Eric's ears.

"You must feel so good."

"I feel okay," he said, shrugging nonchalantly. "I don't mind being a big shot."

"It's something," I repeated.

"Did you meet Miriam?" he asked, wiping a smudge of lipstick from the corner of my mouth.

"Yes."

"She could be a friend of yours."

"She's kind of strange—"

"Sssshhh! She'll hear you," he said, looking over her shoulder.

"Oh, she's way over there," I said, hurt at his reprimanding tone.

"Lisa! I asked you," he said, sighing, "I'm going to be tied up for a while longer. Why don't you go upstairs and look at their Japanese watercolor collection. It's quite good."

"Yes . . . don't worry. It's your night. I'll wait for you. I'm having a wonderful time," I assured him, brushing the dandruff from his shoulder.

He nodded. "We'll talk later," he said.

Just then the pretty brunette came over and grabbed Eric's arm, looking at me like I was an imposter or something. A nerve.

"Lisa, this is Emmy Mendelson."

I rememberd the calendar on the wall in Eric's house. This was Emmy every Tuesday. Up close I could see tiny lines around her eyes. Her skin was smooth and tan.

"Eric's spoken of you, Lisa. You're the writer," she said in this uppity voice.

Eric smiled. "Lisa's first novel is being published."

"About a Jewish princess, isn't it?" she said, looking at Eric.

"Yes," I replied.

"How nice!"

God, was she a pill.

"And you're . . . oh, I don't believe Eric's ever mentioned you," I said.

"Emmy's a painter and on our faculty," said Eric quickly, smiling at Emmy, who was smiling at Eric.

"A painter. How interesting," I said, trying not to sound solicitous. "Where do you show?"

"I don't paint anymore," she explained.

"Uh-huh."

"Emmy goes to the desert, photographs rocks," Eric quickly explained, looking from me to Emmy.

"Rocks," I murmured, remembering Eric's rock collection.

"Rocks," repeated Eric.

Emmy smiled, her eyes on Eric, who looked slightly flustered.

"Rocks are so interesting," I said, aware that Eric was giving me an annoyed look.

"Rocks are . . . well, real," said Emmy.

"I've noticed Eric's little rocks . . . on his mantel . . . so pretty."

"Well, I've got to be going," Emmy said. "I'm leaving for the desert tomorrow. But congratulations again, Eric," said Emmy, kissing Eric. "And when I get back I want to take more photographs of you. He has such a wonderful face, doesn't he?"

"Yes," I agreed.

"Nice meeting you, Lisa," she said, formally shaking hands.

"Yes. Thank you."

When Miss Pill left, there was the tiniest awkward moment between Eric and me. Nothing you could put your finger on, but it was there. I fiddled a second with a loose feather in my hair so that Eric wouldn't notice that I was really bothered . . . on the verge of asking him about Emmy. I pulled the moment together and turned back to Eric.

"I have to talk to some people now," said Eric, kissing me on the cheek. "I'll be back."

"Go ahead," I said, smiling this yucko smile, wanting to swat him and wishing I had the nerve to walk out. But not wanting to make a fool of myself on his biggie night, but most of all to show him that I could love him or leave him, that I had my feelings for him under control.

So while Mr. Cool strutted through the crowd, everyone patting him on the shoulder, touching him, congratulating him, I yakked with a couple of the reporters. After a while I went upstairs and wandered around this big house, looking at the boring Japanese watercolors, still fried about Emmy . . . wondering. Until sometime later, while I was talking to Jacob and Miriam, Jacob raving what a genius Eric was, when, thank God, Eric came over to us and said we had to get going, that he was bushed.

In the car Eric was quiet, like in another world, but he was like that. Could get into his own world. And that night he certainly had the world. He did.

When we got back to Eric's house, we sat in the living room awhile, drinking this rare brandy Eric opened especially for the occasion. Eric gave me a blow-by-blow of the day . . . when he received the telegram . . . what his father said . . . Joshua . . . Ian . . . God, he was proud. He tried to play it down, but I could tell by the way his tone dropped when he told me about the reporters, the telegrams he'd received . . . or the way he stopped and smiled and half closed his eyes like he did when listening to music. It was so nice talking like that, all soft and quiet, close. Max scratched at the kitchen door. The tin "Peace" signs on Eric's front door rattling . . . the rain, light now, tapping the windows. So while Eric talked and talked, going back sometimes to his growing up, something he didn't do often, about how tough it was, always ahead of the others, being poor, unattractive, gawky, how he loved girls but they didn't love him until he was much older and a full professor at twenty-six, then in his thirties met and fell in love with his wife. When he talked about her his voice got all funny and I felt that funny feeling again. But then love even at its worst feels good. Soon between the brandy and the love I began to warm up. After a while we went upstairs and quietly, without any big deal, undressed and got into bed and read the newspapers. Eric's room, rather small, low-ceilinged, kind of monastic, is painted all gray and the plank floors are uncarpeted, a couple of wooden chairs along the wall, a long table stacked with papers, a kind of beat-up dresser on the other wall, its top cluttered with Eric's keys, a glass milk bottle filled with pennies, facing the garden the cell-like small windows all along the wall and covered by short gray cotton drapes, the double bed, attached to the plain wood headboard his and her chrome gooseneck reading lamps. Newspapers were all over the bed. Eric's light was on, shining over his face. I lay in Eric's arms, my head on his broad chest, while Eric read the late-afternoon *Examiner,* holding the newspaper close to his face, chuckling at the long article about him, commenting that the reporter misquoted him. Eric reading quickly . . . sometimes laughing out loud or telling some anecdote about one of his old professors. I loved lying in Eric's arms, the feel of his skin, his calloused, rough feet over mine. It was chilly in Eric's room so I pulled the gray thick quilt over my shoulders, smoothed back the hair from Eric's forehead. Eric read a while longer . . . while reading kissing me on the forehead or touching my hair. . . until he dropped the newspaper on the floor and half closed his eyes.

"Lisa . . . would you get me an Alka-Seltzer . . . in the kitchen cupboard . . . the middle one?"

"Don't you feel well?" I asked, sitting up and touching the side of his face.

"Heartburn," he said, looking nervous and holding his hand over his chest. "All the excitement, I guess . . ."

"I'll get it," I said, starting to get out of bed.

"Never mind," he said, pulling me back beside him. "Let me rest a second . . . just hold you . . . closer . . . like that. . . . I love holding you . . . you feel so good. . . ."

"Baby," I murmured, hugging him. "I love holding you . . . the holding is my favorite thing . . . you feel so good . . . God, you feel good. . . ."

"Maybe I'm a little fluish, Lisa. . . ."

"Sssshhh . . . lie quietly," I said, kissing his mouth. "You've had a spectacular day. The excitement is bound to affect you."

"Tomorrow's another workday," he said gloomily. "And my work is still stuck."

"Eric, for God's sake, why don't you relax? Enjoy yourself? Like you tell me, get other things in your life besides work."

"Like I said, Lisa, I'll extend my sabbatical . . . spend some more time in China . . . with Professor Liu . . . maybe we'll go to Stockholm together for the ceremonies."

"Oh . . . Uh-huh," I murmured, keeping my voice up. "I'll miss you."

"I'll miss you, too," he said softly.

"Will you be home right after the ceremonies?"

"I'm not sure . . . I never plan."

"Oh, sure . . . uh-huh. Well, it all sounds wonderful, anyways."

"Someday we'll travel together," he said, nodding. "Maybe next year."

"Maybe," I said.

"In time we might live together."

"Don't get carried away," I said teasingly.

"I don't want to live alone, Lisa. I don't want to. I want to get married someday. I don't want to live alone," he repeated.

"Oh, Eric . . . the first time I met you, you sang that song. You've been alone fourteen years. Anyways, let's not talk now," I murmured, kissing his serious face. "It's your big night. Let's—"

"I missed you, Lisa," he said, gently stroking my shoulder.

"You did?"

"Yes," he said softly. "I missed your beautiful funny face . . . your warm voice . . . your high spirits . . ." he murmured, caressing along my thighs, my body, all over my body. "And your various body parts . . . right here . . . and our wonderful ass games. I feel sad losing it all. I expect . . . I mean, I hope . . . you feel the same."

"Eric, let's . . I'm going to sleep. I'm tired. You've had a big day and I have one tomorrow."

"O . . . kay."

And then we were quiet. We lay in the dark, on our backs, holding hands, my head resting on Eric's shoulder. You could hear the wind rustling, Max scratching at the door.

"Christ, I have an itch!"

"Eric, go to sleep."

"I can't find it, Lisa."

"How can you have an itch then?"

"Haven't you ever had an itch you can't find?"

"Guess."

"Lisa . . . you found it. Oh, God, that's good. You found it, Lisa."

The next morning, close to eight o'clock, we were in Eric's kitchen. Eric, wearing navy blue cords and a wrinkled faded plaid shirt, was barefoot. He was grinding coffee beans and making toast. I sat at the kitchen table, observing how efficient he was, loving his domesticity, listening while Eric complained about how tired he was and that he was sure he had a touch of flu. The drapes were pulled and the garden looked so green, the trees all shiny from the rain the night before. Max was walking along the edge of the hot tub, and the steam floated into a white puff. The sky was all different colors, parts dark blue. Eric's phone was ringing like crazy, but his answering machine was on and the volume was turned down.

"Lisa, what are you going to do today?" asked Eric, pouring coffee beans neatly into a cone-shaped paper.

"Oh, work. I'm finishing an important chapter . . . it's been driving me up a wall . . . and I have a lot of packing . . . stuff like that."

"Do you want to do something tonight?" he asked, pouring the steaming coffee into two large yellow mugs, one marked "genius."

"I don't think so," I said, smiling at him carrying the tray of toast and our coffee and setting it on the table.

"Okay," he said.

"Oh . . . is that herring?" I asked, ignoring Eric's sulking.

"Yes . . . try some," he said, filling Max's bowl with Friskies. "Put it on your toast," he said, opening the door to let Max in.

"I love herring. My father used to love herring."

"Good, eat," he said, sitting next to me and opening the jar. "I buy it fresh every day at the market. I wash off the salt."

He rinsed the herring in cold water. Then he put a bunch of the herring pieces on his toast and began eating hungrily, like eating was the only thing on his mind. But I could tell he was still sulking.

For a while we ate quietly, our knees touching.

"You'll be busy in New York," he finally said after his second piece of toast and herring.

"Yes."

"Running all over the place. You'll be good on talk shows," he said.

"I hate the way you refer to *Princess* . . . like it's entertainment."

"I'm apprehensive," he said, shrugging.

"Why?" I demanded. "Because you're worried what your friends will think? How the book will represent you? That, God forbid, I'm not Tolstoy or Virginia Woolf?"

"You know how I feel about *Princess*," he said coolly, ignoring my defiant tone, taking more herring from the jar and putting it on his toast. "But I think its publication is a good thing for your career . . . your confidence."

"Your problem," I said, "is that you never read *Princess*."

"Let's not argue. Just have a good time in New York, Lisa . . . with Amy," he said, smiling wistfully. "Spend as much time with her as possible. It's important, Lisa. Kids . . . they're with you . . . then they're gone."

"Yes, I know."

"And get some rest. You work too hard."

"Uh-huh. I'll rest."

"I worry about you."

"Worry? Why?"

"You're too ambitious."

"Maybe I want the Nobel Prize, too."

He smiled and closed the lid on the herring jar, turning it several times, making sure it was tight. Then he poured more coffee. A couple of times he held my hand or touched my hair but then he'd pull away quickly.

"Anyways, Eric . . . you'll be busy today."

"I have to go to the office," he said. "Cope with more press meetings, God knows what," he said with a sigh.

"It's exciting."

"Yes, but I'm still feeling fluish."

"Just rest later."

"I'll double up on the vitamins."

"Your friend Emmy," I said cautiously, sipping the hot coffee. "She's very attractive."

"Yes, she is," he said.

"Have you known her for long?"

"Several years."

"Uh-huh."

"We're just very good friends," he said, his tone like explaining a math problem. "I see her about once a month."

I held the coffee cup close to my face so that the flush on my face would seem to come from the coffee's steam.

"Once a month?"

"Look, Lisa . . . it's allowed."

"Allowed! Everything's allowed! I couldn't care less about Miss Rock Face. It's the way you promise me the moon the night before, say you love me . . . then the next day, act like we didn't exist."

"Oh, Lisa . . ." he said with a sigh, "not today. I have a lot on my mind."

"So what else is new? You always have a lot on your mind, or the flu or your blood pressure, or a pain in your asshole."

"You're not so easy either, Lisa. You think I'm the only one? You're eccentric—"

"Oh. Uh-huh."

"Sometimes," he continued. "I have so many thing I want to say to you. But you're so busy talking about yourself, Lisa," he said sulkily. "Your work . . . You interact only with Anny."

"Okay, so we're both fucked up. Couldn't we still have a good fucked-up relationship?"

He laughed. Then he bowed his head and got all quiet. "If you'd been through what I've been through with my ex-wife—"

"Eric, let it go. My God, you're fifty-one years old! Let it go. We all have pasts . . . hurts . . . let it go."

He got up and went over to the stove and began grinding more coffee beans. He came back and poured more coffee. For a moment he was all quiet.

"You do make me laugh," he said softly, caressing the side of my face, "and I do love you."

"Eric . . . I . . ." I said, smoothing the hair that stuck out at the side of his head, "this isn't a war . . . a win-or-lose . . . I'm not trying to get the last word."

"You always do," he said gloomily.

"Anyways, Eric, I've got to get going," I said, quickly standing up and rushing around the kitchen, getting my things.

"Right now?" he said. "I thought we'd go for a walk."

"I have to get going."

He got up slowly and, carrying the jar of herring, went over to the kitchen counter. He turned and looked at me gently. Then, as if having a second thought, he opened the jar of herring and wrapped the rest of the herring in a big piece of waxed paper and tied the package with a thick brown string.

"Take this home, Lisa . . . it's good. You can have it with your breakfast tomorrow."

"Thank you. I will."

He walked with me to the car then. His eyes were all quiet, and though there was a tension between us, we held hands. But when he kissed me good-bye, I held my lips tight, and when we hugged, I held my body back. I got quickly into the car.

"I'll call you later," he said.

"Uh-huh."

"Drive carefully," he said, blowing me a kiss, looking kind of uncertain. "Lisa, make sure you have enough gas in your car. Oh, I see you do," he said, poking his head in the window.

"Yes. Stop worrying. Take care of your flu."

I drove off.

The next day, at 6:45 A.M., I was waiting for the airport bus. I called Jenny one more time at her apartment.

"Jen . . ."

"Mom! Haven't you left yet? Oh, Mom, I forgot to tell you. Last night I went out with that Joel Ziegler dork."

"Oh. Did you have a good time?"

"He's not bad. We double-dated with this girl Sandra Shtick and she was with a Harvey Schmaltzy something, a dentist. She was a pill. The first thing this Sandra asks me, not even what's my name, is what do you do? So I said I'd gone pro and she said pro what?"

"Oh, God."

"She was wearing this two-tone blue and black angora sweater and diamond stud earrings and had squared nails and drank decaf latte . . . her pinkie up to the sky . . . a real pain in the ass."

"Please watch the language, Jenny. I don't like it."

"Okay."

"You're meeting new people. It's an experience. But what about school? Did you register?"

"You're not even at the airport and you're hocking. I said I would."

"Good."

"Mom, stop worrying. You're always worrying. Have a wonderful time. You deserve it."

"Thanks."

"I love you, Mom," she said.

"I love you, Jen."

Click.

CHAPTER ELEVEN

By the time I arrived at the Waldorf-Astoria Hotel it was past 9:00 P.M. Even though it was the first week of April, it was still cold. So I pulled my red cape closer around my shoulders and hurried into the lobby. My eyes searched the crowded lobby, then I saw Amy and Adam. Amy, wearing a long trench coat and red beanie, rushed toward me and, God, I had butterflies in my stomach. We hugged and hugged over again, Amy crying how much she missed me, loved me. And I couldn't say anything. I was too full of her. After we stopped hugging, I held her face between my hands and just looked at her beautiful face, thinking she looked more sophisticated. Changed.

"Thin . . . much too thin."

"Mom, oh, Mom," murmured Amy, smiling at me, her beautiful green eyes shining from tears. We stared at each other, like trying to connect something.

"I'm here, too. Remember me?" said Adam, tapping me on the shoulder.

"I didn't forget you," I said, hugging. He smelled like expensive cologne, and he was wearing an expensive-looking tweed jacket with flaps in the back, a camel overcoat thrown over his shoulders, his thick brown hair styled like those guys on *Dynasty*.

"You look like a million dollars," I said.

"My Armani suit," he said, stepping back so I could see him. "Barney's had a sale."

Amy gave me this knowing wink. "Adam was the first one in line," she said.

"What are all those gadgets?" I said, pointing to a beeper stuck in his jacket pocket.

"My Sony beeper," he said. "And this," taking another beeper from his pocket, "takes messages from the first beeper. My new calculator watch," he said, pointing to the steel watch around his wrist. "See, Lisa, a tiny TV screen."

"My God, isn't that something."

"You name it, Adam's got it," said Amy sarcastically and looking disgusted. "Mom! I can't wait to hear about Eric," she went on. "A Nobel Prize! Incredible!"

"Come on, let's go into the cocktail lounge," said Adam. "Talk there."

We went into the cocktail lounge. It was so dark it took me a minute to focus my eyes. We sat at a back table away from the tinny piano. The rattle of the cocktail shakers blended with the sound of dice and pieces of soft conversations, laughter, a slight scent from expensive furs and cologne. I took off my cape while Adam and Amy discussed what they wanted to drink. . . . A candle flickered inside a red velvet pleated lamp, throwing shadows across Amy's face. I felt inside a beautiful dream. I didn't want to get out. I couldn't stop staring at Amy's face, my eyes like a camera trying to focus Amy's face into time, to get back all the time. And though Amy looked so sophisticated, no matter how time changes I'd always see the freckles under the makeup, the tiny bump on her thumb from where she used to suck it, or hear the scold in her tone when she'd nurse her broken dolls or boss Jenny, or call for one more kiss. When she took off her beanie, her hair, expertly layered, fell luxuriously past her sholders, complementing her small, beautiful face. When our drinks arrived, we began toasting, all talking at once, our voices rising.

"To Mom . . . my Mom," said Amy, looking at me and smiling, almost shy-like.

"To a star," said Adam, smiling at me.

"Just Mom. Let's toast to Nana . . . Jen . . . the world . . . life."

We clicked our glasses.

"So, Mom," said Amy, daintily sipping her wine spritzer, "tell me about Eric. It's a shock. I mean, here's Mom seeing this celebrity and you hardly ever talk about him. And when am I going to meet him?"

"You'll probably meet him this Christmas. After Eric returns from Stockholm."

"What's he like, Mom?"

"Like," I repeated. "Well . . . he's neurotic as hell, shleppy, fun, sexy, exciting, romantic, and . . . he can be so tender . . . but a difficult person. Really difficult."

"All geniuses are neurotic," said Adam, smiling modestly and looking at Amy.

"Jenny says she likes Eric but that he's arrogant."

"Oh, Jenny would," I said defiantly. "It's just Eric's way. You have to know Eric. He doesn't show his feelings, but he's a pussy cat . . . especially when it comes to kids. He loves kids. But you know Jenny. She's very protective of me. So she's always looking for something wrong."

"When's the wedding?" asked Adam, popping stale nuts into his mouth, ignoring Amy's glaring looks.

"No wedding."

"What's wrong?" asked Amy, looking at me anxiously. Adam was frowning and I'm sure Amy was kicking him underneath the table.

"Nothing's wrong! Why should there always be something wrong? We're having a relationship. And relationships at their best are complex . . . especially ours. Eric's Nobel Prize . . . I don't know what's going to happen. Besides, I'm not ever marrying until it's right . . . absolutely right . . . until I'm really independent. Even then, maybe not."

Silence.

"Anyways," said Amy, glaring at Adam, "everyone at work is dying to meet you. Hear about Eric. You remember Mary? She's having a party for Heather Weisberg's new film about the Indians, and Lynn thinks Eric looks like a cross between Mailer and Kissinger, and wait until you meet my best friend, Andrea . . . you'll love her. And, oh, Mom, last week the Metropolitan gave a twenty-five-year Chanel retrospective. Lynn sent me and Karen, another writer, and said, 'See if you girls can bring me an interview with Karl Lagerfeld.' And guess what, Mom, I not only interviewed Lagerfeld, but I interviewed Pavarotti!"

"Pavarotti! Oh, God, you're kidding! God!"

Adam smiled approvingly.

"I never thought I would. I mean, he's so like . . . well . . . all the reporters were after him. I followed him around all night and caught him alone and tapped him on the shoulder and asked him how fashion influenced his work. And he said he loves colors, style, elegance. Then he pinched my cheek and said, 'Like you.' "

"Oh, my, that must have been something," I said.

"Amazing. He's amazing," she repeated, her eyes all dreamy. "I'll let you know when the show is taped, Mom. You won't see me. I mean, I wrote up the piece but it's Lynn's voice interviewing Pavarotti. But the part when he says, 'Like you,' you might see my shadow. Our cameraman didn't get it all out."

"God, I can't wait to see it! What an experience. Pavarotti," I repeated, looking toward Adam, who was fiddling with his beeper.

She opened the old red leather wallet I'd given her years ago. In it were pictures of me, of Jenny, of Mother.

"See, Mom," she said, looking so proud. "My press card."

"Wow," I said, turning the little blue plastic card with her name and picture on it.

"Amy'll make the big time," said Adam, who most of the time was either clicking his fingers for the poor waiter or jotting notes in a little black leather book.

"No such thing as big time, Adam. Only the work counts," I said. "The rest is bullshit . . . pardon my French."

"You'll change," said Adam, grinning.

"Mom's right," said Amy, looking upset. "I see enough celebrities to know. The committed ones don't need to flaunt."

Silence.

"Anyways," I said, aware of the chill between Adam and Amy, "it sounds exciting."

"Hard, though . . ." said Amy. "The long hours . . . sometimes after a show I'm not out of the office until midnight . . . working in television is incredibly hard . . . especially in New York. It's cutthroat. You don't know, Mom."

"Anything worth pursuing is hard."

"Guess so . . . but Mom, you've never worked under corporate conditions. Lynn is impossible. I'm so sick of making her luncheon reservations at Le Cirque and writing her fashion copy! Then she changes everything I write. Is never satisfied."

"Amy, when you get where Lynn is, you can change copy, too. . . . Meanwhile, you're getting the experience."

"That's true," she said, sighing and drinking her spritzer.

"I want to make the big bucks," said Adam, clicking his fingers and gesturing impatiently for our waiter again.

"You will, Adam, I'm positive."

"That's all he thinks about," said Amy, frowning disapprovingly, not looking at Adam, who was glaring at her.

"Money talks," said Adam.

Then Amy began talking more about her work, excitedly explaining TV cameras, lighting dissolves, slow mos, her small hands dramatically gesturing, her face animated. While she talked—Adam on his third drink, neither one looking at the other—I watched how her green eyes sparkled when she was excited and the way she crooked her little finger when making a point or when pausing how her tongue darted over her full bottom lip or when she was about to dramatize a story—how her voice dropped and her face became intense.

Then we didn't talk for a while. I finished my second martini, wondering why Amy and Adam were so tense.

"How's Nana?" finally asked Amy, sipping her spritzer.

"Oh . . . she's okay. Her leg is bothering her. It's not easy with Bruce home. . . . Outside of that, she's pushing through."

"Poor thing," said Amy, looking sad. "Jenny says that Uncle Bruce is in bad shape."

"Yes."

"Shame," said Adam. "What a case!"

"Don't talk about it now, Adam," said Amy, looking concerned. "Mom doesn't want to talk about it. It makes her sad."

"Oh, that's okay . . . but anyways, Nana is okay. Bruce is giving Nana a surprise seventy-fifth birthday party next month."

"Oh, that'll be wonderful! I wish I could come home for it. Maybe I'll talk to Lynn."

"Well, you'll see."

"Mom, I think Jenny should come to New York. Study acting. Waitress. She's talented. Funny, really hilarious."

"Right now she is doing what she wants to do." I sighed. "She doesn't have the money, and neither do I. Not enough to help her."

"Well, you will soon!" said Adam, raising his glass, clicking his fingers for the waiter to bring another round of drinks.

"Oh, Mom! I almost forgot!" said Amy. "Tomorrow at ten, Mr. Guy—you remember Mr. Guy, Mom—he cut your hair the last time—"

"Yes, yes," I said impatiently.

"He'll cut your hair and do your makeup before you go to Avalon tomorrow."

"No, he won't. I don't wear much makeup, and I don't want my hair cut."

"What do you mean, he won't?" said Amy anxiously, looking at Adam, who was looking at me, both tch-tch-tching.

"Just what I said. He won't."

"Lisa," said Adam softly, taking my hand, "your readers want to see their author as glamorous as your princess."

"God forbid! That princess is a twenty-two-year-old glitzed-up moron. I'm forty-three and proud of it."

"Mom, maybe in California . . . Berkeley . . . you can go around without a stitch of makeup . . . but in New York—"

"Discussion closed."

Adam and Amy gave each other a funny look and nudged each other. Amy daintily sipped her wine spritzer.

"Listen, Lisa, when you go to Avalon tomorrow, do me a favor. Don't sign anything. If anything comes up about movie deals or anything," he continued, his voice taking on a courtroom monotone, "let my firm handle everything. Our firm handles a lot of celebrities . . . Doobie Brothers . . . Tina Turner. All kinds. You have to be careful. Everyone's going to want a piece of the action."

"For sure," said Amy.

"Uh-huh," I said.

"Anyway, I think Mom looks great. She has her own glamour."

"Can't be too thin. Or too rich," said Adam, looking at me closely, then at Amy.

"Glamour, real glamour," I said, "the Hepburn kind, comes from within . . . from the glow within. Her talent. Just her."

Adam folded a cocktail napkin and held it along the side of Amy's

nose. "Look, Lisa . . . with the Streisand bump off Amy's nose
. . . a good plastic surgeon can do it . . . your daughter's a *Vogue*
cover. A beauty. The surgery is only thirty-five hundred bucks.
And I've checked out some of the best plastic surgeons."

"God forbid! Amy, I hope you're not considering such an awful thing."

Amy looked embarrassed. "Well, Nicky . . . the cameraman at
CNN . . . says that on camera my nose looks like—"

"Looks what?!"

"Sssshhh . . ." hushed Amy, looking anxiously at Adam, who
was anxiously looking at Amy, then at me.

"I don't care what your cameraman says. Do you want to look
like one of those Beverly Hills Jewish princesses, all Guccied to
death, shlepping around boutiques with nostrils so big bugs fly up?
Be yourself! Who you are! God!"

"What wrong with Gucci?" asked Adam, holding up his loafers
and pointing to his leather belt. "I wear Gucci."

"God wears Gucci," I said sarcastically.

"Probably," said Adam.

"Anyway," said Amy in an up tone, "what time is your appointment at Avalon?"

"Noon."

"After work we'll go somewhere wonderful . . . celebrate,"
said Amy.

"The Palladium is hot . . . where it's happening," said Adam.

"I'd like to go for a simple dinner, maybe a concert at Carnegie.
After Avalon, I'm going to the Guggenheim. See the retrospective
. . . four decades of American and European art . . . Eva
Hesse's work."

"Oh . . . how is your book coming?" asked Amy.

"Very well . . . hard."

"I never heard of Eva Hesse," said Adam, looking concerned.

"You will," said Amy, smiling at me.

"Anyways . . . in any event, let's meet here in the lobby. Five
forty-five. Under the clocks . . . under the world."

"You're on, " said Adam.

"You look tired, Mom."

"Jet lag. Excitement."

"Get some rest, Mom."

"Amy's right. You do look tired. C'mon, Amy," said Adam, paying the check, then standing quickly. "Let's go. We'll see your mom tomorrow."

I waited with them outside until a taxi arrived. Amy and I hugged, rocking each other back and forth, not caring that people were looking at us and smiling, while Adam sighed impatiently, glancing at his calculator watch and fussing with his beepers. When their taxi arrived, we hugged one more time. Amy shouted out the taxi window for me to get some rest. Suddenly this vertigo came over me, I felt kind of dizzy, like looking down at all the years past. After I checked in, I hurried through the lobby and went upstairs to my room. I undressed quickly, kind of high from the drinks . . . Amy . . . New York . . . too excited to sleep. I wanted to hold the day back a bit longer.

The next morning, after I bathed and dressed in my Calvin Klein black suit, ivory silk blouse, silver earrings, Navajo cuff, black pumps, and pale stockings, the rhinoceros Bruce gave me safely in my pocket, I left the hotel. It was close to noon.

I began walking to Avalon. The day was even colder than the night before. The wind blew hard, whipped over my legs, and my cape floated behind me like a red puff. My lips were so cold they felt stuck. But God, you should've seen the city! So beautiful . . . the sky darkly gray . . . meshes of little brown birds flew between the skyscrapers, tipping their wings, the tops of the buildings touching the sky like pointed crystals. The trees lining the street were getting ready for spring, their leaves sprigs of green. Roasting chestnuts gave off a charred smell. I hurried across the street and went inside the building. I took off my hat, shaking out my hair, and I rode the shaky elevator up to the third floor. The same receptionist sat behind the desk.

"Ms. Perlman, nice to see you," she said, balancing several telephones. A dozen new hardback novels sat inside the glass case. A vase filled with fresh yellow roses sat on the top of the desk, an unopened card beside it.

"How was your flight?" she asked politely.

"Terrible, but I'm a terrible flier," I said, taking off my cape.

She smiled. "Go right up. You know the way. Ms. Goldsmith is waiting."

"Is Mr. Avalon in?"

She nodded but didn't answer.

I hurried up the carpeted stairs, wondering where Walter was. On the top floor I passed his office. His door was closed, but I knew he was in there. When I went into Shana's office, she rose quickly from behind her desk and came toward me, this phony look on her face and her eyes all pointy, giving me the once-over, the air full of resentment. She was wearing this big gray sweater, real expensive-looking—one of those French jobs—and a matching gray mid-calf skirt—real sharp—and matching gray suede boots. Her hair was longer than before, and she wore heavier makeup.

We exchanged one of those no-contact kisses. "Walter will be here soon. He's in a telephone conference."

"It's been a long time," I said, sitting in the blue leather chair in front of her long oval desk. "I'm so happy that *Princess* is ready for market. God, I never thought it'd be finished. Almost two years . . . and I can't wait to see the rest of the manuscript!"

"Yes, yes," she said impatiently, waving her hand, the same wooden bracelets clacking, the traffic outside loud. Her phones rang constantly . . . soft, bell-like sounds. She settled in her swivel chair, pushing her chair closer to the desk. She pulled up her sleeves, her elbows all red, a pilly expression on her face. She opened a bright blue box. "Avalon" on the cover, and took out my manuscript and placed it in front of her. Though not all of it. The little cloisonné clock ticked softly. Footsteps outside the door . . . maybe Walter . . .

"Editing is a slow process . . . a very slow process," she said, sighing like she was so exhausted. "I had to do a lot of cutting," she said, frowning, her face all scrunged, "your endless metaphors, all that introspection. I told you our readers in Iowa don't get off on a flower, they get off on sleaze, action!"

"Well, I certainly gave you that! I couldn't think of anything sleazier than pedophilia—"

"I thought you were going to write me a novel like Judith Krantz," she demanded, thumping her pencil, "that you understood what I wanted. You still have your princess introspecting."

"She has to do something besides polish her nails."

"That's the point! She has to do things! Our princess has to act, not think about her precious feelings!"

"I'd like to see the rest of the manuscript," I repeated. "Eight chapters in two years—"

"I have other authors, too, authors who know what they're doing. And I've been sick . . . I'm tired of making miracles for everyone."

I was just about to tell her what I thought of her miracles when, like an actor on cue, Walter came into the room, all tanned and elegant, wearing this dark suit, his white hair whiter than I'd remembered. I'd forgotten how handsome he was. His glamour filled the room. But I could tell by his dark whispery eyes that he knew, had heard every word between Shana and me.

"Lisa," crooned Walter, kissing me on the cheek, "you look wonderful . . . just wonderful. Doesn't she, Shana?"

"Walter, I've been explaining to Lisa about why it's taken so long editing her manuscript . . . all the cutting—"

"Never mind," said Walter, sitting on the chair next to mine and giving Shana a warning look. He smiled at me, but his probing eyes were enough to give you the creeps. The traffic was really loud outside, and Shana's chair kept squeaking.

"Since Shana's been telling you all the negative things about *Princess*," finally said Walter, his voice all soft, smiling at me, "let me tell you the good news."

"Uh-huh," I murmured, relieved.

"Leonard Serkin read *Princess* and loved it—especially," he chuckled, "the wonderful scene where the violinist rapes the ten-year-old girl." He paused and smiled again. "He agrees you have raw talent, a knack for writing cliff-hangers. And I said to Leonard, you can always tame the raw talent, but if the author doesn't have it, you can't create it."

"Tame . . . uh-huh."

"Tell her about the names, Walter," said Shana, tossing her hair.

"One of the things, Lisa, Leonard wants to go over with you

today at lunch is Anglo-Saxonizing the names, classing them up. Instead of Diane Shapiro, Leonard thought up Swann Duvall."

"Too many Jewish names," said Shana.

"I'll do the talking," said Walter, glaring at Shana.

"Swann Duvall!" I said. "My God! That's gross!"

"It's a wonderful name," said Shana.

"So what's the good news?" I said.

"The good news is that Leonard wants *Princess* for a blockbuster miniseries for this fall."

"Miniseries?" I asked.

"It means more money than a movie," said Walter, smiling. "Not to mention reruns."

"You're very lucky," said Shana.

"Wait a minute—hold it!" I said, looking from Walter to Shana, who was putting on her long dark mink coat. "I don't understand. . . . Why are you talking about a miniseries? I mean, what happens to my book?"

"Well . . . first we'll do the miniseries. Then, if the ratings are good—which they will be," he said with a chuckle, looking at Shana, "you have a presold audience. . . . Then we'll get *Princess* out . . . reruns, perfumes, endless possibilities . . . what every writer dreams of!"

"Who writes the script?" I asked, keeping my voice all even, trying to take this all in.

"Marty Solomon," he answered quickly, "one of Serkin's top writers . . . great track record. Of course," he said nervously, "the credits will read 'from a novel by Lisa Perlman.' "

"Uh-huh."

"After lunch—when we sign the contract and toast our success— we'll call Lester with the good news."

"Lester doesn't know?" I murmured, tapping my foot.

"We wanted you to know first." He glanced at his gold watch. "We'll discuss the terms . . . details . . . at lunch. . . . Mary Solomon is meeting us, too."

"So you mean," I said carefully, my foot tapping harder, "if the miniseries doesn't do well . . . if the ratings aren't good . . . then my book is bagged. . . . But if the series is hot, the book comes out . . . of course, with more changes . . . rewriting—"

"That's no way to talk! Serkin is one of the biggest names in the industry!" said Walter.

"Of course there'll be rewriting," said Shana, looking at Walter. "You're a far cry from Judith Krantz."

"But you can do it," said Walter.

"You're very lucky," Shana repeated, buttoning the three jet buttons on her mink coat.

"A wonderful chance," said Walter, brushing a speck of lint from his sleeve.

"You mean you sent Serkin the whole manuscript?" I asked, wanting all the information I could get out of them.

"Serkin buys scripts on an outline. Eight chapters were enough," said Walter coldly. "Along with a comprehensive outline."

"You sent eight chapters and an outline I've never seen? When my contract specifically says I have complete approval on all changes and publication?"

"Listen," said Walter, his voice almost a whisper, looking mean now and his mouth all pressed tight, "I realize this is your first literary child . . . but Shana and I have assisted in scores of births and we haven't lost one yet."

"Well, you lost this one! I'm not letting any other writer destroy what's left of my book!"

"Now, Lisa . . ." said Walter, brushing his sleeve again and his eyes all still, "you're just upset . . . had different expectations."

"Do you really think that after all the years of writing and rewriting *Princess* that I'd smile and say, 'Sure, Walter, okay, Shana'? Do you?"

"As I've told Lester a dozen times," said Walter, smiling this idiot smile at Shana, who was looking away, then at me, "Lisa Perlman is our favorite author, our most cooperative."

"Not anymore I'm not! I'm pulling out!" I shouted. "I'm not signing any fucking contract. Get someone else to write your slimo series."

Walter cleared his throat a couple of times and Shana's phones were ringing and they were both looking at me like I was this out-to-lunch person and I was feeling this awful feeling in my legs and the floor was going up and down, their faces shrinking into tiny dots. But I sat there real straight and looked them right in the old eyeball, just stared the fuckers down. No way was I going to let them get away with a fucking thing.

"Listen, young lady," said Walter, looking really mean now, "I've paid you ten thousand dollars and you have a three-book option. And speaking of contracts, remember, if *Princess* isn't published, you owe us the ten thousand."

"I owe you nothing! You ruined my book! You hurt my career! You took years out of my life!"

Walter walked back and forth now, but his eyes were quiet and he kept looking at Shana, sitting at her desk, still wearing the mink coat, looking out the window.

"Lisa . . . fame and fortune don't come overnight. A lot of authors would give their eyeteeth for the chance we're offering you. Why the outburst? It isn't like you."

"Because I'm an artist."

Walter stopped pacing and stood in front of Shana's desk, his hands folded, while Shana stood up and kept fussing with the lousy buttons on her coat, giving Walter this look two people have when they're in on some secret. And I was so mad, so mad I was shaking, really shaking. You couldn't see the shaking, it was more underneath the skin, like all the nerves in me came loose and the scream stuck in my throat, all stuck like it was ready to come out. Until I stood and said, "Send the entire *Princess* manuscript to Lester's office and a release from my contract. If you don't, I'll sue you!"

Somehow I grabbed my cape and walked out of the office. Outside the wind was howling and the sky was so dark that some traffic lights were on. But I couldn't hear the sounds. I couldn't. Everything was faded or blurred. I tried to hum and I kept puffing, wanting to scream out but I couldn't. My throat felt stuck, like in a dream when you want to scream and no sound comes out and I wanted to run down the street but my legs wouldn't move. So I stood there a second, trying to catch my breath, get my mind working. I dropped the little rhinoceros into the street and watched it crunch underneath thousands of feet. I began walking then, my feet heavy, like stuck to the ground, pushing one foot in front of the other, my head thumping like Shana's pencil, walking into the gray, faceless crowd until I merged with them, every bone in me aching, my skin sore like when air hits a burn. As I walked, my mind played back every moment, word, gesture . . . the sneaky look in Walter's eyes, the thin smirk on Shana's mouth. Shana never edited more than eight lousy chapters. Oh, God, what a mess. And they expected me to be grateful! The final slap in the face! And Lester—oh, God, Lester—if he hadn't been so greedy, selling my dream . . . if he had paid more attention . . . What a mess, a fucking mess, all because I let it happen, didn't believe in myself, in my book. I'd let them change my manuscript, just like the nebbish princess always changed to please everyone else. And God, the anger was going through me like air leaking from a blown air balloon, so fast, so big, I didn't know what to do with it. I didn't know. So I just kept walking, faster now, my feet pounding the pavement, pounding out the anger, walking by the trees so I could touch their yellowness, feel something real, walking until I felt the blister, an airless puff behind my right heel. And I held my hands in a fist and my mouth was all tight so the scream wouldn't come out all at once.

Finally, I stopped at a corner flower stand. A burst of blooms. Yellows, indigos, their petals puffed out like satin ball gowns just before a waltz. An old man wearing a heavy green quilted jacket— the Chinese kind—and a long red woolen scarf tied twice around his chin, smiled at me. His eyes were dark and sad.

"Violets, please," I said.

He smiled and wrapped the bunch of violets in thin green paper, then twisted a thick red rubber band around the bottom.

I crossed the street, moving faster, the blister burning, my arms, legs tingling, passed rows of tall houses with charred fronts . . . green plastic garbage bags, their knots squeezing shut the stench, piled high on the sidewalk. Clouds dotted the sky . . . the color of the sky neutral. I walked, walked until my blister popped. When I couldn't walk anymore. I went into this cathedral. Inside it was long and dim and cold. The incense burned my eyes. The pews were empty, except for a few nuns and priests, their heads bowed in prayer. For a while I stood there. And as I stood there, looking at the tall gold crucifix, my body shook, just began shaking, like the anger was shaking right through me, wanting to come out, and I gasped until the anger soaked my body, soaked up my body. After a few minutes, I left.

The air seemed darker. Probably a storm brewing. Sirens were screeching and the sound from the traffic was one big boom, the city rattling like an explosion. I bought roasted chestnuts at the corner, but they tasted bitter. I caught a taxi. Inside it was warm. The leather seats were ripped and smelled of perspiration. I asked the driver to take me to the Guggenheim Museum.

I loved the Guggenheim . . . the Frank Lloyd Wright design, all open . . . the circular tiers winding around the light-filled galleries. Usually I'd stop and look at each painting and sculpture. This time I didn't. I only wanted to see Eva Hesse's work, like seeing her work would bring me back to life.

Finally I stood in front of Hesse's massive sculptures. Her work always blows me away. Sure, the critics go on and on about her absurdist view of the world, her psychologically focused art, her sexual string motifs, enough to make you wacko, but inside her massive strings, there's a lightness of spirit. And I thought about her pain, setbacks, God, what she went thorugh shouldn't happen to a dog, and as I looked at her work, the knots, ropes, my eyes drew in her strength, pulling her strength into me, back into me.

Suddenly I wanted to hurry home, back to San Francisco, and finish *Eva,* move into life, my reality. I glanced at my watch. Back to the Waldorf.

The lobby was crowded. Bellboys pushed metal carts piled with expensive luggage, Muzak drifted through the lobby, competing with the swoosh from revolving doors, rattling desk keys, boisterous greetings from conventioneers wearing name tags and carrying tote bags from expensive shops, some dragging whiny kids, clutching postcards. And long lines of tired-looking men and women carrying briefcases or bags strapped across their shoulders waited patiently at the check-out desk. I sat in the back of the lobby on a red velvet curved loveseat, facing the main entrance and the dozens of clocks flashing time from all over the world . . . time, so strange, always seems close, but then when something happens—a disappointment, a loss—suddenly so far away, like it runs away with a part of you. Later I'd call Jenny . . . tell her that I'd be home the next day . . . that the book didn't work out, assure her that I was fine . . . no, probably better if I waited until I got home, because Jenny'd worry . . . she knows how much *Princess* meant to me. Mother . . . poor Mother. Lester . . . I dreaded telling Lester. Eric . . . I didn't want to tell . . . admit . . . oh, God, oh, I'd see . . . right now I'd get through Amy. Anyways, I sat there, pretending I didn't hurt, clutching the violets, until I spotted Amy and Adam. She was wearing the red beanie. Her face was flushed from the wind. Adam was wearing a heavy brown tweed overcoat. When they saw me they rushed toward me.

"Mom! Tell us everything! We're dying!"

I gave Amy the violets. She looked confused, just stood there holding the violets and looking at me.

"Aren't they beautiful? So purple."

"Mom, what's wrong? You look like you've seen a ghost. Mom . . ." said Amy, her voice drifting.

"Lisa," said Adam, "what happened?"

"Sit down," I said. They looked at each other anxiously, then sat down. I told them as clearly, as slowly as I could, what happened at Walter and Shana's, all about Serkin, the whole mess, that I'd refused to go on, while Amy's green eyes slowly filled with tears and Adam frowned and kept shaking his head.

"Mom," said Amy, gently holding my hand. "Oh, Mom."

"My God," said Adam, when I finished talking, "that's the worst thing I've heard. You've got a case, Lisa . . . you could sue the hell out of them. Get some bucks."

"Adam, she doesn't want to."

"And Lisa, would it be so terrible having a miniseries?" said Adam, turning away from Amy. "Give Serkin a shot. You'd make even more money."

"My mom's an artist."

"Artists don't make money," said Adam. "Lisa, maybe if you read Judith Krantz—"

"Adam, how dare you?" said Amy, looking furious and taking my hand. "My mom doesn't need to read Judith Krantz."

Silence.

"Apologize to Mom!" demanded Amy.

"Don't argue. Please stop with the arguing."

"I won't apologize," said Adam, glaring at Amy, "because I'm right. In this business, you play the game. There are only winners and losers."

"What do you know," said Amy, her voice rising, "about years of writing?! My mom's worked like a dog! All you know are your tanning salons and Armani suits and your upper-ten-percent celebrity clients!"

"I'm leaving!" said Adam, his face turning all red.

So, lo and behold, there I was sitting with my hands folded like I just got off the boat, the kids glaring at each other. Until dear Adam, big as life, got up and walked out. Amy sat next to me and then, to top everything, as if things weren't bad enough, Amy put her head on my shoulder and began crying.

"Oh, darling, don't cry. Let's go upstairs . . . or do you want a wine spritzer or. . ."

"I feel so bad for you, Mom," she said between sobs.

"Don't. I'm fine. I really am. Sure, I'm disappointed . . . hurt . . . but I'll get over it."

"Do you have any Kleenex, Mom?"

"Yes. Here," I said, opening my purse, then giving her the Kleenex.

She blew her nose and patted her eyes.

"Adam and I are *kaput* anyway . . . so don't think this is your fault, Mom. We've been having problems for a while."

"My God."

"He thought you'd be a star. And I stayed with him because I don't have enough money saved for my own apartment. He's a phony. He sees other women. Expects me to go along with it. Such an asshole," she said, blowing her nose again. Her fingers were red. "He's changed, Mom. He's not the same Adam I met four years ago. Adam has everything, Mom—he's brilliant, he's good-looking, ever since he's in the law firm and starting to make money all the women are after him. He's changed. I hate him." She burst into tears again.

"Maybe you're the one who's changed. Relationships change. They don't satisfy the same," I said, taking her hand and holding it tight. "You've grown."

"I hurt," she said.

"Of course you hurt. You and Adam have had a lot together . . . a lot," I said, hoping I wouldn't start crying. "Shared a lot with Adam. Of course you hurt."

"I don't know what I'm going to do. He's so selfish. I've left him before. But I have no place to go. I don't have enough money . . . I only make eighteen thousand. By the time I pay the rent . . . my student loan—"

"You can't stay with Adam just because you have no place to go. There's always an alternative."

"I guess I could stay with Bonnie . . . I've stayed with her before. She's one of my best friends at work . . . a writer, too . . . Mom," she said, perking up, "Bonnie knows this guy who has a first cousin who manages this great—really incredible—apartment house on Murray Hill . . . and Bonnie said that if I could come up with a thousand dollars for the key fee I could rent a studio."

"I'll sell 'Fear of Success,' that's what I'll do. Scanga is hot now . . . really hot. Neil Thompson's offered me seven thousand, and . . . oh, what the hell."

"Oh, Mom . . . no . . . you can't," she said, looking relieved. "You're always selling your things."

"I'll express the money to you. I want you to have your apartment. You have to."

Amy wiped her eyes.

"Mom . . . what are you going to do?"

"What do you mean, 'do'? I'm leaving today. I'll stand by for the red-eye."

"I mean, about money? You can't go on just writing," she said anxiously. "You can't, Mom. You have to face it."

"Face what?" I said, concentrating on keeping very cool, not letting Amy see how shocked I still was. "That I might get disappointed again? Of course I'll go on. I keep remembering that Eva Hesse said, 'I know that vision or concept will come through total risk.' "

"Mom," she murmured, shaking her head and looking concerned.

"I'll get a job," I said quickly, aware she was scared, that my words sounded hollow, like a television ending. "Part-time . . . one that will fit into my writing schedule . . . sell art, maybe."

We held hands then, though our fingertips didn't touch. We watched the clocks . . . just watched time flashing in and out of the world. Until Amy said, "I'll try and come home for Nana's birthday party."

"Oh, that'd be wonderful," I said kissing her on the cheek. "A landmark."

"Yes."

I looked away, couldn't look into her eyes. See the wanting.

"Things could be worse," said Amy, sighing. Her eyes were swollen.

"Oh, yes, they could."

Silence.

Amy sniffed.

"I miss having my mother with me."

"I miss you, too. It's hard . . . so far away. . . ."

Silence.

"Will you stay overnight with me? We'll order pastrami sandwiches. Talk."

She nodded.

We watched the clocks until dusk covered the lobby. The rattle of luggage carts, the swoosh of revolving doors, our shadows long. Her hand little. She pulled it away a little, but then I felt her fingertips touch mine. Then we went upstairs.

CHAPTER TWELVE

Phew! If there's a God in Heaven, she didn't like me. I arrived at the San Francisco airport . . . 4:00 A.M. Bleak as hell . . . gray, tired faces. The red-eye flight a nightmare. Never again.

I went into the house, the kitchen first and pulled up the shades. Then I picked up Anny and hugged her real tight. God, she felt good, all warm. I was tired, so tired. I kept picking up my avocado plant and putting it down, not knowing what to do first, just touching things, walking around the kitchen, trying to get my thoughts in order, rattle the shock out of me. For a while I sat at the kitchen table, the avocado plant bouncing up and down in the water, thinking about all those years of rewriting *Princess* and how I'd let everybody fuck up my work.

Suddenly I lifted my foot and tapped the wall, then I tapped the wall harder, then I began kicking the wall, just kicking it, then kicking the cartons with the old *Princess* drafts, kicking the cartons, grabbing pages from the boxes and looking at the passages I'd worked over for years, crying the whole time, crying like a baby. I wanted to get *Princess* out of my life, out of it once and for all. *Princess* only a made-up dream, all made up, no such thing only made up. . . . So long, *Princess*! So I began stacking the *Princess* cartons in the corner, deciding I'd carry the cartons into the garage. Get them out. Old dreams, musty old dreams. Get them all out. I opened the window. The damp air whooshed into the room. I began taking the pictures of Walter and Shana off the bulletin board and dropping them into the cat wastebasket. I watered the rubber plant Aunt Sally gave me last Chanukah, then cleaned off my worktable, re-stacking pages from *Eva,* getting everything ready.

All this stuff took up most of the day, and though I felt really crappy, soon my world was coming back. And the next day I'd start writing no matter how lousy I felt, that much I knew. So I closed the door to the den and decided I'd call Mother, get that

over with . . . then next I'd call Jenny . . . the next day Lester
. . . God, I dreaded talking to Lester, telling him I was firing him,
that I'd had it . . . and Eric . . . I wasn't sure I'd call Eric . . . I
didn't know if I wanted to.

Late that afternoon I called Mother. The phone rang several times,
then Mother answered.

"Hello, hello!"

"Mother . . . Lisa."

"Lisa! How's New York? Is it cold?"

"I'm home."

"Home!"

"Home, Mother."

Pause. My voice broke. Silence, Christopher barking in the background. I covered the receiver so that she wouldn't hear my crying.
I didn't want her to hear my crying.

"Don't tch-tch-tch . . . please, Mother. . . ." I managed to say.

"What happened?"

"It's a long story. But *Princess* didn't work out. And I refused to
rewrite it."

"I should say not!"

I sniffed a few times, catching my breath.

Silence.

Finally in her tiny voice she said, "All along I knew . . . had a
feeling something funny . . . never heard of a book taking so long.
But what do I know? I'm only the mother."

"I don't want to talk about it now. When I see you . . . maybe
tomorrow . . . or the next day . . . we'll have lunch. I just need
a couple of days. But I promise I'll tell you everything . . . every
detail."

"You need rest," she said. "You look like a rag lately."

"Please, Mother."

"Tch-tch-tch."

"Okay."

"All right."

"Okay."

"Lisa?"

"Hmmm."

"Do you need money? I have a little money Sidney doesn't know about. I take it from his wallet while he's sleeping," she said with a giggle.

I laughed.

"Thanks, Mother. But I'll be okay. I have my new book."

"Tch-tch. Where do you think the money's going to come from? From that cheapskate Nobel Prize funny you run around with?"

I sighed . . . popped my tongue. . . . "Margy's Boutique is always asking me to work. So I'll work there on weekends, evenings. Anyways, don't worry. I'll get along. I always do."

"Lisa, Cala Market is selling lottery tickets . . . Sylvia Finkel won five thousand dollars . . . not that she needs it . . . the pill."

"Uh-huh." Pause. "How's Bruce?"

"I dreamed about Bruce. He looked so wonderful, Lisa," she said, her voice drifting, "so I just know everything will be fine."

"Yes, I'm sure. Bruce takes care of himself."

"That boy always gets headaches."

"Shame."

"Birdie just washed some nice shrimps. Bruce and I'll bring you a nice shrimp salad," she repeated. "Or a nice cake. I made a lemon cake."

"No, thanks, Mother."

Pause.

"You're strong, Lisa. You'll do it . . . you'll see. You'll come out smelling like a rose."

"Oh, Mother," I said, sniffing, "do you think so?"

"I know so."

"Thank you."

"You'll meet someone wonderful. Have a normal life. I'll give you my Saks card. Buy yourself nice clothes, not those hippie clothes you wear . . . have a normal life."

"I don't want a normal life!"

"Don't raise your voice. You're too excitable, and high blood pressure runs in our family."

"Uh-huh. Okay."

"I'll drop off the shrimp salad. Have a nice day, dear. Hang in."

Click.

Next I dialed Jenny.

"Extension two-two-one, please. Jenny Perlman."

"Mom! Amy called this morning and told me what happened. I would've picked you up at the airport."

"I didn't want to bother you. I came in on the red-eye."

"Oh, Mom, you poor thing," she said maternally. "Do you want me to leave work and come home?"

"Of course not, darling. I'm fine. Tomorrow I'll start working."

"Give me a break," she said. "Mom, you should rest."

"Today I will."

"What happened?"

"Oh, I'll tell you the story later. But I knew it was coming. It was my fault for letting them change my book."

"Mom . . . I've gotta get back to work . . . but I'll come over after work."

"What about school? Did you register?"

"Yes."

"Good."

"I have a yeast infection."

"My God. After work, go see Dr. Chan. Promise. Don't worry about me."

"Have to get off the phone, Mom."

"Okay . . . but be sure and see Dr. Chan. Call me afterward. Please."

"Okay, okay "

"I love you, Jen."

"Bye, Mom."

Click.

I made a few more calls, wanting connections, familiar voices, consistencies. I talked to Marcie Kaplan for almost an hour, told her the whole story while she cried, murmuring that women still get fucked over and that she was glad I came to my senses and said no and stuck to my guns and what I was writing was more impor-tant and suggesting that I see her new psychic, who works with creative women. And then I called Larry Segal in Los Angeles and told him the whole story while he kept interrupting and yelling that publishers suck and don't know a thing about writers and that he was sick of the whole business and ready to throw in the towel and while he cried I consoled him and urged him never to give up, write his novel, until he promised he wouldn't give up and then hung up. And then I began to feel better. So the rest of the day and evening I busied myself with the little things . . . laundry . . . even cleaned out my closet, putting the unworn things in a box for the Salvation Army . . . thinking about Eric. That night I slept a heavy, dark sleep, Anny next to me.

The next morning I called Lester and made an appointment for noon. He was curt on the phone. I knew he'd already talked with Walter because through his brittle tone I could hear the disappointment.

I parked the car on Union Street. The street was crowded with well-dressed tourists browsing leisurely in the expensive, trendy shops. I locked the car, making sure I wasn't in a yellow zone. All I needed, another ticket. Carrying my briefcase, I hurried along the street, my feet numb, like walking on blocks and kind of dizzy.

I climbed the long stairway . . . humming some dum-de-dum tune, stepping over the loose step, thinking how many years I'd walked up these stairs, dropping off drafts on Lester's doorstep. The hall smelled musty, of paint. Funny how familiar things . . . things you get used to . . . a crack on a wall . . . a loose step . . . smell of paint . . . pieces of life . . . engrain your mind forever.

Even though the door to Lester's office was open, I rang the little old doorbell. Harry's low growl . . . of all days, I thought, that mental dog was there.

"It's Lisa!" I called.

"Come on up!" called Lester.

When I came into the low-ceilinged, narrow room, Cindy, Lester's secretary, gave me a perfunctory nod. Lester hung up the telephone. Wearing a tweed jacket, a blue cable sweater vest, he came toward me, smiling, but underneath his cool poise, you could feel the unspoken tension.

He kissed me, his eyes averted.

"You look great," he said.

"I don't feel so great."

"Sit, Lisa," he said, sitting in his chair, patting gross Harry, tied to Lester's chair by a long red leather leash. I sat across from Lester, a narrow space between us, trying not to look at Harry. Lester opened a bottle of beer—imported beer, the kind wrapped in gold paper with a gold crest—then lit a long, thin cigarette. Along the narrow white-lacquered table were stacked piles of manuscripts, red boxes, above Lester's desk a photograph of Lester with William Styron. Lester watched me through the puffs of smoke. I put on my dark glasses. Not just because the light hurt my eyes, but the red manuscript boxes . . . manuscripts . . . hurtful reminders.

"So!" said Lester, an edge to his smooth voice, still watching me closely and looking at me with forced cheer. "I talked to Walter. He told me that you got a little upset about the miniseries . . . another writer. . . ."

"Uh-huh."

"But I explained to him that sometimes you get a little neurotic . . . emotional." He paused and smiled like an indulgent parent. "But I said, 'Walter, I'm neurotic, too.' I assured him that when I explained to you about the miniseries—all the money you'll make— that you'd make the necessary adjustments."

"I won't make any adjustments! I've already done that. Or sign any contract. I want out! I fired Avalon. I want my manuscript back, or I'll sue!"

He tapped his cigarette with his forefinger twice, as if pressing out the tiny fleck of ash curled around the tip.

"Look, Lisa," he said, his voice all soft, "I have forty-two hard-backs out this year . . . all best sellers. You have a three-book option, a chance for a miniseries, a chance most authors, better writers than you, would sell their souls for. . . ."

"I already did. And it didn't work."

He looked away, sipped some beer. Then he turned and faced me. "Never mind all that," he said. "Just get back to work."

"I am, but not on *Princess*."

"What do you mean?"

"I mean I'm finishing my new book—"

"Who do you think you are?!" he yelled. "I don't have time for this nonsense! I'm trying to make you a star!"

"I don't want to be a star!" I yelled. "You can't package me anymore . . . like a pile of dreams. I'm an artist, not a hack writing rinky-dink glitz!"

"You're not!" he screamed. "You write good commercial shit, and I'm trying to make it marketable! Be grateful for that!"

"For letting Shana take two years out of my life? For letting them sell me down the river? Grateful? For what?!"

"How dare you!" he screamed, opening a blue box marked *Princess* and grabbing some pages from the top of the pile.

"Listen to this!" he shrieked, rattling the page and holding it close to his red face. "Page fourteen, you wrote, 'lust-filled eyes'!" And you call yourself an artist!"

" 'Lust'?"

" 'Lust'!" he screamed, still rattling the page.

"I didn't write 'lust'! Shana did! She loves words like 'lust' and 'fuck'!"

"Stop whining about Shana! She's one of the best editors in New York!"

"She ruined my book!"

"My writers don't write 'lust'! How dare you? You write shit like 'lust' and you have the nerve to sit there and refuse to sign a million-dollar deal! 'Lust'!" he repeated, waving the page again, and wacko Harry going wild and growling, his overbite all pointy. Even Cindy stopped typing.

"Now take this shit out of here!" he yelled, throwing the pages on the floor.

For a second I sat there, frozen, Lester covering his face with his hands, Cindy typing, Harry barking, and the lousy phones ringing. I wanted to say "Up yours!" or something, but I was so mad I couldn't talk anymore. Finally I stood up and said, "If I don't get the manuscript and a release from Avalon, I'll sue. I mean it."

Lester didn't answer. I stepped over the pages on the floor and grabbed my briefcase and got out of there, out of there so fast. My head was spinning. I ran down the steps two at a time.

All gray outside. The clouds floated upside down, broke into pieces, houses with no tops, bottoms, sounds under water, faded, glub, glub. I got into the car, my feet heavy, Lester's voice ringing in my ears, his dream all gone. I drove home.

* * *

When I got home I walked through the house, counting the shadows going up the walls, trying to get my bearings. I felt drained, at the same time relieved that *Princess* was over. I wanted to see Eric, talk to him, be with him. I went to the phone and dialed his number.

"Eric . . . it's Lisa."

"How are you, Lisa? How's the book? What happened?"

"I'm home."

Silence.

"Eric, I need to see you."

"Are you okay?" he asked softly.

"Not really. Kind of depressed. *Princess* is shelved. Didn't work out, I mean. I refused to do it their way. Go along with their sleazo miniseries. Oh, it's a long story. I'll tell you later."

Silence.

"I need to see you . . . talk to you."

"I'd come over and see you," he said, "but I've invited the Reinhardts and the Goldfarbs for dinner. A little Nobel celebration. Why don't you come over? After they leave we'll talk. You'll stay over."

"All right."

"At six."

"Eric. . ."

"Yes?"

"I miss you . . . and I love you."

"I miss you, too."

"Bye, baby."

I soaked in the bath, the warm water soothing, telling myself to pull myself together, that I had a lot of work to do on *Eva*. I couldn't wait to see Eric. Couldn't wait. I was going to let it all out, tell him that I loved him and that I wanted us to work out. Anyways, after the bath I dressed in the jeans, a white rose painted along the leg, my ivory silk blouse and long white feather earrings. Parted my hair in the middle and wound it into two loops secured low at the nape of my neck. Inside one loop I sprayed some silver sequins, the cheap stick-on kind. Then I left and drove to Berkeley.

* * *

When I arrived at Eric's house, he answered the door. His friends were already in the living room. We kissed in the hall and I murmured that I needed to talk to him, that I felt awful. He gave me this silent look, eyeing the white rose. He was cool, like he'd turned off. Even seemed angry at me for needing him, or something. Anyways, Eric introduced me to his friends. And while Eric went into the kitchen and cooked the dinner, I sat and made small talk.

After Eric cooked this really good trout, there I was at Eric's kitchen table, playing anagrams with these five geniuses. Seymour Reinhardt, a chemist I'll call Egghead; his wife, Betty Ann, a slender brunette; Albert, a mathematician; and Holly. And God, you'd think they were playing for blood, screaming out the words before the letters were barely turned. While I sat there with one nebbish word, "gnat," everyone had fought over, including Eric, who claimed he'd called it first. So, with a sicko smile on my face, pretending I was having a merry old time, I screamed out the words along with them like I'd called out the words too late. For most of the evening, during dinner . . . even during the games . . . everyone argued, their voices screeching, about nuclear warfare or birth control in Africa, or about the happenings on campus. Or Betty Ann, in a tiny voice you could hardly hear, explained her creative therapy in prisons, and Holly, who had a voice that could crack glass, monopolized the conversation, going on about her potluck dinners for women poets over fifty. The guys carried on about Eric's Nobel Prize . . . his cellometer, their computers, dartboards, Raleigh bikes, their partridges in their pear trees, while Eric, crabbier than hell and with that poor-me expression on his face, remained sullen and ignored me. Ever since I'd arrived he'd acted funny . . . polite but distant . . . acted like I was someone off the boat. No one special in his life. And during dinner, coughing, almost choking to death from a bone, Seymour Reinhardt slapped my back until I almost keeled over, while Eric just sat there, just sat there like he didn't notice. I ignored him, too, not commenting when every minute someone repeated one of Eric's anecdotes or equations or another little Nobel Prize story. But during the entire dinner, before and after, I could feel Eric's hawk eyes watching my every move and his dumbo ears listening to my every word. Especially when I pontificated about abortion rights while Betty Ann, her mouth full of trout, screamed, "Murderess! Murderess!" God, it was awful. The tension between Eric and me was pretty uncomfortable, but I made the best of it, telling myself as soon as everyone left I'd have my countdown.

Then Holly, a squat blond woman with tiny, close-set eyes in a Miss Piggy face, wearing a too-large U.C. Berkeley sweat shirt, suggested that we all go hot-tubbing.

"O . . . kay," said Eric, scooping the letters from the table and dropping them into a cigar box.

"You're on," said Albert, a pale-faced, skinny blond man wearing horn-rimmed glasses and a bright blue running suit.

"Oh, one more game!" moaned Egghead, the big winner, still adding up his score on a yellow notepad. He was a tall, heavyset man with a red face and a bald head, kind of pointed on the top.

"Oh, come on, honey," said Betty Ann, blowing in his ear. "The water'll be good for your stress."

"How about you, Lisa?" said Eric, looking at me with forced politeness.

"Well, okay, sure, why not?" I said jauntily, pretending hot-tubbing naked with strangers was no biggie. "May as well be a Berkeleyan. Just take off my feather earrings and I'm on my way."

Albert laughed, while Eric gave me a dirty look.

"Robes are in the downstairs bathroom," said Eric, getting up and clearing the kitchen counter, piled with dirty dishes.

So while everyone scurried off, squealing like a bunch of pack-rats, Eric and I cleared the table, exchanging small talk about how Eric made the guacamole. You could feel the scream, the silent scream. Prince Charming's brooding, his silent disapproval, his eyes picking away at me, and when our hands touched, Eric looked away. So after we finished rinsing the crud from the dishes and put them in the dishwasher, we went upstairs into Eric's bedroom and began undressing. Eric turned his back to me and undressed while I crouched in the corner by the bed, watching him.

"Obviously I annoy you," I finally said.

"You do," he said, not turning around, "but I'm biting my tongue."

"Oh, how Nobel . . . how indulgent you are."

"Lisa, I'm getting irritated. I'm not in the mood."

"You're not in the mood! Did you stop to think that I feel shitty . . . that I've had a major disappointment in my life? That I'm hurting? I need you right now! Look at me when I talk to you! Two people are here!"

Eric turned around slowly, reluctantly, and faced me. "I don't like the way you handled yourself in front of my friends. You said some dumb things . . . a poor reflection on me."

"Always you! Worried about what everyone thinks of you! So full of yourself. That's why you're stuck!"

"Maybe it's insecurity," he said, turning away. "But you're always praising yourself. For example," he said in a tone like lecturing his class and pulling off his underwear, "someone mentions art. Right away you say, 'Oh, I know a lot about art.' "

"I do! And your friends don't! All they can talk about are their political slogans—bor . . . ing!"

"Seymour Reinhardt is a very important man . . . a smart man. Chairman of our nuclear program."

"He's a horse's ass."

"He's not!"

"He is."

"I don't like this shit!" he yelled, tying the belt to his robe in a knot twice around his waist. "Stop haranguing me! You know what happens when you lecture me."

"Too bad! If I want to talk, I'll talk! I'm sick of your telling me when to talk, when not to, how to pronounce words, always directing traffic. Even in sex—lick, bite, do—I'm sick of it!"

"Any other complaints?" he said, sitting on the edge of the bed, looking at his feet.

"You don't have the guts to pick out loud . . . give me the privilege of picking back. You're a coward . . . sneaky."

"Look, Lisa!" he yelled, looking up at me. "You're the one who said you didn't want to see me. You dumped me."

"Oh, don't use that Sad Sack stuff on me. You just don't want to admit that I want more than you're willing to give."

"You talk too much," he said, looking at his feet again.

Silence. Eric picked at his toenail, then got up and shuffled across the room. He opened the closet door, then turned and looked at me.

"There's a robe," he said, pointing to a feminine-looking blue dotted robe hanging on the hook inside the closet door.

Covering my breasts, I quickly put on the robe, so small it barely covered my ass, thinking probably Deborah's. Eric had said Deborah is tiny. I followed Professor Shit down the long flight of stairs, practically tripping over the tennis balls, cords, Eric way ahead of me, his rubber thongs slapping against the dusty plank floors, outside to the patio. And wouldn't you know it but the eager beavers were already in the tub, oohing and aahing about the wonderful water, Egghead oohing so loud he sounded like a moose in heat.

"Come on in! The water's great!" he shouted, splashing water over his hairy chest, moving his spindly arms in and out of the water, like swimming. Eric took off his robe and hopped gracefully over the edge, his gladiator body a pale silhouette in the moonlight.

"We won't look," said Holly, covering her eyes with her hand and bobbing up and down like a rubber decoy. "C'mon, Lisa!"

So, squinting my eyes so everyone would shrink into tiny dots, I took off the *shmatte* robe and covered my breasts with my arms, thanking God it was dark and, as quickly as possible, got into the stupid tub, submerging my body in the steamy water.

"Oh, the water is good," I said, the steam curling my hair. And God, the moon was so pale, all distant, like it was floating behind a thin, dark mist. And the crickets, must've been hundreds of them, sounded like a little symphony. Max was creeping around the edge of the hot tub, his tail straight up, enjoying the heat. And for a while everyone bobbed up and down in the water, splashing and moaning their delight, their bodies in the moonlight pale, shadowy things.

"Eric says your first novel will be published soon, that you've been in New York," said Betty Ann politely, her long hair pinned to the top of her head.

"Well . . . I . . ."

"Lisa doesn't like to talk about it," said Eric, kicking me under the water.

"What's it about?" asked Egghead, breathing hard and snorting water, his legs under water moving up and down like riding a bicycle.

"A Jewish princess," said Eric before I could answer, thinking that I wanted to tell them.

Everyone laughed. "I've got a Jewish princess right here," said Egghead, pinching Betty Ann on the ass, while Betty Ann screeched, "Stop it, Seymour!"

"Which house?" asked Holly, her big breasts floating on top of the water like little sails.

"Avalon," quickly said Eric.

"My God! They published *Lust's Angels!* Is your book a romance?" she said in a challenging tone and looking at Eric with an alarmed expression on her Miss Piggy face.

"Quite the contrary. It's about a woman who grows out of her thing for torture freaks."

"Who are they?" asked Betty Ann, looking at Holly, who was poking Seymour, who was blinking nervously and watching Eric, who remained cool as a cucumber.

"The Jewish prince, of course," I said, splashing water on my face and bobbing up and down myself now. "You know, he has the hots for women who torture him. The guilt shtick . . . too much Mom, you know. . . ."

"A riot," said Betty Ann, making this sicko little laugh like she wasn't sure whether to laugh or not.

"Poor bastard," said Seymour, glancing at Betty Ann, who was smiling solicitously toward Eric.

"Hasn't that been done with *Portnoy?*" said Seymour, "and also—"

"The princess has been overdone, too!" shouted Holly.

"We've all been done!" I snapped. "Right, Eric?"

"Lisa's going to get an Academy Award," said Eric, grinning like he was amused.

"Who'd you study with?" asked Holly, assuming a grave expression on her face, like I was some dodo bird.

"Study?" I repeated, feeling nauseated from the heat.

"Lisa studied at San Francisco State," answered Eric, poking me.

"My sister writes romances. Very successful, too," said Seymour.

"Well, I can't wait to read it," said Betty Ann, smiling sweetly.

"Romances make money," said Egghead, winking at Eric.

"It's not a romance," I repeated, my voice rising. "Oooops, sorry I splashed you, Eric. Besides, it's not being published, anyway."

Dead silence. Eric all quiet.

"Good," said Holly, breaking the silence. "Because Albert and I don't read commercial literature, do we, Albert?" lisped Holly, looking at Albert, whose head was tilted back and leaned against the edge of the hot tub.

"Holly doesn't like anything but Gide and Fournier," explained Albert, looking embarrassed, Eric not saying a word.

"That's a crock of shit!" I said angrily, really fed up with Eric, all of them, their pompous tone. "That's like saying there's no music but Mozart."

"There isn't!" said Holly with a laugh, looking at Eric, who remained silent but who had a superior grin on his face.

"So Lisa," said Seymour, breaking the tension, trying to be polite, "are you writing a second book?"

"Yes."

"What's that about?" asked Holly.

"A biographical novel about Eva Hesse."

"Who?" asked Betty Ann.

"A sculptor. Died at thirty-four."

"Oh, I know!" said Egghead, clicking his fingers. "I remember an exhibit at the Berkeley Museum . . . really weird, far-out stuff . . . ropes . . . sexual images . . . weird. . . ."

"Oscar Wilde said art should never try to be popular. The public should try to make itself artistic," I said, splashing Eric.

"A lot of that modern stuff is hard to take," said Seymour.

"Less is more—more or less," quipped Holly and laughed.

"Lisa's upset tonight," explained Eric.

I dunked some more in the hot tub, my contact lenses fogged from steam.

"I . . . I have a book in me . . . just haven't had time," said Seymour. He pointed to his head. "It's all in here. All I have to do is write it."

"Who do you read?" asked Holly.

"Faulkner . . . Mailer."

"Mailer is a hack," said Holly.

"He's laughing all the way to the bank . . . and he's a damned fine writer."

"I agree with Holly," said Eric.

"He writes with guts, craft—"

Eric kicked me under the water. Then Betty Ann and Egghead complained they were getting too hot and lounged their Nautilus bodies on the edge of the hot tub, posed like nymphets. Everyone began arguing about the famine in India, more about Norman Mailer, and then about some eleventh-century Hindu monk-poet. Oh, then to top it, they argued about the best way to travel around the world on two dollars a day, Eric screaming he could do it on a dollar and subsist on rice and banana leaves. Like traveling or having fun was a strategy or a win. While they discussed their student ratings, I dunked under the water, trying not to stare at Egghead's humongous you-know-what, ready to whoops from the heat, until my skin got all wrinkled like a prune.

"So," said Betty Ann after some while and smiling nervously and looking toward Eric, "I think it's so romantic how you and Eric met . . . at the French Hotel, over espressos. . . ."

"We met through an ad . . . the *Bay Guardian*. I advertised for a genius."

"Well, you got one!" exclaimed Holly.

"Lisa's kidding," said Eric, kicking the hell out of my knee and glaring at me.

"I needed material . . . for an article I'm doing on genius princes who answer ads. . . ."

Egghead laughed. "You devil, Eric . . . you've been holding out on us."

"Eric, you didn't tell me about Lisa," said Holly, bobbing up and down.

"Eric's very private," I said.

Holly laughed nervously and the moonlight made everyone look like silver seals.

"I'd be afraid to put in an ad," said Betty Ann, covering her breasts and shuddering like she was suddenly cold.

"You never know," said Holly, shaking her head.

"Oh, the ads are full of victims. Good material," I said, laughing, not caring that my laugh was the only one and rang hollow . . . drifted. . . .

"Is Eric in your book?" asked Seymour, looking sympathetically toward Eric, whose silence was so heavy.

"I don't use my life . . . or the people in it. . . . Besides, Eric is too . . . well . . ."

"Predictable," said Betty Ann, laughing.

"Normal," said Holly, patting Eric's arm.

"Predictably unpredictable," said Egghead.

"My fiction men have pizzazz, sensuous sleaze," I said.

And then there was this awful quiet . . . God, the crickets sounded like a troop of banshees, and the bubbling sound from the water like a crater and everyone was looking at each other, then making small talk about how weird the moon was, pretending they didn't know that Eric was angry. I wanted to break the ice and get the conversation rolling. So I asked, "How'd you meet? I love to hear about how couples meet."

"At a Mensa dance," said Betty Ann.

"Mensa?" I repeated. "What's Mensa?"

"Mensa!" repeated Egghead impatiently and giving me a funny look, then at Eric, who looked embarrassed as hell. "It's an organization of the highest IQs in the country . . . the ninety-eighth percentile . . . top two percent."

"Oh . . . *that* Mensa," I said, kicking Eric back, not caring that they were all silent and looking at me like I was some kind of Dumb Dora.

"We're all Mensans. So is Eric," said Betty Ann. "We met at a Mensa 'Pre-Mensans' meeting. Pre-Mensans are children of Mensans."

"I'm a member of Densa," I said, laughing and not caring that they weren't laughing, too, and that Eric looked like he was ready to go under.

"Densa, that's good," said Seymour, snorting loudly and splashing water on his head.

"Mensa is an excellent organization," said Betty Ann, stretching her long, lithe body, her feet rubbing Egghead's thing. "You meet interesting people. Over fifty-two thousand members."

"I think it's archaic," I said, splashing water toward Eric's face. "People shouldn't be separated . . . God!" I continued, my voice rising. "Who the hell wants to go to a party and say, 'Oh, hi, I'm Lisa Mensa . . . one seventy-two . . . wanna dance?' "

"Enough, Lisa!" shouted Eric.

"Don't yell at her!" said Betty Ann, smiling nervously and looking at Egghead, who was making these moose sounds again and then everyone splashed some more, Betty Ann's breasts flopping up and down, until, thank God, after they talked some more about Mensa this, Mensa that, singing their Mensan troop song, they decided they had it and got out of the tub and went into the house. After I got out of the tub and went back into the house and said good-bye to the group, I went upstairs and quickly dressed.

When I came downstairs, Eric was sitting in the dark living room in the worn leather chair, his legs stretched out and his feet on the footstool. It was quiet except for the sound from Max scratching at the kitchen door and the tin "Peace" signs banging against the windows and our silence noisy with our anger. Eric was smoking a long narrow cigar, looking at me like he was looking through something. Even in the dark, I could feel his hostility. I stood there a second, watching the smoke ring drift across the room, almost blue in the dark. And for a second, a split second, I wanted to scream out, "You shmuck! I love you, you shmuck! I know what you're doing!" But I couldn't, I couldn't. It was over and I wouldn't give Eric his ending. So I stood there a second longer, my hands pressed against my mouth so that I couldn't scream out my anger or let out my tears, my hands feeling as big as an elephant. I gathered up my things then and somehow—don't ask me how—I managed to walk across the room, which seemed endless, careful not to slip and fall on my ass from the slippery floors.

I opened the door and ran down the steps, practically tripping over the stacks of old newspapers, and got into my car, locking the door because I saw Eric rushing toward me. I backed the car from the driveway as quickly as possible, not looking back, not once, not even when Eric called "Lisa . . . Lisa . . . Lisa! . . ." I didn't stop, just kept going until I reached the freeway, then I drove in the slow lane, keeping my eyes wide open, so wide they hurt, because if I blinked I'd cry holy hell. So I just held the steering wheel tight, so tight, and thank God, the moon followed me all the way home.

CHAPTER THIRTEEN

May already . . . God, the rain never stopped. But the leaves were so green, shiny. And I could see spring on the trees, the tiniest pink blossoms. Time softly tapped my window, my face changing, subtle changes. Like all the losses I was finally feeling were coming through my face. Especially in the eyes. Disappointment pressed them deeper, more somber. Tiny creases around my mouth. My face shaping, pulling back, forming another me. Sometimes I'd look in the mirror and squint my eyes, imagine my face years older, the thick dark eyebrows dotted with gray, my hair still brown like my grandmother's, deeper lines between my wide-set eyes, my father's eyes, the bones harsher, tiny red veins growing under my pale skin, Mother's skin. But I liked the changes, even relieved the old face was fading.

After that last night together, I'd refused to see Eric, even when he kept calling, leaving these Sad Sack messages on my answering machine about how sorry he was. When Eric first got to Australia he'd written a whole bunch of letters. Eric's letters were rich with descriptions about the ibis birds, blue mountains, his students, about how much he missed me, wished I were there. And then suddenly his letters stopped. In his last letter—among crossed-out words, like little stammerings—he'd said the trip made him realize how much he loved me, that he couldn't face the thought of losing me and hoped we'd work everything out. After a brief description of koala bears he signed the letter with a flurry of kisses, our special whispers. For days I read, reread the letter, holding it close to the light, trying to see into the crossed-out words, into Eric. But I didn't trust Eric's words, only words, empty words, little skirmishes. I didn't want to go back to the same old things, so I decided that I wouldn't write and when Eric got back I'd tell him that I wanted out, that there was no turning back, that we were over.

So finally I put my hurt and feelings about *Princess* into a new clay pot along the windowsill so I could write *Eva* real, with deeper meaning. And, thank God, *Eva* began to open up, smooth out, come faster, and I was writing past the middle of the book, into the height of Eva's career.

Anyways, a week later, along with the seventy-five-hundred-dollar check from the Oakland Museum, the packers came and picked up "Fear of Success." As they carried out the sculpture, I stood in the hall, tears in my eyes, my mind playing back the day with Leo in Italo Scanga's studio . . . Italo on a ladder yelling in Italian . . . Leo laughing . . . Stephanie, Italo's wife, bringing us coffee. . . .

I sent Amy the money and she moved out of Bonnie's apartment into her first apartment.

Hardly ever did I leave my work. But to make ends meet and pay off some of the bills, on weekends I worked at Margy's Boutique, selling yucko clothes to princesses fresh from the tennis courts, their Vuitton totes slung over their padded shoulders. And Shirley Plotkin came through, gave me a few paintings and drawings on consignment. I contacted some of my old clients, the garbage man Albert Contreras who collects pop art and my two midget friends Wang and Chang who collect unknown California artists. But God, I wondered if there'd ever be a day in my life when I'd pick up my clothes regularly at the cleaners or have my typewriter repaired and not count out eighty lousy pennies for my pork bun.

Anyways, the highlight: Lester called and apologized, not I'm sorry Lisa or anything like that . . . but that he wanted me to know that he still believed in me and even rattled on that Shana had ruined *Princess,* that he was damned angry at Avalon and admired my courage and perseverance and that he'd demand a termination agreement and get my manuscript back and that he'd like to read my new book and hoped that I wouldn't get another agent. So, of course, remembering all Lester's hang-in-there calls, all the years, with even his lousy you're-no-Jane-Austen calls, I was glad we'd work together again, not break the link in the chain. Besides, Lester's a damned good agent. So I sent him the first part of *Eva.*

Somehow word got around the family that *Princess* bombed, and the family stopped calling. Even crazy Aunt Sally stopped leaving her out-to-lunch songs and messages on my answering machine, and the neighbors finally stopped asking about *Princess,* just figured I was this cuckoo bird who sat at a typewriter all day writing these imaginary novels.

Often after work Jenny would come over for dinner. Sometimes she'd cook chicken or fish or bake fresh zucchini bread in coffee cans. Then after dinner we'd sit in the kitchen and eat practically the whole bread while Jenny would tell me about her job at Saks, Auto Jen, or school. And she talked enthusiastically about her classes, especially her English class. She showed me some wonderful little stories she'd written—sensitive, dreamy little stories about horses or spotted woods, the words forming her. And she was so pleased when I encouraged her and repeated how old I was when I began writing and about how long I held stories inside of me and that she had a head start.

Anyways, one Thursday I was writing when Amy's voice echoed over the answering machine.

"Mom! Pick up! Pick up! Pick! It's Amy, Mom! Emergency!"

So I ran to the phone, untwisting the Walkman from my ears, shouting, "Mom's coming! Hold on, Mom's coming! Hello!"

"Mom!"

"What's wrong?!"

"I'm under the bed, Mom," she said, her voice dropping.

"Oh, God . . . God."

"Don't yell, Mom!"

"Tell me! What's wrong?!"

"This man in the building went berserk this morning and started shooting at everybody from his window . . . killed two people. The police caught him but I can't go outside, the building is surrounded by police."

"Oh, my God . . . my God!" I said, crying now. "My God, don't you dare go near the window! Stay under the bed!"

"I told you, they've caught him! But I've been scared to death. It's the most humongous tragic thing."

"You poor thing! My God!"

"You don't know, Mom. In New York this is nothing."

"God."

"This morning I was almost out the door—on my way to work—

when I heard what I thought were firecrackers and the building super, this hideous man, was yelling, 'Stay in your apartments! There's a nut out there shooting people!' "

"God!"

"Mom, stop crying. You're making me upset."

"Oh, sure . . . uh-huh. How's everything else?" Trying to sound cool, shaking like a leaf.

"Terrible," she said.

"What do you mean, terrible?"

"Just what I said, terrible. I miss Adam and I'm broke."

"Broke? But I just sent you money. Talk louder. I can't hear you."

"But that was for the key fee. I have to live. I'm still broke, so for extra money I'm writing sports segments. I called my nerdo father and he said not a cent and hung up on me."

"Are you eating properly?"

"Don't you understand? I don't even have money left over for food, unless I'm taken out. I don't eat."

"You could buy tofu . . . things like that."

Sniff.

"Okay, Amy . . . calm down," I said, trying to keep my voice even. "I know it must be incredibly hard—scary, even—living alone in New York City, supporting yourself without Adam, family. You're very brave. And it will pay off. You'll see. I'll send you a little money . . . a box of goodies."

She sniffed. "Thank you, Mom."

"Sure."

"I miss Adam."

"Sure you do. You wouldn't be normal if you didn't."

"He's such a rat. All along he's been seeing this girl, Jill. Couldn't even be honest . . . a phony, Mom. Here he said he needed the space. Liar!"

"Oh, God. Typical."

"Thank God I have Lucy."

"Lucy? The love of his life . . . his obsession?"

"Yep. Cathouse and all. The cathouse takes up most of my apartment."

"Better hang up. This is costing you money."

"I have MCI."

"Are you still under the bed?"

"Yes. But it's quiet outside now."

"God."

"Anyway, Mom, my apartment . . . you should see it . . . a little kitchen, all white . . . shiny white . . . with little windows . . . so fun . . . shiny and bright. . . ."

"Sounds nice."

"Karen gave me a few pots and Bonnie loaned me towels . . . sheets. I'm decorating in blue and white . . . lots of plants."

"Sounds stunning."

Pause.

"Oh, Mom, did you see the Pavarotti interview?"

"Sure did. The writing was superb. And I saw your shadow. I was crying the entire time. Pavarotti was wonderful."

"He's amazing."

"You'll see. All this will lead to something."

"Mom . . . I have a call coming in."

"Be careful! Another nut could be out there! And remember Sunday . . . Nana's party . . . Jenny and I will pick you up at the airport. Four P.M. We'll go straight to Nana's. When Bruce takes Nana for her walk, we'll all meet in the living room."

"I can only spend the night, Mom. I have to leave the next morning."

"I understand, but it's a landmark. Nana will love your being there."

"Yes," said Amy with a sigh. "Okay, okay."

"Call me the minute the building is cleared."

"I will, I will."

"I love you, Amy."

"Love you, too, Mom." She giggled.

Click.

I went back to the typewriter, feeling that weird, detached feeling I'd often feel after talking to Amy . . . so many miles away . . . so near, yet so far. . . . I sat straight in the chair, put the Walkman back over my head, turned on the Mozart . . . and then I began writing and I was inside the book, watching Eva in the hospital room . . . the geranium pots along the windowsill . . . the photograph of Jackson Pollock on one wall . . . drawings from her collages on the other wall . . . Eva writing in her journal, "Days pass. I do very little. Amazing to see time pass so fast, doing so little. . . ." Eva's ropes and strings, tangled and delicate . . . Cornell's little boxes . . . Nevelson's blocks . . . Hesse chatting with Oldenburg, a light in her eyes . . . then nothing mattered but the work . . . only the work . . . Amy's voice fading . . . the words . . . shadows, pulling at me. . . .

Sunday, Mother's, 6:00 P.M. They were all there, all the relatives. Amy, looking gorgeous in a Betsy Johnson white lace off-the-shoulder dress, a white rose in her hair. Jenny, wearing a pink jersey dress clinging to her voluptuous body, holding a huge bouquet of red roses for Mother. Aunt Sally, wearing a turquoise dress and a rhinestone tiara over her thin hair, clutching my arm and whispering nasty things about the relatives. Aunt Pearl, Uncle Maury, Fat Susan and Keith, their daughter Missie, Aunt Lillian, Uncle Al, the Gottliebs, second cousins on Mother's side, both shrinks, crazies, Bruce dug them up from God knows where. The living room smelled of lemon wax, varnish. The silver bowl on top of the Steinway was filled with orchids Bruce had arranged to have flown in from Hawaii. And Christopher, poor thing, half blind from cataracts and looking like a rat from his recent haircut, stretched in front of the fireplace. The briquets in the fireplace gave off a fake glow. The caterers Bruce hired from Kantor's Catering huddled in the pantry while an accordionist, a hawklike little man with greasy hair, crouched in the hall near the doorway. Birdie, who'd been bossing the caterers and drinking Scotch, stood near the door half drunk, talking to herself.

"Sssssshhhh!" hissed Aunt Pearl, wearing a beige lace dress and dozens of gold chains around her thick neck. "Everyone quiet! Everyone! *Oy!* Any minute, please God, they'll be here. Don't stand too near the door!" she shouted and shoved Aunt Nellie, a frail little woman wearing a red pantsuit.

"Stop worrying, Pearl," said Uncle Maury, his face red and

looking hot as hell, aiming Bruce's heavy movie camera in everyone's face.

"Keep the kid's voice down," said Aunt Sally, pointing to Missie, Fat Susan's daughter, a nasty little redheaded girl riding a hideous bright green spacecar, its giant-size wheels making a crashing sound against the varnished parquet floors.

"Mind your own business," said Fat Susan, wearing a padded red Norma Kamali dress, glaring at poor Aunt Sally. "Keith, make Missie stop," said Susan, popping nuts into her mouth. Keith, looking mad as hell, yanked Missie from the spacecar. The child screamed so loud that Aunt Pearl stuffed a cocktail napkin in Missie's mouth and then Susan and Aunt Pearl really went at it . . . Amy laughing, Jenny murmuring the family was nuts.

"Someone hold Christopher!" shouted Aunt Sally. "He's peeing all over the floor!"

"Should be put to sleep," said Aunt Lillian, wearing a yellow brocade dress and a lot of bright blue eyeshadow, the dress cut so low you could see the crease between her huge breasts, like folded paper. She sat at the piano, her hands raised ready to play "Happy Birthday," while her husband, Al, a tiny, stocky man wearing a white polyester suit and a coral shirt, his belly hanging over like a contentment, repeated every minute, "God bless."

"Stop rattling the ice!" said Aunt Pearl, glaring at poor Sidney, who was setting up the bar. His face was red, all puffed, and he wore a white apron, his name printed in big red letters.

"Oy," hissed Aunt Pearl, waving her arms. "Sssssshhh. Here they come."

Aunt Lillian coughed, Aunt Pearl wheezed, Uncle Al crossed his fingers, snap, rattle. Missie hiccuped, Fat Susan ssshhhh'd Keith, who looked sour as hell, Aunt Lillian's bridesmaid charm bracelets clinked. Mother's heavy footsteps on the stairs outside, Bruce's hum . . . the door opened. Mother and Bruce stepped into the living room. Mother's eyes opened wide, her hand fluttered, raised like pushing back the air.

"Surprise! Surprise!" everyone screamed. Flashbulbs. The moment caught forever. Everyone was yelling "Happy Birthday!" and crowding around Mother, while the drippy accordionist, bouncing up and down, played the theme from *Love Story*. Uncle Maury crouched by Mother and Bruce and aimed the camera in their faces while others took pictures with their Polaroids. Flashbulbs popping all over the place, then more flashbulbs, tiny lights, blinding lights. And Mother looked so pretty in this mauve silk dress and her long pearl necklace and button pearl earrings. Her eyes were half shut, like the surprise was too much for her, and she kept murmuring, "Hell's bells, my God, hell's bells," her hand still raised and grabbing the air, and her mouth in a half smile trembled. Bruce held his arm around Mother's shoulders and kept repeating, "Calm down . . . don't crowd her," his lips pressed tight, nodding approval. And his hair looked so red, almost coppery next to his pale blue cashmere sweater. He had gained more weight, was big as a house, maybe two hundred pounds, but his face was thin, like pinched out, and his shoulders kind of hunched. And everyone was yelling, "God bless!" Tears. Screams. Missie crying at the top of her lungs that she wanted her car, Sidney yelling at Fat Susan to make Missie stop crying and teach her some manners, and Keith was murmuring, "I told you so." And then came the payoff when Amy, who'd been hiding behind the big chintz wing-back chair, pushed through the crowd, the music stopped, everyone backed away and made room, and a hush fell over the room. You could hear a pin drop.

"My God!" shouted Mother, her hands in the air, her eyes full of tears, glazed. "Hell's bells! I don't believe it!"

"Nana," murmured Amy, bending down and hugging Mother, hugging her so tight. Next Jenny went over to Mother and gave her the bouquet of roses. Mother hugged both girls and then Bruce hugged the girls. Then I ran up and hugged Mother so hard I almost knocked her over. God, she felt so little.

"Lisa," she said, looking at me through tears, "that's a very pretty color on you . . . kind of burgundyish, isn't it? And your hair looks pretty today. Simple."

"Thanks, Mother."

"Okay! Enough shmaltz!" said Bruce, waving his hands. "Group picture time!"

We lined up for pictures, taking turns, Mother standing in the center by the piano, all smiling at her, while Bruce shouted, "Keep the noise down!"

"A big smile!" yelled Uncle Maury. "Cheese!"

"Cheese . . ."

And then everyone began kissing, arguing, murmuring "Please, God a hundred more birthdays," while Aunt Lillian played the piano and Uncle Al, plastered out of his gourd, sang "New York, New York" off-key and Missie once again was riding the horrible car over everyone's feet, Fat Susan explaining that Missie attended a French nursery school for gifted preschoolers, while Sidney couldn't mix the drinks fast enough. Bruce stood in the center of the room, his arm around Mother, explaining each detail of how he kept the surprise from Mother . . . arranged the caterers . . . food . . . decorations . . . while Sidney shouted, "All it takes is money!" Everyone had a merry old time. Until Birdie came into the room half smashed and screamed, "Soup's on!" Everyone followed Bruce into the dining room.

A sight for sore eyes. You'd die. The room lit by tiny scented white candles, the centerpiece Mother's Steuben swan filled with birds of paradise, little white swan place cards Jenny'd made set by each place, brightly wrapped gifts stacked in the corner of the room.

Everyone lined up at the buffet table. Silver platters laden with beef, a thin mist of steam floating from silver chafing dishes filled with vegetables, rice, kugel.

"Too much food," said Aunt Sally, tipsy and her tiara falling off her head.

"Eat what you want! No one wants to hear your complaints," said Aunt Lillian, piling her plate.

"No bickering today," said Mother in a singsong voice.

"Everyone shut up!" said Bruce on one side of Mother, Amy on the other, Jenny next to me. Sidney gave the blessing for the wine, everyone murmuring along with him, "*Baruch atou adenoi,* . . ." their voices drifting to the end of the prayer. And Bruce shouted, "Amen! Let's eat!"

Then everyone began eating, murmuring how delicious the roast . . . knocking on wood . . . varnished echoes . . . the chair wobbling . . . Aunt Sally's false teeth clacking . . . Aunt Pearl's funny little wheeze . . . the tapping of silverware . . . Christopher's low growl, begging for food . . . Missie, who sat on top of two telephone books, clutching her noonie, a silk stocking tied in a knot, whining she had to go poops. . . .

"Don't eat so fast," said Fat Susan, slapping Keith on the back. "You're not going to a fire."

"Oh, leave him alone." said Mother. "Eat and enjoy."

"Put the kid to bed!" said Aunt Sally, pointing her fork at Missie. "Phooey! She's driving me nuts!"

"She didn't have a nap today," said Fat Susan in a baby voice. "She stayed up for Grandma's birthday."

"It's not a nap the kid needs," said Aunt Sally, eating rice off Aunt Pearl's plate. "She needs a good crack—"

"No one asked for your opinion!" said Fat Susan, her mouth full of kugel.

"Leave her alone," said Sidney at the buffet, slicing more meat.

"Keith!" shrieked Fat Susan. "Do something besides feed your face!"

"Oh, Susan—"

"Put her to bed," she demanded.

"I want to go wee-wee!" screamed Missie.

"Raise your kids at home," said Mother, giving Sidney a dirty look and Sidney giving Fat Susan a dirty look.

"Kids," murmured Uncle Maury.

"*Nu?* What's the problem?" asked poor Aunt Nellie, her head bobbing back and forth.

"Never mind, eat," said Uncle Maury.

"*Shlepedicha* kid," murmured Aunt Sally.

"Kids," repeated Aunt Pearl.

"Put you in the grave," whispered Sidney.

"This wineglass has a chip," said Mother, frowning and holding the wineglass to the light.

"For Christ's sake!" said Bruce, pressing his lips. "Can't you enjoy yourself? Every minute with the chip."

"Too bad Mark's not here," said Aunt Nellie in a frail voice, her false teeth making a clacking sound, pillows propped behind her.

"He's in the clink!" said Aunt Sally.

"*Oy!*"

"He's not!" said Bruce, who was turning red and giving everyone dirty looks.

"Where is he?" asked Fat Susan.

"He's on a cruise!" said Bruce, giving Fat Susan a dirty look. "In
the Bahamas."

"Oh, nice."

"Hmmm."

"Tch–tch–tch."

"Kids," said Uncle Maury, shrugging and rolling his eyes toward
the ceiling.

"Thank God we have luck with our Mitchell," said Aunt Lillian,
knocking wood.

"You call that luck!" said Aunt Sally, making a sour face.

"So, Bruce," said Uncle Al, raising his voice above Aunt Sally
bickering with Aunt Lillian, "what are you doing these days?"

"Well . . . after my valet dresses me, Prince Charles and I chat
on the phone."

"A riot!" said Aunt Nellie. "The boy should go in show business."

"No business like show business," sang Aunt Lillian.

"And *nu* . . . what's with our little Marjorie Morningstar?" asked
Uncle Maury, smiling at me, his jowls shaking, everyone getting
all quiet and looking at me.

"Nothing's new . . . everything's fine," I said, smiling and ignoring Jenny's kicking me under the table.

"What's with the Nobel Prizer?" asked Aunt Pearl.

"He's a shmuck," said Bruce, making a face.

"Smart as a whip," said Mother, nudging Bruce. "He's working
on a breakthrough for some big disease."

"Is there going to be a wedding?" asked Fat Susan in a singsong
voice.

"No wedding," I said with a smile. "I don't want one."
Silence.

"What are you doing now?" asked Fat Susan, breaking into the
sudden quiet.

"I'm writing another book."

"A very intellectual book," explained Mother. "About the art
world."

"Shmaltzy book," said Bruce, smiling at me.

"'Art, shmart!" said Uncle Maury. "Write romances. That's where the *gelt* is!"

"That's not true," said Amy.

"What's your new book about?" asked Fat Susan with forced politeness.

"Eva Hesse."

"*Oy!* Hitler's mistress!" said Aunt Pearl, looking alarmed.

"Eva Hesse is a very important sculptor," explained Mother. "The postmini movement."

"Minimalism, Nans," said Amy gently, smiling at Mother, who flushed and looked kind of embarrassed.

"That's all right, Mother," I said quickly. "You're close."

"In my book most artists are a bunch of nuts," said Aunt Sally, eating kugel from Aunt Pearl's plate. "One drips paint and dies driving like a nut, another *meshuggeneh* cuts off an ear and it makes history—"

"One thing I can't stand is when people argue about art and they don't know what they're talking about," said Aunt Lillian, addressing Fat Susan, who was nodding and agreeing.

"At least I know what I like," said Fat Susan.

"Lisa works her ass off!" shouted Bruce, pressing his lips, his neck kind of stretched out. "You try and writing a fucking book! She's a goddamned star!"

"Bruce, calm down," I said. "That's okay."

And then everyone began arguing about art, no one really talking to anyone, just arguing about how most art is for the birds, a bunch of hooey, Mother shouting above the racket that you have to be an intellectual like Lisa to understand art, Amy and Jenny giggling and poking each other, Bruce rapping the wineglass for quiet, yelling that Amy wanted to make a toast to Mother. So everyone became quiet then, though Aunt Pearl kept repeating that she hoped Amy and Jenny would have such a husband as Uncle Maury.

Amy stood and made a beautiful toast to her grandmother, not a dry eye in the house. Then Jenny read a little story she'd written about a young girl and her grandmother. And then I read a poem I'd written especially for Mother's birthday. Silver birds, broken clocks, the tide's sweeping time, and then everyone applauded, Bruce yelling, "Shmaltzy!" Mother exclaiming that there were poets on her mother's side of the family, that she saved all my poems.

And then what really got me all emotional was when Mother stood, her hand on Bruce's shoulder, balancing on one leg, and gracefully thanked Bruce for putting together a beautiful party. Then she looked at me, raised her glass, blinking several times, her neck flushed.

"To Lisa," she finally said in her tiny voice, her eyes all teary. "A strong sister! A hell of a lady! Hang in there, Lisa!"

"A shmaltzy lady!" shouted Bruce. God, you could've died. I wiped my eyes with the napkin, Amy nudging me and whispering that my nose was running, Jenny crying her eyes out, Aunt Pearl knocking on wood, and Aunt Nellie exclaiming in her shaky voice, "Lisa's got it."

And then the lights went out. All quiet until Amy and Bruce wheeled in the birthday cake. A long sheet cake, chocolate, Mother's favorite, its top covered in golden sugary stars and seventy-five tiny gold birthday candles. Everyone applauded. The accordionist played "Embraceable You." Holding Bruce's arm, Bruce looking so proud, Mother kind of limped over to the cake, leaning heavily against Bruce, murmuring, "Hell's bells," holding the sterling silver cake knife wound with white baby's breath. Mother, slightly bent over the cake, her face flushed, began blowing out the candles, her cheeks puffed out, Bruce blowing, too, while everyone counted one, two, three, four, until Mother and Bruce blew out every single candle. Then everyone applauded and Uncle Al whistled and the accordionist played the theme from *The Godfather*. Bruce kissed Mother and Uncle Maury yelled. "Make a wish!" Missie screamed she wanted to go ca-ca, Mother squeezed her eyes shut, tilted her head back, kind of shook her shoulders, then with Bruce's hand over her wrist, she made the first cut.

"*Mazel tov!*" shouted Uncle Al.

"Please, God!" murmured everyone.

"A thousand years . . ."

Uncle Maury aimed the camera at Mother's face while Mother divided the cake. Missie screamed she wanted the stars, Aunt Sally yelled, "Shut up, you *shlepedicha* kid!"

After coffee Mother opened her presents. After each gift everyone knocked on wood and passed the gifts, until the candles melted
wax, dripping time. At midnight we left and drove home.

Six A.M. the next day, still dark. Amy decided to take the airport
bus. So, in my sweats, frog shirt, shivering from the morning fog,
I waited with Amy at the bottom of the stairs. Wearing her red
coat and beanie, her green duffel bag slung over her shoulder, Amy
looked apprehensive.

"Mom . . . now, promise you'll go to the doctor's. You look
tired. I'm worried about you. . . . Oh, God, stop crying or I'll—"

"I . . . can't help it," I said, clutching her hand.

"Mom."

"We're always saying good-bye."

Amy took my hand. "Mom," she said, kissing my cheek, "I
love you."

"Amy—"

"We'll be together soon. When you finish *Eva* you'll come to
New York. Who knows what will happen?"

"Nothing will happen."

"It will, Mom. You're just worried about Nans . . . Eric . . .
Jenny. You worry too much. Jenny is doing okay, Mom. She's
going through a lot of changes, but she's doing fine."

"Amy, please eat more. You don't eat a thing. I watched you
yesterday. You're too thin. Only a mother would tell you honestly.
I worry so about anorexia. Just the other day I saw a program on
anorexic girls . . . all bright and atractive like you, overachievers
and, God—"

"Mom, don't. Oh, Mom, don't cry. . . ."

"I can't help it. I worry."

"Now I'm crying."

The bus pulled up and began honking and then the nosy German
woman across the street poked her head out the window and the
lights were going on in all the houses and old Mrs. Nelson shouted,
"Pipe down, you nuts!" Amy and I were rocking and rocking each
other, my head on her shoulder, and I was doing this clutching
thing with my hands, sobbing and making snorting sounds, while
this hideous woman in the bus, wearing an army uniform, yelled

out the window, "Get your ass in the bus! We don't have all day!"
The bus driver honking, Mrs. Nelson yelling "Pipe down!" from
her window, finally Amy pulled away and hopped on the bus. While
I stood there, crying like I'd never stop, the bus drove away.

The next day I was going at it, the words coming hot and fast,
when Lester's voice came over the answering machine.

"Lisa . . . Lester North. Are you behind that machine of yours?
Lisa, darling, pick up! It's Lester!"

"Hello, Lester . . . it takes me a minute to get to the machine
. . . I was—"

"Darling, how are you?"

"Very well, thank you."

"I read the first part of *Eva*."

"Oh . . ."

"I like it. The best you've ever written."

"Oh, Lester! I'm glad."

"A miracle," he said, his voice rising excitedly.

"It's not a miracle. . . . I've been working over a year on *Eva*."

"A miracle," he repeated. "Miraculous."

"Not miraculous."

"I'm very happy," he said.

"And I'm happy you're happy."

"See, Lisa, *Princess* was good practice after all," he said in a pa-
rental tone. "A necessary experience. You learned a lot. If it weren't
for *Princess*, we wouldn't have *Eva*."

"I guess that's a good way of looking at it."

"Ha! Wait until Serkin sees this! Just the other day he asked how
you were coming along and I said you were working on a
new novel."

"Uh-huh."

"And I just love," he continued, chuckling, "the way you cap-
ture the contemporary art world . . . so visual . . . and Hesse's
love affair with her husband is gripping. A hell of a book."

"Uh-huh."

"I talked to Walter the other day. He's agreed to a termination
agreement."

"What kind of termination? You mean I just sign a paper that says Lisa Perlman is free and clear? The three-book option wiped out? And I don't pay back the ten-thousand-dollar advance?"

"Well . . . just about . . . only one minor change. If you ever publish another book . . . and Walter says he'll hold his breath . . ." Lester said with a chuckle, "then you'll have to pay back the ten thousand."

"Over my dead body I'll pay back the ten thousand! Or sign his lousy termination agreement! No way! No, sirree! He'll end up paying me a lot more than ten thousand dollars! Where's the manuscript? I want my manuscript back or I'll definitely sue everyone! I've already talked to a big media lawyer and he says Walter could be in a lot of trouble for breach of contract . . . fraud . . . all kinds of things. So—"

"All right, all right," he said quickly. "Call off the dogs! I'll talk to Walter. And we'll get the termination agreement going. So I can sell *Eva* to a better house!"

"Okay . . . uh-huh."

"Now, dear . . . when will you be finished writing *Eva*? I'd like to have the completed manuscript as soon as possible."

"Soon . . . soon."

"And make sure the rest of the manuscript is as good as the first part."

"Uh-huh."

"And Lisa, I'm glad for you. The book is wonderful . . . a wonderful book. I always knew you were an artist."

"Thank you. I'm glad we're working together again."

"Thank you, dear. It'll be our year."

"I hope so."

"I know so! You'll see!"

"I'll send you the final chapters of *Eva* when they're ready."

"Good, darling! Go! Go! Go! Go! Go! Don't let me disturb you! You'll be a star yet!"

"Uh-huh."

" 'Bye!"

Click.

About a week later, Lester called me and said he got the manuscript back from Walter and the termination agreement and that I didn't have to pay off the ten thousand dollars. So like Jack Robinson I went over to Lester's office, and just as I thought, Shana hadn't edited the manuscript beyond the first eight chapters. God, I got so freaked out, so damned angry. But then after I calmed down and talked to Lester a while—Lester being all nice and everything and reminding me that he wanted to be able to sell *Eva* to a better house—I signed the lousy release so I could get *Princess* and those fucking sharks out of my life.

CHAPTER FOURTEEN

While Dr. Kenner fussed with the *shmatte* pillow behind her back
I watched the slit of light cross diagonally over the rose carpet.
Hard to believe . . . so many years . . . the room familiar, yet
changed. Like looking into your childhood room, all the toys in
place but the time heavy. I could see the time . . . the beige drapes
tinged yellow from the sun, shiny long green leaves grown over
the plant aquarium . . . a room forever implanted into my mind
. . . softly rose . . . dreamy air.

When Dr. Kenner stopped fussing with the pillow I sniffed three
times, did the popping thing with my tongue, sat forward a bit.
Still felt kind of nervous, shy, before a session, like what I wanted
to say stuck.

"Anyways," I finally said, "I miss Eric. And I'm not feeling so
hot . . . my forty-three-year-old hormones are fucked up. Can you
believe, just as I was adjusting to my menopause, I started bleeding?"

"How long have you been bleeding?" she asked, looking concerned.

"A couple of weeks. Probably just stress. I mean, it's been fifteen
months since my last period."

"You should see your gynecologist as soon as possible."

"Yes . . . I will . . . but I hate to take time away from
my work."

"Take care of yourself." she said softly.

"I'll see Dr. Chan. Anyways . . ."

"Hmmm."

I pulled some Kleenex from the fresh box on the table next to
me. I burst into tears.

She fluffed her skirt.

"Sorry about that," I said, looking away, blowing the Kleenex,
my fingers red. "Lately I cry at the drop of a hat . . . for no reason
. . . in the middle of writing or at the bakery. The other day I was

at the stationery store buying typing paper and I bumped into Patty Applebaum looking all gorgeous in her spiffy pink Jane Fonda jogging outfit. My luck, there I was in my frog tee shirt and sweats. When she asked me what's new, I burst into tears."

She fluffed her skirt.

"Old sadness, I guess."

She smiled.

"What about Eric?" she asked.

"I haven't written him. He writes me these I-miss-you-and-when-I-get-back-we'll-talk-and-work-things-out letters."

"How do you feel about that?"

"Feel! What's there to work out?" I sniffed and stuck my finger in my ear, popped my tongue. "You can hardly call Eric and me the normal Hallmark couple. I mean, what's there to work out? That I go on fitting into Eric's life . . . his schedule? The first time I met old Sad Sack he carried on about how much he wanted to get married. Been carrying that line around for fourteen years. But believe me, you don't have to be a genius to know if I said yes, he'd run off dragging his guilt behind him, crying women and Mom want too much."

She laughed. "Exactly." Her brown leather boots made a squeaking sound.

"Uh-huh . . . I'm telling you, I know 'working things out' means Eric controls everything. With Eric marriage is a provision for his old age. Poor thing is afraid of death . . . heartburn . . . high blood pressure . . . especially love. You think you've got phobias? This guy was born with a paper bag over his face! Every minute crying how his mother loved him too much, made him feel guilty, you know the whole shmeer. And oh, the latest . . . he's scared to death of impotence . . . that his thing won't be stiff as a board at any given moment. He can get it up, but sometimes lately it wavers, goes up and down . . . up and down."

"Psychological," she murmured.

"When he comes over with the mushrooms in a paper bag, I get all soft . . ."

"Three mushrooms won't cure that," said Dr. Kenner, fluffing again.

"Men!"

She fluffed.

"Anyways . . . Eric needs a fantasy woman . . . marriage would destroy us . . . make us real."

"Right!" she said, coming to life now, her hand drawing circles in the air. "You're strong enough to hear this now," she said, still drawing circles, "but from the first time you met Eric Blumberg you knew he was limited. You tried to fit him into your fiction."

"Uh-huh . . . Guess Eric and I both tried to fit each other into our fantasy. I'm telling you . . . if Eric Blumberg ever let loose of his feelings, his real feelings . . . like his math equations . . . He stays on the outside . . . observes, then pieces together . . . every minute rearranging the stupid spice rack everything in its little compartment . . . you know what I mean."

"Hmmm. Compartmentalized Intimacy."

"He needs his role . . . victimized genius . . . except in sex . . . that's where he feels."

She fluffed.

"Though, I'll tell you something, most men are underdeveloped . . . poor things . . . you know, the defective male. Women are moving into so many roles and not losing their feminine self. While men hang on for dear life to their one pathetic role, stud/provider. Marcie Kaplan says half the men she meets are bed-wetters."

She laughed.

"When I suggested to Eric we lay off the sex for a while . . . get to know each other . . . he looked shocked . . . like I castrated him . . . accused me of dangling . . . dangling, can you believe? Afraid he'd lose his power."

"Hmmm."

"But anyways . . . I love the shmuck . . . no matter what, I love him the way he is. The Eric all hidden underneath, the shy, insecure little boy. And he has a nice soul."

Silence. The slit of light broke into colored dots.

"God, why can't I love someone like Melanie Finkelstein's husband, Norman? Why do I have to love this little rat person who every time I say 'I love you' scurries into his hole? After that evening, though, in his hot tub with his fellow Mensanites he's lucky if we speak, let alone marry."

She nodded.

"Always so concerned what his friends think."

She fluffed. "If you make it big, he'd be happy to show you off."

"I'll say! Until he acccepts me as a person, a bona fide person, Lisa Perlman, *número uno,* not this sexual thing he's concocted . . . until then, forget it . . . *sayonara.*"

She uncrossed her legs, and her brown leather boots made a squeaking sound.

"But I'll tell you something," I said, squirming in the chair. "I miss him . . . miss him so much . . . and I hate to admit it, but I haven't been so hot in the closeness department. I mean all the games . . . I'm sick of them! Hiding behind my book . . . saving my feelings for my work . . . only giving some to Eric. Like I was this invisible person . . . or Eric didn't have feelings."

"Hmmm."

"So many times I tried to talk to Eric but he didn't give an inch . . . he'd pull back . . . then I'd pull back . . . Push-pull . . . push-pull."

She fluffed.

"Please don't answer that! You know I hate it when you answer the telephone!" One . . . two . . . three . . . four . . . I outstared her until it stopped ringing.

"Sorry about that," she said.

I wrapped the Kleenex around my fingers, tears flowing down my face.

"Would you consider marrying him?"

"Do you think I've shlepped up your stairs all these years . . . paid you my last dollar . . . half the time dressed like a bag lady . . . to marry Eric Blumberg . . . be Mrs. Genius?"

She gave the fish-eyed stare.

"Can you believe I'm saying this . . . the perpetual princess . . . groomed to love, cherish, obey Dr. Poo-Poo?"

She smiled.

"Mother thinks because I'm alone, a struggling artist, I'm this failure, a freak."

"Your mother thinks life without a man is a failure. Earning money is an embarrassment."

"Yes, poor thing. She has no self. Always trying to please everyone."

"You're sad about your mother."

"Yes."

Silence.

"She'll die someday, never knowing she's talented . . . her dreams."

I cried for a while, rolling the Kleenex between my hands into tiny balls. I watched the dust float in the ray of light coming from the window.

Folded the cuffs of my leg-warmers. Shook my hair. Buttoned my big black sweater. On with my gray fedora hat. We sat quietly. Dr. Kenner's eyes steady. A pause that knows quiet. Finally, after a long moment, I sat forward and asked, "Have you ever stood by the sea . . . just let the tide pull you out? Feels like you're not moving . . . but you are . . . right across the sea? . . ."

She fluffed her skirt.

Three days later I was at my gynecologist's office. A late Friday afternoon. Dr. Chan is a pretty woman, about thirty-two, with silky black hair and a beautiful smile. The room so bright . . . plants green . . . everything growing.

"Knees apart."

"Uh-huh."

"Farther down on the edge of the table, Lisa."

"Uh-huh."

"Apart. I know this is uncomfortable." She chuckled. "Always is. But you can do better. Won't take long. That's good. Don't squeeze on the speculum. Relax. All right."

Paper gown rustling . . . tearing . . . my eyes on the glass sky-light . . . rectangular sky . . . blue . . . a vertical shadow fell across the light. Footsteps outside . . . phones softly ringing . . . bells . . . little bells.

"Almost finished . . . just want to check your uterus."

"Uh-huh."

"Are you all right?"

"Uh-huh."

"You can sit up now."

I sat up, my legs swinging over the edge of the table, my face all flushed.

Dr. Chan, slightly frowning and looking concerned, took off the rubber gloves and washed her hands at the sink. "How long have you been bleeding, Lisa?"

"About two weeks."

"Like a regular period, or spotty?"

"Spotty . . . on again, off again. That's why I didn't come in right away. I kept thinking it was nothing . . . stress . . . that it'd go away. God, are my periods coming back? After fifteen months?"

"Usually bleeding like this . . . given your age . . . means one of two things: cervical cancer or pregnancy. I'd like to do a cervical biopsy now. . . . It'll only take twenty-five minutes. . . ."

"Now," I repeated, not knowing what to think, scared out of my wits, not believing what was happening. "Biopsy . . . my God, cancer. . . . And I'm in menopause . . . forty-three . . . I can't—"

"The biopsy is a precaution. It won't hurt. All you'll feel is the Novocain . . . a pinch."

"Oh, God."

She smiled. "Lisa, don't think the worst. Even if it is cancer, if it's caught in time, we'll take care of it. Now lie back," she said. "The nurse will give you something to relax you. I'll be back in a few minutes."

So what was I going to do? Start screaming, run out of there? I lay back on the table, pulling the lousy paper sheet over me, trying not to look at the counter with all the instruments, looking instead at the skylight, watching the birds hopping along the skylight.

Then the nice nurse came in, Marilyn Something, and took my blood pressure again and gave me this yellow pill, murmuring that she was crazy about my bird pants and that she'd like to paint her pants. So while I explained to her how you paint fabrics, she held my hand until I was feeling more relaxed. Then Dr. Chan came into the room.

"All right, Lisa," she said, putting on the gloves and going over to the sink, "I want you to hold Marilyn's hand. But it won't hurt . . . I promise . . . just a pinch," she said, "like I said."

"Uh-huh, sure," I murmured, squeezing Marilyn's hand, my eyes shut, adjusting my feet in the stupid potholders on the stirrups.

"Knees apart. . . . All right, Lisa . . . yes . . . hold your legs apart . . . that's right . . . good girl . . . you'll just feel a slight pinch when I inject the Novocain."

"Ow! God! That hurts!" I yelled, squeezing Marilyn's hand so hard her ring jabbed my hand, because believe me, this was more than a pinch. Pinch, my ass! The nurse patted my forehead and squeezed my hand again.

Then I opened my eyes and watched this lousy bird crap on the skylight, until, thank God, Dr. Chan said, "All right, Lisa. You can sit up now." And boy, did I sit up. Practically jumped off the table.

"Take some deep breaths," she said, her hand on my shoulder. "Take this slip upstairs to the lab and get your blood test. I'll have the results for everything tomorrow . . . four o'clock. If I don't call you before, call me by four."

"Yes."

She looked at the chart gain. "Your blood pressure is down. But we have to talk about that."

"I'll take that over cancer."

She smiled.

"You're a good patient, Lisa. We'll work everything out."

"Yes. Thanks, Dr. Chan," I said, feeling nauseous. "I'll talk to you tomorrow."

When Dr. Chan closed the door, believe you me I tore off the crappy paper gown and took my panties and bra from my purse . . . always keep them in my purse . . . and slipped them on real fast. Next my bird pants, red turtleneck sweater, leather boots, and got the hell out of there.

Outside it was balmy. I walked fast, real fast, watching the clouds break in the sky. Pregnancy . . . death . . . I couldn't die now. Oh, God . . . cancer . . . cancer for others, never for you. . . . My luck, my Blue Cross all canceled, not a pot to pee in. . . . I can see me in San Francisco General, shlepping down the hall with tubes . . . my poor kids crying their eyes out and God knows if that fifty-thousand-dollar life insurance policy I bought from that retarded person at Miz Brown's is on the up and up. . . . What if . . . oh, God . . . a pregnancy . . . no, not possible . . . but all the whoopsy feelings . . . back pain . . . probably from the cancer. . . .

And when I got near my house and saw the pathetic-looking trees, they looked so good . . . the neighborhood, so good . . . even the ya-ya German woman walking her dog. I waved to old Mrs. Nelson shlepping down the street in her walker, wearing a green pillbox hat, then to Doris at the kitchen window, and then I went quickly into the house, screaming, "Anny! Anny!" until the poor thing, half zonked, jumped from her sunspot. I picked her up and hugged and kissed her hard, crying into her fur, her little heart beating. I carried her into my closet and sat there on top of the shoes.

Okay, so there I was in the closet, poor Anny scared out of her mind, thinking about Eva Hesse . . . okay, a brave lady . . . lying in that hospital bed, dying, three little plants along the windowsill, still writing all those brilliant insights about death in her little note-book . . . but you're a coward, Lisa Perlman, you're a coward . . . all I felt was fear . . . fear like you wouldn't believe . . . so big my legs were numb, my back all stiff, and I felt kind of nau-seous. So I got out of the closet, deciding to take a hot bath. Hot baths always calm me down. I went into the bathroom, locking the door, and undressed. I stood on the footstool in front of the mirror, praying to God that I wouldn't fall, the light falling over my body . . . and I looked real hard at my naked body, looking for the changes in my body I'd felt so long, pretending they weren't there.

Okay, yes, my breasts were sore, the nipples tender—ow, they hurt—but then again, you've always had tender nipples . . . big breasts that stick out . . . So what? They're sore. . . . I turned to the side. My stomach was flat, my body even thinner than usual. Then I saw the thick blue vein along one side of my breast kind of underneath, my breasts puffy like they got when I was pregnant. And I held my hands out to the light and the thin gold ring on my second finger stuck into the skin. I got off the stool and ran the bath, telling myself all this could be just the hormone stuff . . . tender breasts, tingly nipples. All I need is to die now . . . and the poor kids . . . their lousy father wouldn't give them the time of day. . . .

I got into the bath and lay still, looking at the bandage on the inside of my arm, remembering the day the doctor said I was pregnant with David's child and that night over dinner whipping up my sleeve and proudly showing David the bandage from the blood test, and the icy look in his eyes and his mouth all tight, champagne cocktails, two red cherries, clicking glasses, silence thick, so thick . . . then . . . and oh, God, I closed my eyes, squeezing Jenny's rubber duck, squeezing the duck . . . squeezing . . . the tears coming out of my eyes, puffing out so hot . . . burning my face . . . I was scared . . . scared shitless . . . wished Eric was with me, his arms around me, holding me tight . . . that it wasn't too late. After the bath I put on the flannel bathrobe, the furry slippers the kids gave me umpteen years before, and went into the kitchen. Even though the clock said 6:10 P.M., it was still so light. God, I hated the lousy Daylight Saving Time, like you're supposed to be this cheerio person all day, never wanting the dark. So I pulled down the shade. I'd write for a while, that's what I'd do. Get my mind off myself. Connect. So I started working, writing, the morning shadows going up the walls, breaking into pieces of sunlight. Until at noon I heard Dr. Chan's voice come over the answering machine. I almost broke my neck running to the phone.

"Hello, this is Lisa."

"Lisa . . . Dr. Chan. Good news! The cervical biopsy is negative!"

"Thank God! Oh, thank God!" I repeated, relief going right through me.

"The pregnancy test is positive."

"Positive? You mean I'm pregnant!"

"Pregnant," she repeated, her voice lilting. "Congratulations!"

"I don't think it's possible. Are you sure?"

"Very sure," she chuckled. "I'd say the fetus is ten weeks—"

"Ten weeks," I repeated, my fingers counting and my mind going back to the Nobel Prize night. "My God! I can't believe it!" I said, relieved and shocked. "I don't see how . . . I mean, I'm forty-three years old. . . ."

"My grandmother was fifty-one with her third child."

"Uh-huh . . . fifty-one . . ."

"We have to talk about you, Lisa. Do you want the baby?"

"Oh, yes!"

"In your sixteenth week I'll do an amniocentesis."

"Uh-huh."

"Make sure there are no genetic defects . . . Down's syndrome
. . . a simple procedure. An ultrasound machine, a slender needle
is inserted into the abdomen . . . won't hurt," she quickly assured
me. "Draws out a small sample—about one ounce—of amniotic
fluid. Then in three weeks, maybe sooner, we have the results."

"Uh-huh," I said.

While she went on explaining the procedure, I figured out that
Eric wouldn't be home by then. My mind played Amy . . . Jenny
. . . Eric . . . oh, Eric . . . Mother . . . the realization that I was
pregnant slowly coming over me.

Dr. Chan was saying that she'd turn me over to her nurse for
appointments, about my diet, exercise classes for pregnant women
over forty, this rush, I can't explain it, went through me . . . and
I couldn't think . . . I felt like floating . . . like those nutso birds
of mine.

"So, Lisa, make your appointments and we'll have a long talk.
See you next week."

"Yes. Thank you."

When I hung up I stood there for a second, staring at the telephone, just staring . . . not feeling anything . . . just guilty that I
wasn't feeling anything . . . except relief that I wasn't dying from
cancer . . . knowing that I was supposed to feel so ecstatic or
something. But how could I? A forty-three-year-old woman marked
menopausal and pregnant feel ecstatic! God, that happened only in
sitcoms, where the women have husbands and dozens of kids all
gathered by the fireplace smiling and crying "Gee, Mom," and
glowing, not shlepping around the house crying. And I was nervous as hell, the anxiety going through me, so I kept pacing through
the house, doing my duck walk, opening and shutting doors,
touching things, doing the breathing exercises I learned after my
paper bag things. I went over to the window then and looked out,
just looked out, rubbing my hands together, a habit I always had
when trying to think out something, squeeze out the feelings . . .
feelings I was afraid to feel. The sunlight was shining across the old

bent trees in front of old Mrs. Nelson's house, shining it all gold. And then I felt a smile and I couldn't stop smiling and the tears, these hot tears, rolled down my face and I kept rubbing my hands and the tears poured down my face and the tears felt good, so good, not old angry tears but tears coming from the glow inside me, because I was having a baby, a baby growing in me, and a feeling like that makes the world go upside down, tilt right over—you feel like you're holding the world up—and then I began kind of a jumping thing, jumping up and down, like I did when I'd first heard *Princess* was sold and I wanted to shout out the window like they do in the movies that I was having a baby and everyone screaming "Good for Lisa!" and smiling . . . tell someone because this glow thing is the kind of thing you can't keep in, can't keep, you just can't.

And, then, slowly, very slowly . . . I guess I'd been trying not to think about Eric . . . but he came over me and I got this funny feeling . . . this feeling that pushed the glow out pushed it all out because I was feeling scared, plenty scared, feeling so many mixed things and plenty scared about what Eric would say . . . what he would feel . . . if he'd blink and run . . . or pull a David . . . or leave and go away . . . the baby wouldn't have a father . . . then the anxiety was coming over me and I was taking these deep breaths.

So I decided to call Dr. Kenner because I wanted to hear her even voice so I could even out what I was feeling . . . even it out. So I called Dr. Kenner, but her lousy answering service said she was with a patient, so after I repeated my telephone number umpteen times, they said she'd call me back. So after I hung up I did the duck walk again and the breathing exercise until about fifteen minutes later she called. And when I heard her gentle inquiry about why I'd called, I blurted out that I was pregnant and she just asked calmly if I wanted the baby, and I said yes, without a doubt, more than anything, wouldn't let anyone or anything take my baby away and that I'd work it all out. Then she said that we had a lot to talk about and that she'd see me at my usual time and then she said congratulations.

But I still couldn't come down . . . I couldn't . . . I'd think about the baby and get all excited and imagine Eric all smiley and happy, carrying me, and lying down together in this beautiful yellow meadow, a kite fluttering in the sky, balloons floating, our kids all glowy. . . .

Maybe I'd call him. . . . No, I'd get too nervous . . . all scared about what he'd say . . . he'd need time, too. . . . I decided a letter would be the best way. So I got my notepad and sat at the kitchen table, drinking a cup of the lousy Café Amaretto, looking at my poor avocado seed sprouting green buds. While I sketched faces I planned out what I'd write Eric. The words were all stuck—wouldn't come out easily—I mean, after all, I hadn't answered Eric's letters, his apologies and request for my answers, about how I felt about him. So now what was I going to say, Dearest Poopy-Pop, Since that lousy night at your hot tub I'm fed up to the hilt with your meanness, your snippy little hurts, your inability to get close, but I forgive you because we're having a baby? No way could I write that . . . not anymore . . . our games were over . . . this was a real baby. . . . I'd write Eric the truth . . . write what I was feeling . . . scrape the bottom of me, the very bottom of me . . . and put the feelings into words . . . not only tell Eric I was glad about the baby and that I loved him, but that I hadn't written him because I knew that not writing would make him want me more and that I wanted to break that old game because I was afraid of getting close, too, and that I wanted us to talk about getting close, at least talk about it, because I wanted him close to the baby, the baby to have a father, and how did he feel about this?

Then I began writing, several drafts, the words not coming easily but each draft closer to what I was feeling, and oh, God, it was something else again, because all the yacking with Dr. Kenner about being afraid of closeness and hiding behind myself was different than doing . . . and I sat there for the longest time, until the shadows broke across the old tile counter, until I had a final draft to Eric. I folded the paper and decided I'd type it the next day, and then I'd feel like I was dreaming again, having this baby was only a dream, not real, and I'd walk around the kitchen again, shaking my arms and doing the breathing thing, like shaking all the dream loose, so I'd feel real . . . God, it was something . . . really something . . . because one minute I'd feel all glowy and then the next

I'd feel like kind of panicked, like I was caught in a dark room and wanted to get out.

But like holding on tight to that rocky boat, you just hold on real tight so you can ride it out. And I had to keep my world going, get *Eva* finished, keep everything going for the girls . . . Mother . . . the baby. . . .

I got up then and washed out the coffee cup and put it in the sink, thinking that as soon as possible I'd tell Jenny and Amy . . . Jenny first . . . not wait . . . because the girls were my lifeline . . . no matter what we'd been through . . . from the mumps to PG&E turning off our lights because I couldn't pay the bill . . . we'd always hung in there . . . kept real close. So the sooner, the better.

So I called Jenny at work and she agreed on dinner the next night.

That night before going to bed I stood naked in front of the mirror again. Now I thought I could see the faint puff in my stomach and the tinge of rose turning my nipples darker. There the whole time and I hadn't noticed, hadn't imagined pregnancy. I laughed, looking at the skin over my breasts tight, taut, like stretching out. I kept staring at my body, turning to one side, imagining my stomach all puffed out, my face fuller. Soon my breasts and feet would be swollen, my hair all rinky-dink . . . but a feeling like no other . . . so full of love.

The next day, I'm telling you, you don't know what I went through . . . I woke at dawn with that floaty feeling you get when you think you're still dreaming. . . . I sat up and looked around the room, saying out loud, "Lisa Perlman, you're a forty-three-year-old pregnant woman. You're having a baby" . . . and God, I couldn't believe it . . . my mind was going a mile a minute, worrying about a million things at once, like if I could be a good mother and handle a career, counting out the days from that night at the Adlers', figuring that the baby would be born December 20, my due date . . . like the girls, right on the button. I felt kind of shaky, woozy, so I held my knees real tight, kind of rocking back and forth, my tongue hanging out like it does when I'm nervous, closing my eyes . . . thinking back when Amy was first born, then afterward in the hospital room when the nurse went out of the room . . . Arnold off somewhere . . . and I unwrapped the blanket and looked at Amy . . . real close . . . afraid to touch her, feeling so shy . . . wondering who she was, who I was . . . playing hide-and-seek with Jenny, Jenny laughing . . . Amy first walking, holding her arms straight out, then plop, falling, and all still for a minute, then crying like hell until I'd rock her, rocking her until she stopped crying. Then the hard years raising the girls alone . . . all the carpools, cooking classes, music lessons, first pimples, first dances . . . Amy crying that the kids made fun of the flowers I drew on her lunch bags . . . Jenny jumping up and down on a trampoline . . . Amy writing "Dear Daddy" letters and never getting an answer . . . Jenny on Parents' Night pretending her father was late . . . the school treating me like I was a third-class citizen. I wanted this time different, better, for my baby not to go through all that hurt. But life doesn't always turn out the way you planned . . . I wanted to marry Eric, but our relationship didn't spell marriage. . . . I loved the little rat person with all his *mishegoss* . . . but even if Eric came to me on a white horse crying, "Lisa Perlman, marry me!" I wouldn't—couldn't—not the way things were between us. . . . Marriage'd be deadly . . . I could just see Mr. Genius running the show . . . everything . . . trying to be the big professor . . . always telling me how to talk . . . even trying to get the baby to talk like some whiz. Anyways, who was I kidding? Probably Eric wouldn't ask me. All this talk about interaction and settling down, wanting to marry . . . a bunch of hooey, believe me. . . . When it comes down to brass tacks, Eric Blumberg is a free agent, always was, always will be . . . likes running around the world, improvising life, sneaking women here and there, keeping all his options open, wanting what he can't have. But maybe . . . oh, God . . .

I took a couple of deep breaths, stretching my arms way out, and then I put on the big yellow down duck slippers and went into the kitchen. After feeding Anny her Meow Chow, I went into the den and began typing a new letter to Eric, the clackety sound from the typewriter breaking the morning quiet. But while I was writing, all those mixed feelings about Eric were boinging around in my head. So the words came out all stuck . . . a mess of lousy birds and purple skies . . . and this was a time for real feelings, direct and honest, not for purple skies or wacko birds. . . . I had to stop hiding behind my words . . . get out what I was feeling . . . stick my neck out.

So after a couple of tries, I finally finished writing a letter I thought was okay. I read the letter several times: "Dear Eric, For once words are hard for me. Especially because I have news that will change our lives. We're having a baby. I just found out I'm ten weeks pregnant. Though I'm still in a state of shock, I'm healthy and happy, so happy about the baby, as I hope you will be. I'm trying to picture your face as you read this letter, feel what you're feeling, and I wish you were here. So much time has gone by . . . I wish I had answered your letters . . . told you what I was feeling . . . kept the door open. I hope that we can work things out, make a go of us, so that the baby can have good parents, a good, loving father like you are with your boys. Meanwhile, I'm doing fine, working hard, and beginning to make plans for my future and the baby's. I want you to know that I don't want nor expect a marriage proposal . . . only that you'll be happy about the baby. There are so many things I want to say to you, but I'll wait until I hear from you . . . until we talk. I hope you're well. I love you. Always, Lisa."

And as I read and reread the letter, imagining Eric's face as he read the letter, I got that funny feeling like when you're looking down from somewhere high, my breath all caught, and I was tempted to tear it up and start another one and tell Eric exactly why I didn't want to marry him, that I didn't trust him and that he was the most difficult person I'd ever met and that he was always giving and taking away and that he made me feel all mixed up sometimes.

But now . . . the news was enough for one letter, and besides, a letter wasn't the place for Eric and me to talk . . . and I had to mail the letter because Eric had to know about the baby before he left Australia . . . the university in Australia was the only address he had given me. Then carrying the letter in my pea coat pocket around 6:00 A.M. when the light was coming into the sky, I walked to the mailbox. When I came home I went right into the den and started working on *Eva* . . . feeling kind of lousy . . . wondering if Eric would call me right away . . . or write . . . but, God, I had a lot of work and if I got off the track even one day, the work would get set back . . . get me out of whack. So I tried to block out everything but the work . . . not think about Eric . . . the baby . . . but as I worked, Eric's face kept coming into my head, like a part of me was with him.

Around five-thirty Jenny arrived straight from her late classes at City College. God, she looked so fresh . . . young . . . she was wearing a pair of tight jeans, a big pink cable sweater, her hair, long now, tied back with a pink ribbon, a big purple backpack slung over her shoulders, her face all flushed. She was carrying a bouquet of pink roses. She always brought me little things . . . flowers . . . little soaps shaped like animals . . . little things.

"Here, Mom," she said, giving me the roses wrapped in green tissue, the roses still damp.

"Oh, Jen . . . they're gorgeous. Thank you," I said, kissing her cheek.

"I'm starved," she said, dropping the backpack on the kitchen chair.

"Well, sit down," I said, unwrapping the roses and putting them in the little glass bowl.

"Mmmm . . . looks good, Mom. I love garbanzo beans . . . my favorite dinner."

"Yes, I know," I said, serving the salad on two white ceramic plates with the rainbows painted in the center.

"And the French bread is just the way I like it . . . with just a little garlic," she said, smiling at me and helping herself to two thick slices.

"Thank you again for the roses, Jen," I said, sitting next to her. "You shouldn't spend your money."

"I wanted to," she said, biting into the French bread. We began eating our salads, Jenny's fork pushing the garbanzo beans in a little pile along the side of her plate, saving them for last. The light from the big pink candle glowed over Jenny's face. Her long, dark lashes curled up at the ends.

"Mom?"

"Hmmm?"

"I've told you about Dodie . . . you know Dodie at work . . . the one who's always asking me for Motron. . . ."

"Oh yes, Dodie."

"She wants to meet you, Mom. Dodie wants to write a novel."

"She'd better start."

"That's what I told her," she said, smiling approvingly and lowering her voice confidentially. "I said, 'Dodie, you don't just sit down and write a novel. My Mom's been writing for years . . . every day.' "

"I'd love to meet her, Jenny."

"Mmmm," said Jenny, piling her plate with spaghetti. "This is great . . . mmmm . . . mushrooms. . . ."

"Good, I know you love spaghetti. Loved it when you were a little girl. You'd always say 'segetti' . . . couldn't pronounce your *p*'s." I laughed.

She giggled. "What was I like, Mom?"

"Oh . . . adorable. Like you are now. Now, eat."

We sat quietly. I pretended I was eating but I couldn't eat a thing. . . . Jenny's so sensitive, and I wanted to tell her gently. Jenny ate with gusto, expertly twisting the spaghetti around her fork, eating neatly and quickly.

"How's your English class?" I asked carefully.

"Okay . . ."

She stopped eating and looked at me with a serious expression on her face.

"My English teacher, Professor Reider, wrote a little note on my paper, said that I have a nice writing style but I should learn how to spell."

I laughed. "He's encouraging you. That's how I got started writing."

She began eating the mushrooms one at a time.

"And how's Kevin?" I asked carefully.

"He's okay," she said, biting her lower lip, and her eyes turned guarded. "I don't see him much because he's busy . . . studying for his broker's license and going to grad school. . . ."

"Sounds like you're both busy," I said.

"I went out with that Joel Ziegler a few times."

"Oh? Did you have fun?"

"He's okay," she said between mouthfuls of spaghetti. "But he primps more than I do . . . every minute he whips out the dental floss . . . or the Certs . . . something about wealthy Jewish guys,

Mom . . . every minute with the decaf . . . born nervous, I guess."

"True," I said.

"Anyway, Mom . . . Nans said if I play my cards right with this Joel dork, she'd buy me a new dress, shoes. . . ."

"Oh, God . . . typical," I said.

"Nans is a classic . . . not a dime a dozen."

"You always say that. I think it's wonderful that you appreciate Nans. When she used to do that with me I'd go bonks."

"That's because she's your mother, I guess, and you couldn't talk to her like I can talk to you."

"True," I said, touching her cheek. . . . "Well, I'm glad you like school," I said laughing, "and meeting new people is fun."

"It's okay," she said, shrugging. "More sauce, please."

I brought her plate to the stove and poured more spaghetti sauce over the remaining spaghetti on Jenny's plate. She liked it heavy and thick. The coffee pot was perking and sounded like an old rusty heater. I had to tell Jenny . . . I couldn't let it go any longer . . . I couldn't.

"Jen . . . I have something . . . well, I have something to tell you . . . it's good news," I said quickly, watching the way she was twisting the spaghetti real tight over her fork. "I mean . . . listen, Jen . . . it's something I'm very happy about."

She stopped twisting the spaghetti around the fork, holding it slightly away from her, looking at me suspiciously, her black eyes narrowed. There was this tiny moment all still—so still you could hear the foil paper fluttering over the casserole dish.

"I'm pregnant, Jen . . . with Eric's baby."

She pushed the mushrooms on her plate into a little pile, then separating the mushrooms, then pushing them into a pile again, like pushing her thoughts into some order. She looked up at me finally with that expression on her face she'd have as a child when trying to cover up a lie or a hurt . . . her eyes all still . . . but I could see by the way she bit her lower lip she was scared . . . and God, I wanted to hold her. . . .

"Mom . . . oh, Mom . . ."

"I know, I know . . . it's a shocker . . ." I said, holding her hand real tight so she wouldn't pull away.

"A baby . . ."

"Uh-huh."

"Oh, Mom . . . why didn't you take care of yourself? . . ."

"I thought I was in menopause, Jen . . . I mean, it happened . . . just happened . . . but I'm happy about the baby, Jen . . . really happy."

"You're happy?"

"Yes, very."

"Like you were with me?" she said, looking at her plate, her fork pushing out the mushrooms.

"Yes . . . only no one can ever take your place. Never."

"But you're an older woman, Mom," she said, still looking at her plate. "Forty-three- . . . almost forty-four- . . . year-old women don't go around having babies."

"I'll be fine. And I really am so happy about the baby . . honestly, Jen."

"Is he marrying you?"

"I've just written Eric . . . I don't know if marriage is right for Eric and me right now . . . if I even want to. . . ."

"I knew he wouldn't marry you," she said, biting her lip.

"That's not true . . . this decision has nothing to do with Eric."

"What do you mean, nothing to do with Eric? He's the father."

"I mean, marriage is something else . . . a separate thing . . . and we have things to work out . . . but the main thing is that we all love each other and this baby. . . . I love Eric very much. . . . He'll love the baby, too. . . . He's a wonderful father, you know. . . ."

"Haven't you heard, Mom? A baby is supposed to come in one package: a father, a mother, and a house."

"Oh, God, Jen . . . I want all those things," I quickly assured her. "But just different houses . . . for now."

"Maybe I should move home and help you."

"You have your own life now, Jen. But I love you for offering."

"All right," she said, sighing and looking at me anxiously. "But I'm going with you to the doctor's . . . help you . . . stuff like that. . . . I don't want you to be alone."

"Oh, that'd be great!" I said, smiling at her, stroking her cheek. "I can't think of anyone I'd rather have with me. You can help me get organized . . . you know what I mean. . . ."

"Do I!" she said, blinking several times.

Then we sat quietly, not saying a word. Jenny pulled her hand slowly away and dabbed her eyes with a crumpled napkin.

"Nans is going to have a shit fit," she said finally.

"Don't tell Nans yet, Jen . . . not one word. Not until I've thought out exactly how I'm going to tell her. I want to talk it over with you . . . Amy . . . it's going to be hard telling Nans."

"And Amy," she said, sticking out her chin. "You know how Amy feels, Mom, about some of your goofy ideas . . . you're hardly Mrs. Brady baking cookies for the Brownie troop."

"I'm calling Amy later—four A.M., our time, so I can talk to her before she goes to work."

Jenny blinked a few more times and fiddled with the napkin. I got up and poured coffee into two ceramic cups with pink and yellow rainbows, the cups Jenny and I bought at an art fair. Jenny stirred three spoonfuls of sugar into her coffee. We sipped our coffee while the candlelight glowed softly around us. Anny was drinking water from her dish, and the rattle of mah-jongg tiles came through the open vent. After a long quiet, Jenny took the backpack lying on the other chair and opened it. She took out a book of Faulkner's short stories, turning to the page where she had stuck a purple silk bookmark.

"Will you help me with a paper?" she said, looking at me cautiously.

"Sure I will. But first . . . I've made your favorite dessert. Tapioca pudding."

"Well—"

"C'mon, Jen . . . I know you love it."

She sighed. "Okay . . . maybe just a little."

At 4:00 A.M. my alarm clock went off. I turned on the light next to my bed. I got out of bed and creaked across the room, my back hurting, and went into the bathroom. I washed my face with cold water . . . my eyes were kind of bloodshot—puffy. I'd hardly slept, thinking about the baby . . . remembering Jenny's face when I told her about the baby and then at the door, the way she hugged me, a lingering hug like when she was a child and wanted more kisses or didn't want me to leave. Telling Amy wasn't going to be so easy, either . . . though Amy, always the old child, on her own so long, was used to talking our lives over the telephone. . . . I wanted to call Amy before Jenny because those two were as thick as pea soup . . . and no matter what Jenny promised she could've called Amy already. . ..

Amy answered on the first ring.

"Amy! It's Mom!"

"What's wrong?"

"Wrong?"

"You never call this early."

"No . . . no . . . I just wanted to call."

"I had the weirdest dream about you last night, Mom. You and Jenny and I were on this big old bus and you were wearing this humongously hideous pink hat with a paper rose on the top and the bus was going nowhere."

"Sounds awful."

Silence.

"Anyways, Mom"—Amy's voice dropping into a confidential tone—"is it Eric?"

"Nothing's wrong."

"Mom—"

"I'm pregnant."

"What?"

"With Eric's baby."

Silence.

"Mom—"

"Uh-huh. I'm so happy, Amy . . . I still can't believe it . . . I'm so happy," I repeated.

"Oh, Mom . . . Mom."

"Of course you don't know what to say. . . . Why would you? . . . I mean, it's not every day your forty-three-year-old Mom is having a baby. . . . But I didn't know how to tell you . . . I mean, I could hardly hop on a People's Express and meet you for lunch."

"I guess not . . . but Mom . . . oh, Mom . . ."

"I was nervous about telling you," I said, waiting for her to say something else.

"When's the wedding?"

"Wedding?"

"Wedding!"

"I don't know if there's going to be a wedding . . . if I want a wedding. . . ."

"No wedding?"

"No . . . not until . . . I—"

"How does Eric feel about it?" she asked quickly.

"I've just written Eric about the baby . . . I mean, we haven't talked yet . . . but I love Eric very much, Amy."

"You haven't talked about marriage?"

"No . . ."

"Tch-tch-tch . . ."

"Stop tch-tch-tching. That's what Nana does."

Silence.

"I don't understand, Mom. . . . If you love Eric, why don't you want to marry him?"

"There are things, Amy . . . I'm not against marriage . . . but Eric and I have a lot of things to work out in our relationship. . . . I mean, after all, this baby wasn't planned . . . I mean, I was this menopausal person. . . ."

"Still . . ."

"But I want this baby so much, Amy. I'm so happy about the baby. And I know Eric will be, too . . . he's a wonderful father."

She sniffed. "How far along are you?"

"Ten weeks."

"Ten weeks!"

"Uh-huh."

"I know you said you're happy about the baby," said Amy carefully, "but you have to be realistic . . . I mean, you are forty-three years old. . . ."

"So?"

"So, you still have time to get an abortion."

"Never!"

"Oh, Mom . . . you know what you went through with David. . . . What if Eric doesn't want this baby?"

"I've always been so sorry about that abortion, Amy. But no one is going to take this baby away. No one!"

"What are you going to do?" she said, her voice dropping.

"Do?"

"Yes, do . . . How are you going to take care of the baby? I mean, you can't let your career go out the window." She paused. "And we were going to work together."

"Oh, Amy . . . we will . . . you'll see . . . nothing's changed. I'm finishing writing *Eva* . . . I'll try to sell more art . . . get a job if I have to . . . I'll make it . . . I always have."

"Oh, Mom . . . I know."

"So don't worry . . . everything will be fine."

"Do you want me to come home? I have three weeks' vacation time I haven't used."

"Oh, Amy . . . that's so sweet. But that's not necessary. I'd rather have you home when the baby is born: December twentieth, I figured."

"I'll stay with you and help you with the baby. . . . Oh, Mom, are you crying?"

"No . . ."

"Oh, Mom, why are you crying? I'm really happy for you . . . about the baby . . . don't cry."

"I'm not crying," I said, wiping my eyes with my sleeve. "I'm just feeling kind of emotional. You and Jenny . . . God, you're so great. I want you to love this baby. We're like those links on this big gold chain. I want us all a family."

"I want that, too. . . . I mean, Mom . . . we are a family. I just want you to be happy."

"I am happy. The rest of the stuff will work out."

Silence.

I could hear sirens in the background like they were so close . . . the rattling of sounds . . . Amy's careful breathing. I missed her so much and I wanted her in my arms, wanted her there. Then Amy said, "What about Jenny? Did you tell her?"

"Last night."

"What did she say?" said Amy, her tone dropping.

"Like you . . . she was great . . . really something . . . happy for me . . . the baby . . . but underneath," I confided, "I think Jenny is afraid I won't love her as much as the baby."

"Jenny needs a lot of extra attention, Mom . . . you have to know how to handle her."

"Yes, I know," I said, touched by Amy's concern for Jenny.

"And what about Nana?"

"I'm telling her soon. Everything'll be all right. Don't worry."

She sighed. "Well, if Farrah Fawcett can do it, you can . . . but she exercised, Mom . . . watched her diet . . . and you eat those humongously hideous French fries . . . I worry."

"Don't worry, I'm fine. Dr. Chan is putting me on a diet. And I'm going to join this aerobics class for pregnant women over forty."

"Good," said Amy, sounding relieved.

"Uh-huh."

"The minute you hear from Eric, Mom, please let me know."

"Of course I will. Meanwhile, stop worrying."

"I can't help it, Mom. I worry."

"And just think, Amy . . . a baby . . . and we're all going to be together at Christmas . . . and meanwhile we'll talk every day. . . ."

Beep.

"Oh, Mom, I have another call coming in."

"Oh, sure . . . sure . . ."

"I'll call you later, Mom."

"Uh-huh."

"Be sure you get on that diet!"

Beep.

"I will. You'd better take that call."

"Bye, Mom! I'll call you later!"

"I love you!"

Beep.

"Love you, too!"

Click.

Three weeks later . . . a balmy June day . . . the day I was going to Mother's house for lunch and tell Mother about the baby. I was nervous, really nervous . . . not so much about what Mother'd say . . . I mean I already know what she'd think, say . . . more because I was damn worried about Mother's health . . . lately she'd been complaining about her leg and about this awful pain in her arms . . . and after all, how many blows could Mother's old heart take? But I'd try to make Mother see that I was so happy about the baby and that I had it all together, so she wouldn't get all nuts about everything, start yelling or crying. But now with the baby coming and all, I wanted to work on making us a real family . . . no matter what Mother's shtick or how difficult our relationship, I loved Mother. I wanted her to be part of my life. This wasn't a time to hide my feelings, pretending they all grew in clay pots along the windowsill.

I hadn't heard from Eric, and I was really getting upset. "Upset" wasn't the word . . . actually, more like frantic. I mean, this awful feeling would come over me, like that feeling I'd get when I thought everything was leaving me, going away. And even though the man at the post office assured me a thousand times that it takes two weeks at least for a letter to get to Australia, every day I'd run to the mailbox, and when I didn't find a letter, I'd start worrying that Eric got one of those awful viruses and was lying sick in the bush with kangaroos.

So after hashing all this over with Dr. Kenner, I finally decided that it might be a good idea to call Eric . . . talk to him . . . face up. So after three weeks went by and still no word from Eric and I couldn't stand it anymore, after talking to this overseas operator, I was put through to the University of New South Wales. The registrar's office said that Eric had left the week before and told them he'd send them his forwarding address but they hadn't heard from him and didn't know where he was. After I hung up I ran around the house wearing the duck slippers, doing my breathing, feeling really lousy, wondering if Eric got my letter . . . if he'd gone on to China . . . where he was . . . if he wasn't answering the letter . . . if he met someone else. . . . I didn't know what to think . . . I didn't. And I hurt.

Anyways, that day I wore a lot of makeup, that Clinique cover-up stuff Mother gave me, hoping that Mother wouldn't notice the splotches on my face. I mean, Mother has eyes like radar, and I wanted to look my best.

I arrived at Mother's house at noon. Birdie, carrying a bottle of furniture polish and a couple of rags, let me in. Birdie, wearing pink bobby socks and white tennis shoes, said that Mother planned luncheon in the garden. So I hurried through the hallway, careful not to slip on the heavily varnished floors and fall on my ass, and went into the garden. Mother was in the back of the garden, clipping roses from the big yellow rosebush that grew along the white wooden fence. The sun was falling over the back of her head, and from a distance her hair looked so pale and shiny.

"Hi, Mother," I said, hurrying over to her.

"Lisa . . ." she said, turning around and smiling at me and taking off her thick white garden gloves. "I didn't hear you come in. Honestly, that Birdie!"

We kissed, a kind of air kiss. Mother's eyes appraised what I was wearing.

"That's a nice blouse. Black is good on you, Lisa. And those tweed pants . . . cotton?" she asked, feeling the material. "Stunning. That's how you should always look," she said, her eyes peering closely at my face.

"Thanks, Mother."

"But your face, Lisa," she said, squinting her eyes and looking alarmed. "Those blotches . . . what are those red blotches?"

"Just stress probably," I said, quickly turning away.

"Use that nice Clinique I gave you for sensitive skin."

"Yes, I have some on."

"Let's sit over here under the umbrella," she said.

And we went over and sat at the white wicker round table by a big floppy yellow and white umbrella. The table was set for lunch, the yellow and white floral linen napkins folded next to white straw placemats.

"Oh, everything looks so nice," I said, admiring the garden. "I can smell the ocean."

She smiled, then rang the bell several times, calling "Birdie!" complaining that Birdie was getting hard of hearing.

"How's Sidney?" I asked, unfolding the napkin and placing it in my lap.

"A rock," she said, crossing her fingers and pressing her lips.

"Yes, he's a wonderful man. . . . And Bruce?" I asked carefully.

"Bruce . . ." she repeated, her voice drifting, opening her napkin, then pressing the napkin on the table, on a tiny smudge. "Bruce is going out more . . . seems he met a nice young man . . . a psychologist . . . not like that other schlemiel." .

"Oh, that's nice. . . ."

"Honestly, Lisa," she said quickly, looking around the garden, "Mr. Takahari didn't spray enough this year . . . the roses look awful."

"Not awful . . . I think they look beautiful."

"They could look better," said Mother, pressing the napkin.

"Amy . . . Jenny . . . send their love."

"I talked to Amy the other day," she said, smiling. "She loves her apartment. Said everything is coming up roses."

"Yes."

"And Jenny calls me every day," she said, nodding approvingly. "And Lisa, I think Joel Ziegler is interested in Jenny. And he's no slouch. Very sophisticated."

"Uh-huh . . . so it seems."

"Did I tell you, Lisa," she said, blinking several times, "that Rhoda Samuelson died?"

"Yes. That's sad, Mother."

"Yes," she said, pressing her lips and looking away. "She was my age . . . such a wonderful lady . . . always did everything so beautifully."

"Yes . . ."

Birdie came into the garden carrying a big white wicker tray with our salads on these beautiful yellow and white salad plates, little rolls, and steaming coffee. We ate quietly for a while, while I went over in my mind just when I'd tell Mother about the baby.

"Honestly, Lisa," said Mother, pouring some dressing over her shrimp salad, "that Sylvia Finkel thinks she knows so much about everything and she's so ignorant. She doesn't even know who Eva Hesse is. I had to explain to her at our bridge game."

"Eva Hesse is so obscure, Mother."

Mother poked her fork at the tiny shrimp over the endive. "She's still a pill," she said, looking guilty.

"Yes," I agreed.

"So, what have you heard from Eric?"

"Oh . . . he's fine," I said in my most up tone, looking directly at her, my arms all tingly. "He's fine," I repeated, Mother watching me closely.

"Everyone . . . the family . . . asks me when you and Eric are getting married. I never know what to say."

"Mother, Eric and I need more time together . . . it's a complex relationship. Eric is a complex person . . . difficult. . . . I am, too. We're both involved in our work."

"Why you always have to pick the funnies, I'll never know!"

"Mother . . . I have something to tell you."

Mother blinked a few times, looked up at the sunlight, and blinked. I kept watching her face . . . the way she kept blinking, pressing the napkin . . . watching her closely . . . afraid . . . scared to death she'd get sick . . . or maybe even die. Until I just said as softly and directly as I could, "I'm pregnant, Mother . . . I'm pregnant with Eric's baby."

She looked at me then and I sat all still, hardly moving, and her eyes were so yellow in the sunlight, all still, like they'd get when she was upset, like closed off. She pressed the napkin a few times on the table and cleared her throat and blinked several times like blinking away what I'd just told her.

"Mother . . . I'm happy about the baby . . . I'm happy . . . and I want us, all of us . . . you especially . . . close with the baby. Mother, I . . ."

"Now he has to marry you, Lisa," she finally said, still pressing the napkin on the table and blinking. "You'll settle down . . . lead a normal life."

"Uh-huh. Normal."

"When is Eric coming home?"

"Mother, I've just written Eric. I haven't heard from him yet."

"So, they have telephones in Australia! Tell him to come home."

"I don't want to pressure him."

"Pressure him! When's the baby due?"

"December."

"Still plenty of time to have the wedding. . . . I'll have it here . . . in the garden and—"

"I don't know, Mother . . . what Eric's going to feel . . . or how I feel. . . ."

"Know! What's there to know?!"

"We have to know our feelings."

"This isn't a time for feelings, Lisa. You women libbers are for the birds with your feelings."

"This has nothing to do with women's lib, Mother . . . I mean, I'd like to get married . . . if it's right. . . ."

"Right! Make it right! Play your cards right! For once, Lisa, listen to your mother. Be smart. I've had two wonderful husbands. I know what I'm talking about."

"Yes, you have," I said. "And . . . oh, Mother . . . I'd like that, too. . . . It's not that I have anything against marriage . . . maybe in time. . . ."

"Make it easier on yourself, Lisa. . . . What are you trying to prove?"

"Prove! I just want to do what's right for me . . . the baby."

"So you think it's right for the baby not to have a father?"

"But the baby will have a father . . . a loving father. I'm sure of that. Eric loves children, Mother. He raised two good sons."

"Tch-tch-tch," she said, squinting her eyes and looking at me curiously, like trying to see through the sunlight.

I watched a bird perch on a tree and the roses looked so beautiful . . . shiny. . . . We looked at each other like two women eyeing each other from opposite sides of a fence.

"Mother . . . I love Eric very much. I promise everything will be all right . . . you'll see . . . I promise. I really want this baby, Mother."

She nodded a couple of times, like assuring herself. She waved away the air then, like some imaginary bug.

"Lisa, make sure you wear a good bra," she said, lifting and dropping her shoulders and squinting her eyes at me, "so you don't get saggy. . . ."

"That's true."

"I thought you looked bigger. And you'll have to watch your weight, Lisa . . . not get so big, like you did with the girls. Nowadays, Lisa, they have such wonderful things. . . . I'll take you to my lingerie girl at Saks . . . she'll fit you in a decent bra."

"Uh-huh."

"On television I see these gorgeous pregnant movie stars."

"Uh-huh."

"And rest. You need rest, Lisa."

"Yes, rest. I'll rest more."

"Are you feeling all right?" she asked, frowning and leaning forward and peering closely at me.

"All right . . . I mean, I'm kind of tired . . . you know, the usual first-trimester stuff. But I'm fine."

"Do you have to sit at the typewriter all day writing? Can't you rest?" she said, tch-tch-tching.

"It's my work, Mother."

"There are more important things than work."

"Yes. Uh-huh."

"Believe me, Lisa . . . if you play your cards right, your Eric . . . genius or not . . . will be putty in your hands . . . it's up to a smart woman—"

"Uh-huh."

"Does your doctor give you vitamins, Lisa?"

"Oh, yes . . . and she's already put me on an excellent diet."

"Tomorrow I'll call that dummy, Mr. Takahari, and tell him to spray the roses . . . summer is a nice time for a garden wedding."

"Uh-huh."

She pressed the napkin again on the table. We sat quietly until the sunlight rolled into a strip of shadows and broke across the trees. . . .

CHAPTER FIFTEEN

Almost the end of August and God, the days were foggy . . . but the trees all green . . . really beautiful. I had the amniocentesis and the baby, a little girl, was healthy and growing. I listened to the baby's heartbeat through Dr. Chan's stethoscope and I could feel the baby moving in me and sometimes when I felt those little flutters of life I'd stop what I was doing and hold my hands over my stomach, like holding the baby close to me . . . so close . . . I'd imagine that the baby and I lived inside this beautiful pink bubble, all warm and safe . . . looking out at the world . . . and my dreams were full of babies . . . always the same baby, wrapped in a pink blanket, looking at me through Eric's dark eyes.

The baby puffed out my face and I'd gained seventeen pounds and I was carrying real high, like I did with Amy and Jenny. My legs were swollen, zipped with tiny blue veins, and I walked like you do when you're pregnant, kind of backward on your heels, like looking up. I mostly wore slacks and these loose cotton tops I'd made and painted with faces of dolls and flowers, and my comfortable pink rubber sandals. I'd decided that I wanted as natural a childbirth as possible . . . not that I'm into this midwife thing, having the baby at home while my picture was taken for the *Whole Birth Catalogue*, not that . . . but I'd want to feel this birth. Dr. Chan said okay, given my age, hypertension, edema, some other things, natural childbirth might not work out, but we'd try fo⁻ it. So I joined this class at the Jewish Community Center and three evenings a week I shlepped my mat, towel, and practiced having babies with all these young couples . . . a few older women . . . learning prenatal exercises . . . pushing positions . . . breathing exercises . . . looking at films on natural childbirth . . . the whole bit. And God, it was something watching these nice young couples, the way the father would be all concerned and everything, and those times I missed Eric so much, wished he were with me.

I missed Eric like crazy . . . dreamed of him making love to me

. . . caressing my growing belly . . . kissing me all over . . . and I was kissing him all over, the baby stirring inside me. Sometimes I'd undress and stand naked in front of the mirror, looking at my body—the way my belly was growing round and my breasts turning all full and the veins getting thick—and I'd get that breathless feeling I'd get when I'd look at a beautiful painting or special light because I'd never seen anything so magical—so wonderful—as a baby growing.

But even though I had this ache in me, after the first few months and the dizziness and nausea stuff passed, I felt really wonderful. The baby gave me new energy. A lot of times after writing *Eva* all day I'd go walk along the ocean, thinking about the baby, collecting seashells, old rocks, pieces from the earth, saving them in a glass jar . . . or I'd go into baby shops and look at all the infant things, this glow in me . . . sometimes buying little things for the baby, a lovely cloth book or rattle, keeping the things in a big wicker basket. In an antiques shop on Clement Street I'd bought an old wooden cradle and was stripping the wood and planned on painting a big rainbow along the side. So even though by body felt heavy as a cow and I was no beauty with my face covered with these yucko red splotches . . . God, I felt close to the baby . . . sometimes so content I hated leaving my little contained world . . . resented the slightest intrusion.

On the nights I didn't have art clients I'd sit in the living room with my sketch pad and felt pens, drawing faces, imagining what the baby looked like . . . drawing Eric's squashed nose, Sad Sack eyes, my thick eyebrows, Eric's frown and curled lip when he'd get into those pilly moods . . . or I'd write little poems for the baby, saving them in shoe boxes. And then I'd open the wicker basket and look at the things I bought for the baby . . . smiling and remembering Jenny in the playpen, sucking her pacifier, Amy swinging back and forth on the electric swing.

And one day in the stationery store when I was buying typing paper, wearing the white denim top I'd painted with a big owl, I bumped into Patty Applebaum, looking all spiffy in her purple Calvin Klein jumpsuit and when she said what's new, Lisa, I smiled and happily said I was having a baby. I guess she didn't know what to say or didn't really understand that I was so happy about the baby because she turned away, just went away. But after a lifetime of thinking I needed everyone's approval, always be what others wanted, it was wonderful not worrying about what others thought about me, like I'd let go of the old script and at last was living my own lines. At last accepted me . . . Lisa Perlman, this person wearing bird pants, loving cats and being alone.

The telemoaners were great . . . Larry Segal called a lot from L.A. and after complaining about the lousy life of a writer, we'd talk about our work and then he'd listen while I complained about my swollen feet and back pains . . . and Andrea Mandelbaum called all the time, though she said if it were her having the baby she'd jump out the window . . . and Kathy said she couldn't wait to baby-sit . . . and Marcie Kaplan called every minute asking how I was feeling and bought the baby all these adorable little stretchies . . . and Amy said she'd give the baby her first gold locket. Jenny was knitting the baby a big purple blanket . . . and when I'd go over to Jenny's apartment she'd open the old blue vinyl toy box and show me which toys she'd give her new sister . . . then, biting her lower lip, she'd sort out the toys and put them in a wooden box.

I tried to spend extra time with Jenny, doing the things she liked, going to Golden Gate Park and looking at the penguins or the planetarium, where we'd pretend we were on the moon. And Mother in her own way was accepting the baby, buying these fancy layettes, always hocking me about getting married or my weight. . . but so touching the way she'd shop for just the right baby things, listening quietly while I talked about the baby, her eyes all wide, like she was trying to see into me.

Mother explained to the family that after Eric returned from sabbatical the wedding would be at her house and that really with-it people did things differently these days. Anyways, Mother put up a damned brave front, and believe me, she had plenty of her own *tsuris* . . . more than ever. Of course, Mother had leased Bruce a new Porsche, with the promise that he wouldn't drive it until he got his license. But Bruce, one night wanting to see his Rick, the psychologist, sneaked his new Porsche out of the garage and driving too fast, ran a red light and was picked up for speeding and driving without a license. So Bruce was in a whale of trouble, and Sidney was raising holy hell, yelling his head off that Bruce was costing a bundle and that he wanted Bruce out of the house and that the car had to go, while Mother cried her eyes out and argued that Bruce wasn't well enough and that Sidney should be more understanding. Meanwhile, Bruce, back to his old ways, ran up a whole mess of bills on Mother's charge accounts until Sidney took away and closed all Mother's charge accounts and cut her allowance again.

So Bruce spent most of his time in his room watching old movies and listening to opera tapes, sometimes going out on errands with mother, or to Dr. Heindrich. I'd go over and visit Mother and there'd be Bruce in his monogrammed blue bathrobe, looking like death warmed over, and Mother'd be fixing her little bridge lunches or playing the piano, fussing over Bruce, and giving him money on the side. But when I tried to talk to her about Bruce's spending so much money, she'd get that funny look in her eyes, all angry, and say that Bruce needed his things because Bruce lost his father so young and never had a girlfriend, a sick boy and so lonely. So I butted out . . . an old story, anyways.

I cried. I mean, sometimes I'd remember poor Bruce walking to school, one of those hidden private schools, the parka zipped up to his chin. Then after school, lying on the water bed with one of his headaches, the vials of medicines on the table next to him, the room dark except for the fluorescent glow from the fish tanks. After Daddy died, except for Bruce's extravagant birthday parties, he never went anywhere, just driving Mother around in her Cadillac, his learner's permit inside an expensive alligator wallet. I'd get so sad. Because he was stuck. Always stuck.

A couple of times Bruce came over and helped me file drafts, fix my typewriter—he loved to fix things. But then he stopped coming over . . . fizzled out. Things stayed the same, in their places, like Mother's porcelains. Mother swept away the catastrophes just as she swept out the old dust.

So things were a little tough in the family department, and the worse they got, Mother only got older, more fragile, more involved in her little rituals, her errands, her roses, her silver, always covering up. But then Mother could be really wonderful, so generous, always ready to help. And when I'd confess to Mother that I still hadn't heard from Eric and that I was plenty worried, Mother would say in her baby voice that I had to keep the faith and that she had a feeling in her bones when Eric got my letter he'd rush right home and we'd live happily ever after and that plenty of movie stars have beautiful weddings after the baby is born and that Sylvia Finkel could go to hell.

And things were going well in the writing department. Finally I wrote "THE END" on the bottom of the page and three stars after. I felt kind of funny, like you do when something you're used to suddenly goes away—isn't there anymore—a mixture of relief and sadness.

But Eva had made me think a lot about art and work and I didn't agree with Eva that "art and life are a total person." I think art is about a lot of things, not one single idea or ideal, and that work is only a part of your life, not the whole picture. But like Eva says, if you take "total risk" and never get off your path . . . believe in yourself . . . your work . . . no matter what . . . you can make something true, and I think art is something true.

The next day I got right back to work on *Eva* because now I had to do the polishing and smoothing out, and that would take some time.

Anyways, Lester was up to his old tricks, calling every minute and hocking about when I'd send him *Eva*'s final draft and why was I taking so long and to get the show on the road.

Meanwhile, the bills were piling up. But my art clients were picking up . . . a lot of referrals. . . . I was selling some expensive California art, making enough money to pay off some of the old bills that cropped up during *Princess,* but I had to make more money . . . and God knows what would happen with *Eva* . . . a long way down the road . . . so I called Neil Thompson at the Oakland Museum and we met at Neil's office. Neil was so nice when I told him about the baby and asked me if I'd work on a special project with California artists . . . so I decided that after I had the baby and arranged for baby-sitters, I'd work part-time. God, I was excited because I loved the work and though the money wasn't great, the job would help support the baby and my writing.

So I began looking at places in Oakland, not only so I would be closer to work but also so the baby would be closer to Eric . . . her father.

The third week of August . . . Sunday . . . the fog rolling over the city, and the sky dark. I loved San Francisco foggy days . . . the cold summers . . . the foghorns' hollow sound . . . so private. That day I'd felt really lousy . . . I hadn't slept well and had been up most of the night, every minute running to the john. My back was killing me, like the baby was trying to press through. So that morning I did a lot of pelvic floor exercises and deep breathing and after that I decided it was time to get to work. Then I went at it, typing like crazy, and soon nothing mattered except the work . . . even the back pain was somewhere else. I was in the middle of polishing this gripping scene when Eva's ex-husband comes to the hospital.

I heard the doorbell ring so I stopped typing and sat there real still because I was on a roll and didn't want to be interrupted. Then I remembered Marcie Kaplan said she might come by, that she had a gift for the baby, so I peeked out the shutter to see if it was Marcie, lifting one slat slowly, carefully, so she wouldn't hear me.

Eric was standing on the porch. I couldn't believe it . . . I thought I was standing in some long dream . . . watching him through the narrow shutter . . . not moving a muscle . . . for fear the slightest sound, breath, would make him turn around. . . . I didn't want him to know I was standing there, all shaky and hardly breathing . . . looking out at him. So I moved the shutter slat up and then slowly down . . . I wanted to go in all directions at once . . . run into the bathroom and comb my hair and change my shirt . . . but if I took too long, Eric might go away . . . might never come back . . . so I just started walking, like in slow motion, kind of on my toes, so my rubber sandals wouldn't make that squishing sound, still hardly breathing, my arms all held out, like balancing something, until I reached the door. I took another deep breath, pulling my frog tee shirt down over my stomach, panicked that Eric might not have received the letter. I opened the door.

"Hello, Lisa," Eric said. Just like that. "Hello, Lisa." Not another word.

"Hello, Eric," I finally said, my voice so soft it hardly sounded like me, wishing it were dark so Eric wouldn't see the splotches on my face, looking at the dots of gray in the stubble along his chin. I moved back a bit, away from the door, just kept moving back into the shadows, my sandals making that squishing sound. Eric came into the hall and then shut the door. He had a big green duffel bag on a thick beige strap slung over his shoulder and he was wearing one of those *shmatte* quilted coolie jackets and a black tee shirt with gold Chinese letters on the front and brown leather sandals, his loopy hair long and out to the sky. He dropped the duffel bag on the floor . . . buttons from China were pinned all over the side of the bag, and Chinese newspapers and magazines stuck out from the top.

We stood in the shadows looking at each other, Eric sniffing like maybe he had a cold or something, and I kept pulling at my shirt, wanting to run into his arms and at the same time hide.

"Lisa . . . I . . ."

"I . . ."

"Lisa . . ."

"When I didn't hear from you . . ."

"I came as soon as I could . . . I got your letter two days ago . . . in Nankai. . . ."

"Nankai?"

"I was traveling around China until Nankai."

"I can't believe you're here."

He was looking at my stomach. "You're so big . . . beautiful . . . more beautiful than ever," he said, his eyes all soft.

"I look awful . . . I . . ."

"Are you okay? The baby?"

"I'm fine . . . and the baby's a girl, Eric . . . a healthy girl."

"A girl . . . oh, my . . . my . . ."

"Isn't it something?"

"Oh, my . . ."

Then in one fast step Eric moved toward me and took me in his arms and held me close . . . so close . . . his hand gently on the back of my head. I slowly put my arms around his neck, but I curled my hand into a tight fist because I didn't want Eric to feel it shaking. We kissed . . . a warm kiss . . . our kiss . . . and then Eric said, "Let's sit down."

I took Eric's hand and we went into the living room and sat down on the old white couch. The blinds were open and strips of light made these zigzag shadows along the wall. I kept touching Eric's face, like trying to touch what I was feeling and couldn't get out. Because there was so much to say . . . but the words got all stuck. So we just kept holding hands and looking at each other. But Eric's hand was all still and I kept mine slightly curled because it was still shaking.

"I want to talk to your doctor," said Eric, looking concerned and gently kissing the side of my face. "Make sure you're okay."

"Really, I'm fine," I said, kind of rattled. "At first I was sleepy all the time . . . cried a lot . . . and I had cravings galore."

"What kind of cravings?"

"Anchovy pizza . . . French fries . . . probably why I have these splotches."

"I love your splotches," he said, touching my face gently.

"You can have them."

"Lovely and pregnant," he said, grinning.

"At least pregnant."

"Are you scared?" he asked, suddenly looking serious.

"No . . . I want this baby . . . so much, Eric."

"When's the baby due?" he asked softly, his hand on my stomach.

"December twentieth."

"How do you know the twentieth?"

"I counted."

"Lisa, you know you can't count!"

"I can count this: I figured from our last night."

"Lisa! I feel the baby . . . she's moving! I feel her, Lisa!"

"Isn't it something?" I said, putting my hand on top of his.

"Oh, my . . ." he murmured, his mouth half open, like holding his breath, just keeping his hand on my stomach, pressing it. "Does she move a lot?"

"No . . . not yet . . . just little tap dances. Soon she'll be kicking."

"I can't get over how wonderful you look. . . ."

"You look wonderful, too," I said quickly.

"I lost about ten pounds," he said, patting his stomach. "Caught some bug in China."

"Oh, no . . ."

"But I'm okay now . . . drinking a lot of herbal tea."

"Oh, God."

"How did the girls take it?" he asked, looking concerned.

"Like you'd expect. I mean, it threw them for a loop. But they were great. And now they're excited about having a sister."

"Your mother?" he said, looking pensive.

"She was shocked, of course. But she's been great, too . . . supportive. But I worry about her . . . I really do, Eric."

"I'll call her . . . talk to her," he said.

"And Ian," I said, keeping my tone light. "Did you tell Ian? Joshua?"

"Ian went on to India, but I wrote him on the plane about the baby. . . . I'll call Josh . . . my father."

"Oh, God . . . they'll die "

"They won't die," he said quietly.

"Anyways, Eric . . ." I said, loving the feel of him, his smell . . . nearness. "I'm so glad to see you . . . so glad. . . . I still can't believe you're here."

"Neither can I," he said, putting his arm around my shoulder and pulling me closer.

"I hadn't heard from you for such a long time, Eric . . . I didn't know what to think . . ." I said, holding his hand tighter.

"I met a lot of people . . . got busy."

"Uh-huh," I murmured, his hand getting all still in mine. "Did you meet someone?" I blurted.

"No," he said, looking away.

"Why didn't you write, then?"

"Look, Lisa," he said, looking at me, but his eyes guarded, "you're the one who dumped me. Then you didn't answer my letters. So what was I supposed to think?"

"Oh, God . . . Eric . . . I wanted to write you . . . tell you what I was feeling . . . I didn't . . . I was afraid to . . . I mean, every time I'd try and get close to you . . . tell you what I was feeling . . . you'd pull away, run off . . . and the last time we were together, that night at your house, when I was hurting so much . . . you . . ."

"O . . . kay," he said, "let's not talk about that now. Talking about it makes me uncomfortable."

"Eric . . . we have to . . . start talking about our feelings . . . admit them."

"Look, Lisa," he said crabbily, "I just got off a sixteen-hour flight . . . I'm tired. There are a lot of things I want to say   but don't talk at me . . . don't pull them out of me. Let me sort out my thoughts."

"Sure . . . uh-huh. Okay," I said, tapping my foot.

"We'll talk later about our marriage plans," he said crankily.

"Marriage plans?" I repeated, tapping my foot harder, trying to keep my voice even.

"Of course, marriage plans," he said, looking at me closely.

"But I'm not marrying you, Eric. . . . I already said that in my letter."

He kind of sat forward and moved his neck and pulled his hand out of mine. He sat so still and I could see the little muscles in the hollow of his cheek go up and down. For a moment I didn't know what to do . . . so I made my hand into a fist, so when I looked at Eric's angry face I wouldn't get all scared and give in to him.

"Can't or won't?" he said finally, looking at me, his eyes all cold.

"Both."

"Because of your career?" he said sarcastically.

"My career has nothing to do with us," I said, tightening the fist.

"What then?"

"We're not ready," I said, trying to keep my voice even. "We're not ready for marriage, Eric . . . but in time . . . I mean, if we're honest . . . really love each other . . . in a real way . . . stop playing cat-and-mouse games . . . but not until . . ."

"Until what?"

"Until you look at me as I am."

"Don't be analytical . . . stubborn!" he said angrily. "I want my child to have a proper home . . . parents. I have an important position, Lisa."

"Proper for whom?"

"Cut it out, Lisa! You know what I mean! What's everyone going to say?"

"Who cares, Eric? You care too much about what people think. I'm not going to be Mrs. Nobel Prize . . . someone to fit into your world. . . . We need more than that, Eric. We do."

"Oh, Lisa . . . you offer me no alternatives."

"I do. We just haven't talked about them yet. Like having different houses . . . but being together when we're with the baby."

"I want to think about this. I don't like it."

"I'm not marrying you now."

"You'll marry me, Lisa. In time. I'll buy a bigger house . . . your own study . . . my own bathroom . . ."

"Eric, don't," I said. "I'm moving to Oakland. And we'll be closer to you there."

"Oakland?"

"After the baby is born, I'm working at the Oakland Museum. I need money, Eric . . . while my book goes to market."

"You finished your book?"

"*Eva*'s finished."

"Amazing," he said, like saying it to himself.

"What's so amazing? You just don't know me very well."

"Maybe not," he said softly and looking pensive. "It seems that you've thought of everything . . . but the father."

"That's not true. If anything, it's the other way around. I want us to be good parents. . . ."

"Maybe after you have the baby, Lisa, you'll have time for other things . . . for me . . . not work so hard at being a writer."

"Oh, Eric . . . don't," I said. "Don't pull away now . . . I need you. . . ."

"You always want the last word . . . control . . ."

"Oh, Eric, we both do, I mean, I'm not so hot in the relationship department . . . but we're not playing a game anymore."

And then I couldn't help it, like everything I'd been feeling came loose in me, and I started to cry, the tears puddling down my face, and I could feel the splotches turning redder, bigger. . . . Eric put his arms around me and held me close and stroked my hair and I could feel his body all stiff, like he was holding himself back. Until after a while I felt Eric relax more and we held each other tighter. I kissed him on the mouth.

"Lisa, I feel kind of fluish."

"Poor baby," I said, kissing him again, loving him so much.

"Let's lie down. I want to hold you," he said.

"Let's hold each other," I said.

The shades were down, and the room was dark. We lay naked, touching our bodies, just touching, settling in our love. We held each other for the longest time, lying still, so still. Holding my breath, I wanted to keep the moment forever, all still. Close.

"She's moving again, Lisa . . . she's moving . . . I can feel her heart beating. . . ."

"Uh-huh. She knows we're loving each other."

"Parents, Lisa . . . we're parents. . . ."

I laughed. "Isn't it something?"

"But I'm a sick old man, Lisa."

"Oh, stop with the sick every minute. You're a tough old bird, mean and tough, and you always will be."

"You're beautiful . . . so beautiful," he said, kissing my breasts. "Your nipples . . . full and brown."

"Oh, God . . . they're getting hard."

"Our daughter is going to look like you," he said, kissing me along the stomach. "Your dark eyes . . . wonderful, uneven face . . ."

"And your loopy hair," I said, pushing back the loop of curls that fell along his forehead.

"Erica's a nice name," he said. "Erica Blumberg . . ."

"Uh-huh . . . Kiss me again, please."

"I'll kiss you for the next fifty years. . . . I'll never stop kissing you . . . here . . . right here . . . my favorite place . . . where you're all wet . . . warm. . . ."

"Don't you think that Eva Perlman is a lovely name?"

"Maybe Eva . . ."

"Let's try a new position . . . I saw these films in my natural childbirth class."

"Natural childbirth?"

"Yes."

"Lisa, you're too old!"

"I don't want to miss a moment of this birth, Eric. Not a moment."

"Oh, Lisa . . . you're so sweet. . . ."

"What do you think of this way?"

"O . . . kay. That's good . . . now I can see . . . touch your belly . . . my baby . . . ," he said, stroking my belly.

"Do it more, Eric. Put it all the way in. Don't be afraid . . . you won't hurt the baby . . . way in . . . don't be afraid . . . slow . . . real slow . . . yum . . . God, like that . . . fuck me harder."

"I love you, Lisa."

"Don't love me, Eric . . . just fuck me, please. . . ."

"Oh, you terrible woman . . ."

"Put it in . . . way in . . . stop being so careful!"

"For a pregnant lady, you talk terrible."

"Fuck me more!"

"O . . . kay."

"Oh . . . that's wonderful."

"Raunchy . . . oh, God, Lisa . . . oh . . ."

"God . . ."

"Don't get too excited!" he yelled. "You can't come too hard!"

"Eric . . . oh . . . I'm coming. . . ."

"Come . . ." he said, holding me gently.

"Coming . . . oh, God . . . what a come . . . I . . . I . . . I . . ."

And then we lay still . . . so still . . . our bodies damp and my hair sticking to the side of his cheek . . . the pillow all wet. For the longest time we didn't move, not a word, nothing. Eric closed his eyes and rested his face on my stomach and kept pressing the palm of his hand on my stomach. . . . I stroked the loopy hair

. . . and the quiet came through . . . and I could hear the beating of our hearts . . . our three hearts . . . and God, it was something . . . really something.

The following Sunday—the air still and muggy—Eric and I were driving in Berkeley on the way to his house along a narrow, tree-lined street. It was almost evening, but the light was all white. Eric and I'd spent most of the afternoon at the cottage I'd leased in Oakland, a darling little house Marcie Kaplan had found two days before. The rent was a little more than I'd wanted to pay . . . somehow I'd manage. Of course, Eric wanted to pay for everything . . . but finally, after a lot of going back and forth, we agreed that we'd share the costs for the baby and I'd pay my own expenses. And Eric would pay for Eva's education and all our doctor bills.

I knew the last week had been hard for Eric . . telling the family that we weren't getting married . . . and his colleagues and friends that he was almost a new father . . . his Nobel Prize pushed aside . . . but underneath his pilliness was a begrudging gentleness . . . God, he loved the baby. I loved him for that . . . loved him more than ever.

I put my hand on his leg and looked out the window at the way the trees were so still and the sky smooth as glass. Eric'd been complaining about the house and worrying about how I was going to support myself . . . ranting on and on that *Eva* was a long shot.

"Where you're going to put all your crap . . . the art . . in that small house, I'll never know," said Eric crankily, slowing the car down and glancing out the window at a beautiful house with a "For Sale" sign on the front.

"When I fix it up, you'll see, it'll be adorable . . . and it's near you."

"It's okay . . . temporarily," he said gloomily.

"Uh-huh."

"I'm buying a second set of baby furniture," he said, pulling the visor down so the sun wouldn't get in his eyes. "Keep the crib in Josh's old room."

"Good idea."

"I'm checking out a bigger house . . . with a garden . . . hot tub . . . pool," he said.

"Uh-huh."

"I also think I'll put an ad in for a wife," he said, a deadpan expression on his face.

"While you're at it, make sure you ask for a baby-sitter."

He laughed.

"Did you get a letter from Ian yesterday?"

"No," he said, turning the corner. He sighed. "I wish he'd settle down . . . stop traveling . . . but I think he wants to get away from Dianna."

"He'll settle down," I said, stroking his hand.

"Kids . . ." he said.

"That was nice of you, taking Jenny to dinner the other night."

"She's an okay kid," he said with a shrug. "Just takes time."

"And the way you handled Mother was wonderful," I said, pressing my hand on his thigh.

"O . . . kay. . ."

"Anyways, I can't wait to meet your father. He sounds wonderful on the phone . . . so funny. And Josh and Amy'll be home, too."

"Everyone's staying at my house, Lisa," he said. "I've hired a nurse for you and the baby."

"A nurse . . . uh-huh," I murmured.

"I'll do the cooking," he said, "and the nurse can take care of the baby . . . you. . ."

"Uh-huh. That'll be lovely."

"You need rest, Lisa. You're not twenty-one."

"Eric, can't you just see us at our daughter's graduation . . . in our walkers?"

"I'll be an old man with a long gray beard," he said, grinning. "But you'll still be beautiful," he said wistfully, squeezing my hand.

"You'll be a cranky old bird with equations in your pocket . . . solving the universe."

"Look at that house!" said Eric excitedly, stopping the car in front of a stately white house. "Looks worth checking out."

"Uh-huh."

"Nice, isn't it?" he said, looking at me for approval.

"Very nice."

Then he drove on, real slow, like he was slowing up on purpose, and I could see the hollow in his cheek going up and down, feel the flip of his mood, his sudden silence.

"I still think that cottage is too small," he finally said. "The baby needs a house to move around in."

After a couple of blocks Eric stopped the car in front of the old Berkeley Rose Garden, one of our favorite places. He turned off the ignition, turning the key twice before taking the key out of the lock. He kissed me lightly on the mouth.

"Let's go into the garden. It'll only take a minute." He got out of the car and opened my door.

I grabbed his hand and he tugged me out of the car. We crossed the street. Eric's hair in the light looked almost auburn. He held my hand tight. He was wearing a new tan corduroy jacket he'd had made in China, the threads hanging from the sleeves . . . and I was wearing a white denim loose top with clouds painted on the front, and the new silver bird necklace and bird earrings Eric brought me from China, a violet ribbon wound inside my long braid.

We went into the garden . . . just rows and rows of rosebushes . . . hundreds of them . . . the roses sparkling like little rainbows. The garden . . . shaped like an amphitheater . . . faced the bay, and the sun was so white I held my hand over my eyes.

"So beautiful . . . aren't the roses so beautiful, Eric? Like jewels."

He smiled and touched the side of my face. His eyes were shiny with light, and in them I could see roses.

"Remember, Eric . . . when we first came here a year ago? The Sunday after the concert."

"What a year," he said, looking reflective.

We walked along the paths holding hands, admiring the rosebushes, roses like you wouldn't believe . . . romantic roses . . . magic roses . . . funny roses . . . fragrant roses. The gravel crunched under our feet. I walked slowly, kind of puffing, my breath getting shorter, a pulling feeling across my back . . . like the baby was pressing on my back. Eric was still in a mood. I squeezed Eric's hand but we didn't say anything . . . we didn't have to. . . . We'd just stop and kiss or look at each other or touch and admire a particular rose . . . until we stopped at the bottom of the garden and watched a butterfly—a Monarch, I think—perched on the most beautiful white rosebush, its wings in the sunlight transparent and all different colors, like stained glass. The butterfly suddenly took off, at first flying low, like floating, kind of fluttering up and down, then drifting off into the sky. A pink mist . . . so thin and fine . . . hung over the ocean and gave everything a pinkish glow. . . .

"Wait here, Lisa."

He went over to a white rosebush and looked first to the right, then to the left, making sure no one was looking, and then in one grand swoop with the little knife he snipped off one perfect rose. He put the rose under his coat, then came over to me.

"Let's go home," he said.

Six weeks later . . . another Sunday . . . one of those hot, earthquakey October days . . . the air still. Eric was helping me finish up the packing. The movers were coming the next day. God, it was sad . . . after all, I'd been there fourteen years. I'd told the Pons I was moving, Mrs. Pon cried while Mr. Pon yelled that I'd pay for the holes in the walls, and then Mrs. Pon yelled at Mr. Pon in Chinese and that morning Mrs. Pon gave Eric and me a big tin box of fortune cookies.

Anyways, cartons were all over the kitchen. Eric was cutting strips of masking tape, laying the strips across the kitchen table, while I was taking the rainbow dishes from the cupboards and wrapping the dishes in newspaper.

"Lisa!" Eric shrieked. "Don't reach!"

"Stop fussing," I said calmly. "You know they said in childbirth class about your not getting too excited. . . . Do your breathing exercises."

"Breathing exercises!" he muttered, smoothing a strip of masking tape across the bottom of a box. "I have a paper to write . . . my acceptance speech . . . and you have me going to childbirth classes. . . ."

"You're so cooperative," I said, smiling at Eric looking so funny in green cotton dungarees with the drawstring around the waist and the black tee shirt.

"My ass! You just know how to get around me. Next Erica will be doing the same thing."

"Eva Erica . . . remember? We agreed."

"Eva Erica Blumberg," he said. "Not Perlman."

"Yes . . . of course."

"Eva Erica Blumberg . . . Harvard Ph.D.," said Eric.

"Harvard? Why Harvard?"

"Where else? My daughter's going to Harvard!" said Eric, neatly stacking some boxes in the corner. "The Nobel Prize money will go in Eva's account . . . help pay for Harvard."

"Oh, Eric." I said, touched by the way he was fussing with the masking tape while at the same time he was grinning and scowling. I went over and kissed him.

"Okay, enough of being touched all the time. Get to work! I want to get out of here. I'm an important man, remember. I have a lab, an office, papers, students."

"Is Ian definitely meeting you in Stockholm?" I asked, dropping the paints and brushes into a box.

"His last letter says so."

"And Josh?"

"Josh will come with my father."

"Take lots of pictures . . . for Eva."

"I will. I wish you would come with me."

"No, you don't. I'm as big as a house. I could just see me, curtsying to the king. You'd be so embarrassed."

"Lisa! I told you, you can't just throw things in a box like that! Now I have to take everything out," he said crankily, pushing me aside and taking the paints out of the box.

"You make me nervous."

"Lisa . . . where's the Alka-Seltzer? I have a stomach ache."

So while Eric finished the boxes, stacking them in the hall, I sat at the kitchen table, sipping a Tab, huffing like a horse. God, it was hot, and my legs were twice their size, and the tiny gold ring I always wore on my second finger was grown into my finger.

I loved watching Eric while he worked, smoothing the masking tape across the boxes, making everything perfect, the muscles in his arms moving up and down. I tried not to look at the old ink stains on the wall . . . scuff marks on the linoleum from Jenny's old doll buggy . . . the marks of my past . . . because when I did I got scared . . . got that woozy feeling.

"Okay . . . that's it!" said Eric, looking approvingly at the boxes. "The boxes on this side, Lisa, are coming to my house. You don't have room for all this at your place, and when we move, it'll make it easier."

"Uh-huh."

"You look tired," he said, kissing the top of my head.

"A little."

"What's that?" he asked, looking closer at the white rose, turned brown by now, I had collaged under a thin layer of chiffon, then painted over with silver paint and mounted on a canvas.

"It's the white rose you picked for me that day in the rose garden . . . remember?" I said, caressing his arm.

He shrugged and looked away.

"I'm hanging it by the baby's crib . . . it's a romantic rose. . . ."

"It's only a rose, Lisa," he said quickly, and scowling. "Talk in concrete language . . . remember what I've told you. Here . . . let me take that. You take the avocado plant and Anny. I'll carry the *Princess* manuscript . . . it's heavy."

I stood there a second, looking at the trees, already turning autumn colors. Old Mrs. Nelson's walker was in front of her house. But I didn't look back . . . I couldn't . . . I was ready to go. . . .

CHAPTER SIXTEEN

December 3 . . . and a nip in the air . . . Eric, Jenny, and I had gone to Mother's house for Thanksgiving dinner and Birdie cooked one of her famous turkey dinners and we had this really nice time. Eric was busy teaching and lecturing and practicing his acceptance speech. He was leaving for Stockholm on December 8, coming back right after the ceremonies. I was sure I'd have the baby on the twentieth, so we planned that Amy, Ian, Joshua, and Eric's father would come home for the holidays and the baby's birth. So it was going to be merry. And though I'd gained over thirty pounds and carried just like I had the girls, big as a house, and the baby was kicking like crazy, I was feeling well. My new doctor at Peralta Hospital set Eric and me up with this great childbirth class in Oakland, where I was practicing more Lamaze breathing and learning about breast feeding . . . and Eric was coaching me and taking over . . . real in with the other fathers . . . generally running the show . . . and God, it was something.

Eric made all the arrangements with Peralta Hospital in Oakland . . . a special room so he could stay with the baby and me. I wanted to have the baby in the birthing room but Eric said no, he wouldn't have it, argued that he'd gone far enough, so I agreed on the delivery room. Dr. Graham, my new doctor, was very nice and said she thought everything was going well and that I'd probably be able to have natural childbirth.

Anyways, Anny and I were comfortably moved into the cottage. And God, I loved it . . . its teeny garden, old blue-tiled kitchen, its small high-ceilinged rooms. There was a big old apple tree in the back, a lot of pretty shadows, and a patch of yard where Jenny and I'd planted tomatoes and put out Amy's old electric swing. Eric bought these really nice walnut bookshelves, which held my art books, stereo, knickknacks, my growing shell collection. Two bright green and white chintz print chairs sat in front of the fireplace across from the old white couch, looking brand new with the bright yellow felt pillows Jenny'd made. A fluffy white rug covered most of the wooden floor and gave the room warmth. The wall above the fireplace was covered with pictures of my girls . . . Amy's first by-line . . . Jenny's little story about the horse . . . my parents . . . grandparents . . . Bruce . . . my family tree.

I'd framed a copy of an old *Life* magazine article about Eva Hesse and Jackson Pollock, along with the photograph and article about Lester. Eric and Jenny helped me paint the cottage white . . . I'd loved decorating the cottage—especially Eva's room—all white, too, except one wall, on which I'd painted these big clouds floating in a bright blue sky. A few of Eric's students made this big wooden mobile for the baby . . . stars . . . planets . . . numbers . . . geometric shapes . . . a whole universe floated over her cradle. And hanging above the old wood dresser I'd had as a child was the white rose I'd mounted, next to this wonderful picture of Eric and Eric's Nobel Prize telegram.

Jenny came over a lot . . . we'd bake bread in old coffee cans or pick apples or drive over to the campus to see Eric. And Jenny said she liked Eric better, said that he wasn't as dorky as she thought. Jenny fussed over me a lot, not letting me reach or bend, and when she'd come over she straightened out my closet or neatly rearranged the toys she'd given the baby in the big wicker basket.

Several times Jenny brought Mother over to the house, and Mother, hobbling on her cane, said she thought the cottage was a very cheerful place but she agreed with Eric that it was too small for the baby but since it was temporary and I'd be marrying Eric soon it was probably all right and thank God Eric had some sense.

Anyways, Amy called me every day and after we'd talk about the baby, Amy would tell me about her new boyfriend, Bill, a newscaster, all about their relationship. And she said she was thinking seriously of maybe moving to California, that it was time for her to move on in her career and she wanted to live near me, her family. But I'd tell her that I thought she should move only if the job would be an important step in her career.

So after all the years of writing and not doing much else but writing, the smallest events became big . . . a slow walk . . . a pottery exhibit .   . discovering new interests like photography . . . having lunch with an old friend . . . planting a rosebush for Eva . . . and I was painting this huge canvas with pots and pots of these big flowers. God, it was fun . . . a real gas . . . everything so new. Sometimes I felt like old Big Bird, just landed on earth.

Polishing *Eva* was a bitch . . . I went crazy over every page, every detail, getting up in the middle of the night and going through the manuscript, trying to tie up all the loose ends, filling in the holes so *Eva* would be one whole piece. Until finally I let it go, telling myself that I'd put everything I'd learned, all my new insights, into my next book. . . .

I mailed the manuscript off to Lester, who sent it to New York. After I mailed *Eva* I cried . . . after all, *Eva* had been my closest friend, like a real person. But Lester yelled that there was nothing to be scared about and that I was a professional and that *Eva* would make a hell of a movie. But when I'd think about the manuscript making the rounds, read and reread from top to toe, I'd remember *Princess* and I'd get this breathless feeling, the floor going up and down . . . but only for a minute . . . just a minute . . . because change won't let you go backward . . . not real change.

Anyways, I was getting ready to write another book. I'd learned from *Princess* you don't put your life on hold, you go on with your work . . . and even if *Eva* didn't get published, God forbid, I'd write the next one. And so I was always watching people's gestures . . . the way they'd walk . . . end a sentence . . . close their eyes . . . look away . . . listening for new sounds . . . to what they didn't say . . . pieces of impressions I'd collage into something whole someday. I'd go on these long walks, kind of waddling along, enjoying the leisure, watching the birds float on the air, their wings all shuddery, or the special way the light fell over the trees, imagining the shadows were castles, the sky all mine, the world a jar of paint. Then every morning I'd write all the new things I had seen and drop the pages into a grocery carton marked "New Novel." And at those times, with Anny lying beside me in a box of pages, jam jars filled with more seashells next to my typewriter, Mozart playing softly, the baby kicking in me, I'd feel so content . . . so utterly content . . . like my world was all inside the cottage.

And I was selling some paintings and drawings from the cottage
. . . the art stacked against the bookcases, print bins in the dining
room . . . Neil Thompson, a real doll, was always sending me a
bunch of new clients . . . so I was making ends meet and I was
enjoying the work.

And Eric was a real daddy . . . I mean, you should've seen his
house, filled up with these wonderful baby things . . . I'm telling
you, it was something . . . this old buggy Holly and Albert gave
us . . . and this lovely crib with ducks painted on it in Josh's room
. . . and Ian's old mahogany dresser filled with lovely little blankets and diapers and the tiniest little shirts and things . . . I mean,
Eric was going wild . . . even a live rabbit in his backyard . . .
and a big red swing and slide.

But my Eric wasn't always wine and roses, believe me . . . I
mean, he still had plenty of his poopy-pops, working longer hours,
always complaining about now that he was a Nobel laureate everyone wanted something from him, and about how his work wasn't
going so hot, that getting older was shitty, and that life never went
right anyways.

Sometimes, without our old defenses and games, we'd get these
awkward silences between us and I'd feel really shy, like at my first
boy-girl party, hiding underneath the table pretending I was looking for my napkin so that no one would see that I wasn't asked to
dance. But gradually Eric and I got more comfortable with each
other, closer . . . I mean, the change wasn't really noticeable, but
like change, it was there, softly . . . in our gestures . . . little ways.
Eric didn't correct my mispronounced words as much, or when I'd
get all dramatic and go off on one of my trippy stories about the
wacko birds and Eric would say talk straight, Lisa, I'd swallow my
hurt, not jump at him. I guess just knowing all the poopy-pops
makes love real . . . acceptance makes room for the love to grow.
And on Sunday, lying on Eric's couch, I'd listen while Eric played
Bach fugues on the piano or Mozart on the clarinet, his eyes half
closed, and God, the guy played music like he made love . . . gentle
but direct . . . the romance underneath . . . hardly seen . . . but
there.

After Eric would play his music, sometimes we'd lie in bed, my belly so big I'd have to lie on my side, Eric gently caressing my belly, feeling Eva kicking, while talking about what we thought Eva looked like, over three hearts beating. And those special times, I knew no matter what course our lives took, the baby bound us forever.

Anyways . . . that Friday night, December 3 . . . I was in the kitchen, doing my Chinese cooking—the wok, the whole bit—the cookbook Amy sent me was open to this beautiful colored picture of a lavish Chinese banquet. . . . I was chopping vegetables, having a wonderful time, making this special dinner for Eric. It was one of those solemn gray days when you think every minute it's going to pour cats and dogs but only turns darker, gloomier. My back was hurting a lot, and Eva was kicking up a storm, so I'd stayed home all day, just puttering . . . making a tuna noodle casserole for the freezer . . . rearranging Eva's closet again . . . going through the old Christmas tree ornaments Jenny and Amy'd collected . . . planning Eva's first Christmas. This silvery frost stuck all along the old windows, and the fire in the living room fireplace was going and the little kitchen was all warm. Anny was curled in a ball on the stool next to the refrigerator . . . Mendelssohn's Violin Concerto in D was playing from the stereo, and the exquisite music filled the cottage.

I was chopping the vegetables, kind of standing backward because my back was hurting so much, humming with the music, when suddenly my water broke—it was running down my legs— and I felt this shortness of breath . . . my feet turning all cold. I stood there holding on to the counter, telling myself not to panic, that I was early, reminding myself that the labor coach said that no matter what, don't panic. So breathing deeply, I went into the bathroom and cleaned myself up, took a shower, and then called Dr. Graham, who said she'd meet me at Peralta Hospital. I sat down a minute then because the backache started pressing . . . pressing like the baby was pressing out of me . . . and I had this urge to lie down on my side and push . . . push out the baby . . . and I was getting scared, really scared.

So after the contraction stopped I called Eric who, thank God, was just leaving his house to come over, and told him that I was getting ready to go to the hospital. He said that he'd be right over and that I shouldn't panic. I went into the closet and took out the little suitcase I'd packed months before for the hospital and put on my big red cape. I sat in the living room on the couch, breathing deeply because I was getting another contraction and my legs were getting these funny cramps in them and I was feeling kind of nauseated.

When Eric arrived he looked a little green though he was trying to be Mr. Cool, even wearing his camera around his neck so he could take pictures of the baby. But I knew he was nervous, so I tried not to show that I was having trouble breathing and this contraction was starting and the pain was getting pretty bad. But in the car on the way to the hospital, the contractions got worse. God, so hard, like this long spasm went through me, and I wanted to push, push out the baby, and so I started the shallow breathing thing, praying that I wouldn't push out the baby in the car.

"Use your paper bag, Lisa!" screamed Eric, driving like a nut toward the hospital.

"I don't . . . don't need . . . the paper bag. . . ."

"You're hyperventilating! In class they said use your paper bag!"

"I'm having a . . . a . . . con . . . traction . . . I'm not . . . hyper . . . ventilating . . . oh, God! . . . God! . . . oh . . . God!"

"Don't panic!" he shrieked, turning the corner at full speed.

"God . . . oh, Eric . . . I think . . . oh, God! . . . I hope another one doesn't come. . . ."

"Don't panic!" he repeated.

"God . . . oh, Eric . . . thank God . . . it stopped. . . ."

"I knew you miscalculated!" he yelled, pulling into the hospital parking lot, the tires screeching.

Somehow we got into the hospital. Eric was yelling that I was having the baby soon and that they'd better get me to delivery and he never heard of such a thing as a woman my age going through natural childbirth. So, thank God, while the nurses got me ready for labor, they made Eric wait in the room at the end of the hall because he was making everyone crazy. Then Dr. Graham came in the room and examined me and said that I was dilating seven centimeters and that soon we'd go to delivery. And God, then the contractions started coming longer, longer, long and so hard. I couldn't breathe and I was trying to do everything like I'd learned in childbirth class, until my breathing rhythm started and God, then the contractions got real close, five minutes apart, and I was yelling my head off, yelling like hell, my face all scrunged up and red.

Eric came back into the room and held my hand. All the training he had learned in childbirth class left him. During one of my contractions Eric started yelling that the nurses should give me an epidermal and that I shouldn't be so crazy and the nice nurse with big round hazel eyes squeezed my hand and said, "That's right, Lisa . . . keep breathing . . . you're doing it . . . that's right, Lisa . . . you're doing fine . . . you're almost there. . . ." But then the pain was so big, like it was bigger than me and I kept on yelling. And I just held on to the nurse's hand so tight, staring at the tiny black specks around her dark irises, imagining my purple birds and yellow skies . . . birds flying all around . . . until the contraction, the pain, got a little better and everyone clapped. And, thank God, Dr. Graham, a nice lady with soft brown eyes, came in and examined me and said I was fully dilated and ready for delivery and that she'd meet me in the delivery room and God, I was relieved. So they wheeled me on a gurney down a long corridor and into the delivery room. Eric, wearing his green scrub mask and the camera around his neck, his loopy hair sticking out from underneath this green cap, sat on a stool next to me.

They adjusted the mirror attached to the other end of the table so we could see between my legs. While Dr. Graham scrubbed up at the sink, putting on a sterile gown and gloves, Eric kept telling me to relax and that I was doing great and that he was with me, while the nurse with the nice eyes and round face wrapped my legs and put my legs in the stirrups and draped me with sheets and Eric adjusted the pillows behind my head.

"Put your hands on these hand grips," said the nurse. "That's right . . . so you can push."

"Oh, God . . . I think . . . I . . ."

"Lisa," said Eric, "Lisa . . . remember . . . push."

"Oh, God . . . Oh . . . it's awful . . . awful . . . I'm having another contraction . . . I can't . . . stand it. . . ."

"Bear down, Lisa," said Dr. Graham.

"I can't . . . oh, please. . . ." And then I heard myself hollering that I couldn't stand it anymore and the chrome lights on the ceiling were floating in and out, in and out, and Eric was yelling, "Push, Lisa! Hold your breath ten seconds, Lisa! Ten seconds, before pushing, Lisa!"

"I can't . . . I can't breathe. . . ."

"That's right, Lisa," said Dr. Graham. "That's right . . . push . . . push . . . take two deep breaths . . . two deep chest breaths. . . . Good girl, Lisa. You're doing fine . . . just fine."

"I'm tired . . . I . . . oh, God . . . I'm tired," I said, relaxing my hands and breathing deeply until the next contraction, watching Eric's face in the mirror, only his face, while he fussed with the towels under my shoulders and whispered in my ear that he was with me, that I was doing great. And then the pain started again, this time a faster pain and a burning feeling along my legs, my back pressing out of me, out of me, and the burning feeling was so awful. But I forced myself and took two deep breaths, holding the third, pushing out, my hands pushing out the grips, pushing and pushing, my head all forward, my eyes open . . . so wide they hurt, on Eric's face in the mirror, on Eric's scared face, pushing my body out of my body.

"Don't stop, Lisa," said Dr. Graham, "we're getting there . . . good!"

Then the pain stopped and I inhaled deeply, imagining the dumbo birds whirling around, so I wouldn't hurt so much, so I wouldn't stop breathing and get scared. Until the next contraction started and this time it was so awful I felt my body go away from me. My head lurched forward and I screamed so loud and I was scared because I felt like all my breath was gone.

"Lisa, don't stop your breathing!" yelled Eric, his face turning red.

"Bear down . . . push . . ." said Dr. Graham.

"Exhale through your mouth, Lisa," said Eric.

And so I pushed, while Eric kept whispering to me that I was doing great and that he loved me, until the next contraction . . . that time I really lost it . . . and Eric was yelling for them not to make me push anymore . . . and I kept pushing the hand grips like trying to push the breath out of me, all out of me.

"Give her some oxygen," said Dr. Graham.

"No . . . I don't want it."

"Just a little," said Dr. Graham. "You're tired and we need you to push."

Then the nurse put this rubber mask over my face and I practically gulped in the oxygen, and for a second I was floating, but then they took the mask away and I hurt, my body felt like it was going to burst open, and the pain in me was so big . . . and I heard Eric saying, "Give her more oxygen" and the pain in me was so big . . . like pressing me out . . . and I was yelling . . . I could hear me yelling . . . and Dr. Graham repeating, "Now, a big push, as big as you've got," and I pushed and pushed and Eric was holding the back of my head and then I held on to the hand grips and I pushed and pushed and, God, it hurt, like everything in me was coming out and I didn't think I could stand another minute . . . another minute . . . then I saw the top of Eva's head, this black patch of hair, Eric's face in the mirror all still, like he was holding his breath, his hands holding my head and Dr. Graham said, "Push, Lisa, push." Then Eva's head came out more.

"Oh, God . . . God!" I yelled, trying to push . . . so tired.

"Here she comes!" said Eric, kissing my face, his eyes on mine in the mirror.

"Good, Lisa . . ." said Dr. Graham.

"She's a beauty!" cried Eric.

"My God!" I yelled. "I can see her . . . my baby . . . I can see her . . . I can see Eva!"

"Keep pushing, Lisa," said Dr. Graham in her gentle voice.

Then I watched Eva slowly come out of me, her head tilted kind of downward, her nose this blob, perfect little eyebrows, her tiny arms tucked at her side. And Eric and I were all still . . . all still . . . Eric holding my hand so tight . . . both of us watching Eva being born . . . this little person coming out of me. It was something.

Then I was crying and not caring that I was making a slob of myself. Eric was yelling, "She's a beauty . . . a beauty!" And then

I heard Eva's strong, wobbly cry . . . that cry . . . I'll never forget it or Eric holding my head and kissing me, crying, too. Until after a while Dr. Graham put the baby at my breast. I held Eva real close to keep her warm . . . real close . . . Eric bending over me . . . both of us all still again, caught in the moment, looking into her little face all scrunged up and tiny and mottled pink and with a mass of dark hair and a squashed nose and a mouth like Eric's . . . exactly like Eric's. God, I couldn't believe it . . . I'd never seen anything so perfect . . . so wonderful.

"Ten fingers, ten toes," I murmured, checking the baby's feet and tiny but long fingers, the fingernails with perfect little moons.

"My little girl . . ." murmured Eric, his big hand holding Eva's little thumb. "Daddy's here . . . Daddy's here. . . ."

"Isn't she something," I said, touching the side of Eva's cheek.

"My little girl," said Eric.

"Mommy's going to feed you soon," I whispered.

"You're a great beauty," Eric whispered. "A knockout . . . like your mommy. . . . I love you, Eva. . . ."

"I love you, too," I said, laughing now at Eric, who was making these gooing, suckling sounds, and enjoying Eva's warm little body on my breasts.

"Isn't my little girl beautiful?" said Eric, looking at the nurses and at Dr. Graham, who was finishing the episiotomy.

"Certainly is," said the nurse, patting my forehead and smiling.

"I always wanted a little girl," said Eric, his big hand still holding Eva's thumb.

And then they wrapped Eva in blankets and put her in this portable heated crib and wheeled the crib over by me and Eric took a bunch of pictures of Eva in the crib, then of me, going on about how Eva looked like her mother, then murmuring that Eva Blumberg was a very special child . . . and I felt this glow in me . . . a peaceful glow . . . and I kept touching my stomach, making sure that I wasn't in a dream. I was floating, just floating . . . and I didn't want to close my eyes, not for a minute, because I was afraid I'd come out of the dream then. . . .

"Lisa," said Dr. Graham, unwrapping my legs, "we're going to take you to the recovery room in a few minutes, and you can nurse the baby."

I became drowsy . . . I tried not to close my eyes . . . just enjoying Eric stroking my face . . . my arms . . . whispering . . . until they wheeled us to the recovery room, baby and all.

I had no idea what time it was . . . close to dawn, I think . . . but I could see the stream of light coming through the print curtains. The nurse propped the pillows behind my head so I could breast-feed Eva. Eric stood by the crib, taking more pictures. The nurse took Eva from the crib and put her in my arms, telling me just to relax and that she'd be back in forty minutes. Eric lay beside me, his arms around me. Eva was sleeping but her little mouth went right to my nipple . . . she really went at it, her little mouth sucking my breast, her tiny fingers curled under. While Eva sucked, Eric kept kissing me and Eva's little cheek, and I kissed Eva's little mottled pink face, and her eyes under the closed eyelids so long and oval, beautifully shaped. Eric was whispering to Eva that he loved her mommy and kissing me, then Eva, until the nurse came back and took the sleeping Eva and put her back in the crib.

I lay my head on Eric's shoulder and felt really sleepy . . . all floaty . . . and then I closed my eyes and, holding Eric's hand, drifted off . . . like floating . . . a dream . . . into this wonderful place   all silver . . . with these gorgeous birds flying around. And I slept.

When I awoke several hours later, Eric was sitting beside me. Eva was sleeping in her crib, and the room was all light. And this enormous bouquet of balloons, all different shades of pink, floated on the ceiling.

Eric leaned down and kissed me. "You look wonderful."

"I feel wonderful," I said. "Did you sleep?"

"I've been busy . . . making calls . . . looking at my beautiful Eva. . . ."

"She is beautiful, isn't she?" I said, looking at the crib. "Oh, Eric, the balloons . . ."

"Amy and Jenny sent them," said Eric, kissing me tenderly. "Did you see the pink roses over there? They're from your mother and Sidney."

"They're beautiful."

"I have a surprise for you," he said.

"Another one!"

"Amy is getting an early flight . . . she'll be here later today."

"Oh, my God! My God, Eric! I'm so happy!"

"Amy's going to take her vacation time," he said, smiling. "I told her she can stay at my house with us."

"Oh, I'm so happy," I said, brushing a tiny flake of something from Eric's bottom lip.

"I'm glad you're happy . . . so am I," he said softly, lying down beside me. "I'm very happy."

We kissed, and then we just lay still . . . in our contentment . . . looking at the sleeping Eva. Then I nursed Eva again, Eric lying next to me, his arms around me and holding Eva's tiny hand, practically on top of us, telling me just how to move my nipple . . . the sleeping Eva smelling so sweet, her little mouth sucking at my breast, her eyes opening, then closing. The nurse came in, carrying more flowers . . . the most beautiful little pink arrangements from Eric's department . . . a telegram from Josh . . . messages from Marcie Kaplan, Kathy, Lester North, Eric's father.

We had breakfast together and then I showered and washed my hair and put on the pink lacy bed jacket Mother gave me.

Eric was sitting in a chair next to the crib . . . Eva was still sleeping . . . he was wearing his old corduroy jacket and the camera was still around his neck . . . rolls of film lay across the nightstand. Eric looked so tired . . . his hair sticking out all over his head . . . but his eyes were so clear. . . .

"Definitely, Lisa," said Mother, wearing a rose-colored woolen suit and looking up from the crib, "Eva looks like my side of the family . . . the Hellman bones . . . coloring. . . ."

"Uh-huh," I said.

"She has the Blumberg mouth," said Eric.

"Definitely your mouth," said Jenny.

"Lisa says Eva's hair will turn light, like mine," said Eric, cooing like an idiot at the sleeping Eva.

"I think Eva looks like Mom," said Amy, smiling at Eva and still wearing her red snow boots and heavy green coat.

"Mom's-shaped face," said Jenny.

"Your great-grandmother's skin," said Mother.

"More like Mom, though," insisted Amy.

"Mom and I look alike," said Jenny, biting her lower lip.

"She looks a little like Ian, too," said Eric.

"Definitely," I said.

"O . . . kay . . ." said Eric, wiggling his fingers at Eva. "You look like Eva Blumberg, don't you? Don't you, my sweetheart?"

"She's so beautiful . . . just like my other girls," I said, looking at Amy, who was nudging Jenny.

"When will I meet your sons?" asked Amy.

"After we get back from Stockholm," said Eric. "You'll stay at my house with your mom and the baby . . . Ian . . . my father . . . everyone'll be there."

"I'm staying at Mom's," said Amy.

"Me, too," said Jenny.

"Your mother's staying with Eric," said Mother.

"I'm staying at my house with the baby."

"Listen to Eric!" said Mother.

"Oh, it'll all work out," I said.

"Lisa," said Mother, coming over to the bed and lowering her voice, "I think you and the baby should stay at Eric's until you're stronger."

"Mother, I'm fine."

"Lisa won't listen," said Eric, smiling sympathetically at Mother.

"The girls will help me . . . stop worrying," I said.

"Mom looks great," said Amy.

"Yes, she does," said Mother. "Your blotches are better."

"Eva's incredible," said Amy, bending over the crib.

"Eva Erica," said Eric, still cooing.

"Personally, I like Erica Eva Blumberg," said Mother, smiling at Eric.

"Whatever she's called, she's perfect," said Eric.

"Mom's naming the baby after Eva Hesse, Nans," said Jenny to Mother.

"I still like Erica Eva," said Mother.

"Lisa and I are going to talk to a rabbi about naming the baby and having the ceremony at my house."

"Oh, that would be nice," said Mother, looking pleased.

"I think that's great," said Amy.

"As soon as Eric and his family get back from Sweden, we'll have the naming at my house," I said. "Just the family . . . a little luncheon afterward. . . ."

"Your house! Your house is too small," said Mother, looking at Eric and tch–tch–tching.

"That's what I told her," said Eric.

"My house would be better," said Mother.

"No, I'll have it at my house," said Eric.

"Well, Eric's house would be better," said Mother.

"Uh–huh," I said.

"I'll bring Birdie," said Mother happily, "and make some of my gorgeous potato salad."

"Wonderful!" said Eric.

"When are you going to Sweden?" said Amy.

"The eighth. But I'll be back right after the ceremonies."

"We'll take care of Mom and Eva while you're gone," said Jenny. "Don't worry."

"I'm counting on you," said Eric, cooing again at the baby.

"Wait'll I show Sylvia Finkel and the other girls these pictures," said Mother, looking at the pictures Eric had taken of Eva. "They'll die."

"For sure," I said, looking at the pictures with Mother.

"Lisa," said Mother, her face close to mine, her voice a whisper, "don't ever let Sylvia Finkel or anyone in the family know how you met Eric. I told everyone you met through friends."

"Uh–huh."

"I think Lisa needs some rest," said Eric, coming over and kissing me, smiling at Mother.

"You look like you could use some rest," said Mother, looking at Eric with a concerned expression on her face. "Maybe you should eat something."

"I'll eat later."

"I'm hungry, Nans," said Amy.

"You could use some food . . . you're thin as a rail," said Mother.

"So why don't we all go and eat something, Nans?" said Jenny. "Then come back later with Sidney."

"Good idea," I said.

"And Eric, I'll tell the family that the naming is at your house," said Mother.

"Yes . . . just family. We'll talk."

"Good," said Mother.

"Uh-huh," I said.

And then Eva coughed and they all made a beeline for the crib, all talking at once, Eric all worried about Eva's cough, Mother assuring Eric that all babies cough, Amy and Jenny nudging each other and giggling, and the balloons floating softly . . . so pretty.

December 19 at my house, a rainy Sunday afternoon, Eric back from Stockholm eight days. Eric and I stood in front of the fireplace, Eric holding Eva, crying to beat the band, while Rabbi Rhoda Weiss—a tall woman with long red hair and wearing a bright blue robe—repeated the blessings, the family standing around in a big circle.

"May she bear this name, Eva Erica Blumberg, with Jewish dignity and honor through a long and useful life."

"Amen," said Solomon Blumberg, Eric's father, a good-looking man wearing a three-piece dark suit, with white loopy hair and Eric's Sad Sack eyes, standing on Eric's right, next to Josh, a tall, handsome boy with blond curly hair and a sensitive face.

"Sshhh," hushed Aunt Pearl, wearing a pink flowered dress, poking Uncle Maury, who kept taking pictures with his Polaroid.

"May she so live as to find favor in Thy sight," continued the rabbi.

"*Mazel,*" said Sidney, standing next to Mother on my left, and Mother so pretty in a mauve silk dress, standing next to Amy and Jenny and Bruce.

"And in the sight of Israel and all mankind," the rabbi's voice rising. "We are humbly grateful for the life bestowed. We give this child, Eva Erica Blumberg, the Hebrew name Chava Avrasha."

"Amen."

"*Mazel,*" called Solomon Blumberg.

"Sshhh," said Eric, giving his father a stern look.

"Let us pray," said the rabbi.

And then we all bowed or heads and prayed silently, my hand on Eric's arm, and Eva still crying and so adorable, wearing a pink

stretchy, a strand of her hair tied with thin pink ribbon. I stood real
straight and held my breath so my stomach wouldn't stick out—I
mean, my stomach was still kind of swollen, but I'd squeezed myself into this black wool midcalf straight skirt and my white silk
blouse.

"Amen," said the rabbi.

"*Mazel tov!*" said Eric, looking proud in the *shmatte* velvet jacket
and ruffled shirt, holding the baby close to him, kissing me, then
Mother, Jenny, Amy, Ian, Josh. And then everyone was kissing
everyone, going wild with the *mazel tovs,* Eva really crying, Rabbi
Weiss shaking hands, then explaining that she had to leave because
she was officiating at a wedding.

"Don't crowd her!" said Bruce, wearing a blue tweed jacket,
standing in front of Eric and the baby, his arms out like a traffic cop.

"Bruce is right," said Eric nervously, his hand protectively on
the back of Eva's head. "The baby's had too much excitement."

"*Oy* . . . a doll," said Aunt Pearl, pressing her fleshy face close
to Eva.

"Be careful, Pearl," said Eric, looking worried. "There's a lot of
flu going around."

"My sister's beautiful," said Amy, looking gorgeous in this hotshot
Perry Ellis white wool dress.

"Beautiful . . . like my *machetayneste,*" said Solomon, smiling at
Mother.

"I told Lisa . . . definitely the Hellman side," said Mother, smiling back at Solomon and moving closer to Eva.

"She looks like your father, Lisa," said Aunt Sally.

"Eric looked just like Eva when he was a baby," said Solomon,
stepping in front of Bruce and kissing the baby's forehead.

"Looks, shmooks! As long as the kid's healthy," said Aunt Sally,
adjusting her tiara.

"Everyone! Don't crowd!" said Eric. "Please!"

"Gorgeous thing," said Uncle Al, wearing a maroon leisure suit
and a toupé, standing on his toes, and looking at Eva.

"Too pretty for words," said Birdie, wearing a big sprig of
Christmas holly pinned to her aqua suit.

"Not bad for fifty-two," said Eric, grinning.

"At fifty-two I was a bull," said Solomon, "and at eighty-five, I'm no slouch."

"Okay, Pop," said Eric, sshhhing Josh and Ian, who were laughing.

"Why is her face all broken out?" said Fat Susan, wearing this thick Japanese-style dress, layers of material.

"Mother's milk," said Aunt Pearl, looking at Mother, who was looking closely at Eva's face.

"Looks like a rash," said Mother.

"My Eva doesn't get rashes," said Eric, stroking Eva's pink face.

"Already spoiled rotten," said Aunt Sally. "The minute the kid squeaks, Lisa sticks her breast in the kid's mouth."

"In the old country, that's how they did it," said Aunt Pearl.

"You're not in the old country!" said Aunt Lillian, looking disgusted.

"Sucking makes them crazy!" said Aunt Sally.

"Never mind," said Solomon. "A good breast never hurt anyone."

"Please, Pop!" said Eric.

"Kids . . ." murmured Solomon.

"Kids! What kids!" said Aunt Nellie in a shaky voice, adjusting this big crocheted shawl around her thin shoulders. "Lisa's way over forty and Eric's pushing sixty."

"Eric was a nice baby," said Solomon in his booming voice. "Smart as a whip . . . genius level," he said, looking at Eric, who glanced up annoyed, then went back to cooing at Eva. "But his mother spoiled him," Solomon continued, lowering his voice and turning to Mother. "Fussed over him too much . . . made him *meshugge* . . . but he's a good boy."

"I think he's wonderful," said Mother.

"My other son's smart, too . . . genius IQ. He'd be here, but he's giving a big talk at his university tomorrow."

"We have geniuses in our family, too," said Mother, sitting next to Solomon.

"If we do, I haven't met them," said Aunt Nellie, sitting on a card-table chair and swaying back and forth, like praying, her eyes behind her thick glasses watching every move.

"My first cousin Waldo is a famous physicist," explained Mother, smiling charmingly at Solomon, who was winding this gold watch on a thick chain. "He lives in Oak Ridge, Tennessee . . . worked on the atomic bomb."

"Waldo's a nut," said Aunt Sally.

"Tell him about Jack London," urged Sidney.

And then Mother began telling Solomon the whole story about Jack London and about all the artists in her family. "And Lisa's very smart, too," said Mother.

"Shmaltzy," said Bruce, sitting next to Mother.

"At three years old," said Solomon, putting the watch back in his vest pocket and leaning back in the chair and looking around the room, waiting for everyone's attention, "Eric's mother and I were told that Eric was a genius."

"Pop, please."

"Don't shake the baby, Eric! She'll get nuts!" said Aunt Sally.

"Eric knows how to hold Eva," I said. "Stop worrying."

"Smile, Mom," said Jenny, standing in front of us and aiming her camera. She was wearing this bright red woolen dress and her hair tied by a red and green ribbon.

"Cheese," everyone murmured.

"O . . . kay . . . enough pictures. Eva's upset," said Eric, sitting on the couch and rocking Eva in his arms.

"Daddy, you're holding the baby too tight," said Josh.

"Never mind, your father knows what he's doing!" said Solomon. "You should only know so much."

"Okay, Grandpa," said Josh, rolling his eyes upward and looking at Ian, who was strumming his guitar.

"So *nu,* big shot, how was Stockholm?" said Aunt Pearl, sitting across from Eric.

"Fine," said Eric, looking suddenly modest.

"Let Lisa show you the Swedish newspapers I brought her," said Solomon, smiling at me. "Stockholm went crazy over Eric. The newspapers were filled with Eric's achievements."

"And all about my little sweetheart," said Eric, cooing at Eva.

"Mom keeps a scrapbook on Eric," said Jenny. "Saves every article."

"I sure do," I said.

"Why not? It's incredibly exciting," said Amy.

"Exciting," echoed Fat Susan, looking like she was about to die. "Isn't it, Keith?" in a singsong voice, her eyes all squinty.

"What? Oh, yeah . . . great . . ." said Keith, cracking Uncle Maury's back.

"The king was very impressed with Eric," said Solomon.

"Pop—"

"When Eric gave his acceptance speech," said Solomon, ignoring Eric's protests, the kids all giggling, "I could see the Royal Family was lapping up every word."

"Big shot," said Uncle Maury.

"Eric *is* a big shot," I quickly said. "It's not every day you get a Nobel Prize."

"You should've seen Daddy's face," said Josh, "when he forgot you're supposed to walk backward from the King . . . and Daddy just turned around and walked back to his seat."

"Everyone was laughing," said Ian.

"Never mind," said Solomon. "Everyone loved your father."

"O . . . kay . . . enough," said Eric.

"Solomon, why don't you pass around the pictures of Eric with the Royal Family?" I said.

"Oh, Lisa . . ." said Eric.

"I'll pass all the pictures around," said Solomon happily, taking three yellow packets from his inside pocket.

"Royal, shmoyal!" said Aunt Sally.

"The Royal Family congratulated me about Eva," Solomon explained to Aunt Pearl.

"Isn't that something?"

"Eric, show Pearl the medal," said Solomon.

"Jenny took it."

"I gave it to Aunt Lillian," said Jenny.

"Not real gold," said Aunt Lillian, biting the medal, then passing it to Aunt Sally.

"It's for Daddy's sweetheart," said Eric, wiggling his fingers at Eva.

"You must be so proud, Lisa," said Fat Susan.

"Of course."

"Are you still writing?" asked Fat Susan.

"Lisa finished her book," said Bruce before I could answer.

"Eric says it's a wonderful book," said Solomon, smiling at me approvingly, "that Lisa has a fine style."

"Yes, she does," said Eric, nodding approval. "Lisa uses concrete language . . . her style is rich . . . interesting."

"Thank you," I said.

"Very shmaltzy," said Bruce.

"Intellectual," said Mother.

"So what intellect !! I hope it sells," said Uncle Al, fiddling with the thick gold chain around his neck.

"What happens now?" said Aunt Lillian.

"It's making the rounds," I explained. "You know, the publishers are reading it. . . ."

"They'll love it," said Mother.

"What are you going to write next?" asked Solomon.

"Well . . . I—"

"She'll have plenty to do with the baby," said Aunt Pearl positively. "She won't have time to write."

"For sure," said Fat Susan.

"Plenty to do," repeated Aunt Nellie, swaying again.

"Lisa will always write," said Eric. "She's a writer."

"She's a smart girl," said Solomon. "And a beauty, too. Eric always knew how to pick them."

"Okay, Pop . . . that's enough," said Eric.

"Can't say a word these days," said Solomon, turning to Mother, who was tch-tch-tching.

"When's the wedding?" asked Fat Susan, looking at me suspiciously.

"In time . . ." said Eric, looking at me, his eyes all still.

"Uh-huh . . . in time . . . maybe . . . we're going to see . . ." I said, kissing Eric.

"What did I tell you!" said Aunt Sally, poking Fat Susan.

"No picnic for older women alone these days . . . let alone raising a child," said Aunt Pearl, turning to Fat Susan.

"I'll say," lisped Fat Susan. "Gigi Ginsberg, my best friend, got dumped by her so-called future husband after three years . . . he left her for a younger woman . . . then bought a car telephone . . . a fifteen-thousand-dollar Rolex watch."

"Soup's on!" called Birdie from the kitchen.

"Eric, why don't you put the baby in the cradle for a while? So you can eat something . . . relax," I said.

"O . . . kay . . ." he said reluctantly, putting Eva in the cradle.

And everyone got up and rushed like a house on fire to the table. And you should've seen, my plain wooden table was all covered with Mother's white lace tablecloth from Switzerland, and these darling wicker baskets all filled with the most exquisite pink flowers, their petals like little butterfly wings. And the food . . . you wouldn't believe . . . Mother had insisted on going all out . . . platters of little caviar and salmon sandwiches . . . jumbo prawns, Mother's special hot sauce . . . two kinds of pâtés . . . cheeses . . . all the fancy salads . . . a silver bowl with Mother's potato salad . . . along with Aunt Pearl's kugel . . . Aunt Sally's cranberry mold . . . Aunt Lillian's *challa* bread. Stanley stood at the end of the table, carving this huge roast beef, while Birdie carved an equally large turkey with chestnut dressing. Stacks of brightly wrapped gifts for Eva were piled in the corner, along with a five-foot teddy bear from Lester North.

I sat on the couch, rocking the cradle . . . Eva all quiet now, finally sleeping . . . Anny curled up beside us. Eric came over carrying our plates, his filled with Aunt Pearl's kugel, roast beef, potato salad, mine with only a few lousy wheat crackers and a tiny scoop of cottage cheese.

"Eric . . I'd like some of Aunt Pearl's kugel," I said.

"Lisa, you know you have to lose weight," he said, giving me the plate and sitting next to me.

"Weight . . . oh, that . . . sure . . ." I said, picking at the cottage cheese and trying not to look at Eric's kugel.

"Bruce, please bring me a little more potato salad,"said Mother, sitting across from us and holding out her plate to Bruce.

"What about your diet?" said Bruce, pressing his lips.

"Please, Bruce . . . only a little . . ."

"All right," said Bruce, getting up.

"Wonderful kugel, Pearl," said Uncle Al, his mouth full.

"The turkey's tough," said Aunt Nellie, arranging pillows behind her back.

"Tastes wonderful to me," said Solomon.

"Not bad," said Aunt Lillian, wrinkling her nose, like studying the food.

"C'mon, Birdie, sit with us," said Amy, sitting by the fireplace along with Jenny, Josh, and Ian, patting the pillow next to her.

"Your hair looks very nice, Lisa," said Aunt Pearl, looking up from her plate.

"Isn't it gorgeous?" said Mother.

"Not so stringy," said Aunt Nellie.

"I always liked that blouse on you, Lisa," said Mother.

"Motherhood agrees with her," said Aunt Lillian.

"And *nu*, the necklace?" said Aunt Pearl, leaning over and looking more closely at my bird necklace.

"Eric gave it to me . . . it's from China."

"Very arty," said Fat Susan.

And then everyone began eating like there was no tomorrow, some sitting on folding chairs in front of little TV tables Mother brought . . . Aunt Nellie still muttering about the turkey, her false teeth clacking . . . Amy and Josh arguing about Africa . . . Ian telling Jenny about gurus . . . Birdie putting in her two cents . . . Aunt Pearl wheezing . . . Keith making these smacking noises, his face close to the plate . . . Solomon looking over at Ian and Josh and smiling proudly . . . Anny purring softly.

"I had the piano tuned yesterday," said Eric, putting his plate down and looking at me.

"Oh, wonderful."

"I thought you'd like to play," he said.

"Oh, I would . . . especially Mozart," I said, kissing him.

"How can you play it when you can't even pronounce it?" he said with that deadpan expression on his face.

"You pronounce it, I'll play it," I said, brushing some dandruff from his shoulder.

He grinned.

There was this silence, until Eva started yelling again.

"Why is that kid always screaming?" said Aunt Sally.

"Lisa!" said Eric, getting up and bending over the cradle. "Eva's wet . . . and I think she's hungry."

"I just fed her an hour ago."

"Spoiled rotten," murmured Aunt Sally.

"You're telling me," said Aunt Nellie.

Eric took the screaming Eva out of the cradle and we went into Eva's room. Eric put Eva on the bassinet, her face all red and scrunged up and wet from tears. I took off her soaked stretchy and dropped the Pamper in the basket. I picked Eva up and held her sweet little body so close to me, so close, loving the feel of her warm little body next to me, covering her with a blanket.

"You're so lovely," said Eric, looking at me tenderly.

"Thank you," I said, kind of shy, looking at Eric's dark eyes.

We kissed . . . a warm, gentle kiss . . . our lips barely touching.

"And you, my little sweetheart," said Eric, kissing Eva's little face. "You're a knockout . . . like your mommy."

"You're crazy, Eric."

"Not as crazy as you are."

"We're both crazy."

"You have crazy parents, Eva," said Eric. "Are you tired, sweetheart?"

"No, I'm fine," I said, putting Eva down on the bassinet.

"It's been a long day," said Eric.

"A nice day . . . wasn't it, Eric?" I said, taking a fresh Pamper from the box.

"Okay . . . but Eva was the star."

"She sure was," I said, kissing Eva.

"Weren't you, Eva?" said Eric, clucking his tongue, his face close to Eva's. "My little sweetheart . . . Daddy's little girl . . ."

"Sweet little Eva . . ." I murmured.

"Lisa, didn't you notice at my house the other night how well Eva slept?"

"Uh-huh."

"Lisa! Watch what you're doing! You're not folding the ends right! Here, let me show you," said Eric.

"Uh-huh . . . sure," I said, stepping aside and loving the intense expression on Eric's face.

He held Eva's little legs. "First my little sweetheart likes talcum powder," he said, sprinkling the powder on Eva. "See Lisa—thicker on the ends—she likes them this way. . . ."

Then Eric pressed the edges of the Pamper, making sure the ends were folded evenly, talking to Eva in this really strange language—words like you've never heard—his eyes half closed . . . and his big hand holding Eva's little hand.

And then I began singing this dopey song I made up for Eva, Eric still talking to Eva in that strange language . . . and I swear, Eva looked at us like we were crazy . . . really bonkers . . . God, it was something.